BLOOD

"An intriguing tale of murder, espionage and betrayal. It's a thriller that deserves to be read."
—UPI

"Kilian writes about today's Russia and its communist heirarchy with shrewd insight...Riveting...and a totally unexpected ending."
—*Washington Post Book World*

"A fast-paced run-for-it saga."
—*Austin Star*

"A fun book...(with) the scrappiest heroine in recent memory."
—*West Coast Review of Books*

"Splendid reading. Few writers around these days can tell a story quite as well, or with as much panache, as Michael Kilian."
—*Washington Times*

By the same author

Northern Exposure
Who Runs Chicago?
The Valkyrie Project
Who Runs Washington?

BLOOD
OF
THE
CZARS

Michael Kilian

St. Martin's Press/New York

ISBN 0-312-90079-1

For Pamela, and Moscow nights

BLOOD
OF
THE
CZARS

PART ONE

'Tis not easy, brother mine,
In a foreign land to live.

—old Cossack song

1

The unexpected slam of the screen door meant that someone was coming out to her, which at that particular hour
of the morning was forbidden. Tatty Chase was not an un-
reasonably demanding hostess, even by the permissive
standards of the Hamptons, but the guests at her place in
East Hampton were subject to three strictures: they could
not invite anyone else to the house without Tatty's permis-
sion; they had to contribute to the liquor supply; and on
sunny days between ten A.M. and eleven A.M. they were
to stay off the back lawn, for that was where and when
Tatty sun-bathed in the nude.

The ritual was in part a professional consideration.
Tatty was an actress—not quite as successful and active
an actress as she would have liked, but for all her wealth
a hard-working professional member of Actors Equity
who had had some good parts on Broadway and still
enough television and summer stock work to stave off
rumors of a failing career, and who had never used her
family's name, money, or her own body to further her
ambitions, except to keep her body and face as attractive
as possible.

She possessed a lovely body. Her first major role, at
eighteen, had been that of a slender blond ingenue. She
had now just turned thirty, and was still playing slender

blond ingenues. With the dedication of a professional, she had kept her figure just so, and these regular sun-bathing sessions kept her tan just so.

She could hear the swish of approaching feet in the too long grass, but because of the screen of hedges she had planted for privacy, she could not see who it was. All she could view was her private section of sky, the limitless blue of a few minutes ago now retreating before a gathering veil of cloud.

If it was one of the two men who were staying at her house that weekend, she would send him packing back to New York City on the next train.

Tatty closed her eyes, waiting for the intruder's voice, not making a move to cover herself. One of the season's Lotharios had made a boorish comment upon seeing her close her eyes at the beach. Tatty's Anglo-Saxon features were English country-garden perfect, a harmonious proportioning of delicate chin and lips, aristocratic nose and brow. But her cheek bones were high and wide, almost Asiatic. When her blue gray eyes were open, the Lothario had observed, her face seemed "an illuminated palace."

"But when you close them," he had said, "you are just a Slav."

She had not given the ass an opportunity to see her with her eyes closed again.

"Tatty?"

She looked up to see Gwen Alderidge, a thin, freckled, auburn-haired woman her own age, barefoot, wearing a thin, billowing summer housedress, and holding a package. Tatty sat up. The sky was going quickly to gray.

"I wouldn't have bothered you, but this just came special delivery."

Gwen had once been considered as beautiful as Tatty, when they were young and close friends in Greenwich, Connecticut. They had been childhood playmates, boarding school roommates, debutantes together, had made their first trips to Europe together, and double-dated in college. The Alderidges had never really had all that much money; her father had been an industrial manager who lived entirely off his salary. When Gwen's young architect husband died six years after their marriage, she had been left penniless and compelled to support herself by teaching school. When school was not in session, she lived with Tatty, at Tatty's request.

"Thank you," said Tatty, taking the package. She thought at first it might be a script someone had sent her. "I'll be having lunch at the house today. I'll be in shortly."

"They all will, I'm afraid," Gwen said, with a faint, troubled smile, a frequent expression. "They're predicting rain."

Tatty nodded, but said nothing more. Even as Gwen turned to walk away, Tatty was staring transfixed at the return address on the package: *Mme. Mathilde Iovashchenko Hoops, Pommel Ridge Road, Braddock Wells, N.Y.*

Mme. Hoops was Tatty's grandmother, now nine years dead. The address was that of her grandmother's huge, tottering old country house in Westchester, now a religious home of some sort.

The screen door slammed shut as Gwen reentered the house. Tatty held the package closer, staring hard at the handwriting. It looked like her grandmother's, even to the fragile shakiness. Mathilde had had a series of small strokes in the weeks before she died. Tatty recalled the terrible, trembling grip of her grandmother's hand the last time they had been together, just a few days before her death.

"Never forget that you are Russian," she had said, pulling Tatty close as she uttered her raspy, imperious command, ice gray eyes as wide and mad as those of the principals in Eisenstein's *Ivan the Terrible.* "You have the blood of czars, Tatiana. Your people have ruled the land that is the center of the world. You are Russian. You are Iovashchenko. Never forget."

Tatty Chase, a product of Miss Porter's and Smith College, descendant of a member of the Continental Congress and step-daughter of R. Hastings Chase, one of the wealthiest bond lawyers on Wall Street, had disobeyed her grandmother's command as much as possible. She felt no affinity for this Russian blood. With her grandmother and mother chattering in it constantly, she had been compelled

5

to learn the Russian language as a child, but with no relish. She never spoke it in public.

The label on the package that bore Tatty's name and address—*Tatiana Alexandra Chase, Sandrow Road, East Hampton, L. I., New York*— was quite old and worn in places like rubbed velvet. She turned it over. It had been opened once before and resealed. Almost violently, she began tearing at the paper and tape.

Inside was an old leather-bound manuscript, but nothing to do with Broadway. The pages were handwritten, largely in French, with occasional phrases and notations in Russian or English. *Les Morts Russe—Russian Dead—* was the title. It was subtitled *Murders of My Family.*

A large, cold drop of rain struck Tatty on the back of her neck. The blue was utterly gone from the sky.

She began leafing through the pages, struggling with both Russian and French. She had heard of this book of Mathilde's, but had never seen it. It had not been found among her grandmother's possessions. Tatty's mother, Chloe, herself now dead, had been extremely upset by its disappearance, calling it the most important writing to have come out of the Russian Revolution.

She paused at one entry: "The Murder of the Princess Denzhevsky."

The Princess Irina Arkadyevna Denzhevsky, a striking beauty who had studied the dance with the great Tamara Krasavina and who performed at court as well as at entertainments for guests at her estate near Petrograd, was the wife of my mother's brother, General Mikhail Ivanovich Denzhevsky. When the Revolution broke out, he was at the Galician front in command of a division of Imperial Polish troops. She refused to leave Petrograd until he could join her, and when the Bolsheviks seized power from the Kerensky government eight months later, she was unable to flee the city and so took refuge with a maid in the home of Madame Dulski, a milliner she had for years richly patronized. The Princess remained with Madame Dulski until the spring of 1918.

6

The handwriting was difficult to read so she abandoned an exact translation and began glancing quickly over the passages, following the story as best she could. The princess had managed to reach an estate once owned by friends near Novgorod, on the Moscow Road. Her first hope had been to get to Finland, a former province that the Revolution had rendered an independent and neutral country. But the civil war with the Whites was underway and the Bolsheviks had sealed off that escape route. Instead, the princess decided to attempt a much longer route south and west to Poland, where she still had wealthy friends. Had she disguised herself as just another peasant refugee, Tatty gathered from the text, the princess might have succeeded, but instead she hired a car and driver in hopes of making speed, paying him with one of the many jewels she had sewn into her clothing when she had fled Petrograd.

No more than a hundred miles from Novgorod, they were stopped by a patrol of Red cavalry and turned over to a local unit of what ultimately became the Cheka, Lenin's state security police. The driver apparently told them about the hidden jewels.

Her grandmother's account of what had followed was so compelling that Tatty now found the French and Russian words easily returning to her.

They dragged the Princess and her maid to a room at the rear of a farm house. It was a low-ceilinged chamber, rude, with a dirt floor. Animals were likely kept there in the wintertime. They accused Irina Arkadyevna of theft of property of the Congress of Soviets, meaning her jewels. When she denied this, she was thrown to the floor and her clothing was pulled from her and torn and slashed to shreds with knives and other sharp instruments.

The same treatment was accorded the maid, though no jewels were found. The jewels yielded by Irina Arkadyevna's hat, cape, dress, and corsets filled a small basin. As the two women huddled naked on the floor, Bolshevik police inventoried the jewels and made entries in a ledger. The maid was then given some filthy peasant clothes to wear,

7

was told there were no charges against her, and was allowed to leave. One of the policemen escorted her to a nearby forest and shot her once in the back. Wounded only slightly, she feigned death until he was gone, and then made her way to a woodcutter's hut. She recovered from her wound, and eventually reached Poland.

The body of the Princess Irina Arkadyevna, naked, riddled with bullets and stab wounds, and with blood still clotted in her beautiful blond hair, was found along the bank of the River Velikaya. She was buried by peasants, but the grave was left unmarked lest the Cheka discover what they had done. All this is fact and was later recorded in an official report to Admiral Kolchak, head of the White Government. This was the fate of the Princess Irina Arkadyevna Denzhevsky, my aunt-in-law. Her murder has not been avenged.

A drop of rain again, and then another. More fell on the page. Tatty closed the manuscript, and her eyes.

She felt her damned Russian blood again, flowing forth in its mad, dark, Asiatic richness. Her grandmother had reached out to her once more, just as she had from her deathbed. Her grandmother, or someone else who knew her well. Who? And, for God's sake, why?

A heavy rain began to fall. Tatty pulled on her robe and stood, tying it closed. Clutching the old manuscript tight against her breast, she walked quickly to the house, her head lowered.

Her guests were all in the kitchen. Gwen was at the stove, stirring something in a large pot. Helping her was Becky Mather from down the road, a tiny young woman in Bermuda shorts and a Beethoven sweatshirt. Becky had gone to Endicott College for Women in Beverly, Massachusetts. Her father owned a restaurant and motel near East Hampton. Her sister ran a boutique in Southampton. They were descended from the same Mather family involved in the Salem witch trials.

Witches. Cold, wet forms raised from the tidal pools dead and dripping, tied and slumped in crude wooden

8

chairs teetering on long stout poles, showing the pleasure of God.

The Princess Denzhevsky, sprawled on a river bank with blood thick in her hair. Tatty shook her head.

Amanda Ensor, an artist friend, was in the far corner of the windowed breakfast nook, still wearing her morning caftan and reading a small book, her very long red hair falling over her brow. Next to her this weekend, not wearing his military uniform, thank God, was Captain David Paget, a longtime friend of Gwen's from Westchester who had ardently dated her while in college and had pressed a continuing correspondence over the years in the vain hope that she would marry him, first as an alternative to her architect husband, and then as one to widowhood. He was a few years older than Gwen and Tatty, a thin, fair-haired, muscular man with a nice smile in a scarred face, whom Tatty found strangely attractive. He was a Special Forces officer, rumored to have killed some people somewhere in Latin America, but had also had poems published in *The New Yorker* and the *Atlantic*, poems about death. He was arguing now across the table over some point of history with the other male guest at the house that Labor Day weekend, Cyril Greene. She presumed Paget would prevail.

She did not like Cyril Greene. She was fond of his brother, Sid, a fitfully successful and earthily warm-hearted New York producer who had hired her for her two best roles. He had not had occasion to hire her for anything at all the past two seasons, but they were still close enough to exchange Christmas presents. And there was a new production Sid was putting together for the fall, a very contemporary morality play set during World War I. There was a part for her, possibly: a young British noblewoman pacifist. Tatty had a very good British accent.

Cyril Greene had a British accent, among his many other failings. He was a pitiful example of the futility of attempting to be something one was not—in his case, utterly not. He carried leather-bound copies of the classics about with him, and sometimes wore knickers on the streets of Manhattan. He had no real job. Having graduated from Columbia, he had continued attending classes all his life—in medieval painting, hibachi cooking, needle-point, Yugoslavian cinema, Portuguese, Kung Fu—end-lessly, and without significant success. He occasionally earned money as a tutor, dog walker, sales clerk, or something of the sort, but lived mostly off his brother, other well-off relatives, and their friends. Like Tatty.

A pink-faced man with weak blue eyes and reddish blond hair, he had not been all that bad looking as a young man, but in his thirties had gone to fat and now had two chins. He had tried to offset this with a silly mustache, but it only worsened the effect. He looked like a red-haired, Jewish Oliver Hardy.

Cyril had more or less invited himself out to Tatty's that weekend, though he had contrived to have Amanda make the invitation official. Tatty suffered him for a number of confusing reasons: because she was Sid Greene's friend, because there were times when Cyril Greene was actually quite charming, because she was beginning to fear Sid Greene would never offer her a worthwhile part again.

Cyril had brought a woman with him this time, a rab-bity little creature named Clara. She sat next to him in the breakfast nook, nibbling on bread and lettuce, listening raptly as though Cyril were actually besting Paget in the argument, which he demonstrably was not.

Alice Mettering, a newspaper writer friend of Tatty's who had the month before divorced her second husband, was on a wooden chair by the corner windows, applying a violently red nail polish to her toes and sipping from a can of beer.

Tatty put down her head, hoping to pass through the kitchen without having to speak to any of them, but Alice ambushed her in midstride.

"A hair ribbon, Tatty?" she said, peering over the rim of her beer can. "You're lying out there naked yet still wearing a goddamn preppie hair ribbon? I swear you'll go to your grave in a hair ribbon, and maybe a plaid wrap skirt."

Tatty hurried on, but was caught again.

10

"I'm making pea soup," said Gwen, with that same faint, worried smile. "Your favorite."

"That's fine, Gwen," Tatty said. She paused. Cyril Greene was staring at her, his imagination doubtless dispensing with her robe. She wanted the sanctuary of her room. She wanted to read on in this strange, terrible, fascinating, and mysterious book. She found herself extremely nervous and agitated, on the verge of trembling. She would have a drink. It was close enough to lunch.

"I think I'll have a gin and tonic," she said to Gwen. "I hope there's gin."

"There should be."

But there wasn't. The antique liquor cabinet was empty but for a large bottle of Pernod and a few other liqueurs. The gin, vodka, Scotch, bourbon, and rum that had been there had vanished. It was Sunday, and the liquor stores were closed.

Cyril was talking quite volubly.

"The rule here is that everyone contributes," Tatty said, loudly, noting that no one except Gwen returned her gaze.

Cyril grinned, looking down at the table. Paget abruptly rose and went out into the rain. Tatty snatched up the Pernod, took a clean glass from the sink, and, letting her anger show in her stride, left the kitchen, climbing the broad front stairs to her room.

It was a corner bedroom, a quite large chamber with a fireplace and a view of the sea. She filled the glass with the strong pale green liqueur, and nestled in a big armchair by the sea-view window, opening the manuscript once again. Now she was trembling. She drank, tasting licorice and wincing as the Pernod seared its way to her stomach.

"God," she muttered to herself. The rain was now drumming on the roof. She began reading again, from a chapter describing the fate of a Prince Vasily, godfather to Mathilde. He had stayed with his regiment in Petrograd until the Bolshevik takeover.

There was a knocking at her door, polite, but firmly insistent.

"Gwen?"

"It's David Paget."

Fuming, Tatty left her chair and went to the door, wrenching it open and slamming it back against the wall. His face impassive, he held a bottle. Vodka. Stolichnaya. Expensive.

"I had this in my kit," he said. "Consider it my contribution."

She calmed herself. He was always doing nice things like that.

"That's expensive vodka," she said.

"I paid nothing for it. A souvenir from Nicaragua."

"Souvenir? Stolichnaya?"

He handed her the bottle.

"I can get more," he said.

She wondered if he was trying to impress her. He seemed so matter-of-fact.

"Thank you, Captain," she said, even more matter-of-factly. "I'll join you all later. After I'm dressed."

With a quick smile, she shut the door. Before returning to the manuscript again, she sat a long moment, sipping the Pernod, staring out at the sea. She had planned such a wonderful weekend. A novelist friend of hers and his wife were to have come but had had to decline her invitation at the last moment. So had a ballet dancer, a favorite friend. She'd been left with the old crowd, a military friend—and killer—and Cyril Greene. And her grandmother's bloody book. She picked up the manuscript and continued reading.

Prince Vasily had been arrested in his own home by the Cheka. They had tied him to a chair in the central hall, harangued him with charges and accusations for several hours, then blown out his brains with a large caliber pistol. This, too, was officially entered in the records of the White Government's special commission.

A cousin Dmitri, a renowned botanist with no firm politics anyone knew of, was dragged off a train in the Urals and, with his fellow passengers, machine-gunned to death in a snow-filled ditch. An Uncle Misha was beaten to death in his home by a Red mob. Cousins Sasha and Boris, little more than children, disappeared on a cold night in

Petrograd. Colonel Alexander Borisov, a distant cousin, was captured in civil war fighting in the south of Russia and executed.

The Countess Valentina, elder sister of a close friend of Mathilde's, had been shot for her elegant clothes in the winter of 1919. The Duchess Marie Pavlovna Gamov was caught in Pskov and burned alive in her car.

Tatty was interrupted by another knock at the door, followed by Gwen's voice. She entered, bringing lunch on a tray—a large bowl of soup, thick rye bread and butter, and a pot of tea. Tatty accepted it gratefully, touching Gwen's arm. Gwen left quietly. As Tatty was biting into the bread, it struck her how Russian the meal was. It was becoming Russian Day. Soup. Stolichnaya. A book full of dead Russians. What would be next? The only Russian thing in her own life was the fact that her stepsister Chesley's ex-husband, a newspaperman named Jack Spencer, had been transferred from Washington to Moscow, and had recently sent a postcard, addressing her as "Czarina," as he often had in the past. She wondered how the postcard had gotten out of the Soviet Union.

She ate most of the bread and soup, but left the tea, returning to the Pernod. If it was going to be an odd, ridiculous, utterly insane sort of day, she would behave to suit it. The rain was continuing, even harder than before. As she sipped the liqueur, she remembered a little song Chesley had sung when she was a child and Chesley a teen-ager:

> *All night long, the glasses tinkle,*
> *While outside, the raindrops sprinkle,*
> *Do you think another drink'll*
> *Do us any harm?*

Tatty's grandmother Mathilde had married Elwood Hoops, a well-to-do Westchester surgeon, shortly after arriving in the United States as a refugee. As his daughter, Tatty's mother Chloe was a descendant of one of the oldest families in America, but Mathilde brought her up as though she were one hundred percent Russian, as though she had never left St. Petersburg.

Mathilde was pleased when Chloe became an actress—the arts were the only profession suitable for the temperament and station of a Russian aristocrat—but unhappy when Chloe married a military man, an Air Force pilot and very handsome Virginia gentleman named Bobby Shaw.

Chloe had stuck with Bobby, from air base to air base, their infant daughter Tatty in tow. In 1963, Bobby was shot down on a special mission over Laos. He was later discovered to have been tortured to death in a Communist prison camp run by Pathet Lao. A year after that, Chloe, having resumed her stage career, married a wealthy admirer, R. Hastings Chase.

Chesley was Chase's daughter by his first wife, who had died in pregnancy along with her second baby. Tatty supposed that she in a way had become that second daughter he had lost. Hastings Chase had been inordinately kind and generous to her, more so perhaps than he was to Chesley.

Jack Spencer was socially acceptable enough, from Bedford in Westchester and a well-to-do family; but he drank all the time and was an incorrigible philanderer, as Chesley must have known. She could only wonder why Chesley had suddenly decided to divorce him, after having been so complaisant about his flaws for so many years. It may have been merely that he was getting old.

At any rate, Chesley had divorced him.

And now he was in Moscow.

Her mind was entertaining implausibilities, impossibilities. Jack Spencer could not have sent the manuscript. He was a witty man, who liked his little jokes, but was not the sort for anything so ghoulish. He or Chesley might have come upon the book in the Chase family summer place on Cape Cod, where Mathilde had been a frequent visitor, but they would have forwarded it to Tatty or her mother at once. The package bore a postmark dated just two days ago, a Braddock Wells, New York, postmark. Spencer had been in Moscow for several months.

14

She poured herself a full glass of Pernod, stared at the manuscript's cover for a long moment, then drank and began to read again. She must be done with this thing, but she could not be done with it until she had read it all. It was as though her grandmother's strong, trembling hand were still gripping her arm, holding her close.

The next chapter was about a family Chernevkov, cousins to Mathilde, St. Petersburg gentry who lived off income from mines in Siberia and a factory in Kiev, neither a place they ever went near. When the czar abdicated, they fled Petrograd at once, traveling by rail east toward the Urals. It took the family four years to reach their ultimate destination in China, Shanghai, and by then only Nathalie Chernevkov and four of her children were alive of a family group that had numbered fifteen. Nathalie herself committed suicide in Shanghai in 1936, a death Mathilde, with great invective, blamed on the Bolsheviks.

This mad, bloody procession of uniquely Russian tragedies continued inexhaustibly. The cumulative effect of the recountings seemed to increase Mathilde's zeal for the writing. Tatty's was the opposite response. She remembered something James Boswell had jotted in a notebook: "Saw three men hanged; effect diminished as each went." It was happening with each turn of a page. What was at first shocking became tragic and then merely pathetic and finally all but comical. These poor, ridiculous, ancestor-worshiping aristocrats had been utterly unable to comprehend the wrenching social dynamics that were tearing their medieval social system apart. Feckless in the face of it, clumsy and frantic in their attempts at escape, they succumbed to the ultimate horrors like frightened animals, mewing and bellowing. Tatty could only half convince herself these people were her relatives. She was no liberal. She was in fact a Republican who had kept a George Bush bumper sticker on the rear of her MG-A since the 1980 primaries. But there was nothing more logical in what she knew of world history than the Russian Revolution. She sometimes damned these Russian ancestors of hers. They and those like them had so foolishly made the Revolution inevitable, made it possible for a minor if ruthless fringe

15

political group to swiftly seize such massive power. They were directly responsible for the catastrophe brought upon themselves, for the tyranny the Communists unleashed upon all Mother Russia, and the further tyranny that they now threatened to inflict upon all the world.

Midway through an account of the drowning of a little girl, a distant cousin of hers through some connection, Tatty closed the manuscript and went to stand at the window. The rain had abated, but the haze was thick and gloomy, the sea visible only as an ill-defined grayness above the line of trees. She emptied her glass, noticing that she had already consumed more than half the Pernod.

The rain began again. It was imprisoning her in this house. Judging by the volume of voices, all her guests were still downstairs, trapping her in this room, for she was in no mood for the frivolous and contentious yak that had been the fare that weekend. She was trapped with this book and the memories it provoked—and a half bottle of Pernod.

She took the manuscript to her wide old canopied bed, and sat on its edge, turning on the lamp on the bedside table. There were so many characters, too many characters, and not just in the book. This assemblage of dead princesses and royal colonels was an unwanted intrusion, but no more so than the clutter of people downstairs, than the clutter of all the people in her life. Now they were crowding her, obscuring her, drowning her lines with their chatter. She had thought that in using her money to become mistress of this huge house she could more firmly control her life and surroundings, but her circumstance was little different from being caught in a crowd on a New York street. She should have taken Gwen's advice and bought instead a small cottage, something not in the Hamptons. Perhaps Montauk, or on Nantucket. Or in France.

No, not France. No longer France. *Plus jamais.* It hadn't been willingly, but she'd removed France from her life forever.

She lay back on the bed, thinking of her sister's ex-husband, and her little-girl love for him. Had Jack

16

Spencer been irrevocably removed from her life, as small a part of it as he had shared? Moscow was a million miles away, and Chesley had so thoroughly, almost viciously, discarded him.

Tatty had been married once, several years before. At times, she almost forgot the man's name. It was Dirk.

She sat up again, turning the book's pages until she came at last to an unread chapter. It opened with an old photograph firmly pasted to the paper, one of two young women in World War I–era dresses and wide-brimmed hats, standing with parasols in what looked like a formal garden with other figures walking in the background, including several men in uniform. Both girls—looking closer, Tatty decided they were teenagers—were strikingly attractive. The one on the left, a blonde with large eyes and a staring, serious expression, was her grandmother Mathilde. She did not recognize the one on the right, though it struck her, strangely, that the girl somewhat resembled herself. The hair was too dark, but the eyes were as wide and luminescent as her own, and the lips, chin, and nose were much the same. The cheekbones were exactly the same.

She looked to the handwritten caption at the bottom of the page. The girl with Mathilde was the Grand Duchess Tatiana Nicolayevna Romanov, the second daughter of the czar. The photograph had been taken in 1915, when Tatiana Romanov was eighteen and Mathilde two years younger. Tatty's mother had once told her she had been named for a daughter of the czar, but Tatty had dismissed it as more Russian mumbo jumbo.

The text on the following page began with a complicated genealogy that linked the Iovashchenkos with the royal Romanovs as cousins of cousins, descended from a common ancestor. From Tatty's mother, this would have seemed just so much theatrical nonsense, but Mathilde was too fiercely serious about her heritage and tireless in her research for this passage to be anything but the truth.

Tatty sat fully erect again, feeling tipsy now. "I am a cousin of the Romanovs," she said. "I am of the blood of czars." It sounded so silly, so melodramatic. She drank again. Everything sounded silly.

As Mathilde related, Tatiana was the tallest, slimmest, most elegant, and—though only second eldest—most commanding of the royal children. Mathilde quoted an Imperial Guard officer as saying, "You knew at once she was an emperor's daughter." Auburn-haired with deep gray eyes, she was the closest to the Czarina Alexandra, the dominating figure in the royal family, and shared her mother's zeal and drive. She excelled at French, at the piano, at theatrics, and was the most active in society. She was the decision-maker. She reminded Tatty of Chesley.

Page after page followed filled with details of Mathilde's social encounters with the imperial family. Most of these occasions were quite formal and involved large numbers of guests, but Mathilde had apparently achieved a genuine if not overly intimate friendship with the Grand Duchess Tatiana, who had several times had Mathilde to the family country retreat at Czarskoe Selo without inviting any other guest. In gratitude, Tatty gathered, Mathilde had responded with the fullest measure of devotion. Had there been no revolution, Mathilde might have become a favorite at court.

Had there been no revolution, Tatty would never have been born. All those millions of people slaughtered, and thus Tatty lived.

Tatty was growing weary, and, she supposed, not a little drunk. She'd not had her shower, which would revive her. Finishing this last glass of Pernod and leaving her grandmother's book on her bed turned to an unread page, she went with some clumsiness to her adjoining bathroom, shed her robe, turned the water to as high a temperature as she thought she could tolerate, and stepped into the shower. She stood there for a long time, head back, eyes closed, the steamy water cascading over her entire body, until its temperature began to lessen, a sign that the basement hot water heater's capacity had been exhausted.

Turning off the faucets, Tatty returned to her bedroom without pausing to dry herself. She lay down on her bed, every muscle relaxed. The effect of the shower had been just the opposite of that desired. Without another thought of Russia, she quickly fell asleep.

She was half awakened by a rattling sound, which she thought must be rain against the window. Struggling to escape her woozy sleep, she opened her eyes to darkness and realized that there was no rain. The sound was a rapping on her door.

"Yes?"

It opened to noise from downstairs and Gwen's unmistakable silhouette against the hall light.

"Tatty? Are you all right?"

"Yes, sort of."

"There was a call for you. Two actually. From the same person. A woman. A secretary, I think."

Tatty rubbed her eyes.

"Secretary? On Sunday?"

"A man's secretary, a friend of yours. She said he'd be coming out here this weekend. I came upstairs the first time she called, but you were in the shower. The next time I came up you were asleep."

"Gwen. What is this man's name?"

"Oh. Ron."

"Ron? I don't know any Ron."

"That's what she said. Actually, the way she pronounced it, it sounded more like Ran, but I never heard such a name."

"Neither have I. She said this weekend? Tomorrow's Labor Day. The weekend's almost over."

Gwen shrugged.

"It must be some mistake," Tatty said. She sat up, brushing her hair back from her face with her hands. Gwen came and sat on the bed beside her. Here she was naked again, with Gwen looking at her.

"Tatty, you're all right?"

"Yes," she replied, reaching for her robe. "I . . . I've done something very silly. I've been drinking all afternoon. It's this book. It was in that package. My grandmother wrote it. It's about all of her relatives, my relatives, too, I guess, who were killed in the Russian Revolution. I've been reading it all day, and drinking. I'm sorry."

Gwen touched her shoulder.

"It's all right. It must make you very sad."

"Not really. I never knew them. Who's here? It sounds like quite a crowd."

"Allan Michaels and his wife came over," Gwen said, referring to a New York magazine editor who lived nearby. "And Dexter."

Dexter Johns, a Wall Street customer's man and another neighbor, had proposed to Tatty at a party the week before. It was the third time he had done so that summer.

"Actually, we're having a good time. Joe Walsh is here, too."

Walsh was one of the town policemen.

"What on earth are people drinking?"

"Cyril found some wine and a case of beer in the cellar. You must have forgotten it. Will you be coming down?"

She could hear laughter. Cyril was performing.

"I don't think so."

"Do you want something to eat? David's brought some pizza and clams."

"No thank you. Just leave me to my Russians. I'll see you tomorrow."

She waited until Gwen had closed the door, then turned on the lamp again. The chapter Mathilde had written about Tatiana Romanov and her family was an extremely long one but apparently the last. She would finish it that night.

She began to read, then froze, her jarred memory finally performing its function. The name was not Ron, or Ran. It was Ram, as Gwen should have known. She and Tatty had met F. Ramsey Saylor on Cape Cod the summer before their sophomore year in college.

No wonder the secretary had been working on a Sunday. Ramsey was an officer of the Central Intelligence Agency.

Tatty went to the window and stood a moment, then began pacing back and forth, two fingers pressed to her lips in nervous habit. She had not spoken with Ram Saylor in more than a year. Not since France.

She brought the glass and the vodka bottle to the night table, and then Mathilde's manuscript to the bed. Loosening her robe, she climbed beneath the covers, turning onto her side and pulling the book into the lamplight.

The March revolution had caught the czar on his military train near the front and his family at Czarskoe Selo. The country retreat almost at once became a prison. Mathilde anguished voluminously over their plight, though it seemed a not uncomfortable house arrest.

After his abdication, the czar was quickly reunited with his wife and children, but their imprisonment at Czarskoe Selo continued without interruption, as the Provisional Government led largely by Alexander Kerensky continued to debate their fate. In August 1917, with the knowledge of only three others in his government, Kerensky finally arranged to have the imperial family taken by secret train to Tobolsk, a friendly town in Siberia.

In November, as the Siberian winter began to close on their new prison, Kerensky's Provisional Government fell.

In January 1918, a new unit of soldiers came to guard them. Many were brutes and oafs, who took perverse pleasure in carving obscene words into the wood of the swing used by Tatiana and her sisters. They endured this until April, when Red cavalry arrived with orders to return the imperial family to Moscow. The commander's plan was to do so by taking a circuitous rail route that would avoid Ekaterinburg, a town on the eastern slope of the Urals that had long been hostile to czarist rule and was filled with Bolshevik militants.

The Red soldiers took the czar and the czarina separately, leaving the four girls and the hemophiliac boy Alexis behind under guard. Tatiana had them sew a fortune in jewels into their clothing, but that cleverness was to prove pointless. As Lenin had secretly arranged, the train carrying the czar was turned back onto tracks taking it into Ekaterinburg. There, they were brought to "the house of special purpose" that had been prepared for them. Tatiana and the other children followed soon after.

21

The family's happiness at being reunited swiftly changed to despair.

Armed guards with big pistols, hard-core revolutionaries from the town, sat outside their open bedroom doors while they slept at night. These coarse brutes followed Tatiana, all the girls, into the lavatory when they used it. They drew filthy pictures on the walls depicting the monk Rasputin and the Empress engaging in perverse sexual acts. They were animals, making every moment of this imprisonment a torment. One guard, who had warmed to the children, tried to prevent some of this. He was shot.

On July 4, on discreet orders from Lenin in Moscow, the local guards were replaced with another unit. The new men were well-disciplined, correct, even courteous. They were Cheka, Lenin's secret police, and they had been carefully selected for their mission.

At this point, Tatty set the manuscript aside. She took a strong drink of the vodka, letting it fill her stomach with its heat, then sat a long moment, running her hands over her face, listening to her own heavy, unhappy breathing.

She did not want to read on, though she knew she must, as her grandmother had intended. It was not that she was squeamish. Had she not herself killed another human being? It was that she desperately did not want to have happen what had already happened nearly seven decades before. In her fuzzy state, it almost seemed logical to her that, if she did not turn the page, the violent, cruel, awful act would not ever have occurred.

She turned back to the old photograph, looked deep into those wide, gray, beautiful eyes set in the face that was so much hers. This tragic young woman had done nothing, had starved no peasant, imprisoned no dissident, ordered no father from his suffering family to the front. She had no involvement in politics, no involvement with any vile, corrupt Rasputin. She was just a young woman, still waiting for the fullness of life's joys and wonders. She was not quite twenty-one. It was quite possible she had not yet even been in love.

22

Again vodka, and again. Then Mathilde's words, the French perfectly clear.

On the night of July 16, around midnight, the Emperor and his family were awakened and told to dress at once, because the White Army was nearing Ekaterinburg and they had to be moved for their safety. The family believed this deceit, and did as they were told. When ready, they were escorted downstairs and taken to a very small basement and told to wait. At the Emperor's request, three chairs were brought, allowing him, the Empress, and the sleepy Alexis to rest. Behind them stood the four girls, the family doctor, and three servants. When the guards returned, they were carrying those huge military revolvers.

The leader said, "Your relations have tried to save you. They have failed and we must now shoot you."

It is reported that the Czar tried to rise to stand in front of Alexandra and Alexis and protect them. He was shot through the head. The Empress was shot through the breast and died at once. Tatiana was hit by a fusillade of bullets, striking her in the chest and stomach and head. She fell with two of her sisters. The doctor and two of the servants were also slain in the shooting. The maid, Demidova, had not been hit. As they were out of ammunition, the killers took some rifles with bayonets from an adjoining chamber and chased her about the room, clubbing and stabbing her until she ceased her wild screaming and died. The fiends clubbed the family spaniel to death. When Alexis, who had only been wounded, regained consciousness, they kicked him in the head and one who still had bullets fired twice into the boy's ear. The youngest daughter, Anastasia, proved to have only fainted. They dealt with her with bayonets and rifle butts. Then all were dead and the room was silent and the floor was a river of blood, czarist blood.

All this has been recorded by Bolshevik historians and is in archives in the Kremlin.

The fiends tried to hide their awful crime. The next day, they began chopping up all the bodies with axes and burning the pieces in gasoline. The bones that would not burn were soaked in acid. What was left was thrown into a deep

23

abandoned mine shaft. That was the grave of this beautiful, holy family.

The White Army retook Ekaterinburg eight days later, and saw the evidence of the shooting in "the house of special purpose." Admiral Kolchak, the White leader in Siberia, ordered a thorough investigation, which uncovered much of what is related here.

The investigators reclaimed hundreds of articles of evidence—jewelry, religious crosses, belt buckles, small icons, fragments of clothing, eyeglasses, and a military badge—all known to belong to the Imperial Family. They found charred bones in the mine shaft, and the still unburned body of the family dog. A severed finger was also found. On it, too tight to remove, was an emerald ring. It was Tatiana's ring.

The jackal Sverdlov, the Lenin lieutenant who masterminded the czar's removal to Ekaterinburg and arranged this bestial crime, was mysteriously murdered six months later. Ekaterinburg was renamed Sverdlovsk in his horrible honor. The criminal Lenin died of a stroke six years afterward, but that by no means sufficed. The murders of my family have not been avenged.

Tatty drank more vodka, but it was insufficient to the task. Letting the manuscript fall to the floor, she turned and pressed her face into her pillow, and cried. At length, she was rescued by sleep, but it took a very long time.

2

Tatty awoke at the first light of morning, a cool breeze gently stirring the curtains. It seemed much too early for the air to be that restless. Her mind toyed with the word *ghosts*.

She rolled onto her back, closing her eyes tightly and rubbing them, as though she could rub away the images of the night before, the bloodied bodies in long dresses, the face of the young woman with her grandmother in the old photograph. The Pernod and vodka had left her more sickened and depressed than she had been in months, or years. She lay still, perfectly and desperately still.

But there was no going back to sleep. She had spent too many hours on this bed. Overriding the nausea and depression was the urge for freedom and escape.

Tatty sat up, swinging her tan legs over the side of the bed and dizzily gripping its edge. She wanted a brisk cold shower, but the noise would awaken her guests, and she was in no mood for company this morning. Good God, what if she went down to the kitchen and found Cyril? She quickly brushed her teeth, then pulled on a pair of khaki shorts and a blue blouse, slipping her feet into a comfortably worn pair of Topsiders. She would bathe in the ocean, after her run. Gingerly picking up the half empty bottle of vodka, Tatty made her way quietly down the stairs to the kitchen.

It was extremely neat and clean. Gwen must have stayed up after all the partying to tidy things—even the ashtrays had been washed. Tatty made a Bloody Mary of sorts with a small amount of vodka and some V-8 juice, almost spilling it when she heard someone come into the room behind her.

"Did you have a good sleep?" Gwen asked, moving to wipe clean the countertop where Tatty had spilled juice. Gwen could only have had a few hours of sleep herself. She was barefoot, and wearing another shapeless housedress, doubtless with nothing underneath.

"That wasn't my problem," Tatty said. "I've had too much bloody sleep, and much too much to drink."

"I imagine everyone will have hangovers. Cyril found more cheap wine downstairs. Do you suppose it belonged to the previous owners?"

Tatty looked to an empty gallon jug visible at the top of the full trash basket.

"That woman who called yesterday," she said, "the secretary, who said to expect a Ron?"

"Yes," said Gwen, moving now to put the juice away.

"I believe she meant Ram."

"Ram?"

"Ram. Ramsey Saylor."

Gwen paused and blushed, as well she might. Ramsey had been the first man Gwen had slept with. He had seduced her on Cape Cod's Nauset Beach that long-ago summer, when she was nineteen. This carried little stigma with Tatty. Ramsey had performed the same service for her a few nights later.

"Such a long time ago," Gwen said.

"I've seen him more recently. Quite recently. Last year, in fact."

"Oh? Where?"

"In the city. And in France."

"Did you invite him out here?"

"No. I don't know why he might be coming. I don't

26

think he is, really. There's nothing left of the weekend. That call was probably some mistake."

"I hope so. All we need out here is Ramsey Saylor."

Tatty took two compulsive gulps of her drink, coughed, took a deep breath, then drank again.

"Gwen. Do I look Russian?"

Gwen smiled, as though sharing a happy secret. "Sometimes. But sometimes you look very English. And sometimes just yourself. You have a very expressive face, Tatty. After all, you're an actress."

"There are so many Russians on my mother's side of the family. I just wonder if it's beginning to show through more as I get older."

"You look beautiful, Tatty."

Gwen's expression was one of adoration. Tatty hurriedly finished her drink.

"I'm going for a run," she said. "Would you hide this vodka some place where Cyril and Amanda won't find it?"

"I'll put it in the dishwasher. What shall I do if Ramsey Saylor does show up?"

"Shoot him."

"That's a joke."

"Kind of. I'll be back in an hour or so. Don't let our hungover guests run amok."

"Tatty. What did Ram Saylor do to you?"

"Nothing. Nothing you need worry about. Relax, Gwen. I'm sure he's not coming."

All of August had been cool. This September morning was almost chilly, the cloudless, crystalline sky meeting the darker blue of ocean at a sharply etched horizon. Tatty removed her shoes when she reached the beach, breaking into a fast-paced run when at last she came to the hard, surf-packed sand; but not long after she slowed down, coughing. Her damn fool drinking. The poisons would have to be driven from her body slowly.

She trotted east toward the sun, squinting against its shattering brightness, her breast heaving as her need for oxygen turned discomfort into pain and pain into agony. She ran on anyway until she couldn't take another step.

Then she collapsed rolling onto the sand, lying limp and weak on her back, listening to the scree of nearby seagulls with her eyes closed, the cold splash of shallow waves reaching to her feet.

The questions still clung to her mind. Who had sent her that horrifying manuscript from her grandmother's grave? When was Sid Greene going to call her about the new play? Why was Ramsey coming? Was he in fact coming or had she made too much of a wrong number or some secretary's mistake?

She rolled over onto her stomach and looked idly at the sand, drawing in it with her finger, finally writing his name, as she recalled doing at Nauset Beach that first summer on Cape Cod, only that time she had spelled his last name "Sailor." He had been her first man who was not still a boy. Their sexual experiences were not only her first, but her best. She had never again encountered a man as tender and artful as Ramsey had been that summer, and when they had their second affair years later, it was as wonderful.

Tatty turned onto her back once more, her hands behind her head and her eyes on the sky and a high-flying gull. She had not slept with a man since France, and the need sometimes became oppressive. She blamed Ramsey for that.

If he were to call right now, Gwen would answer, and Gwen professed to despise him. Tatty, totally unable to control herself, had stolen Ramsey from her that summer. But Gwen chose to hate only him for it. When he had left Tatty at the end of that summer, as Tatty had half expected him to do, it was Gwen who became furious.

Tatty wanted to see him now, Gwen or no. France or no.

There had been no calls from anyone. Tatty lingered about the house after breakfast, but the phone remained silent. Embarrassed by her attendance upon it, she drove to Sag Harbor by herself for lunch, and then took her sailboat out into Noyack Bay for an hour. But only that. Hurrying back, she found that a neighbor had called inviting her to a party a week hence. No one else.

Amanda and Becky were going to the beach. Tatty decided to join them, and asked Captain Paget and Gwen to come along. Gwen, pleading fatigue, stayed behind, which irritated Tatty. Despite his profession, Paget was as nice a man as Gwen had ever met; certainly better than she could expect in the years to come.

Paget recited poetry to her on the beach, Robert W. Service, and, of all people, Elinor Wylie. He showed off for them, diving repeatedly into the surf, which had become quite heavy. His back muscles were lean and corded, contorted in places by a long curving scar. Tatty made herself stop looking at them.

"Mr. Greene called while you were away," Gwen said, when they returned.

"Sid Greene?" Cyril's head snapped up in the manner of a dog whose name had been spoken.

"Yes. He wants to have lunch with you on Friday."

"Did he say where?"

"Yes. At the Plaza, the Edwardian Room, at one o'clock. You're to call his office tomorrow to confirm."

"That's all he said? Nothing more?"

Cyril was grinning again.

"No, Tatty," said Gwen.

Tatty started toward the dishwasher, then halted.

"No one else called? No one came by?"

Gwen's fleeting, troubled smile came and went.

"No. No one."

Tatty continued to the dishwasher. Dirty dishes there were in it, a jumble of them, but not the vodka. Tatty looked back to Gwen, who sadly shrugged.

"All right, you miserable sponges," Tatty said, her eyes darkening. "I thought I made myself clear. I'm not going to finance all of your drinking problems. This is not Hollywood."

"We went all the way to Southampton looking for an open liquor store," Alice said. "They're all closed for Labor Day."

" 'The Liquor Stores of Southampton Are Closed,' " said Cyril, dramatically. "A tragedy in one act."

"You could have gone Saturday."

"But Tatty," said Becky. "We did."

"Not a tragedy," said Cyril. "A farce."

Tatty leaned back against the sink, folding her arms. She was not going to let these people turn her into a shrew. No one had ever called Tatty Chase less than a lady.

"We'll get ourselves all the liquor we need," said Paget, slowly. He reached beneath his chair and pulled forth the bottle of vodka, pouring what little remained of it into what appeared to be a glass of Coca-Cola. He had preceded her into the house while she had put the MG in the garage.

"How?" said Amanda, her eyes flirtatious beneath pointedly lowered lids.

"We'll steal it."

Paget picked the perfect beach party, eight or nine people seated in a semicircle around a large bonfire, facing the ocean. A long plank with a number of large bottles had been set to the side, the side nearest the entrance to the beach.

Paget and Tatty dropped to a crouch and then flattened out into a crawl, moving silently but with surprising swiftness through the now cold sand. About thirty or forty yards distant from the plank, Paget halted, lifting his head slightly to study their target.

"No dogs," he said. "*Bien. Rien de chiens.*"

"I feel silly," she said.

"No you don't. You're enjoying yourself. Have you ever done anything like this before?"

"Just some pranks in college."

Paget began moving forward again. A tall woman by the fire stood up, turning her back to the flames, seemingly looking at them. But she saw nothing, and soon a man in a sweatshirt pulled her down again. Paget smiled, the flicker of the fire in his eyes. They soon reached the outer circle of light, and waited.

Amanda's primal scream came precisely on time. Repeating it, more a long screech this time, she lurched along the sand at the water's edge, stumbled, then tottered on, screaming one more time.

Paget touched Tatty's arm and they began to creep forward again, toward the firelight. Tatty heard a slow thudding, and looked to see Becky come by, riding bareback, having somehow coaxed her old horse into a lumbering canter. All was going according to plan.

They reached the liquor plank unnoticed. Paget silently took two half-gallon bottles of what appeared to be whiskey and slipped them under his arms. Tatty less silently pulled a similarly large bottle of what she hoped was gin into the sand, and snatched at a smaller one that looked to have rum in it. They began to ease themselves backward, back toward the sheltering darkness, Tatty's breath coming fast.

She was enjoying this. She was enjoying Paget.

Once again in the shadows, they paused to make certain they were undetected, then turned and ran to the bluff. A basket was there. After dumping the bottles in it for Gwen and Alice to haul up to the top, Paget slipped his arm around Tatty's waist. She let him keep it there until, laughing in celebration of their wonderful triumph, they reached the road.

When Gwen and Alice joined them with the basket a moment later, Gwen said nothing. She let her eyes linger on the two of them, and then nodded, as though in blessing. They all walked on slowly, giving the others a chance to catch up. Cyril and Clara were the last.

Chattering happily, they were caught suddenly by a flare of headlights at the next curve in the road. With Cyril in the lead, the others scrambled over a stone wall into the trees to their right. Gwen, struggling with the heavy basket, was the last to disappear. Tatty and Paget remained where they were, even when it was obvious the approaching car was a police cruiser. It stopped beside them, and Joe Walsh rolled down the window.

"Tatty! Where you going? You're missing a hell of a party."

"Party?"

"Back on the beach. Augusta von Letzendorf's party. She's got a whole crew of Europeans with her this summer."

Tatty had heard about them. "I wasn't invited," she said.

"I was. And she told me to bring friends."

Joe Walsh was invited to some of the best Hamptons parties. Consequently, those events never had trouble from police, or outsiders. Walsh was a decent sort, bluff and cheery and with some wit about him, a charitable fellow with always an open arm for the extra or unwanted woman of a weekend. People who snubbed or cut Joe Walsh because he was a mere policeman were often snubbed or cut themselves.

Tatty wanted to go home, but the others denied her the opportunity. Seeing that the policeman was only Walsh, they hurried back over the stone wall.

"Did you say party?" said Alice. Others made it a chorus: "Party! Party!"

Tatty sighed, feeling like some primitive tribal matriarch. "All right," she said. "For a little while."

Trooping back along the road behind Walsh's slowly moving police car, Tatty asked Paget where Gwen had gone. Tatty had guessed, but she was curious about how much attention Paget was paying.

"She went back to the house with the booze," he said. "Someone had to do it. And when someone has to do it, there's Gwen."

"Does that bother you?"

"That's not what bothers me about Gwen."

As Tatty fully expected, the party Walsh led them to was precisely the one they had just raided. The tall blonde who was Augusta von Letzendorf welcomed Walsh, telling him about the mysteriously disappearing liquor and the strange occurrences of screaming women and night-riding horses. Walsh, with a grin, only shrugged. The von Letzendorf woman looked at Amanda with uncomfortable interest, but said nothing. Tatty took a seat off by herself, where she could watch the waves break out of the blackness. A pleasant-looking man in a sweatshirt and ragged cut-offs made her a gin and bitter lemon, which she accepted somewhat guiltily. He seated himself next to her and, with a well-bred German accent, introduced himself as Paul.

He was a prince—literally. Tatty knew about him, about all of them. They were all princes or archdukes or countesses or something, if only by marriage. Augusta, once a model, was a baroness by marriage. Her group here had been featured in an article on the Hamptons in the most recent issue of *W* magazine.

"It is a warm night, yes?" the prince said. "For the end of summer."

The low surf was cresting white and gold in the firelight. Paul had serious eyes, but an innocent face, a person to trust.

"It's lovely," she said. "I wish I weren't going back this week."

It was a lie. Her urge to return to her apartment on East Fifty-seventh Street was almost frantic. It was as though a few days back in Manhattan would somehow enhance her prospects for her Friday luncheon with Sid Greene. Staying here, she was holding back time.

"I am going back tomorrow morning," said Paul. "Erik and I." He nodded toward a thin, blondish man talking to Amanda. "Would you like to come with us? I have a very large Mercedes-Benz sedan. You could sleep if you liked, in the back."

Augusta was dancing, or at least swaying back and forth, accompanied by her own loud humming.

Tatty was as good as these people, even by their standards. What had Mathilde been? A princess? A countess? In any event, a relative of the Romanovs. She had the blood of czars.

She declined the man's invitation. Finishing her drink, she excused herself. She ran all the way back, not so much in haste as in a need for release and freedom, her head back, her bare feet pattering over the asphalt, her breath rapid but easy.

Reaching her almost darkened house, she took a seat in the most distant of the canvas chairs set out on her side lawn, tilting back her head, drawing the night and its sounds close around her. It could be hours before the others came back from the beach party. It was a pleasing prospect.

Tatty lost track of time. The sound of approaching footsteps surprised her as they came from the left, from the town, not the beach, a man walking with a brisk, military pace. The sound stopped, and a moment later Ramsey Saylor stepped onto the lawn. Though Tatty was off in the shadows, he saw her immediately, and came toward her with the purposefulness of someone approaching a bank teller.

He was dressed as she might have expected: a tan poplin suit; white shirt with button-down collar; and muted striped tie, doubtless all of it from Brooks Brothers. He carried an under-the-seat overnight bag with the handle of a squash or tennis racquet protruding from the side. He set it down silently as he eased himself into the chair next to her.

"Tatty, Tatty," he said. "God, but it's good to see you. And in so irenic a circumstance. I feared you'd be surrounded by houseguests, engaged in some Hamptons romp."

Ramsey was a handsome man as F. Scott Fitzgerald had been handsome, with extraordinarily clear blue eyes. His complexion was very English, flushed cheeks visible even beneath his tan. His lips were a trifle feminine, with a droll turn at the corners appropriate to his style of speech. Though Ramsey had a surprisingly high-pitched voice, he spoke in a long, Westchester drawl. Tatty recalled that he was now thirty-three.

"You've arrived rather late, Ramsey," she said.

"I am awfully late. I had business in Center Moriches. God, I've never had business in Center Moriches before in my life."

Tatty remembered that the Philippine president had established a luxurious hideaway there. It was the only point of interest in Center Moriches.

"Have you now become an Asian expert?" she said.

34

The droll corners turned up, revealing a flash of perfect teeth.

"Clever Tatty," he said. "No, it has not to do with Marcos. A colleague from Langley, actually. Summering there. God, what is the Agency coming to? Center Moriches."

He leaned to look into her face, into her eyes. He touched her cheek and smiled.

"I trust my presence is not invasive," he said. "You Hamptons types live such perennative lives. I shouldn't have thought you'd mind another old face turning up again."

"I'm sure Gwen will find your presence invasive, and then some. She's inside."

"Ah, sweet Gwen. I suppose she found me invasive from the very beginning." Another flash of teeth.

Tatty frowned. "What do you want, Ramsey? Are you here on some errand for the Agency?"

"As a matter of fact, yes. My superiors were quite upset about what happened to you in Marseilles last year. They want to make it up to you."

"Nearly a year later."

"It took some time to arrange something meaningful, don't you know. After all, you don't need mere money. And your gravamens in this case are quite compelling. I think you'll be quite pleased, when we talk about it tomorrow."

"Tomorrow."

"Yes. God, Tat. No need for major discourse tonight. Actually, I was going to come see you about it after you returned to town, but since I was in the area anyway, well, how could I stay away?"

"Ramsey. I do have a houseful of guests. They're all down at the beach."

"Yours is a commodious dwelling, Tatty. Surely you can provide me with some wretched corner and scrap of blanket."

"All right," she said.

"You're the kindest person I know," he said, his smile remaining in place. He leaned toward her, and put his hand gently on her bare knee, rubbing it softly with his thumb. "Dear, dear Tatty. It's been eleven years. Can you imagine? Eleven years since I first sang to you that song from *Hair,* 'Smith girls are delicious.'"

"The proper lyric was 'black girls.'"

"Tatty. You are the very antithesis of every black girl in the world. Have you ever stopped to ponder that? You are the whitest woman I've ever known. And without question the most beautiful."

She wondered how annoyed she should be, but before she could decide, he had lifted her to her feet. She was fearful of what was coming, but didn't want to stop it. He kissed her. She tried to remain stiff in his arms but it was hopeless.

It was a mistake to let him do that, and a mistake to let him do it again. But, unnaturally perceptive, he had read her perfectly again. Before she could quite figure out what to do about it, he had slipped his hand beneath the waistband of her shorts and, finding no obstructive underwear, had moved with practiced swiftness to remembered places, and then to the most perfectly wonderful place. She was helpless against this man she had once, twice, so passionately loved.

"Not here," she said, between heavy breaths. "In back. I have a place. There's a hedge. Ramsey. You're a bastard."

He lifted her with an easy swiftness. She had forgotten his remarkable strength.

"To the hedge," he said. "And then to the gin."

Afterward he was gentlemanly enough, or at least clever enough, not to ask her how long it had been. To her chagrin, she had made it more than obvious how long.

3

The morning came much as had the one before it: a pinkish sky beyond the window, a cool breeze moving the curtains, the unhappy residue of too much drinking too evident. What was different was the foreground presence of Ramsey Saylor's bare back and dark head.

Pausing only for a few words to Gwen, who greeted Saylor with only the most brittle courtesy, they had taken gin to Tatty's room, and, after an interval of drink, talk, and fitful sleep, had made love once more.

He lay quite still, his breathing the quietest wisp of a sound. She did not know if this was a matter of physiology or another of his practiced skills, whether he was being considerate of her or merely professionally cautious, but Saylor did not snore. Gwen once said it was the most likeable thing about him.

Moving carefully, Tatty slowly sat up, then gently swung her tanned legs over the side of the bed. Ramsey did not stir. She eased herself to her feet. Ramsey still did not stir, but he spoke.

"My darling Tatty. There is nothing so bucolic about the Hamptons that warrants rising at so chthonic an hour."

"Do you have to talk like William F. Buckley all the time?"

It was something of an insult. Much as their politics and mannerisms coincided, Ramsey considered himself Buckley's superior—intellectually, physically, and socially. Ramsey's father had of course been nothing more prestigious than a well-off arms exporter, but the Saylors were Episcopalian and the Buckleys Catholic. In Ramsey's world, that still counted.

"Your remark is a rhetorical nullity," he said, still motionless. She could not see, but guessed he had his eyes closed. "Tatty, let us go sailing this afternoon."

"To chat?"

"Yes."

"To chat professionally. About the Central Intelligence Agency's generous offer?"

"Yes."

He was studying her body.

"God, Tatty, you're still the golden girl of the beach. Come back to bed."

"Ramsey, my houseguests are leaving this morning. I must say good-bye." She glanced at his shoulders. He had been a wrestling champion at Princeton, and looked as though he still could be.

She locked the bathroom door behind her.

Saylor was as good as his name, the best yachtsman Tatty had ever known. Buckley had crossed the Atlantic in a large boat with a large crew and servants, writing of the experience as though it were an epic voyage rivaling Brendan the Navigator's. Ramsey had crossed the Atlantic several times, in much smaller boats, and once by himself, treating all the adventures as routine, as though it was expected of sailors to cross the Atlantic. He had won a Newport-Bermuda race, among many others.

With its forward staysail and jib, Tatty's thirty-foot cutter had a painfully heavy weather helm when sailing close-hauled, yet Ramsey tacked into the strong easterly with an almost effortless grip of the tiller. He had few words for Tatty other than commands to shift and trim sail. The strong wind and heaving spray were not conducive to conversation. Both were wearing foul-weather jackets, Ramsey's imprinted with the word BERMUDA and a map of the island.

At length they came abeam of the channel that led north from Cedar Point, and Ramsey fell off to a broad reach as he turned into it, lessening the cut of the wind and making for a gentler passage. He leaned back, relaxing, squinting forward over the pitching bow.

"All right," she said, "what do you want to say to me? If this is all leading up to another of your patriotic recruiting pitches, Ramsey, I can't think of a sillier approach."

His flashing smile froze in place. It was an acting technique. Putting the face in neutral while the mind raced ahead.

"Tatty, I can't think of anything your country would welcome more than to have you assisting the Agency on a full-time basis."

"And I can't think of anything I'd welcome less. After Marseilles."

"Under the circumstances, your reluctance is certainly understandable."

"That thug tried to rape me, Ramsey. He damn near succeeded. You assured me I'd be protected every step of the way. Yet you let that bastard get into my hotel room. He broke my wrist. He hit me in the face."

"We haven't forgotten that."

"He could have killed me."

"You dealt with that possibility magnificently."

"I blew his bloody brains out! That disgusting mess, all over everything, all over me. God, what you made me do, Ramsey. I could throw up all over again just thinking about it."

Ramsey pushed the tiller away from him slightly, pointing the boat back up into the wind, its increasing sound filling the silence that came between them. They were well out into Gardiners Bay now. Ramsey was steering toward Orient Point, far across the roughening open water.

He took her hand.

"I'm not trying to recruit you, Tatty. My concern over your daisegnonian lifestyle is quite genuine. Almost fatherly."

"You're all of three years older than I am."

"You often make me feel quite fatherly nevertheless. Perhaps it's because you're an orphan."

"For God's sake, Ramsey."

There was a rain squall visible to weather, far down the bay, or possibly farther east, in Block Island Sound.

"Ramsey. What is it you came to say to me?"

"You're curious as to what it is the Agency would like to offer you, by way of compensation."

"You thought I'd never ask."

She had felt so close to this man, just half a day before. Now he seemed someone she scarcely knew. For a third of her life they had been friends and sometime lovers, from the last reach of childhood until now, the last of her youth. She could not comprehend why he seemed so distant and forbidding. She kept her friends too long.

"Tatty, we'd like to offer you a job."

"I told you. Nothing could interest me less."

"I don't mean Agency work. Not really. We have in mind something altogether suitable for your profession, something theatrical."

"Shakespeare? Shaw?"

He treated her to another quick smile as he paused to haul the main sheet in tighter and point the bow up to the very edge of irons, heeling the boat till the rail touched the hissing rush of sea.

"Not Shakespeare," he said, raising his voice against the humming and drumming of the shrouds and sails, increasing its register to a remarkably high pitch. "Harriet Beecher Stowe."

"What?"

"Ready about!"

It was a command. He was going to come about, shift the bow through the wind and change course for the south. It fell to her to slack off the jib and staysail and haul them to the starboard side. She moved to the winches. "Ready!"

He swung the tiller. "Helm's-alee!" She worked the winches quickly, then waited to see his point of sail before setting the sails in trim. He was falling off to the south-west, back toward Sag Harbor.

"Harriet Beecher Stowe," Ramsey repeated. "The State Department has arranged for some dramatic readings abroad. *Uncle Tom's Cabin.* Walt Whitman's *Leaves of Grass.* Abraham Lincoln's speeches. Harriet Tubman. Frederick Douglass. Stephen Crane's *Red Badge of Courage.* They want an actress, and haven't decided on one. We thought of you. It's a month's work."

"Why the Civil War?"

"Russian people are extremely interested in American slavery and the Civil War. Their Kremlin masters are fond of indulging this interest. They love to draw egregiously spurious parallels to the serfs and their own civil war."

"These readings are to be done in Russia?"

"Two weeks in Leningrad. Two weeks in Moscow. The pay is fifty thousand. It comes from a foundation grant."

"Why do you want to indulge the Kremlin masters?"

"I don't. It's strictly State Department. More of their cultural exchange foolishness. It helps keep us supplied with defecting ballet dancers."

"What is your interest in this?"

"You might do us a favor or two while you're over there, but it mostly struck us as a wonderful opportunity for you. We have a number of media contacts, of course. We might arrange some publicity for you. I shouldn't be surprised if you received some sort of pleasant write-up in one of the news magazines."

"I'm not interested."

"It's only four weeks. The money is quite generous. We feel very obligated to you, and here you are spurning our gesture of gratitude and concern."

He was into a broad reach again, steering for Cedar Point. The wind sound had fallen almost to silence.

"The man I killed was a Russian agent," she said. "You told me that yourself."

"He was, but of the most minor sort. A hired troll."

"But their troll nonetheless. And you would send me to Russia! Are you really trying to get me killed, Ramsey, or am I just becoming paranoid in my old age?"

"I fear friend Gwen has been playing the makebate."

"She has not! Whatever that means."

"Tatty. That man you killed was the only Russian who knew anything about you. He made no report. We've confirmed that. The KGB made only the most cursory investigation. They lose a dozen miscreants like that every day."

"Ramsey. I have absolutely no interest in visiting Russia. Not for the rest of my life. And certainly not at your invitation."

"I'm only thinking of your career, Tatty. You've not exactly had a great deal of work, lately."

"That's subject to change. This week."

"Perhaps. I hope so." His blue eyes held kindness. "I'll leave our offer open. The Russian tour is not to begin until early November. We can deal with the paperwork quite quickly. All of this can be attended to with the utmost celerity. Quite remarkable for something involving the Soviet Union."

She hugged her bare knees. Her legs were becoming unpleasantly cold.

"I'm sorry," she said. "I appreciate your good intentions, if that's what they are. But I'm quite leery of things Russian just now. Especially after yesterday. This extraordinary book came in the mail. My Russian grandmother wrote it, years ago. It was a handwritten, leather-bound manuscript, the only copy, an account of how my grandmother's relatives were killed in the Revolution. It had completely vanished. Yet there it was, in my mail."

"I know," said Ramsey. "I sent it to you. Ready about!"

Sid Greene was late for their luncheon at the Plaza, making Tatty all the more nervous. The maître d' recognized her, and led her to a table by one of the windows facing the park, but the waiting proved unpleasant. It lasted for two long sherries. A few people glanced her way, but there was no one in the room Tatty knew.

Sidney entered the room with the tentative aggressiveness of a bull trotting into a *corrida*. He glanced warily about, then broke into an enormous smile upon seeing

Tatty, and charged toward her table. She rose in time for his embrace, and he stepped back to hold her at arm's length, admiring her beige suit, matching Ferragamo shoes, and Henri Bendel purse.

"Class, class, class," he said, as he always said.

He took his seat after Tatty, and then took command, summoning the waiter, ordering cocktails, lunch, and wine for them both. He ordered well, but even if he had not, she would not have said anything. He talked volubly, with great gestures, about his summer; the early autumn weather; Vienna, from which he had just returned; a new gallery exhibit. Nothing about the theatrical season.

"Well, Sidney," she said, alarmed that they were nearing the end of the main course. "Is this a luncheon at which my agent should be present?"

"Tatty. With you and me, an agent is always a formality."

"And?"

"Yes?"

"The World War I play. The British part."

"I have a great part for you, Tatty, and it's a British part. Noel Coward. *Hay Fever.*"

"Sidney. That's his worst play. What are you talking about?"

"Coward's coming back. The critics love Coward. Anyhow, we'll start you in Washington, at the Arena. It's a season ticket house. But if it clicks, on to Chicago."

"Chicago? With Noel Coward?"

"Liz and Dick were SRO there in *Private Lives.* Tatty, I can't think of an American actress who can do Noel Coward better than you. If there is the kind of Coward revival they're talking about, you could click."

"Chicago. Who's my co-star? Forrest Tucker?"

"Tatty, right now, it's that or the dinner-theater circuit. And you're not even a has-been."

"When do rehearsals begin?"

"Next spring. Maybe late spring. June. The Arena has a couple of Off-Broadway things they want to put up first."

"What about on Broadway? What about Macabee's World War I play?"

Sidney lifted his hands and eyes to the heavens in a bad parody of Zero Mostel.

"That's completely out of my control, Tatty. They're going with Dahlia Symmes."

"Dahlia Symmes?!!" Tatty half rose from her chair. "She's a goddamn rock singer!"

"Pop singer. But she did well in that Gilbert and Sullivan thing last year. And she is British."

"Cockney."

"It's out of my hands, Tatty. The money man. Dahlia's a sure thing."

She set down her fork. She had no more taste for food or wine. She felt suddenly extremely tired.

"So all we're talking about, Sid, is probably two weeks in Washington doing bad Noel Coward."

"Possibly Chicago."

"And not until nearly a year from now."

He shrugged, actually better than Zero Mostel could have done, under the circumstances.

"Larry's got a made-for-TV movie going," he said. "A 1920s thing. Gangsters. I could work you into that. Legs Diamond's socialite girlfriend. It would mean three months in L.A."

"Thank you, Sidney. But no thank you."

"Tatty. These are hard times. You gotta go with sure things."

"I said thank you, Sid."

He touched her hand, but Tatty, staring at her plate, did not respond. Greene usually had a brandy after lunch, but now he just called for the check.

Outside, on Central Park South, he hugged her. She merely let him. She did not respond. When he at last pulled away to charge toward the taxicabs parked across from the fountain, she asked herself with some pain if she would ever see him again, if she ever wanted to see him again. She started walking west, into the golden light of the New York afternoon sun, only because it was the opposite direction from that Sidney was taking. In a moment, Ramsey Saylor was in front of her.

"Why, Tatty!"

"Oh for Christ's sake."

"What a wonderful coincidence. I was just thinking of you."

"Just stop it, Ramsey. This is no coincidence. You're just going to haunt me all fall, aren't you? Like some creep on the street."

"Well, actually, I was thinking you might be passing this way."

"I'm sure you've been lurking here for hours. Pushing your Harriet Beecher Stowe tour again."

"I'd like to talk to you again, Tatty. Let's hop into the Oak Bar. You look like you need a drink. A need majuscule."

He was particular about their table, demanding one by the window. It provided a good view of the street and the entrance to the bar, and also of the huge painting that dominated the room. It was of the fountain sculpture in the plaza outside, a nude woman of perfect form and classic Roman features. Jack Spencer had once told her that the model for that statue had in her old age been the desk clerk in a cheap apartment hotel where he'd lived in the East Thirties. Her name was Vera, and in her youth she'd been an actress in the Tenderloin.

There were tears flooding Tatty's eyes. There was no point in her trying to hide them.

"That was your producer friend?" Ramsey said, having ordered Courvoisier for them both.

"Yes," said Tatty, dabbing at her eyes with a beige handkerchief.

"He turned you down."

"Not entirely. He has something for me next spring."

"On Broadway?"

"No. If I'm lucky, Chicago."

"God," he said, touching her cheek. "You must be absolutely devastated."

"Your concern is touching, Ramsey. Pardon me for being suspicious."

"What do you mean?"

"I'm feeling very vulnerable now. What better opportunity for you to make another pitch for this Russian trip?"

"Have you changed your mind?"

"No."

"Then I won't say another word about it. But there's something else I'd like you to do. Come up with me to Westchester for an afternoon."

"Why? Where in Westchester?"

"Near Braddock Wells. That old Russian duke who had your grandmother's book? He'd like to meet you."

"You mean he's alive?"

"Of course. Didn't I make that clear? He's ninety-five or ninety-six now, but he gets around. His memory is quite intact. I mentioned that he's done some work for us, didn't I? No? Well, he has; quite a bit. That's how I came to know him. He has a wonderful knowledge of the old Bolsheviks and what they did. He served in the White Army in the underground, well into the 1920s. A very brave fellow, actually. He—"

"Ramsey. I don't want to see him."

She sipped the cognac, wondering how she would spend the rest of her day and evening.

They sat for a very long time in silence. Finally, Saylor signaled for the check.

"You don't want another one, do you, Tatty? Actually, you really ought to ease up a little. You were outdrinking me on Long Island."

She looked away.

"Well then, Tatty. I suppose this will be it for a while. I have to go back to Washington next week."

They rose, Ramsey taking her arm.

"Where are you staying?" she asked.

"The Beaton Place Hotel," he said. "I always stay there now. It's just a few blocks from our United Nations mission. I do a lot of work there."

No doubt. Spencer had told her the U.N. was perhaps the biggest spy nest in the world.

"I'll call you before you leave," she said.

"To say good-bye?" he said.

"I may change my mind. About the Russian duke. But I doubt it."

Her apartment was near the East River, but the view from her living room window was over Fifty-seventh Street. It was an opulent view, the window high enough to take in a northerly sweep of the Upper East Side. She sat by the window, staring morosely, but not at anything in particular.

There were two parties that evening, one at Amanda's place in the Village, the other at Elaine's still terribly chic restaurant. Tatty had no interest in going to either. If Sid Greene had given her good news, if he had not pronounced her talents as meager compared to those of a Cockney pop singer, she might have gone to the one at Elaine's. It might have been something of a triumph. Tatty Chase, back on the stage. Back in action.

She would go to a movie instead. There was a new Claude Lelouch film in the neighborhood. It would keep her from drinking. God, how she had been drinking.

Who was a person like Sidney Greene to trifle with her life so? Was she not the descendant of czars?

She didn't make it to the movie. That night, she called Ramsey Saylor and told him she would go with him to visit the old Russian duke.

4

Ramsey hated driving. To Tatty's knowledge, it was his only manifestation of cowardice. She picked him up in her MG-A, having to wait until he emerged late and grumbling, then spent the next half-hour fighting surprisingly heavy Saturday morning traffic all the way out of the city. An easier hour after that, they were in upper Westchester, descending the hilly curve that led into the three-century-old village of Braddock Wells. Ramsey slept most of the way.

This warm, golden September afternoon, hinting at the explosion of bright color soon to come, reminded her of the beginnings of school terms so many years before. Westchester had always been an ill-manicured, rough-edged, somewhat unsettled version of her part of Connecticut, a wilderness of sorts for a Greenwich girl, the state line at Banksville a true frontier. She had come up here only to visit her grandmother and for odd dates and parties. She had also come for her grandmother's funeral. Her last visit had been her mother's funeral.

Tatty drove the MG around the Braddock Wells village green then pulled to a stop in front of a hardware store, where she remembered having been horribly overcharged for some things for her grandmother years before. She poked Saylor awake. He opened his blue eyes, instantly recognizing where they were.

"Six or seven houses down Pommel Ridge Road from your grandmother's is a dirt road going down to an old mill," he said. "You recall it?"

"Yes."

"Past the mill, across the stone bridge and all the way up to the top of the hill, there's a great stone house on your left."

She remembered it vaguely. In her youth they had said it was haunted. Tatty had once petted in a Jaguar XK-140 roadster backed ever so carefully into the house's lower driveway.

"The duke lives there?"

"He has since 1931. Let's get up there, please. I think he had in mind a late lunch."

The driveway ascended from the road to the summit of the hill in a great sweeping curve that lost sight of the house. It was a bizarre construction, high wooden eaves and stone turrets set chockablock; ivy, vines, and overgrown gnarled trees obscuring most of it. Unlike most houses of its size and place, it boasted a porte-cochere that was less an imposing entrance than a welcome protection against the clutching overgrowth.

The bell rang sonorous chimes deep within. When the great wooden door was finally, closely, swung open, it was by the old duke himself. Tatty caught her breath at the sight of him.

He looked as old as Ramsey had said, his skin the color and seeming consistency of ash. Yet he was an enormous and certainly a once very strong man, easily six foot six, with huge hands, shoulders, and head. He was stooped, to be sure, but still towered over them, and his strong jaw was still square and jutting. The long teeth in his hanging smile were healthy and his own. His cheekbones and brow were massive, framing huge, piercing gray eyes that reminded Tatty uncomfortably of her grandmother's. Great age or not, they were full of vision, like a staring old cat's.

He was dressed in slippers and gray flannels, a gray wool sweater pulled over an old white shirt with long, frayed collar, and a strange, old-fashioned, high-collared green jacket with military pockets and epaulets. A strand of some sort of jewelry was visible at the base of his wattled, old man's neck.

"Your Excellency," Ramsey said, "as I promised. This is Mathilde's granddaughter."

Ramsey then drew himself full-up, militarily, almost comically.

"General Vladimir Mikhailovich Suvorov, I present Tatiana Alexandra Iovashchenko Chase."

It was well that Ramsey did not use the Russian patronymic, what with Tatty's grandfather having been christened Elwood, and her father Bobby. Bobbyevna, indeed. For a bizarre moment, Tatty almost laughed. But then the duke took her hand, and there was no thought of laughter.

The old man had a cane she had not initially seen, but seemed in little need of it. As he conducted them down the wide hall, he pointed with it at several oil paintings on the dark, oak walls, portraits mostly, including those of Czar Nicholas and his wife, and one of Mathilde as a young woman, or at least a woman no older than Tatty's age. Mathilde looked quite striking, far beyond the flattery of the artist's brush. The slightest flush came to the old duke's face as they looked at the painting, and he stood even straighter.

"Your grandmother, as you must recognize," he said, his speech slow with age and his accent. "As you may know, we were somewhat related. Distantly. But through the Romanovs."

Tatty had never heard of the duke before Ramsey's revelations of the weekend. She wondered why there were no servants about. If he could afford this great house, certainly he could afford servants. At his age, he would need them.

It was at this point that she began to hear the music, very Russian music, with a great many people singing, perhaps with only people singing. Their voices were so rich she could not tell if there were instruments. There was no evident source of this music. As he led them into his library, the sound grew louder, but again she could not divine its source. There was no phonograph visible, no speaker. There was a fire, not a small, glowing fall afternoon fire but a full roaring blaze feeding on several large logs. The duke took a seat in a huge armchair beside it. Tatty, feeling a diminutive Alice in Wonderland, sat in a huge matching chair opposite. Ramsey went to a corner shelf where there were glasses and several decanters, and poured Scotch whiskies and water, with no ice.

"Forgive my seeming presumption," he said, handing them around, a very small glass for the duke. "I come here quite often. You don't mind Scotch, do you, Tatty?"

She minded it without ice, but was reluctant to complain. The duke was staring at her, but with what she took to be a friendly expression.

"Tatiana Alexandra Iovashchenko," he said. "Granddaughter of Mathilde and daughter of Chloe. You favor them both. But you favor better, someone else."

His wrinkles and wattles pulled themselves up into a smile. Then he slowly rose and moved to a near bookshelf, reaching with the ease and familiarity of a blind man for a leather-bound album. He brought it to Tatty and leaned over her, somewhat painfully. It was an album of photographs, all of the same person: Tatiana Romanov, as baby, child, girl, and young woman. The book contained an extraordinary number of them, but the duke kept turning the pages, until at last he came to the one he sought. The grand duchess was wearing winter clothing, a heavy, high-collared coat, and a large fur hat that came down close over her auburn hair, showing only a curl of it on either side of her face. The face, thus delineated, was embarrassingly beautiful. It was Tatty's face, exactly.

"Is astonishing, yes?" he said, after laboriously reseating himself and taking a small sip of his whisky. "Mathilde had told me of the resemblance, but I thought she had, as you remember she did, exaggerated. But no, she was so right. Is astonishing."

He closed his eyes. For a moment, she thought he had fallen asleep. Then she feared he had become ill, though his breathing did not sound labored. At length he revealed that he had only been concentrating.

"I cannot recall the exact relationship," he said, his eyes again open, and fixed on hers. "I cannot recall so many things. But you are as close a relative of the Romanovs as am I. You and the Grand Duchess, she would now be almost as old as am I, you and she would be, were, cousins. I will show you all this in another book. Is in another room. Later."

His voice trailed off and his eyes closed again. Tatty quickly realized that this time he was asleep. She looked to Ramsey, who put a finger to his lips, shrugged, and flashed his droll smile. She cupped her glass with both hands and stared into the fire, letting the music command her attention and then completely overwhelm her. It seemed there were a thousand people singing, the voices of strong, long-suffering men and women, voices rising from Russia's rich and bitter soil. She leaned back her head and closed her eyes as well.

"What is this music?" she asked. "Where is it coming from?"

"That's the Sveshnikov Choir. Russian peasant music. This particular oeuvre is, I believe, 'The Broad and Rolling Steppe', or possibly, 'From a Distant Land.' The house has a tape system. Our people bring back recordings from the Soviet Union and I put them on tapes for him. He keeps them playing twenty-four hours a day. He's very nostalgic."

She pondered that.

"I don't recognize the instruments," she said.

"They're not using any. The Sveshnikov performs a cappella. A Russian talent."

Ramsey moved to the fireplace and leaned against the mantel, swirling the whisky in his glass. In his perfectly Westchester tweed jacket, gray flannels, gray sweater vest, striped tie, and button-down collar shirt, he looked more the master of this house than the old duke. He certainly acted it more.

"You're certainly on familiar terms with the duke," she said.

He smiled over the rim of his glass, his eyes deadly serious. "Tatty. I am now number three in the Soviet section.

52

His Excellency is a marvelous resource. And, after all, I grew up here. If you had visited your grandmother more, you might have met the duke years ago."

The duke was still sitting in his chair, still holding his glass in both hands, but still deeply asleep.

"Mathilde never mentioned him once," said Tatty. "Are you sure he's all right? He's so still."

"He sleeps quite a bit. Great age is at best a constant struggle against somnolence. The whisky acts as a soporific, of course, but it's very good for his health. He takes a small glass three times a day. This is his second."

"Ramsey, why has he no servants?"

"He has four, five if you count the gardener, who drinks considerably more than three whiskies a day. I have them sent away when I'm here; when the duke and I are working. They usually go down to the village, or to the gardener's cottage."

The duke stirred slightly, his shoulder twitching. He opened his eyes with a great deal of blinking, looking first at Ramsey, then at Tatty. He smiled.

"Astonishing resemblance," he said, pausing to cough and clear the crack and rattle from his old voice. "Astonishing." He noticed his glass of whisky, and sipped from it, coughing again. He sat straighter. "I must show you now many things, granddaughter of Mathilde Iovashchenko. Come. *Pozhaluista.*"

He seemed to gather strength the farther he went, though he passed by the main staircase of the house and led her to a small elevator in the rear that took them to the top floor. There was not a whisper of the Russian music once the elevator's doors closed, though it resumed with full vengeance when they reopened. Taking her by the hand now, he proceeded into a huge room off the upstairs hall. It had probably once been the master bedroom of the house, but had been transformed into a sort of shrine. The emerald drapes had been opened to reveal the windows and the view beyond, but the drapes, the paneled walls, and the rugs were so dark that the room was only meagerly illuminated, as though the light dared not intrude. But for a narrow, triangular bookcase in one corner,

53

the walls were lined with oily dark icons. The only furniture in the room were two scarlet velvet Victorian armchairs and a number of mahogany chests, one of them bearing a collection of Russian Palekh boxes. The others were covered with fringed oriental cloths.

"*Dochka. Pridi.*" He pointed to one of the chairs and then, despite its great weight, dragged the other close to it.

She paused before sitting, halted by the brilliant autumnal panorama glimpsed from the window.

"The view from the house is all to rear," he said, enjoying her appreciation of it. "Mathilde liked it much more than that from her own. She would come here sometimes . . ."

Tatty thought, "often."

". . . and walk with me in the rear garden. There was a pond. Is still there. And the view is of fifteen miles."

When she was seated, he went to the bookcase and pulled forth a thick, leather-bound album. It proved to contain not pictures but a genealogy, the most elaborate Tatty had ever seen, page after page of thick, costly paper inscribed in an elegant, old-fashioned hand with lists of names and diagrams of family lineage. It was written in French. The old duke turned quickly to the proper passages, pointing out proudly the linkages of Mathilde and Tatty to the czarina and the Romanov daughters, and to himself. He went on then, with some evident excitement, leading her with gnarled finger on a tour through the families, stopping for discourses on the most famous and most interesting, including a general at Balaclava, a freed serf who married into the aristocracy, and a countess who went for long summer walks in the woods—in the nude. Tatty was most interested in her own ancestors.

"According to this, I'm as much related to Kaiser Wilhelm as I am to the czarina."

"Yes, but that is irrelevancy. Here, let me show you clearly how Russian you are, through Mathilde, that is." He smiled, very broadly. "Otherwise, you are so American, so English. Hoops, Shaw, Chase." He laughed.

She recognized only a very few of the Russian names

he cited, and those few she remembered only as vague snatches of little-girl conversations with Mathilde. She was relieved when he finally put the album away and went to open one of the chests.

At length, he retrieved a small wooden box and brought it to her, setting it gently on her lap and wearily lowering himself into his chair.

"Yes, *dochka,*" he said, again calling her "daughter." "Open it."

She did so with considerable care, curious as to why he accorded it such special attention. Inside, nestled in the folds of very old wine-red velvet, was a very old-fashioned gold and emerald ring. She inhaled sharply at the strange beauty of it.

"Please, *dochka.* Take it out. Its history is very sad, but remarkable. It belonged, Tatiana, to the Grand Duchess, whose name you bear."

Tatty held it close to her eye. The emerald was not extraordinarily large, but perfect in its cut and color, gleaming even in the room's darkness. The filigreed design of the band and setting was exquisite, but on one side it was marred by a deep, ugly gash.

"If you have read Mathilde's book," said the duke, "and you have of course, yes? Then you know of the terrible end of the imperial family in all its lamentable detail."

"This gash. They tried to cut it off her finger?"

"Yes. I, I have always thought this such a tragic thing to keep. But now, there, in your hand, by your face, the face that is so much Tatiana Romanov's. I feel—how can I say, *dochka*?— I feel I have returned it."

"Sir, I . . ."

"There are many Romanovs around," he said. "From the Czar's side. There are many in New York. Grandchildren of the Czar's sister. Others. Some are decent people. Some are merely pretenders. They consider the Russia before the Revolution a civilized place, a civilized time. They have no understanding of what destroyed imperial Russia. You have this understanding. I know this from Mr. Saylor, from Mathilde. There was . . . once, one night in the winter, in St. Petersburg, I brought home this freezing, starving old man I had found. My family thought it was a joke, an amusement. I kept him in my room and fed him until he died. It was only a few days. I was very young then. I . . . Tatiana, they indulged me as though I had brought home a stray animal. You would not have thought it a joke. The Grand Duchess would not have thought it an amusement. She was her mother's daughter, very proud, but so very kind and warm."

He was touching her hand, looking at the ring rather than her. She stared at his monumental Russian face.

"What I mean to say, Tatiana Iovashchenko, is that . . . you see, Mathilde was the Grand Duchess's friend, her best friend after her sisters. And you are related. You are of common blood. I want this ring to go to Iovash-chenko, not Romanov. I wanted Mathilde to have it, but she would not. I want you to have it, Tatiana."

It went onto her finger with an ease that amazed her.

"You see, *dochka*. Perfect."

Later, after they had lunched on soup, cheese, bread, and tea, she took him for the long slow walk to the pond at the edge of the rear lawn. She imagined Mathilde there in various styles of dress—a young woman in long skirt and straw hat, an older one in cloche and flapper shift, a matron in the frilly frumpiness of the 1930s, a grandame in the 1950s, returning to the long dresses of her youth. He sat while she walked around the pond, hopping over the brook that poured from it over the brow of the hill, pausing to take in the full magnitude of the view. She had visited her grandmother many times, had grown up nearby, yet had never known of this romantic place.

"It's glorious," she said, turning back toward him, but he only stared into the pond's dark, still waters, saying nothing. She feared he might be cold. Saylor, who supposedly had stayed behind in the house, stepped out from behind a hedge and went to the old man's side.

"We must go back now, Your Excellency," he said. The duke rose slowly, obediently.

They returned to the library. As Ramsey restocked and restirred the fire to its former blazing intensity, the duke seated himself on the long, soft couch opposite, inviting

Tatty to join him. She did so feeling very girlish and daughterly, the ring a magic, commanding presence on her hand, the emerald glittering brightly with the light of the flames.

Then at once he slept again, this time snoring quite loudly, his head fallen onto the back of the couch. Tatty ignored Ramsey, letting the taped Russian music fill the minutes. The sunlight from the windows faded and dimmed as the afternoon slipped to evening. Ramsey brought her a whisky, which she accepted with a nod. He poured a stronger one for himself and then another small neat glass for the duke. When the old man again awoke, Ramsey greeted him with it.

"We must go soon, General. Will you join us in a farewell drink? It's a special occasion. I'm sure the good doctor will not mind."

"Yes, *spasibo, gospodin* Saylor."

He took the glass with one hand and then her hand with his other. The room was dark now but for the fire. The Sveshnikov Choir had returned, the voices softer, singing in a slow cadence, receding as a male alto came to the fore in clear and lilting tones. She had never heard Russian words sung so beautifully before.

"It sounds like bells," she said. "They're singing like bells."

The duke nodded, smiling.

"The name of the song is 'Evening Bells,'" Ramsey said.

"Is a song for the twilight," said the duke. "The man you hear singing is hearing the sound of evening bells, and they remind him of the evening church bells in a distant village where he once lived. When he is no more, after he is dead, he knows the sound of the evening bells will still be heard."

When the music at last was done, the last singer's long note fading into a momentary interlude of silence, Tatty squeezed the old man's hand. "I will come back to see you," she said. "Would that be all right?"

"Yes, *dochka.* Indeed. Very much. I am so sorry that

it was not possible, not appropriate, for us to meet before this. Now I am very, very happy."

A door slammed at the rear of the house.

"That will be the cook," said Ramsey. "We must go."

"*Chto?*"

"We must go, Your Excellency."

"Yes. *Do svidaniya, moi sin, moya doch.*"

They left him looking into the fire. She held that image of him in her mind until Ramsey halted them in the hall to point out one of the smaller paintings, a portrait of a young officer in imperial uniform. The face was bold, sharp, and aristocratic, more striking than handsome, the hair and cavalry moustache blond, the unmistakable staring eyes the same arresting gray.

"How old was he then?" said Tatty, in a near whisper.

"In his twenties, I imagine. He said it was done just before the Revolution. Your grandmother must have thought him quite a dashing fellow."

Ramsey again refused to drive, irritating Tatty, for she would have much preferred lolling back in the passenger seat with her thoughts on the long trip back to the city. There was still a fair measure of light along the western horizon. When she turned her MG south onto the Bedford Road, it brought a dim sparkle to her ring.

"I wonder whether to believe half of it," she said. "Or any of it."

As they crested a small hill, she could see the moon rising through some trees to her left. Upper Westchester was not only wilder than her part of Connecticut, but in its eerie way more beautiful.

"We've found him quite reliable," said Ramsey, slouching in his seat with his knees up against the dashboard. He clasped his hands, his two index fingers pressed together and pointed at the road ahead like a gun. "A most veridical man. You might question his memory at times, but never his honesty."

"Could this really have been the grand duchess's ring?"

"The leading expert on the subject just gave it to you."

"I feel guilty wearing it."

"It fits you perfectly, as though they'd made it up for you at Tiffany's. Cinderella's slipper."

"I feel it belongs with the family."

"Tatty. He explained all that to you. You are family."

There were headlights behind her, approaching at some speed. She was traveling at exactly the limit.

"It must be a very expensive ring."

"Priceless. I shouldn't flash it about on the IRT, or for the IRS either."

"Why wouldn't my grandmother have mentioned him? She talked about Russia constantly. Why wasn't he at her funeral?"

"Tatty, not to be indelicate, but there were rumors about your grandmother and the duke. I remember hearing them as a child in the village."

"What are you talking about?"

"Scandalous rumors, Tatty. I'm sure she didn't want to do anything to encourage them. Certainly not with her own family."

"I find that very hard to believe."

"You will note a certain fondness on his part for her." He slouched further down in his seat. "I'm going to sleep a while now."

"Again?"

"I've been working rather hard, lately. Don't speed."

"Ram. There's a car behind us."

"Imagine."

"It came up fast, then slowed to match my speed. It's had several chances to pass, but doesn't."

"They're friendlies, my dear. Associates of mine. I keep them with me constantly now, at a discreet distance. They're a perk attendant to my new position. Not to worry."

"Ramsey, do you swear this Russian junket you're offering me isn't some covert action?"

"Oh, some higher-up in the HumInt section might try to take some advantage of it, but nothing that would personally involve you. All you'd have to do is perform your readings brilliantly as always and be nice to the Sovietski."

"Take advantage how?"

"I've no idea. But your glamorous presence will certainly attract attention, and with so many Russians looking agog in one direction, our fellows might well find opportunity to busy themselves in another."

"Busy themselves?"

"Tatty, we always take advantage of a distraction. When Nixon was in Moscow, the Agency was able to clean up all sorts of old business. During the Moscow Olympics we had an absolute romp."

"And this is why you want me to go on this tour?"

"No."

"I suppose you'd like me to do a striptease at the end of each reading. That certainly would hold their attention."

"Tatty, for God's sake. I'm merely trying to give you honest answers to your questions. I can't promise that one of our gentlemen won't seek some benefit from this. I can't. But I can guarantee there'll be nothing involving you personally. This venture is legitimately and genuinely a State Department cultural exchange. I just saw this as a good opportunity for you. One you need. One we owe you."

"How could I ever doubt you, Ramsey? What's an attempted rape by a crazed KGB agent among friends?"

"Don't be so churlish. If you don't want to go on this, don't. But whatever you decide to do, don't worry about this being an Agency mission. I swear to you it isn't."

She drove on a ways in silence. The car behind her kept pace. They were nearing Bedford, just a few miles from the interstate. In an hour they'd be back in New York City, and she'd be free of Ramsey Saylor. She could be free of him forever.

"Why would you pay me so much money? Sid Greene isn't that generous."

"It's not out of line for this kind of thing. Foundation grants are often generous. You'd be representing your country; presenting some of its greatest literature. And with your talent and speaking voice, there'd be a good return on the investment."

60

The road led on in shallow curves, then straightened for a direct climb of a long hill.

"I'm going to sleep now, Tatty."

If he did, she could not tell. She glanced at his profile in the flare of headlights as a car came by in the opposite lane. The thickly lashed eyes were closed, but he could have been fully alert, listening to every sound she made. Her thoughts, though, were still her own, and they were of Russia, a Russia she now seemed to see as her grandmother and mother had seen it. Her one schoolgirl's tour of it had been brief and unpleasant. She had been hurried through The Hermitage in Leningrad scarcely understanding that it had once been the czar's Winter Palace. Illness had kept her from an excursion out to Czarskoe Selo, the imperial country retreat. Her distaste for her own Russianness had been very strong then and colored every impression. She had been told of the beauty of Saint Basil's on Red Square when it was floodlighted against a cold, starry winter sky. She had seen it on a hot, gray, rainy day when she was suffering from an upset stomach. And so many years ago. So briefly. Mathilde might have prayed in that church; so might have the grand duchess.

On the other side of the hill, the road narrowed, curved, and became the main street of Bedford Village. She followed it past the village green, heading west toward the interstate.

Jack Spencer was in Moscow. Unmarried. Free of Chesley.

"Ram," she said, as she pulled away from a stop sign. "I think I'm going to accept your offer."

Ramsey's talk of an article in the news magazines was ridiculous, but *The New York Times* would probably write something about her tour. Sid Greene never missed a day of the *Times*.

Saylor did not stir, did not seem even to open his eyes.

"We should talk about this, Tatty," he said. "There's a restaurant coming up just on your right, the Village Inn. It's quite good. Let me buy you dinner."

"Is there still time? For the visa and everything?"

Ramsey all of a sudden rearranged his body into an upright position. "As a matter of fact," he said, "ever the optimist, I've already arranged that." He pulled forth an envelope from his jacket pocket. "I had to forge your signature on the visa application, but I'm a superb forger. You'll have no trouble from the Russians."

"You're such a swine."

"But still your friend. There's the restaurant." He returned the envelope to his pocket.

"When do I leave?"

"In about a month."

"And that's all?"

"Oh no. You're dealing with the government, after all. First, you must come to Washington. But I can promise you a glorious round of parties."

He put his hand on her knee and then abruptly ran it up the length of her thigh. She was turning into the restaurant parking lot and almost struck a Cadillac Seville.

5

By New York standards, Ramsey's "glorious round" of Washington parties proved to be stuffy and dull, though he excitedly dragged her from one to another as though they were events in some royal jubilee. The only one approaching splendor was a Swedish embassy reception decorated with two thousand roses and the presence of Henry Kissinger, who in a brief introduction charmingly pretended to know who Tatty was.

For the others, her highest accolade was "interesting," with "enervating" and "irritating" also included in the review. At a British embassy reception—which Ramsey thought the best of all—a roomful of rumpled men and overdressed, frumpy women talked about British politics, boarding schools, and gardens with equal boredom. At a Mexican embassy luncheon, the satin-skinned Latin ladies were overdressed in the manner of a cabaret dance troupe, and talked disdainfully of both Americans and Mexican peasants. An exhibit opening at the Corcoran proved a more genteel occasion, the assemblage one of quiet-spoken men and women in evening dress, whom Ramsey described as local aristocrats, though Tatty recognized none of their names. No one at the exhibit wore running shoes. In New York, at least one man in a tuxedo would have worn his Adidas.

Tatty had been in Washington before, but only as a touring theatrical performer, with little mingling among the local population. Now that she was among them, they seemed as two-dimensional as the paintings in the Corcoran. They dressed uniformly rather than fashionably; during the day the men in dark pinstripes and the women in Stanley Blacker suits, at night the men only in the most circumspect black tie and the women in evening gowns Tatty presumed to be off the racks at Garfinkel's, though she saw an occasional Bill Blass or Oscar de la Renta. Names and job titles were more magnetic than wit or charm. Gossip and inside information did for new ideas. At her last New York party, she had talked for some time with an old Viennese gentleman about the universal human affection for balloons. At the best of Ramsey's gatherings, all anyone cared to discuss was the expected administration job changes after the next elections. One man, upon learning she was from New York, asked if she thought Mayor Koch would run for federal office again. As politely as she could, she replied that she had never had any thoughts on the subject.

The party this night was a very high-powered affair at the Canadian embassy to which Ramsey had somehow contrived a last-minute invitation. He had originally planned to take her to the Kennedy Center, not realizing how much a Washington opening of a new play bound for New York would depress her until she emphatically told him. The Canadian ambassador's residence was imposing enough, a large brick mansion just off Massachusetts Avenue overlooking Rock Creek Park. The guest list was imposing as well, as Ramsey spelled out: the French ambassador, the publisher of the *Washington Post,* the White House chief of staff, the head of the FBI, the deputy director of the CIA, two Supreme Court justices, and a dozen or more Canadians of equal rank. There were some unnamed others. Tatty supposed she and Ramsey were "others."

The dinner was served at tables set up in several rooms of the house. Tatty was fortunate in hers, at least in the man seated on her left, a charming older gentleman with a touch of Scots accent. He had been identified by Ramsey as the commissioner of the Royal Canadian Mounted Police, but they didn't discuss that. Refreshingly, he preferred nongovernmental topics. She thought of bringing up balloons, but was soon given no chance. The empty chair on her right was taken by a latecomer, a very blond and unpleasantly effeminate younger man who introduced himself as an official at the embassy. Once seated, he kept talking, his jabber leading eventually to rumors that the new Russian leader was seriously ill. Wouldn't it be marvelous if he died? Upsetting the Sovietski apple cart before it had even been set up? Didn't the commissioner agree? And the lovely lady?

The commissioner said he had little knowledge of Russia. He reminded the embassy aide that intelligence functions had been taken from the RCMP and that he had no interest in Russians unless they robbed Toronto banks. The young man then began engulfing Tatty with talk about Russia, drawing out of her that she had once been there and was, yes, part Russian, and, yes, she might return someday, possibly soon. The ambassador announced demitasse and cordials in the drawing room before the young man could ask anything more.

Tatty moved quickly from the table, taking a Cointreau from a butler encountered in the foyer, and hurried on into the drawing room. She stood off by herself, examining one of the Oriental figurines that were everywhere in the house. Someone halted behind her, and touched her bare back. She feared it was the blond Canadian, but it was Ramsey, brandy in hand.

"An amusing evening, don't you think?"

"You certainly seem at home here."

"I do move in some social circles still, Tatty. There is a society in Washington."

Jack Spencer had once likened the society in Washington to that of an Old West mining camp—the governmental equivalent of gamblers, swindlers, speculators, drifters, and dance hall hookers—the pecking order determined by whoever was flush at the moment.

"Ramsey, I think I'll go back to New York tomorrow.

65

There's nothing left for me to do at the State Department except talk to the assistant secretary of cultural affairs. I have my tickets and papers. They even provided me with a lovely leather bag full of lovely nineteenth-century literature."

"You're seeing Cultural Affairs in the morning?"

"Yes."

"You must stay at least through the afternoon. I want you to come out to Langley. There's something I want to go over with you."

"Here it comes."

"Not business, Tatty. Not official business. There's something I have to show you."

"About Russia?"

"In a way, but about your father."

"My father? What do you know about my father?"

The blond young man was upon them, mostly upon Ramsey, who looked quite startled. The Canadian was gripping his arm in the mode of a Roman gladiator about to begin ritual combat.

"The prettiest lady in the house and of course she's yours, Rammo. Aren't you the lucky one. *Comme toujours.*"

"Miss Chase is an old friend. This is Bill Newcombe, Tatty. He's with—"

"The Canadian embassy. I know. We were at the same table."

"It was delightful, Rammo," said the Canadian. He released Saylor's arm, moving away, trailing his smile, which Tatty did not return.

"Who is he, Ramsey? I don't like him."

"He's one of the Canadian foreign service's famous fairies. Very second echelon."

"You seem quite chummy."

"Come on, Tat. He does work for us. Small, cheap work. Filching scraps from the ambassador's wastebasket and the untidy like."

Ramsey halted one of the butlers and procured another cognac and Cointreau.

"He kept rattling on about Russia over dinner."

"I'm sure he does work for the Russians as well. And for the Chinese. And for the British. And for—"

"Ramsey, what is it you want to show me about my father?"

"It's inenarable, Tatty. You must see for yourself."

He smiled, but the smile abruptly vanished as he caught sight of something or someone across the room. Tatty followed the direction of his gaze, even as he looked away. It was a short, neat, dapper man with perfectly combed white hair, metal-rimmed glasses, and cold gray eyes, which were fixed on Ramsey, who now turned away completely.

"Does he do work for you, too?" Tatty said.

"It's quite the other way around. He used to be a top drawer nabob at Langley. Retired early, but keeps getting called back as a consultant. I believe he's displeased to see me here, among so many of his fellow nabobs. And he doubtless was displeased to see me chatting with Newcombe." He glanced over his shoulder, waiting until the white-haired man had moved away. "He probably has no objection to you, Tatty. He's quite the ladies' man. His new wife is no older than you. Though Madeleine's beauty pales before yours, to be sure."

Tatty finished her Cointreau.

"Let's leave," Ramsey said. "I know a much better party. One where we can relax."

It was at the Irish embassy. The hour was late, but the gathering looked as though it might continue another hour or two. People were gathered around the ambassador's piano, and there was a lot of singing and drinking. Young Irishmen in ill-fitting dark suits kept refilling her glass with straight Irish whiskey. She wished Ramsey had brought her here earlier, or did until a tall man who had been standing next to her in the group around the piano began to speak. The Russian accent was unmistakable. Tipsy now, Tatty looked about desperately for Ramsey, finding him in a corner in deep conversation with a Catholic priest, of all people. She went to him, taking his arm and pulling him to her side in a demonstrative manner she hoped would dissuade the Russian from following. She was so demonstrative that the priest, with some amusement, left them.

"There's a Russian here," she said.

Saylor glanced over her shoulder. "Yes. That's old Selyutin. He's with the Russian trade section here. He's something of a fixture at these small legation affairs. Russians at the big social events stand out, and not only because of their atrocious manners. But they find it comfortably discreet to appear at these lesser shows, especially Third World national day parties. I suppose it's where they get most of their gossip, and they trade in gossip as much as everyone else. I was at a Congolese party not long ago that had no fewer than six Russians including the plodding Selyutin."

"If you knew he was going to be here, why did you bring me?"

"I didn't know he was going to be here, but Tatty, the Russians do know you're coming, after all. It's not a military secret. They've issued you a visa."

"I want to go home, Ramsey. Or somewhere. What time is it?"

"It's late, but not oppressively so. Can I get you another drink? Hmm, perhaps not just yet. Perhaps a perambulation is in order, a walk over to Georgetown. You haven't seen my house, Tat. You can't go home without doing that. I think you'll be quite surprised."

"I need some air."

"Air, indeed, Tatty." He took her by the hand as he might a small child's.

They walked down the hill to Massachusetts Avenue, but her sleepiness troubled him, and he stopped a cab. She nodded off against his shoulder on the short drive, and was fast asleep upon their arrival. He shook her shoulder gently and, when her eyes opened, kissed her. She coughed and looked past him out the window at the tall brick house that apparently was their destination. She knew enough about Washington to realize that Ramsey Saylor had apparently become a very wealthy man, as he had never been in Westchester.

"This is yours?"

"Don't be condescending, Tatiana."

She kissed him back, as an apology.

The interior was more surprising than the imposing façade. Given Ramsey's orthodox WASP tastes in clothes, music, books, and friends, she had expected the orthodox colonial decor. Instead, the rooms were filled with Victorian extravagance, red velvet couches and settees, horsehair chairs, great dark mahogany tables, enormous satin draperies. There were potted ferns everywhere, and Aubrey Beardsley prints on the walls. Above a plump crimson sofa in Ramsey's sitting room was what looked like an original oil painting—three beautiful nineteenth-century ladies in dark finery, reclining in a lush jungle of a garden. She stared in wonder at the huge painting, then glanced down at the nameplate. It read "John Singer Sargent."

"Good grief, Ramsey."

"Isn't it fantastic? It's the most precious thing I own."

"How much did it cost you?"

"Not so much as I couldn't afford it. They're my true mistresses, those three." He put his arm around her. "Admire it. I'll be back in a moment."

He went to what she presumed was the bathroom, returning at length with another brandy and Cointreau, poured in generous measures. He had a fire already prepared and lit it. When it was blazing to his satisfaction, he seated himself on the sofa beside her, slipped off his patent leather pumps, loosened his tie, and leaned back with a happy sigh, cradling his brandy glass.

"Paradise, Tatty."

"You're not looking at your painting."

"I know it's there."

"I'm here, too."

He took her hand. "Paradise."

"What am I to make of this?"

"What you will."

"I mean of us. Of this."

"You mean, of me." He lowered their hands until they were resting on her lap, his touching her pelvic bone.

"Ramsey, I've never known what to make of you."

"Is that disapproval?"

"Certainly not. We used to call you the wild man of Westchester in college, but it wasn't disapproval."

"I should die in the scorn of your reproach, Tatiana Chase."

He moved his hand to the back of her neck, and deftly undid the clasp of her gown. She leaned forward as he pulled down the zipper, then stiffened.

"Will you please tell me what you know about my father?"

"Not now, Tatty. It won't make you very happy. Let's leave it until tomorrow, and avoid the nocent remark."

"I'm not very happy as it is. I don't suppose I've been happy for years."

He lowered the gown's straps from her shoulders, then reached to deal with the clasp of her bra.

"I'm aware of that, Tatty."

"I am not a frivolous, superficial person."

"No you're not, Tatty."

He gently pulled the dress and bra down from her chest, exposing her breasts.

"Yet I've surrounded myself with frivolous, superficial people. I've made for myself a frivolous, superficial life."

Ramsey paused to drink more of his brandy. He set down his glass and moved the freed hand to her right breast, sliding his fingers over her nipple.

"That's why I helped you out in France last year, and the time before that," she said. "It struck me as a way to be useful."

"An accurate perception, Tatty." He leaned to kiss the breast. She raised a hand to touch his hair, and pull him closer.

"I'm so unhappy, Ramsey."

He pulled her down on the sofa, and then rolled himself up beside her, slipping his hand beneath the waist of the gown and down over her belly.

"It will be better for you, Tatty. The Russian tour will be good for you."

His hand moved to her buttocks, and began a gentle caress. She pressed herself closer to him.

"I don't trust you worth a damn, Ramsey."

"Darling, darling Tatty," he said, kissing her. "It will be different after Russia."

He took her back to her hotel at an hour touched with the first pale gray of dawn, driving his long Mercedes himself, slowly, and rather clumsily, hitting the curb twice while making right hand turns. Both devoted their scant energies to the gritty task of staying awake, and did not speak. When he lurched to a halt before the hotel's entrance, she only touched his hand in farewell.

"Lunch," he said, with a weary amiability. "Maison Blanche."

She nodded, at him and at the sleepy doorman who had opened the door. She stumbled going up the entrance steps, thinking with a grimace of the romantic advertisements depicting laughing people in evening clothes at dawn. She wanted nothing more than to get to her room, but the elegant lobby was small and she had to pass close by the front desk to reach the elevator. Her box held messages. Mustering whatever dignity she still possessed, she asked the desk clerk for them, haughtily ignoring his overly curious stare.

There were two from Gwen, in Connecticut. Nothing that required a return call at five in the morning.

Wearing her most expensive suit, a soft gray Valentina, suppressing her hangover, and straining her acting talents to the utmost, Tatty managed to survive her meeting with the assistant secretary of state. She had assumed he would be another Gucci-clad monsignor in the diplomatic priesthood, as suavely arrogant and disapproving as all the other State Department officials Ramsey had inflicted upon her. To her surprise, this man was not a professional diplomat at all. He was, in fact, a former motion picture producer from California. A friend of the president, he had been given the cultural affairs job as a reward for his enthusiastic political fund-raising efforts. Tatty recalled his movie work: profitable but shoddy horror films and adolescent sex comedies. He knew her work as well, and

71

mentioned her two best plays, though he got the years wrong.

He was a small man, expensively but ill-fittingly dressed, his wrists too thin for his cuffs, his shoulders too small for his suit jacket. He had thick dark hair and moist, nervous, darting dark eyes. He licked his lips as he talked, reminding her oddly of Ramsey.

His manner was polite, indeed respectful. He thanked her effusively for agreeing to the tour, saying they would have had to settle for an unknown or an aging has-been if she had turned them down. He said he himself disapproved of the project, as he disapproved of sharing anything with the Russians, likening American entertainment to American technology. He then launched into an inchoate speech on the virtues of free enterprise and the menace of communism. It was a long harangue, and Tatty twice caught herself on the brink of nodding back into sleep. He invited her to lunch. She was relieved at being immediately able to claim another engagment without having to search through her sodden mind for an excuse. He gave her a souvenir pen with the State Department seal on it. She feared he might also hand her an autographed photo of the president, or of himself.

Ramsey was very subdued, staring into his cocktail glass until lunch was finally served, only picking at his expensively prepared salmon. He made little effort at conversation and fended off her attempts to learn the cause of his distress, staring tragically off at what looked to be a side door. At last, Tatty decided to make the most of the situation by getting some questions answered.

"There are some things I still don't understand," she said. "Why can't I have someone go with me? Gwen would love the trip."

"The Soviet authorities prefer that you come alone. I don't know why. There's no understanding them. But you'll have people watching out for you until you get on the Aeroflot plane in London, and there'll be someone from our embassy with you all the time in Russia, along with your Intourist guide, whom I expect will be a lady. You'll be fine, Tat."

He looked off again at the door.

"Why do I have to fly to London on Air India and change planes?"

"The Soviets, as a friendly gesture to Madame Gandhi, are subsidizing Air India by using it for the trans-Atlantic leg in their tourist packages. The State Department is trying to be friendly to Madame Gandhi as well. Your seat is first class. You won't notice much difference. Unless you order the curry dishes."

"No thank you. When am I to be paid?"

"I've no idea. Does it matter? Tatty, you're a woman of—"

"I'm a professional actress."

"Yes. I'll make the necessary inquiries."

"The money is to be paid to my agent."

"Yes, Tatty. Shall we go?"

"Why are you so unhappy today?"

"Let's go to Langley."

Tatty was impressed by the ease with which Ramsey was admitted through the gates and surprised at the immensity of the building as it came into view in the midst of the Virginia woods. He obtained a visitor's pass for her with similar ease, explaining as they walked on toward the elevators that he had prearranged her clearance.

"You're in the computers as a part-time employee," he said. "Courier."

"How wonderful."

He did not respond to the sarcasm of her tone, appearing not to notice it. His countenance was utterly dark and somber now, and he did not speak until they reached his office. His secretary, an attractive older woman, rose to greet them, but without a smile.

"Mr. Twill has been looking for you, Mr. Saylor."

"Well, don't let him find me, Elizabeth. I'm going to be in my office with Miss Chase for some time."

"Mr. Saylor, Mr. Twill is in your office."

There were three men waiting there. Seated at Ramsey's desk, rising with the other two upon seeing Tatty, was a large, athletic man with very short hair and a dark Washington suit that cramped his massive shoulders. Nearby, unfolding himself from a leather chair, was a tall, cadaverously thin old man who blinked at her through thick glasses with heavy black rims, the same color as his hair, suit, and tie. In a corner by the window was the white-haired man they had seen at the Canadian embassy the night before, dressed in a perfectly pressed gray suit and looking younger in it than he had in black tie. He was also friendlier, bowing his head to Tatty with a polite smile. Ramsey introduced him as Hugh Laidlaw. The spooky man in black was Freddy Mendelsohn, and the brawny one was William Twill, Ramsey's boss.

"Miss Chase has assisted us in the past, as you may remember," Ramsey said, seeming nervous in his superior's presence. It was so odd to see Ramsey in the company of someone he felt inferior to, as he would put it, a "rara avis."

"Twice, as I remember," Twill said. "Thanks. Sorry about the rough stuff in Marseilles."

"We regret it very much, Miss Chase," said the man named Laidlaw. He had an extremely cultured voice, with a very exact touch of New England accent.

" 'Ah, my Beloved, fill the Cup that clears Today of past Regrets and future Fears,' " the spooky one recited. He was smoking, with a holder, exhaling as he spoke. The expended cloud hung about his face like a veil. "*The Rubaiyat of Omar Khayyam,*" he added, with an eery smile. "A less remembered passage."

"Miss Chase is going to Russia," Ramsey said.

"For the State Department," Tatty said. "To do dramatic readings."

"Yes," said Twill. "We know." He looked unhappily at Ramsey. "We need to have a little powwow, Ram. Beaucoup schnell."

"Certainly," Ramsey said. "Uh, Miss Chase . . ."

"We'll go back to my office," said Twill. "Miss Chase can wait here."

With Twill leading, moving in a sort of rapid trudge, they filed out; Ramsey gave an unhappy backward glance. Mendelsohn paused at the doorway, as Tatty seated herself on Ramsey's leather couch.

" 'Serene, I fold my hands and wait,' " he said.
"What?"
He smiled. "John Burroughs."
She stared at him.

> *"Serene, I fold my hands and wait,*
> *Nor care for wind, nor tide, nor sea;*
> *I rave no more 'gainst time or fate,*
> *For lo! my own shall come to me."*

He backed out, pulling the door behind him. "A pleasure, Miss Chase. *Proshchaite.*" The door closed silently.

The office's decor was most unlike Ramsey. The paintings were all modern, some quite stark. The furniture was contemporary as well, though comfortable. When Ramsey's absence grew to fifteen minutes, she slipped off her shoes and put her feet up on the couch. After a half-hour, she let herself fall asleep, her last thought a curious one about what sad thing he was going to show her, and what it could possibly have to do with her poor dead father.

Ramsey shook her gently awake. "I'm sorry, Tatty. There's a big to-do. The Soviet general secretary is ailing and everyone in the White House and Congress is turning to us for answers as to what might happen next." As she sat up, he eased himself beside her. "We, of course, have no idea."

"They seemed angry with you."

"I've been somewhat inattentive to duty these past few days." He took her hand and squeezed it, but did not look at her. His long-lashed eyes, deadly serious, were fixed on the carpet. He sighed. "Well, let's get this done with then. Please, come sit by my desk."

As she did so, he went to a locked file cabinet, opened it, and with great solemnity removed a bound folder. He placed it carefully on the desk, as though it contained something fragile.

"This is in the nature of a remarkable coincidence, what I'm about to relate to you," he said. "It's not a happy one."

She felt chill. She had left her shoes by the couch. Without them, she lacked not only warmth but dignity.

"You read your grandmother's memoir. Do you remember the man Jakov Sverdlov? He arranged the murder of the Romanov family.

"He was himself murdered by a Moscow laborer some six months after the regicide, presumably with the connivance of the Soviet. Lenin honored him nonetheless by renaming Ekaterinburg 'Sverdlovsk.' He had an illegitimate son, this Comrade Sverdlov. A party camp follower was the mother. He was looked after, even by Stalin. All the right Bolshevik schools, if you know what I mean. His name is Valeri Jakovich Griuchinov. He is sixty-seven years old and is now a member of the almighty Politburo. He is in charge of all Soviet agriculture, and is unusually competent. You don't follow these things, of course, but Soviet grain harvests have improved significantly every year since he took over. This success has taken a great deal of internal political pressure off the military to be less extravagant with the Soviet exchequer. They are so pleased with him he stands a good chance of ascending to the throne if the present secretary should succumb. It's all in this report."

She only glanced at it. "What has this to do with my father?"

"Valeri Jakovich Griuchinov was not always so important. Twenty years ago, he was only an agriculture specialist in the Soviet foreign service, assigned to the Russian embassy in Hanoi as an advisor on rice crop production. This was deep cover. He had been an intelligence officer in World War II, working as liaison with our OSS. You're familiar with the OSS, the original incarnation of the Agency?"

She nodded.

"His real function in Indochina was counterintelligence, with particular attention to Laos. In the early 1960s, the Agency was waging its famous 'secret war' there against the Pathet Lao. It was a discreet affair, but very nasty."

She hugged herself for warmth, half-seriously wondering if Ramsey had deliberately turned off the heat, or whether she was coming down with some illness.

"We had a number of American pilots flying reconnaissance for us. Mostly free-lance, but a few serving military officers. Your father, an extremely brave man, was among them, TDY from the Air Force. These were not stratospheric U2 flights, you understand. They were low-level missions, always very close-run things."

"My mother told me about that," she said, very softly.

"Your father was shot down over the Plain of Jars and taken to a Pathet Lao camp near Muong Soui. There was a Soviet operative at that camp, in functional control of that camp and Pathet Lao operations in the area." He took a photograph from the file and set it on the desk in front of her. "Valeri Jakovich Griuchinov."

The photograph, a slightly blurry enlargement, was of a stoutish man with a pleasant, almost handsome face. He was wearing a short-sleeved tropical shirt and standing in front of thick, exotic-looking foliage. There was a holstered pistol on his belt.

"Mr. Griuchinov, son of the murderer of your czarist ancestors, was your father's captor, Tatty. He was in charge of your father's execution. It happened August 3, 1964."

"Yes." Her voice was softer still.

"Our side overran the camp that afternoon," he said, consulting another official-looking paper. "They took prisoners who had witnessed everything. They took photographs."

He reached again into the folder, but stayed his hand, hesitating. Again he sighed.

"Tatty, I loathe the idea of putting you through this. It has preyed upon me ever since you agreed to the Russian tour. But I think that, under the circumstances, it's quite necessary, for you see, it's quite likely that on this tour you will encounter this Griuchinov among other members of the Politburo. Socially."

"Socially."

"Receptions, dinners, public occasions and private ones. The entertainers we send over there are invariably treated that way. Do you remember that cowboy actor, Chuck Connors, with Brezhnev?"

She shook her head.

"It was embarrassing. Brezhnev kept hugging him whenever he had the chance. At the airport, he climbed Connors like a telephone pole and hugged him for the benefit of the news cameras. You would have thought them newlyweds." His smile flickered and went out under Tatty's unhappy gaze.

"Are you saying I'm going to be hugged by the man who killed my father?"

"No. But if you go through with this it's likely you'll find yourself in his company, along with several of his colleagues. You're a very beautiful woman, and a celebrity. They are Russia's ruling elite and will consider fellowship with you their *droit de seigneur,* pigs that they are." He leaned forward, looking at her very earnestly now. "Tatty, this is something you're going to have to have very clear in your mind. If you make the final decision to go, it will mean more than just meeting Griuchinov and being civil to him. You will have to be nice to him. It's part of the protocol."

"This is why you brought me here? To tell me this? To show me Griuchinov's photograph."

"I regret that's not all, Tatty."

"You said it was something in, inen . . ."

"Inenarable. I'm afraid that it is. Before you make this decision, it's important that you know all that there is to know. Unfortunately, Tatty, that means you must see all that there is to see." He paused once more. "Your father was tortured and then executed," he said, drawing out another photograph. "The method of execution was decapitation."

He set the photograph in front of her.

6

The photograph put her into shock. He took her to his couch and covered her with his coat, summoning a nurse from Langley's medical section, who put her hand on Tatty's forehead, took her temperature, and asked Ramsey if he wanted to give her a sedative. Tatty recalled Ramsey saying no, emphatically. She remembered other people coming into the room, especially the cold, calm face of the white-haired Hugh Laidlaw. When they were gone, Ramsey called for an official car and driver and took her back to her hotel.

He held her close in the back seat, but she kept her face averted from his, staring out the window at the rhapsodically beautiful autumnal Virginia countryside, finding it suddenly bleak. Brown and white highway signs flashed by at the approach of bridges over deep ravines falling to the Potomac on her left. Spout Run. Windy Run . . . Run.

She was able to walk into her hotel, but collapsed on her bed. He undressed her, covered her gently, and went to a chair in the corner, as though to see her through the night. In a moment, she flew into a rage, ripping the sheets from her bed, throwing an ashtray at him, knocking over chairs, pounding on the window. He subdued her as best he could, holding her down until she at length relaxed. Then he let her sit up and got her to drink a large glass of Scotch. He stayed with her until she was asleep and was there when she awoke again hours later. Then, he took her off on a mad round of the loudest discos he could find in Georgetown, till her mind was numb from noise and drink. When they returned once more to her room, he stripped her clothes from her again and mercilessly put her through the most athletic sexual acts he could devise.

The rest she could recall with great clarity. They lay side by side, trembling with fatigue, covered with sweat, too tired to speak. Yet he embarked on a dissertation on the essentiality of aristocracy and the importance of family lines and breeding. He said that his overriding regret about never marrying was that he hadn't fathered a child—a son, an heir. He said he could think of no woman more perfect to be the mother of a child of his than she. He said that, as long as Tatty was alive, he could not stand to have another woman bear his child.

Confused, shivering from the evaporation of her perspiration, she had sat up and pulled the blanket around her. She told him, hesitantly, that it was doubtful she could bear children, that she had an irregular menstrual cycle and ovulated only infrequently. She wanted to say she did not love him, but hesitated. He had said nothing of love. She hugged her knees and stared at the wall. The nightmare photograph of her dead father was still much in her mind, though she was now drained of any emotion with which to respond to it. It was as though she were in some way dead herself.

Ramsey was watching her. She looked away. She let him take her hand and hold it gently.

"Your father should be avenged," he said. "So should all your murdered relatives."

"Yes," she said. Her voice was the merest wisp of a sound.

"I have a way."

She looked at him again, into his steady, gazing feminine eyes. She knew what he was about to say, but could find no anger with which to stop him.

"A way?"

"It would involve you."

"Yes. That's what all this has been about. That's why you want me to go to Russia."

The flat, emotionless sound of her voice seemed odd to her, as though she were listening to someone else talking, as though she'd been hypnotized.

"What I want doesn't matter, Tatiana. What you want is to bring suffering upon those who murdered your father, and I know a way."

She slid back down beneath the covers and turned away from him. He let a long, long silence pass. They could hear the shrill, distant call of awakening birds in the park below. If they turned out the lights, the pale beginnings of dawn would doubtless be visible through the window.

She sighed. "What is it you want me to do?"

"Not very much more than what we discussed. You would do your readings, and you would be nice to your Soviet hosts. But that would have to include Valeri Jakovich Griuchinov."

"How nice to Valeri Jakovich Griuchinov?"

"Enough to compromise him, but it wouldn't mean what you think. Appearances would suffice, certainly."

"Appearances."

"If he seeks you out, as we think would be a strong probability, we'd want you to allow yourself to be entertained by him, socially, and privately."

"How would I keep 'privately' from becoming another Marseilles? You've told me he killed my father. You've shown me how horribly he did it. How do you think I'd feel if he touched me?"

Ramsey took his hand from her back.

"You wouldn't have to permit that. I'm sure you've kept legions of theatrical producers from doing that. You are an exceedingly resourceful woman. We just want to be able to record that you met with him privately, secretly."

"Record how?"

"We have means."

"Photographs?"

"Simply arranged. Even in Moscow. After your tour, we would make them available to extremely interested

81

parties in the Kremlin, along with information attesting to your being an employee of the Central Intelligence Agency and your being a linear descendant of the family Romanov."

"And that I killed a KGB agent in Marseilles."

"If necessary. For emphasis."

"And what would happen then?"

"You would be back here, safe, sound, and fifty thousand dollars to the good. Tovarisch Griuchinov would be dispatched to a gulag, or with luck, executed in the Lubyanka."

"What do you and your employers get out of this? What's my father's death to you?"

"We would be extremely pleased to see Tovarisch Griuchinov removed from the succession to the party leadership. If we can do something for you at the same time, it would be most gratifying, for all of us."

"Tell me why you would be extremely pleased to see him removed."

"Your father has not been his only victim. If Griuchinov were to become premier, there would be more, possibly millions more. We think he's the most dangerous man in the Politburo."

"The others are all enlightened reformers, with western sympathies?"

"Did you read the piece in this week's *Time* about the new Soviet hierarchy?"

"I turned to the theater section first, and didn't go back. I'm not much interested in politics, anyone's politics."

"A failing, Tat. Although the *Time* article would have misinformed you. There are not eight in contention for the party chairmanship should something truly unfortunate befall the ailing premier. There are only four. Griuchinov, unfortunately, has the best chance, barring a massive corn blight. Of the others, and they're all basically swine, the best is Felix Alexyevich Popov. You're familiar with him?"

"I think so. He's the deputy premier."

"Felix is something of a bumpkin, but he has argued in meetings of the Politburo for increased talks between the two Germanys, for some limited forms of Hungarian-style capitalism in the Soviet domestic economy, and for détente with both the People's Republic and ourselves. Lamentably, Felix is seventy-four years old. The premier made him deputy so that none of the stronger rivals could be number two. With Felix about, there really isn't a number two."

She closed her eyes. She wanted to send Ramsey away, but kept listening.

"The third possibility is General Viktor Vasilevich Badim, as I'm sure you know, chairman of the Committee for State Security. He's actually a civilian. He carries the general's rank as head of the KGB, but he's basically a diplomat and a spy. Far, far more westernized, sophisticated, and educated than Andropov was purported to be, which is why he's been given the same idiotic reputation for liberalism. In fact, he's quite ruthless, a rotten son of a bitch. He's backed the Red Army in everything it wants and has filled the gulags as they hadn't been since Stalin. I shouldn't like to be one of his guests."

He coughed. She wished he would put on his clothes.

"Badim has only a slightly better opportunity here than old Felix," Ramsey continued. "Andropov came out of the KGB and there's resistance to establishing that as the traditional step to party leadership. And Badim's western posturings have made him somewhat obnoxious to some of the hardliners, though he's really one of them. Also, he's Latvian. He was born and reared in Riga."

The image of her dead father's staring face flitted across her mind. She reopened her eyes, focusing them on the night table.

"The fourth candidate is the sleeper, and our secret trump. He's already made some discreet, unofficial diplomatic contacts with us and has given us reason to believe that he'd work with us in neutralizing Iran, among other exigencies, should he come to power and should we make certain concessions. His name is Yevgeni Ivanovich Kuznetzov and he's a career soldier, Marshal Kuznetzov, now, and defense minister. He used to be head of the GRU. You remember the GRU?"

83

"Vaguely."

"GRU. *Glavnoye Razvedyvatelnoye Upravleniye.* The Chief Intelligence Directorate of the Soviet General Staff. The 'clean' Soviet spies."

"They don't rape helpless women in Marseilles."

She sensed his smile. "I'll conclude. If the premier should die, Griuchinov is the likely winner of any fight that would ensue. If Griuchinov should himself succumb to an untimely end, his civilian supporters in the Politburo would probably move to old Felix, if only to purchase time, but Badim and the Kremlin marshals would likely retaliate at the earliest opportunity, perhaps one of their own scheduling. If Griuchinov were disgraced and discredited, however, we think the turn would be to our man Kuznetzov. Griuchinov's faction would not dare try to enthrone another of their own, but they would have enough strength to block the Latvian Badim. Kuznetzov would be the natural compromise: a creature of the army, but liberal enough for the rest of the *apparat.* More usefully to us, he'd have the strength to entrench himself in power, unlike Felix."

She rubbed her eyes with the heel of her hand.

"Tatty?"

She sighed again. "What?"

"Does this interest you?"

"How long ago did you think this all up?"

"It came together as something of a quadratic equation: Our obligation to you for Marseilles. The State Department's deciding on this tour. The illness of the Soviet premier. My finding that photograph of your father in the files. The logic was impelling."

She rubbed her eyes again. "Why didn't you tell me from the start?"

"I wanted you to come upon your decision slowly, with a full understanding of what this means."

"The first time you promised me an exciting adventure."

"This time I promise you revenge. And your complete safety."

He waited.

"Tatty?"

She said nothing.

"Tatty, what's your decision?"

"Go away now, Ramsey. I'm going to cry. I can't help it. Go away. I want you to leave me alone."

Trembling, she controlled herself until she heard him close the door behind him.

The Air India flight left New York at ten P.M. Tatty had taken dinner by herself at Altri Tempi, a quiet Italian restaurant on the Upper East Side that was a longtime favorite of hers. She had no interest in the meal the stewardesses in their saris began serving almost immediately after take-off. They had a decent cognac aboard, and she was interested in that. She sipped it modestly but frequently, turning to peer down at the flickering lights of New England as the huge 747 groaned on toward the sub-Arctic on its great circle flight-path across the ocean. When dinner was finished, they would dim the cabin lights for the movies, and she could be alone with her jumbled thoughts.

The first-class section was nearly empty, and she was happily spared the company of some stranger in the seat next to her. The economy class behind her was quite full, about evenly divided between Indians in turbans and saris and American tourists organized into groups, little red, blue, or white tags dangling from their carry-on baggage.

She recognized one couple, taking seats near her in first class, as distinctly English, and four men who boarded after, three short and round, one tall and thin, as distinctly Russian. One of the short round ones dropped off into a seat in first class. The others, moving as though in step, disappeared into economy.

Now, reclining further in her seat, she saw only darkness below. The aircraft was probably crossing a brief stretch of the Atlantic before the next landfall at New Brunswick. After that would come Newfoundland and then Cape Farewell, Greenland. She had made so many of these crossings that the isolated outpost was now a routine reference point, as familiar as any of the commuter stations between Grand Central and Greenwich. On one flight, with the clear northern skies aglow with the aurora borealis, she had actually seen the few dim lights marking the Cape Farewell settlement. It had seemed so cold, lonely, and forbidding then. Compared to her destination, it now seemed friendly and familiar.

Farewell. There had been a song about good-bye. About wishing someone love. She had sung it a lot to herself when she had first come to the Hamptons. Farewell. Sweet sorrow. Tears. She tried to put the song from her mind, but voices continued to sing it, over and over.

Shortly after returning to New York, Tatty had driven up to Westchester to the bank of the small river where her mother's ashes had been scattered. It had been a bright clear day with the autumn sunlight intensifying every color, but as she looked down at the stream, dropping roses slowly one by one onto its steady surface, she thought she heard the depressing sound of rain. It was only the leaves, falling. She said to herself that the trees were crying.

Finishing her brandy, she leaned forward to press her cheek against the coldness of the window. When this Russian affair was over, she would go away, far away, perhaps to California. That was about as far from reality as she could possibly get.

There was bustling in the cabin. One of the first-class stewardesses was distributing earphones for the movie, which in this section was another dreadful Glenda Jackson comedy. Tatty shook her head when the stewardess came by. The girl lingered, asking in heavily accented English if she minded if a few people from the tourist section came into first class for the movie, as it was the only place the film would be shown. They would be sent away immediately afterwards, she said. Tatty said she didn't mind, and turned away. She wanted to sleep.

Before she could, one of the passengers from economy class, a turbaned Sikh with a coal black beard, took the seat beside her, adjusting the earphones with some difficulty. The movie started and she closed her eyes again, only to have the man jostle her.

"A thousand pardons, *memsah'b,*" he said, with Kiplingesque exaggeration. Then he jostled her again. She was about to reply, angrily, when he put his fingers to his lips, leaned close, and whispered, "Relax, Tat. Just because I'm from economy doesn't make me an untouchable."

She glanced quickly across to the Russian on the other side of the cabin. He had his earphones on and was watching the film. She turned back to her seatmate.

"Your makeup is very good," she said. "I almost wonder if I should make you prove your identity."

"What? Quo warranto? Very well. You have the faintest small birthmark on the inside of—"

"Stop it, Ramsey. Aren't you taking a risk? There are four Russians aboard. There's one just over there."

"Actually, there are seven of them on this flight. But no one particularly worrisome. At any rate, I shall be dropping off at London. I've a bit of business there."

"I'd expected you to show up, you know."

"Did you?"

"I thought you'd pop up in London, or in Russia somewhere."

"That would hardly do for a man of my station in the Soviet section. They'd snatch me five minutes off the plane and haul me off to the Lubyanka. If there was anything left of me when we finished chatting, they'd then barter my remnants for whichever of their leading lights we have locked up, or worse, persuade me to defect. I'd take death to that, Tatty. Nothing patriotic, mind you. It's just that life in the great workers' paradise and pigsty would be all the same to me as rotting in the grave."

That comment alone would have assured her of his identity. Ramsey hated communists more than anyone else on earth, and he hated many, many people.

"Do you have anything new to tell me?" she asked. "You're not calling this off?"

"Heavens no. I just wanted to reassure you that we're watching out for you. And I wanted you to have a little bon voyage gift."

He placed a small package on her lap.

"Open it on the Aeroflot flight to Leningrad. It's meant for good luck. It was the duke's idea."

"Open it on the Aeroflot flight to Leningrad. It's meant for good luck. It was the duke's idea."

She studied the package, and then looked at the antique emerald ring the old man had given her.

"Ramsey . . ."

"The Russian has noticed us. He's taking off his earphones. I need to make an appropriate exit. I'm going to kiss you, Tatty. I want you to push me away and then hit me in the face as hard as you can."

"What?"

"I'm an obnoxious wog, missy. I've been pestering you. I'm doubtless drunk."

He opened his mouth and pressed it against hers in what could be described as a slobber. She felt his saliva run down her chin. Though never so realistically, she had played this scene many times. Shoving him as hard as she could, she struck him hard in the mouth, hurting her fingers and causing his lip to bleed. The emerald ring.

Ramsey rose, his earphones hanging comically from one ear, and leapt back into the aisle, spewing out mouthfuls of whining curses and apologies in a language she thought and hoped might be Hindi. Then he fled.

An anxious stewardess rushed to Tatty's seat, hands aflutter. Tatty asked for a wet towel and another brandy. After those were brought, she requested a pillow and blanket. Brandy, warmth, softness. They might bring sleep.

But they did not. When she closed her eyes, she heard the sound of leaves, falling like rain.

She did not see Ramsey for the rest of the flight. At Heathrow, the Russia-bound passengers were given time to refresh themselves and relax in the international terminal lounge. The bright neon lights pained her eyes, which had looked horribly red in the mirror of the dim airplane lavatory. She bought a pair of unattractive but serviceable sunglasses at a notions counter, then went to the duty-free shop to see if there was any clothing that interested her. There wasn't. Buying a copy of the *Times,* she went to the café and settled down at an empty table with tea, biscuits, and a sour orange juice. It was then that she noticed

Ramsey, reading a newspaper himself off in a lounge area. She watched him steadily but he never once looked her way.

He was waiting to make sure of her decision, that she would continue on. Once she boarded the Russian aircraft, it would be irrevocable.

With sudden haste, she set down her cup, snatched up her coat and carry-on bag, and hurried to the customs exit, starting toward the Nothing To Declare line, then retracing her steps.

Ramsey was still in his chair, still reading the newspaper. She moved quickly back to where the American tour group was being assembled for transfer to the Russian flight. He did not follow. He didn't need to.

They were passed through a checkpoint with the worst sort of British officiousness, two blue-uniformed women counting passports and noting, "One male, one female. One female. Two males . . ."

From the gate, they were taken not out to the plane but down onto the tarmac, where their luggage had been placed in a large rectangular pile between two white lines. There were four men standing nearby, all quite Russian, two of them in brown leather or vinyl trenchcoats. When the passengers approached, the men moved to take position at the corners of the rectangle. One of them gestured to the first of the passengers, and demonstrated what was wanted. The passengers were to take their individual luggage by themselves over to another space between white lines on the tarmac. The point of this idiocy, apparently, was to match luggage with person. But what else?

Tatty did as instructed. As someone traveling with the tour group but not part of it, she was made to wait until last. She had Gucci luggage—a very large tan suitcase, a smaller one, and her makeup case, plus her carry-on bag. It took her two trips. She looked up at the nearest leather coat when she was done. He nodded once at her, and then again at the waiting aircraft, and looked at his watch. She hurried aboard, and the heavy-set stewardess quickly reached to close the forward door behind her.

The interior of the plane, the Soviets' closest approximation of transport luxury, was funereal—dingy gray walls, stained, dark blue seats and carpeting. The three stewardesses were large, square, and grim, lending the impression they were chosen more for their abilities to subdue passengers than to charm them. As with Air India, they began serving the meal almost immediately after take-off, from a huge chipped and peeling white metal cart that looked as though it had done duty in a nineteenth-century Russian army hospital. The food was a match. Tatty declined it, accepting only a glass of extraordinarily bad wine, a wine so awful she almost didn't take a second sip.

Thoroughly intimidated, the other passengers sat in dumbstruck silence, acting more like cowed inmates than the boisterous tourists they had been aboard the Air India plane. Tatty ignored them, even the nice old couple in the two seats next to hers. She took Ramsey's gift from her handbag, recognizing the wrappings as Tiffany's. The small box inside was Tiffany's as well. She opened it clumsily, surprised and enchanted by what it contained: a small, gold and red enamel pin bearing a crest and coat of arms. The design was very old fashioned, as antique as the emerald ring that the old duke had given her, but the pin was quite new, as though it had been made up to special order very recently. It was elegantly beautiful. It was the imperial double-headed eagle of the family Romanov.

It was pinned to what proved to be a piece of notepaper folded many times over into a very small square. The message, in Ramsey's hand, was only a few words long.

"I love you, as you cannot know."

She affixed the pin to her jersey, letting her wool jacket fall back over it, hiding it. She would look at it in private glances. She finished the execrable wine in three quick gulps, then went to sleep.

She awoke to a graying dusk. The plane, losing altitude rapidly, was banking over a dull expanse of water, a bay or large lake. One of the stewardesses, in commandant style, announced over the public address system that they were nearing Leningrad and warned against the taking of photographs out the cabin windows. Tatty yawned, amused by the notion. There was nothing to see but an endless darkening expanse of green-brown-gray merging to black in the east. The country at the center of the world, her grandmother had called it, a land of limitless horizons. Beyond one was the Arctic; beyond another, the United States; beyond others, China, the Middle East, and Europe. Both Mathilde and Tatty's mother Chloe had cherished their Russianness; Mathilde had a passion for the physical state of Russia, for the land and trees and skies, for the extraordinary space of Russia. Mathilde and Mathilde's Russian friends had called it a magical country, the most magical country in the world, in all history.

She would see. The touring schoolgirl remembered mostly hurry, sickness, and drabness, and falling asleep at the opera. Tatty the mature, worldly woman should find more. She would try.

She saw a sweep of trees as the ground rush came. The airplane landed roughly, bumped along for a great distance, then swerved sharply as it headed for the terminal. There were a few other aircraft about, some military, but none moving. At last theirs rolled to a stop.

"Flight is over," said one of the stewardesses, in a gruff, thickly uttered monotone over the intercom. "Good, bye."

They opened the cabin door, revealing a soldier in fur hat with a submachine gun standing just outside.

The terminal building was poorly lit and drafty, the customs and passport clearance procedures confusing and inefficient. One of the aimless porters took Tatty's luggage and disappeared with it. After finally escaping the suspicious stare of the soldier in the passport control booth, she had to spend many minutes frantically searching for the porter, finding him at last trying to load her bags onto one of the buses assigned to a tourist group. A Russian word came back to her, the word for idiot.

"*Idyot!*" she shouted. The porter, smiling, continued piling them in. Obviously, there were no idiots here. Just him. "*Idyot! Eto moi bagazh!*"

It was then that she was joined by her welcoming committee of one, a youngish man who looked very American and very State Department, complete to his chesterfield topcoat. He introduced himself as Dixon Meadows from the embassy, then hurried off to deal harshly with the porter, who, submissive in the face of authority, even American authority, began to pull Tatty's bags off again.

Once they were in the back seat of Meadows's embassy car, the driver departing the airport at great speed, Meadows reintroduced himself, this time more elegantly and comprehensively. He was with the USIA section at the embassy in Moscow, and specialized in being "nanny" to visitors such as herself. He would be at her service from beginning to end of her tour, as much or as little as she wished. The Russians had also assigned her an Intourist guide, a woman named Raya Postnikova, who would accompany her during her free periods, but he was to be her escort at all official functions, of which there would be a great many. That night, after she had rested from her journey, there was a small dinner at the American consulate in Leningrad. The following morning, there was a press conference for the Russian media, and afterward a small one for a few American reporters who had come up from Moscow. That evening, after her performance, the Soviets were giving a party for her at the Union of Societies for Friendship and Cultural Ties with Foreign Countries.

"And, as the Russians love to say, and so on and so forth," he said. "When we shift to Moscow, it will start all over again, only on a much grander scale. The ambassador is planning a dinner for you, and I'm sure the Soviets will reciprocate handsomely. Oh, my dear, you'll find yourself treated quite like a princess."

"Or grand duchess."

"Yes, all the same, my dear. You'll be pleased."

He kept patting her hand in reassurance. He had curly brown hair he wore combed over his ears, light, darting eyes, and a mouth as feminine as Ramsey's. She guessed Dixon was a family middle name he used in State Department affectation as a first. Mischievously but unrealistically, she hoped his first name might be Moe.

"You say you're the assistant cultural attaché?" she said, as though she had expected a higher rank.

"Yes, quite the junior man," he said, "although I often report directly to Washington, frequently to the man who recruited you for this tour. He's quite concerned that this be a success and that you have a pleasant time of it." He patted her hand again. "He's threatened dire consequences for me if things go awry."

Meadows might as well have written it out in neon lights. He was an Agency man, working for Ramsey, and the cultural job was cover.

He handed her a small but surprisingly heavy package. "He sent you this little gift. Chocolates. Chocolates you cannot get in the Soviet Union. Your favorite kind, in fact."

She glanced at the package and then quickly back at Meadows. She didn't have a favorite kind of chocolates. As Ramsey certainly must know, she never ate them. She started to speak.

Meadows put a finger to his lips. "He remembered the brand from France. When he sent this package in the diplomatic pouch, he told me he had memories of France and you very much in mind."

The weight of the package now frightened her. Watching her eyes, he put his finger to his lips once more then patted her hand. "I'm sure you're going to have a lovely time."

"What, what about make-up? Rehearsals? A stage manager?"

"The Russians are taking care of everything, my dear. You've only to show up at the recital hall two hours before your first performance. Don't worry. Theater is what the Russians do best."

He then prattled on about the city, as she was sure the woman Raya would prattle on about it the following day. She turned and looked at it out the window, recalling schoolgirl memories, not of her first trip but of her readings of Dostoyevsky. Modern times and autos or no, Leningrad with its eighteenth-century buildings and dimly lit streets still seemed the St. Petersburg of droshkies and troikas, gentlemen's carriages and Cossack patrols, hereditary aristocrats replaced with Bolshevik ones, but still a city of the elite. They were driving north toward the Neva River, skirting the center city, but at one point they crossed the grand boulevard that was the Nevsky Prospekt. Tatty remembered Mathilde's many descriptions of it, and now found it quite the same. She had a sudden feeling of kindredness for this place. She was being absurd, of course. She was only a quarter Russian, after all, and that very Russian grandmother of hers was as much Prussian as anything else. But however much Russian she was, she now felt at last very glad of it.

"I tried to get you into the Astoria," Meadows said, as they crossed the dark river. "It's down by the Winter Palace and by far the most elegant hotel in town. Did you know Hitler once issued invitations for a victory banquet there that the fortunes of war never permitted him to hold? But the Soviets insisted on putting you up at the Hotel Leningrad, where they like to put all foreigners. It's deluxe. More modern than chic. Built by the Finns. The plumbing works. I got you a suite on the river side. It has a sunken tub and a view of the Winter Palace. I'm sure you'll find it charming."

He patted her hand again as she left the car, then handed her the package of chocolates she had left behind.

"Tonight's dinner isn't formal. Cheerie bye."

The suite looked high-class Cleveland, the bath only high-class Toledo, but it was warm and comfortable in its wood-paneled, contemporary way, and the view was extraordinary, even at night.

She then discovered a reason to be very fond of the Russians indeed. On top of her bureau was a basket of fresh fruit and cheeses. Next to it was a bucket of ice in which had been set a large carafe of vodka. She ate and drank somewhat greedily, then remembered the package of chocolates, opening it with some difficulty. As she expected, its second layer contained not candy but a small white-handled automatic pistol. And a note, from Ramsey, written in his cryptic style:

To spare you a fate worse than death.

She presumed that, once she was out, someone would search her room, someone certainly practiced enough to find a gun. What they would make of that, and do with her, she could only imagine with a shudder. She would take it with her to the dinner, and return it to the solicitous Dixon Meadows.

Pouring more vodka, she wearily took off her travel clothes and drew her bath. There was indeed a commodious sunken tub—she wondered if this was the honeymoon suite—that she quickly filled with hot, steamy water. Soon she was enjoying the happiest moment of her long day, although her pleasure was somewhat dampened when she reached for her towel. It had the consistency of facial tissue and the texture of fine-grained sandpaper.

To her surprise, she slept only fitfully, her body's time clock apparently knocked completely askew. Putting on her dinner clothes, including the czarist pin Ramsey had given her, she pulled a chair to the window and had one more glass of vodka.

"Grandmother," she said, lifting it in toast to the Winter Palace. "I am home."

She had said "Grandmother." What she had meant was "Cousin." Cousin Tatiana Nicolyevna Romanov.

By the time Meadows rang from the lobby, she had little interest in going to the consul's dinner. She was in fact half tipsy and quite content to sit by the extraordinary window and become entirely so. But she was a dutiful person more than anything else, and dinner with the consul was precisely the kind of duty her family had brought her up to honor.

Meadows seemed impatient. When she realized she had left the box of chocolates and their interesting surprise back on her dresser, he refused to let her fetch them, insisting that they were too late. So she left a pistol on her dresser. The hotel had taken her passport. She wondered if she might be dragged into some horrid prison that very night.

But she wondered that frivolously. She was in a surprisingly good mood, and did manage to get entirely tipsy at the dinner party. Relying on the reflexes of breeding and social discipline to prevent herself from behaving too embarrassingly, she hoped the consul—a pleasant, circum-spect man in his mid-forties—would attribute her conver-sational excesses to jetlag and theatrical bohemianism. He seemed not to mind in any event, although Meadows got quite sharp with her when she began going on about Valeri Griuchinov, asking if he wasn't a monster like Stalin and hadn't he committed all sorts of war crimes in Asia. The consul said only that he thought Griuchinov to be a very nice man, and then Meadows changed the subject.

Upon her return, she found that the maid had come to turn down her bed and take away the uneaten fruit and cheese, but otherwise the room seemed perfectly unmo-lested, the package of chocolates untouched. She put it, the pistol still inside, into her make-up case.

She attempted some reading before going to sleep, choosing Harriet Beecher Stowe's *Uncle Tom's Cabin* as the easiest, but slipped off into the dreamiest of states after only a few pages.

There was a call sometime in the dead of night, a silence on the other end at first, and then the voice of a Russian man speaking angrily and quickly. Not quite awake, she could not understand his words, but a moment later he hung up.

PART TWO

You cannot make a revolution with silk gloves.

—Josif Vissarionovich Dzhugashvili
(Joseph Stalin)

7

Raya the Intourist guide arrived promptly at eight A.M., finding Tatty most unpromptly still abed. Apologizing, Tatty told her she would be down in the lobby in fifteen minutes. She arrived in twenty-five. Raya, who did not need to identify herself, was standing in front of the elevators, arms folded, looking as though she was there to prevent Tatty's escape.

Raya was a magnificent blend of things. A very large woman, with a square face and button nose, she was nonetheless quite attractive; by Soviet standards, glamorous. She had red hair and green eyes that would have been Irish in another face. She wore a red suit, thick red coat, and the most fashionable Russian high-heeled red vinyl boots. Tatty was dressed not dissimilarly. She had chosen a black suit and red silk blouse, black boots and a black Russian fur hat from Bergdorf Goodman's, but her Christian Dior coat was as bright a red as Raya's, except for the black fur cuffs and collar. Bolshevik chic.

"It is bad to be late for breakfast," Raya said. "The waitress girls are very slow." She smiled, a brief revelation of a secret friendly nature, then shifted her face into its customary gruffness. "Come."

Breakfast included smoked sturgeon, sausage, herb cheese, thick dark bread, mineral water, and eggs. Tatty took a few bites of each. Smoking constantly, Raya managed to finish everything on her plate. Despite her commanding presence, she wasn't as old as Tatty had first thought, perhaps only thirty or thirty-five. Meadows had told her Raya was a member of the party, one of the elite, a Soviet aristocrat. She certainly acted it, reminding Tatty of not a few actresses in New York. She quickly explained she was a guide only to celebrities like Tatty—"Veeps," as she pronounced the term "VIPs." She said she had been in charge of handling the American press for the Vice President Bush visit. She was entrusted with and had a special license for escorting Russians privileged enough to travel to Paris and London. She had access to special stores.

The press conference was to start at ten-thirty. Tatty asked if they could go across the river for a visit to the Winter Palace first.

"When you are with me," Raya said, lighting another cigarette, "you can do anything you want."

Raya had a car, a small red Zhiguli that was cramped and confining but, according to Raya, no more so than the taxis. It would be hers as long as she held her Intourist job, which she said would be forever, as her brother was a general in the Soviet army. She drove very rapidly, and with great assurance. When they pulled up at the palace and Raya parked near one of the grand entrances, a soldier—Raya called them militiamen and said they were the same as police—tried to make her move on. No doubt dropping names, she bullied him down without even showing identification.

Tatty paused a moment, looking out at the broad square that adjoined the palace. Mathilde had told her of this bloody place, Dvortsovaya Square. She had read of it and seen photographs taken of it that day in 1905 when a hundred thousand people bearing petitions for the czar had been fired on by soldiers, Cossacks, and hussars. More than a thousand men, women, and children had been cut down. It had been in a way the first Russian revolution, and the wisest of the aristocrats and czarist officialdom began to leave the country soon after. The czar had not ordered the shooting, had not been in the city; but ultimately that had made no difference.

"Come," said Raya, opening the car door. "Here we have all the best paintings. Rembrandts, Impressionists, El Greco, da Vinci. Hermitage is best museum in the world."

"I'd like to see those, yes. But mostly I'd like to see it as it was when it was a house."

"A house," said Raya, contemptuously. "It has one thousand forty-seven rooms, all built for one parasitical family."

"It wasn't the only such house," said Tatty.

Raya snorted and swept on with her tour, moving through the endless rooms and endless corridors at a speed that rendered any lingering contemplation of a painting or exhibit impossible. Raya knew all there was to know about all the paintings, about all the czars. She went on lengthily about Czarina Catherine the Great's sex life with horses.

"There was a throne room," said Tatty. "I was here once before, more than ten years ago, on a school tour."

"I know. That is recorded on your visa papers."

"I remember that throne room. I didn't pay much attention to it then. I'd like to see it now."

"Of course. There are no longer thrones, you know. They were removed in 1917. What is enthroned there now is all of Soviet Union."

It was called the Saint George Hall in Mathilde's time, and served as the large throne room, a chamber lined with forty-eight Italian marble columns and so huge Tatty could not distinguish the faces of the tourists at the other end. She could certainly distinguish the enormous map, however. Made of semiprecious Ural stone and rare jewels, it was, according to Raya, three hundred square feet in area. It showed all of the Soviet empire, with Moscow marked by a hammer and sickle made of diamonds. Tatty tried to imagine it with thrones there instead, and the hall filled with elegant people in court dress.

"My grandmother was here once," she said.

101

"Yes. Thousands of people visit Winter Palace and Hermitage every week."

"No. I mean when the czar ruled."

Raya made a face. "You should not talk of such things."

The press conference was held at the House of Friendship and Peace, in a room too small for the two dozen or so Soviet journalists. She presumed they were journalists, though a number of them might have been some sort of police. There was only one television camera unit there, with an old-fashioned sound-on-film camera. She laughed. This was more press attention than she had ever received in the United States.

The questions were odd: Did she think Thoreau antisocial? Could *Uncle Tom's Cabin* be published today? Wasn't Lincoln a traitor to the proletariat from which he had come?

Then one of them really got down to business. With so much economic and police violence against black people in the United States, did she not think these writings just as appropriate now as before the American Civil War? Did she not think it would be more appropriate for her to read them in American cities such as Chicago and Washington, D.C., instead of in the Soviet Union, where all races lived together as brothers?

In the Soviet Union, journalists and police were much the same thing.

"I am here as a guest of the Soviet Union," she said, as icily as she could. "I am here as an actress, to read the words of these fine Americans, to share them with the Soviet people. I do so without any political consideration, just as I would not intrude such political matters as your forced labor camps when I am performing Chekhov. I should make the observation, however, that the works I am going to read from were written when both of our nations practiced slavery."

Meadows looked extremely pleased with her response, but the Soviets did not. They ended their segment of the news conference. After the Russians were cleared from the

102

room, four American reporters were brought in. Meadows had briefed her on who they would be. Two were from wire services, one was from *Newsweek* magazine, and the fourth needed no introduction.

She had not seen Jack Spencer in two years. He was beginning to show his age. His sandy hair was going gray and there were weary lines around his eyes. Still, he was an unusually handsome man. Tatty had once told him that he would look like God by the time he was sixty. He had replied that, by the time he was sixty, he would look like he had deeply offended God.

They smiled at each other warmly, but he gave no other greeting. Most of the questions were asked by the others. One wanted to know how the Russians had reacted to her, though she had yet to give her first performance. Another didn't seem to know precisely why she was there. Jack at last came to her rescue, asking if she didn't think efforts like hers on the cultural front were every bit as important as new trade agreements in improving Soviet-American relations. She was not familiar with new trade agreements, but she said yes. He asked if the Soviets ought not to reciprocate by letting the Bolshoi tour the United States again. Tatty said it would be a lovely idea, realizing without regret that her answer would irritate her Soviet hosts, who had kept a tight grip on the Bolshoi because of all the defections and the hostility arising from the Soviets shooting down a Korean civilian jet. As the other reporters were scribbling in their notebooks, she assumed she had just given them a news story.

The Soviets intervened to bring the conference to an end. Spencer held back as the others walked out of the room.

"Hello, Czarina. We have to stop meeting like this."

"I was hoping we would meet, but I didn't expect it to be at a news conference."

"Dornfeld of *Newsweek* and I were going to come up by ourselves, but the two wire-service lads then decided to come along for fear they'd miss something. Your Bolshoi remark will probably make their reports."

"You mean your Bolshoi remark. Will you be in my audience tonight?"

"Yes, but I'll have to leave immediately afterwards to catch the train. I have travel orders." Both Raya and Dixon Meadows were approaching. "I have to go. There's a press luncheon with their culture commissars. We can talk about the Bolshoi."

He squeezed her hand, then stepped away.

"But when will I see you again?"

He took another step. "In Moscow. We can be free spirits in gay old Moscow." He smiled and bid farewell with his odd salute, bringing two fingers laconically to his brow.

In the little car, on the way back to the hotel, Raya said, "You know that man?"

"Oh yes. Quite well."

"He is a foreign correspondent. He does theatrical reviews?"

"No. He's just someone I've known for a few years. I met him in New York."

She did not want to go through the effort of explaining her relationship with Spencer—that he had married her stepsister, that he was no longer married to her, that Tatty had always thought him more than a brother-in-law, very much more now. Raya would only ask more prying questions. A divorcée herself, Raya had already asked Tatty about her sex life with her ex-husband.

Her Leningrad performances were in the Gorky Drama Theater in the Fontanka Naberezhnaya. The great writer had founded it himself in the first year of the Bolshevik revolution and Tatty felt quite honored. The theater staff was very respectful toward her and unexpectedly helpful and efficient, complete to the fresh flowers in her dressing room. Before the revolution, Raya informed her, such flowers in winter were available only to the nobility. Tatty only smiled.

The lighting, she was assured, was perfect. A small chamber orchestra was on hand to play introductory music and bridges between her readings, mostly Aaron Copland. It worked very well in their one rehearsal.

"You were divine," Meadows said, at its conclusion. "You will be divine."

She was nervous, more so than she could remember being at any of her New York performances except her first. She had wondered if the Russians in the audience would understand English. It became clear very quickly that few of them did. They had been given translations of what she was to read and, disconcertingly, not in unison, kept turning the pages. Some read on ahead. Happily, there were some American tourists seated in a group toward the rear, and they followed her rather raptly, if only because they were so glad of English words after having been treated to so much Russian. Tatty tried to play to these American faces as much as possible, but her eyes kept wandering. She was well into her program when she finally caught sight of Jack Spencer, finding him shunted off to bad side seats with his three colleagues. He smiled when he saw her eyes upon him, causing her to flush and falter in her delivery. Later on, in the midst of one of the more moving passages of Stephen Crane's *Red Badge of Courage,* she faltered again, though not because of Spencer. She had let her eyes lift to the boxes. Only the nearest of these were occupied, mostly by older men, though a few had brought their uniformly round and frumpily dressed wives. In the box nearest to her on the right sat a man alone. His somber, staring face and longish white hair caught the light from the stage, but with his dark clothing he was so enveloped by shadows that his head seemed almost disembodied—the head of a ghost. Peter Stolypin, the czar's reformist prime minister who Mathilde said might have prevented the revolution, had been assassinated in a theater. But it was not here that he had been shot; another city, Kiev perhaps. Good Lord, how had she remembered that? Who was this ghost?

Though the Russians seemed not to notice, she lost her place. Blushing, holding her hand in front of her mouth as though she had paused to stifle a cough, she finally regained it, proceeding flawlessly enough until her glances caught the man in the box again. His expression was friendlier now, perhaps encouraged by her second direct look, but the face was still disembodied. With his slight grin, he now seemed less a ghost and more the Cheshire cat. She found herself less frightened, vaguely amused.

Not for long. As she let her voice warble on into a melodramatic rendering of "Oh Captain, My Captain," something began to bother her as might an increasingly perceptible cold draft. Her eyes were attracted to this strange figure because of something inexplicably familiar about him, and it was bringing out the wrong emotions in her.

As the orchestra began the musical bridge that preceded her finale, Copland's "Fanfare for the Common Man," she stood, head high, waiting, and looked to her right again. The grin had become a fatherly smile, the patriarch observing his favorite daughter. He bowed his head in recognition of her gaze.

Tatty snapped her head back sharply. The feeling of familiarity was now wholly one of fear. He was the man in Ramsey's photographs. He was Griuchinov. He had come to her already.

As she reached to hold the page she was about to read, that infuriating tremor again ran across the back of her hand. She clenched her fist and began again.

When she finished, she stood with lowered head in a silence that grew embarrassingly long. Then the Russians realized she had concluded the performance and rose to give her thundering applause. Spencer nodded with emphatic approval, then waved farewell again with his two-fingered salute as he followed his colleagues up the aisle as they were led away for their train. She had an impulse to run after them, to cling to Jack, to let him drag her away.

They brought a bouquet of flowers onstage for her, the flowers from her dressing room, to which she hastened as the applause quickly dwindled. There was little for her to do there but put on her coat and hat, but she had to wait for Raya and Meadows. Pacing back and forth, trapped, fearing Griuchinov might enter at any moment, she labored desperately to compose herself, without success. Instead, she began to cry. At the sight of his face, she knew

106

she would scream. Ramsey's intricate plot, her own revenge, her theatrical tour, it would all be a shambles.

She slumped into the hard wooden chair by her dressing table, choking back sobs, finally regaining control of herself just as someone knocked at the door. It opened, and a man entered.

"Divine," said Meadows.

They drove in Raya's little car through surprisingly busy streets. The night air was cold and crisp with a scattered flavoring of early snow. Tatty rolled down her window to bring it against her face. When they reached their destination, she stood a moment at the curb, savoring this touch of winter Russia, thinking of droshkies and troikas, of her grandmother and imperial balls. The Friendship and Cultural Union party inside was no such gala. A hundred or more people were crowded into a long narrow room, milling and swarming in a sort of Alice in Wonderland caucus race along and around a long table heaped with food. The room was too hot. In addition to the smell of people were those of fish, cheese, and Russian tobacco. She was given no opportunity to remove her coat, until she almost screamed at Raya to take it from her. She happily accepted a cold glass of vodka some happy-faced Russian pressed upon her.

"Marvelous," said a tall Russian woman whom a returning Raya introduced as one of the country's leading stage actresses. "Marvelous. Marvelous, marvelous." It was apparently her only English word.

The American consul general was there, and she was glad of the familiar face, though it was quickly lost to her in the moving crowd. A troupe of ballet dancers was introduced to her, and seemed to dance by, one by one, as she shook their hands. A military man with enormous amounts of braid and medals came up and stood talking to her in Russian, gripping her hand. At length she was able to turn gratefully away in response to someone tapping her shoulder. It was a woman in Russian evening clothes, a slender and perfect blonde with wonderfully large blue eyes and one of the most beautiful if gaunt and tragic faces Tatty had ever seen, a face not greatly unlike that of her mother, Chloe. Without the slightest change in her sad, sad expression, the woman stood on tiptoe to kiss Tatty slowly on both cheeks, then stood back and slipped away, as much into the vapors as into the crowd.

The human crush was becoming oppressive. Raya stuck close by, though Meadows had disappeared somewhere back by the door and none of the other Americans was in reach. A number of Russians were obviously and ardently trying to reach her, but their efforts to do so only pressed the crowd more thickly around her. One big bulging-eyed aspirant was struggling forward much like an American football player, but the strength of his effort ultimately undid him as people to her left gave way and he was carried off obliquely by his own momentum. Another Russian man, a small, round, cheery, and quite drunken fellow with a bright red nose and shiny bald head, was able to move to her from the table with little effort at all. Very politely, he placed a small smoked fish in her hand and, nodding enthusiastically, said, "*Pokushyte.*" Eat.

She shrank back, flustered. Not for anything would she put tongue or teeth to the thing, which still bore its little head. Yet she dared not drop it on the floor for fear that she might offend the little man, or worse, that he might simply pick it up and hand it to her again. The table was beyond her reach. She could give it to Raya, but then there would still be her greasy hand, and she had nothing on which to wipe it but her evening dress.

"Tatty."

Meadows had at last rejoined her, but he had brought a guest. The somber ghost, the Cheshire cat, and the kindly father now had a body, an older man's body, to be sure, but taller and trimmer than most Russians'. She looked into his dark, glittering eyes, so close now, and the fear came back to her in a great rush.

"Tatty," said Meadows. "I should like you to meet Mr. Griuchinov, Chairman of the Council of Ministers."

The crush of people around Tatty evaporated, leaving her alone and exposed. She worried about what must be the cold look on her face, for she could no longer control it. Without a word, he reached to take her hand as though to kiss it, like some damned Prussian count, but abruptly halted when he found it full of fish. His quizzical look turned to humor. Impulsively, he brought her hand, fish and all, to his lips, then gently lowered it, standing erect. He began to laugh. Trembling, her lips quivering, she began to do the same, a nervous, faltering laugh that uncontrollably began to rise higher in pitch and volume. Soon everyone around them was laughing. In a moment, the entire room was laughing. She let the fish fall to the floor.

When the din subsided, he spoke at last, a surprisingly mellow and cheerful voice.

"Miss Chase," he said, pronouncing it "Meese Chess." "On behalf of our government and Soviet people, I welcome you to our country and say that you are very beautiful and talented person and that we are very, very grateful that you have come to read to us these beautiful writings of your countymen."

The laughter had vented her fear and nervousness. She found herself the mannerly person she had always been. She even smiled, though no more than diplomatically.

"I am very grateful for your having me," she said, wanting to say it in Russian, but not quite certain of enough of the words.

"We shall look forward to seeing you again while you are here," he said.

Still smiling, she stared hard into his eyes.

"That would give me great pleasure, Mr. Chairman."

He left her less the admiring father and more the Cheshire cat. With Raya gobbling food behind her, Tatty hastily departed as soon as Meadows said it was acceptable to do so.

Back in the hotel, alone in her suite, the Winter Palace the centerpiece of her view, she drank herself to sleep with three large vodkas.

"I want to go to Czarskoe Selo today," she said to Raya at breakfast the next morning.

"The town is called now Pushkin. He came from there."

"I don't want to see the town. I want to see the palace."

"There are two palaces."

"I want to see the main one, where the czar and his family spent their summers, where they were kept under arrest after the revolution."

"The main one is the Catherine Palace. Is closed now, for renovation project. You would like better the town of Petrodvorets. It was called Peterhof when czars went there. It is on the sea and has two beautiful parks. There is also there the Mon Plaisir palace of Peter the Great. We can go there tomorrow, or next day."

"Fine. Today I want to go to Czarskoe Selo and see the Catherine Palace, where Nicholas and Alexandra stayed."

"Why?"

"I want to make sure I see it. Something came up the last time I was here and I missed it."

"Is not on the schedule."

"Raya, I don't have a schedule, except for my performances."

"I have made a schedule for you. Today you are to see Smolny Institute, where Lenin planned the revolution."

"I'll see the Smolny some other time. Tomorrow, if you like, instead of Peterhof. But today I want to see Czarskoe Selo. It's such a lovely day, Raya."

Tatty had awakened to find a night's fall of snow on the ground and old women with brooms and shovels clearing the sidewalks. The overcast had broken and all of Leningrad glittered in the morning sunlight.

"Is closed. I am sorry."

"Raya, you said you were a party member, that you could do anything. Prove it."

Raya lighted a cigarette and made a face, coughing.

"Okay," she said. "We go to Pushkin. But we must be back in afternoon so you will not be late for performance."

"My performance is not until eight o'clock."

"We must not have you stranded out in countryside. Soviet government is being very careful of you, Miss Chase, to make sure nothing goes wrong for you. It is not well that you make surprise."

Tatty reached and patted Raya's hand. "Somehow I

110

think that your thoughtful Soviet government shall not lose track of me."

Czarskoe Selo turned out to be only some fifteen miles from Leningrad, less than an hour's drive. Raya had to show a uniformed guard identification, and she added to it a very official-looking letter that Tatty presumed was a temporary grant of special privileges. It commanded instant respect from the soldier, who shouted something to a comrade and then bade her enter the grounds with much deference. Raya grunted.

Mathilde had always spoken of Czarskoe Selo as the Romanovs' country place and Tatty expected exactly that, a country house, something along the lines of a hunting lodge. What she found seemed almost to eclipse the Winter Palace, an awesomely grand Russian version of Versailles. The further Raya drove onto the grounds, the wider they seemed to extend, almost to every horizon. They parked directly in front of the wide entrance steps of the Catherine Palace without challenge, as might the czar's chauffeur have done seventy years before. Tatty got out, still awestruck, and a little troubled. The Winter Palace had been what amounted to the seat of government, and its immensity a justifiable extravagance. This monstrosity was a creature comfort, just for one family. A railroad from the city had been built—solely for the family's use. She had thought it good fortune that the Romanovs had been caught by the revolution in this place, and not in the city; that they had had their interlude in this warm, familiar home before their removal to Siberia and its horrible consequences. But now it seemed the worst luck of all, to be held here in this mammoth symbol of all their indulgences while the revolution boiled and festered around them. No wonder the revolutionary soldiers assigned as their guards were so brutish.

"What do you want to see?" said Raya.

Tatty looked up at the three balconies above the grand portico, and the four grotesque statues bordering the three front doors.

"They have restored the Great Hall," Raya said. "It is worth seeing."

111

To rub the capitalist lady's nose in it, Tatty thought.

"There were family quarters," she said. "A private wing. Where they were kept during the first days of the revolution. It was near a park, where the czar cut wood. I would like to see that."

Raya huffed and grimaced. "That is at the Alexander Palace. It is a long walk."

It was a walk through the pristine snow, red vinyl boots trudging to the fore, plowing a path for Tatty's black leather ones. Raya seen from behind looked a very strong woman. Tatty had an impulse to pound her back, to hear the muscles thump.

It was not a walk; it was a trek. They should have driven, but Raya was apparently intent on being perverse and difficult. It was almost as though she knew of Tatty's czarist blood, and was falling into the role of the revolutionary guards of 1917, behaving as correctly as ordered but subjecting her ward to petty irritations and humiliations. Nevertheless, Tatty was enjoying the outing. She had felt confined and restricted from the moment she had arrived in Russia. For the first time now she was feeling the space of the place.

When they reached the Alexander Palace, she felt as though she had crossed half the country, and there was little vigor left to her stride.

The palace was nearly as large as the other, but its lines were graceful and less imposing, less flagrantly imperious. Tatty stood with hands clasped behind her back, studying the palace facade.

"Don't you want to go in?"

Inside would be the empress's mauve boudoir, the children's playroom and schoolroom, the study where the czar had first received Kerensky, the bedroom in which Tatiana had recovered from typhoid, the rooms Tatty remembered from her grandmother's telling and from recent reading, rooms too intimate and personal, too depressing.

"No, Raya." She began walking, her boots kicking up small sprays of snow. At the far corner of the long building she came to a raised, covered veranda with ornately carved balustrades, a structure more balcony than porch.

"Is empress's balcony," said Raya. "Private for her."

"Raya, when the grand duchesses entertained their friends, when they gave garden parties, where would that have been?"

The other woman shrugged, then pointed to some distant hedges.

"There maybe. Those are formal gardens of park."

"No. It would have been a place nearer the house. A place where the girls would entertain close friends, or relatives. Where they might serve refreshments."

"Around the other side, maybe. That would be close to the kitchens in this wing."

They went around the next corner, two women in red against so much whiteness. With the snow and so many decades passed, there was no way of telling where the flower beds might have been. Tatty walked about until she had a view of the house that resembled what she remembered in the background of the photograph in her grandmother's bloody memoir. She stared at the house for a long time.

"It could have been here. It could very well have been here." She scuffed at the snow until she had cleared a patch of moist black earth. Scooping up a handful, she held it close, finding it as black as her glove. She clenched it tightly, then scattered it in lumps across the snow at her feet.

"*Kuzina,*" she said.

"What did you say? Did you call me your cousin?"

"No. Let's go. I've seen what I came to see."

They did not speak again until they were in the car and driving away. Raya, going too fast in the snow, kept shaking her head, as though puzzled by the folly of this excursion.

"Those grand duchesses," she said, finally. "They were parasites."

Tatty leaned her head against the window. She would escape Raya by closing her eyes and feigning sleep. But, before she could, something glittered at the periphery of

113

her vision, sunlight reflecting on the chrome bumper of a parked car. It was an American car, sitting back down an unplowed side road in an avenue of tall, bare trees, exactly the same color and model of car as that which had welcomed her at the airport.

She meant to ask Meadows about that quite directly on the way to the theater, but he did not appear. Instead, there was Raya in the lobby, Raya without her little car.

"Tonight we are driven in Soviet government car," she said, leading the way outside to a black, gleaming Ziv with a chauffeur.

"Comrade Griuchinov?" Tatty asked.

"You have very much impressed him."

"Lucky me."

Griuchinov was not in the audience that night. Neither was he waiting in the car for her when the performance was over. So it went for the next several nights. On the evening of her next to last performance in Leningrad, the routine changed. Raya was not in the lobby. There was only the military chauffeur. And in the rear seat of the Ziv, smiling generously as she leaned forward to enter, was Griuchinov. She hesitated, but there was no point to that. It was far, far too late for that.

"Good evening, Miss Chase."

His pronunciation had improved slightly. She was no longer "Meese Chess." Now she was "Meese Chass."

"Good evening, sir," she said, in as gracious yet cool a tone as she could muster. "This is most kind of you." She lowered herself stiffly into the plush seat, gathering the skirts of her evening dress away from the door just as the chauffeur swung it shut.

"Is my pleasure, Miss Chase. Is wrong that such a great actress should be conducted through our streets in such little car as Tovarisch Postnikova's."

"You're too kind." She was doing her best frosty Grace Kelly. It was her most perfect role. Grace Kelly movies were what had attracted her first to acting.

"I enjoyed very much your first performance. I am told tonight you are reading from new works. Yes?"

114

He stayed well to his side of the car. She was afraid he would reach to kiss her hand again, or start patting it like Meadows.

"Yes. I'm including some writings by Frederick Douglass, and Abraham Lincoln's Cooper Union speech. I'm dropping *Uncle Tom's Cabin.*"

"I am not familiar . . ."

"Frederick Douglass was a slave who won his freedom and became an abolitionist lecturer and eventually an ambassador. It's said Lincoln's Cooper Union speech won him his party's presidential nomination."

"And *Uncle Tom* . . . ?"

"The book was very important in its time. But it's too juvenile." She paused, then smiled, frostily, adding, "For your sophisticated Russian audiences."

"Yes. So your recital becomes more political."

"In a nineteenth-century sense, I suppose that's true. But it's good politics, isn't it, Gospodin Griuchinov? Opposition to slavery?"

He seemed unfazed by both her use of the czarist-era term for gentleman and her oblique reference to the gulags.

"Yes, yes, Miss Chase. But is no matter. All words are beautiful when you speak them."

Now she let her frosty Grace Kelly lapse into Vivien Leigh's fluttery Scarlett O'Hara.

"Mr. Chairman, you are just so sweet."

She had touched his arm. She pulled her hand away.

"You are leaving Leningrad soon, Miss Chase?"

"My last performance is tomorrow."

"I am returning to Moscow myself. I shall be looking forward to seeing you there. I am wondering if tonight, after performance, if you might be liking to join me for dinner?"

"I can't."

She uttered the words reflexively, without thought. She had to be with him somewhere, someplace more compromising than a chauffeured car in a public street, or a public hall. But not now. She was not yet ready to cope with that moment. She must keep the monster trailing along.

115

"I've already eaten," she said, lying. "I have quite a nasty headache, and I'm just utterly exhausted, as I'm sure you understand. If I'm to be any good at all in Moscow, I simply have to have a thoroughgoing good night's sleep."

His expression had become somber, his glittering eyes hard and serious. In the darkness, he seemed a great bear peering out from the recess of a cave.

"So what about tomorrow night?" she said, with an elegant Grace Kelly inflection. Before he could respond, she put a fluttery hand to his arm again. "There's a restaurant, the Baku? In Sadovaya Street? Raya says it has the best *zakuski* in Leningrad. Yet we have not been. I should be delighted to dine with you there." And not in some plush, old man's hideaway. "That is, if you haven't more pressing business?"

"Oh no. Nothing that cannot wait. No. This makes me most very happy, Miss Chase. I shall be envy of all Soviet Union."

With good bloody reason, she thought.

At the theater, he kissed her hand again, his lips lingering overlong. She did not smile at him until he finally released her.

"No fish," she said.

"Yes. No fish. Ha ha ha."

She ran into the theater.

He was most attentive during the performance, especially when she read the Douglass and Lincoln speeches directly to the box where once again he sat alone. He did not appear afterward. There was only the chauffeur, and Griuchinov's empty car. He had apparently taken another, as though fearing that if he came into her presence again now he might say or do something to make her change her mind.

The next morning, Tatty got rid of Raya, feigning a need for more sleep that proved real once she returned to her suite. She awakened again after eleven, then went for a solitary walk along the river. Moored to the quay alongside the Pirogovskaya Embankment was a warship. It had been part of the view out her window but she had assumed

116

it was just another ship of the Soviet navy. As she looked at it now, it seemed much too old-fashioned for that. And there was no crew visible aboard; only a militiaman in a fur hat standing outside a sentry box by the gangway. The name on the bow, in Russian letters, was *Aurora*.

The cruiser *Aurora*. Mathilde had told her something about this ship. It had to do with the Bolshevik rising. The *Aurora* fired the guns that had begun the Bolshevik rising and driven Kerensky and the Provisional Government from the Winter Palace. And here it was, on display, just like the U.S.S. *Constitution*.

Tatty looked at the guard and gestured toward the ship. *"Razreshayetsya?"* He nodded curtly. It was open to the public.

Finding little of interest on the deck, she ducked through a hatchway, discovering that the old ship was maintained as a museum. Throughout the interior were artifacts and enlarged and mounted photographs of the revolutionary period, not only the two uprisings of 1917, but also of the 1905 disorders. On a lower deck was a massive photograph of the bloody demonstration outside the Winter Palace, the enlargement intensifying the deadliness of the soldiers' weapons, the panic and desperation on the faces of the fleeing people, the horror of the dead.

She felt confined, and oddly frightened. This ship could serve as the perfect prison for her, a Dantean hell for the claustrophobic, crowded with searing reminders of the blood and misery that was the reign of czars and the end of czars. She went back to the stairway and hurried up it, up past the main deck and all the way to the bridge, glad as she stepped out onto it to be returned to the space of the sky, river, and city.

The ship was moored almost directly opposite the hotel entrance. Standing there, watching her, was a man in a brown leather overcoat. A block down the street was Raya's small red car, a figure in red visible inside. A hundred yards in the other direction was another man in an overcoat, leaning against the wall of the embankment. This wretched, stupid country. Even if it had been as bad under the czars as they said, nothing had changed. All

117

those millions of people, including her cousin Tatiana Nicolayevna, had died for absolutely nothing. All that had changed was the name of the secret police.

She stomped her way out of the ship and down the gangway, stopping to give an exaggerated *spasibo,* or thank you, to the young militiaman, who seemed embarrassed by her. Then, walking with long, quick strides, she crossed the river to the Kutuzova Embankment and went west toward the palace. She assumed they were following her, but didn't look back to see. Reaching the broad expanse of Dvortsovaya Square, she marched out to the center of it and then whirled around to face the palace and the balcony from which the czar had so often spoken to his people. She stood defiantly, her hands on her hips, legs apart, watching as the little red Zhiguli car pulled to a peeking halt just around a corner of the palace, feeling suddenly a great joy in her czarist blood.

Then she walked rapidly back across the square, and into the museum entrance of the Winter Palace. They would catch up with her, of course, but it would require some inconvenience. Moving through the exhibits at a tear, she did her best to make it a considerable inconvenience, complete to ducking out a side exit that said, in Russian, No Exit.

Back at the hotel, she went up to the foreigners' bar on the top floor for a drink, and stayed for an expensive lunch she had to pay for in American dollars. Back in her suite, she had another drink, forsaking the chair by the big window to pace about her sitting room. Finally, she did sit, on the edge of her bed, holding the rim of her glass against her lips.

Like most theatrical people, she was a person of habit—routine and ritual. When she was indulgent and disorderly, even that followed a pattern. Ramsey had told her in France this was a dangerous failing.

But now it had a value. It told her that something was amiss, out of place. She looked about the two rooms. They had been victim to the maid's clumsy neatenings, but the maid would not have touched her suitcase. Someone had. It was set many inches away from where she had set it

118

down snug against the side of the bureau. And it had been turned with the zipper and lock side facing out, instead of against the wall as she had left it. The combination lock was set, but the three rolls of numbers had been turned to only a few numerals distant from the combination, and not spun wildly as was her custom.

She opened it, reaching immediately for the small pistol. It was gone. It was nowhere in the suitcase; nowhere in the room.

She returned to the edge of the bed, nervous, sipping her drink and trying to calm herself. If they were going to arrest her for some weapons infraction, there would have been militiamen awaiting her upon her return. Perhaps they were merely being discreet, in their totalitarian way. Firearms were forbidden. As she had one, they simply took it, no questions asked, no questions needed. They may well have relieved previous theatrical guests of drugs in the same fashion.

In any event, she was now without Ramsey's charming little gift. She laughed. She had not much need for it. The only one threatening her with "a fate worse than death" was old Griuchinov, and she certainly wasn't going to shoot him.

That she was going to leave to the Russians.

She pulled on her coat. She would go out to the street now and march right up to Raya's little car. She would make Raya take her to the Fortress of Peter and Paul, the Zoological Museum, all sorts of places. She would make Raya perform as a tour guide, and then some.

But when she went out, the red car was not to be seen.

Her performance that night, though her finale in Leningrad, was her worst. It was in fact execrable. Doubtless those following along with the Russian translations didn't notice or care, but New York reviewers would have hooted her off the stage. She was wooden and clumsy, hurried and slurred. She wanted only for the show to be over with, so she could go and dine with Griuchinov and get that over with. And soon—get Russia over with.

The seats, fittingly enough, were sparsely filled, with

Griuchinov the only occupant of a box. He, too, appeared impatient.

In the car he held her hand and talked volubly about Moscow all the way to the Baku restaurant, which was not far away in Sadovaya Street just off Nevsky Prospekt. The main dining room was on the second floor and, by Russian standards, quite elegant, if noisy. There was a dance orchestra and singers, and a boisterous response to the music from the many diners. Griuchinov had obviously been intent on making a discreet entrance, but the restaurant manager and his staff reacted to their arrival with a frantic, nervous deference that Nicholas himself could not have commanded before the revolution. A quiet corner and three tables had been set aside for them and the security entourage that had materialized from following cars. Their table was quite large, but the only two chairs at it had been set close together. Tatty had prepared for that. She had prepared herself for every eventuality.

The menu given her was in both English and Russian but she spoke her choices to him in the latter, ordering amply of the Azerbaijani dishes, commencing with smoked sturgeon and pickled peppers. She also asked for a large carafe of vodka. He smiled at this, as though he thought it augured well for his plans for the night, not knowing her mind.

"You speak our language well, Miss Chase," he said, lighting what looked to be an English cigarette. "Is surprising."

"My grandmother was Russian."

"Yes?" He seemed much interested in this.

"An immigrant."

"Not Jewish." He said it in the manner of a little joke. For a moment, she had an impish impulse to say that she was, but there was the possibility that might frighten him away.

"No. She was of the Russian Orthodox faith, though in the United States she became a Catholic."

"You are then Catholic?"

"Oh no," she said, smiling as though this was all the most wonderfully witty dialogue. "Worse. I'm Episcopalian, as much as I am anything religious." She quickly found another subject in the music. A woman was singing now, a ballad very haunting and moody, yet a song that could only be Russian.

"What is that song?" she asked.

" 'The Pear Tree.' Is country song. Very much romantic, yes?"

"Yes," she said, allowing him to hold her hand again, but taking it away when the waiter hurried up with the next course.

She drank thirstily of her ice-cold vodka. So much hand holding with the old Russian gentleman. The word applied to Griuchinov, for, all else aside, he was as courtly a fellow as the old duke in Westchester. It was just unfortunate he was a courtly old murderer.

He began coughing violently, the spasms not easing until he took several swallows of water and then some vodka.

"Excuse, Miss Chase," he said, grinding out his cigarette. "These are what killed Brezhnev, and here I am doing same thing to me. Doctors make me stop smoking, but I thought for tonight, for special occasion, I indulge myself."

"Do I provoke you to indulgence, Mr. Chairman?" She fluttered her eyelashes.

"You are very provocative, Miss Chase. No, I mean, very beautiful."

"Do you think I look Russian? From my Russian grandmother?"

"A little, yes. But you are not beautiful in way of beautiful Russian ladies. You are more something special."

"My mother was said to look quite Russian, and I'm told I favor her greatly. Do you resemble your father, Mr. Chairman?"

He blinked his eyes, and looked down. "My father was killed in Revolution, in war against White Armies. He was Red Army officer. I remember him not at all." He lifted his head again, letting a happier expression seep back into his features. "And as my father never came to be an old man, is now impossible to say if I resemble him."

She poured and drank more vodka, digging into the hot spicy food. She was so close to him. It would be an instant's business to drop some poison in his drink, or snatch up the knife beside her plate and plunge it into his throat, sawing and slashing until the neck was rendered an approximation of her father's. The little goon men at the other two tables would be helpless to prevent her, and for that they would go to the gulags, or bloody worse. If they did not gun her down right there, she would also be in for bloody worse, bloody awful worse.

But that fate was not for her. That was no fit end for a Miss Porter's girl. So she would sit here and munch her *zakuski* and swill her vodka and say her sweet little flirtatious lines so that Ramsey could spring his nasty little trap. Then she would get her sweet little czarist buns the hell out of this wretched, beautiful country.

She asked for more vodka.

"Have you traveled a great deal, Mr. Chairman?"

"In socialist countries, yes. In West, only Vienna and London. Oh yes, I was once also in Canada. In Ottawa, and Saskatchewan. Very much like Soviet Union. Big country, and cold."

She drank.

"You've never been in Asia, Mr. Chairman? I thought I'd been to absolutely all the places that there are to be, but then it occurred to me I'd never been to Asia, not even Hong Kong. Have you been to Asia? To Hong Kong?"

"Not to Hong Kong."

"Well, where in Asia were you, Mr. Chairman? Were you in Southeast Asia? Vietnam?"

"Miss Chase, there was war there with your country. We should not speak of these things. Let us talk of Moskva. In Moskva, I will take you on personal grand tour of Great Kremlin Palace."

She turned away from him to look at the orchestra, and sip more vodka. They were playing an old song, bright, happy, and vibrant in one passage, sweetly sad in the next. Singers came on and sang it with great passion, a very small dark-haired woman doing the melodic solo.

"Is 'Samara Town.' Very old song."

122

" 'Samara Town,' " she repeated, not pronouncing it right. She was having trouble pronouncing anything right now. She reached and drank more vodka. Through all the happy songs, she reached and drank. Through all the sad ones.

Woozy, she tried to set down her glass, but it kept falling over. And finally, so did she. The alarmed Griuchinov grasped her arm, but was far too late, not in time to keep her perfectly wonderful beautiful face from falling smash into her plate of *zakuski.*

Tatty awoke feeling so horrible her hotel suite might as well have been the torture chamber at Lubyanka Prison, or the drunk tank there, which might be much the same. It was only a little after six A.M., but she felt too sick to try to go back to sleep. With some struggle, she sat up. Someone had removed all of her clothing, every piece. But she could not possibly have been capable of a sexual act. Of any act.

She would be leaving Leningrad that day, that morning, by train, an arrangement made by Intourist and agreed to by Meadows, though she could not understand why. The trip was five hours by train, only an hour by air. Perhaps they wanted her to see a bit of the Russian countryside.

Her eyes focused on the distant darkened windows of the Winter Palace. Whether things went well or badly, she would not be returning to Leningrad, ever. What remained that she needed to see?

Emerging from her bathroom feeling not much better, she dressed clumsily, noting that someone had also packed all of her things for her. The hotel provided so many extra services, pistol removal, packing of things, stripping of clothes.

Gathering up her red coat, she went out into the hallway, closing the door too loudly behind her. The *spasibo* lady, as Tatty called the floor concierges stationed in all the hallways of Russian hotels, looked up, glowering. Tatty went up to her, and in fractured and slightly slurred Russian, asked if she had been on duty during that night.

"*Da,*" the woman grunted.

Tatty asked, as best she could, who had taken her into her room.

"Red-haired woman," was the reply.

Tatty handed her her room key, as was required, and this time didn't say *spasibo*.

Getting directions from the sleepy desk clerk, she stepped into the sobering cold outside and walked east along the embankment, turning left after two blocks. There was the last memorial in Leningrad that she had to see, a railroad station, the Finland Station. In 1917, the Germans had sent the exiled Lenin into Russia on a special train, as someone had said or written, injecting him into the body of Mother Russia like a bacillus. Here he had arrived, and here the disease had inflamed and begun to spread. The czar was doomed from that moment. Tatty walked back to a point where she could see both station and Winter Palace. This city was such a small stage for so much to have taken place, for so much horror.

The Moscow train was overheated and slow, the roadbed almost as bad as those of American railroads. Tatty and Raya Postnikov had been given a compartment on a wagon-lit that looked as though it might have predated World War II. The compartment was spacious enough, wood-paneled with wine-dark dusty curtains at the window sides and an actual upholstered chair.

Tatty lay on one of the worn plush seats, boots off and knees up, her head against the cold window pane. She had quickly tired of the scenery, which consisted entirely of snow and pine trees. "Don't take photographs out the window!" party member Postnikov had warned her. What nonsense. Tatty could photograph exactly the same scenes on any Christmas tree lot in America.

Raya chattered in her heavy way about Moscow, all the important people she knew, and what grand things there were to see. Tatty responded only with occasional groans, wondering if some porter might be fetched to make up one of the bunks. Though they would be in Moscow by dinner, she desperately craved a bed. An empty one.

124

"Was very bad for you to get so drunk with chairman," Raya said, lighting yet another cigarette. "He was very upset."

"He didn't seem to mind my getting drunk until I passed out."

"He was being very nice to you."

"He was putting his hand on my very nice knee."

"Why do you drink so much, Miss Chase? A woman like you?"

Raya said it not as a rebuke, but with a discernible note of concern in her voice. If she'd been able, Tatty would have smiled at her.

"That's a fine question coming from someone with a big slug of Stolichnaya in her hand."

Raya looked down at her glass. "Sure, I drink, but I don't fall onto table. Never with chairman of council of ministers and deputy general secretary of party."

"Try it. You'll like it." Tatty giggled, then groaned again.

"Be serious, Miss Chase. You drink too much."

"Normally I don't, Raya. But this has been a very bad year. Very frustrating. Very sad. Very boring."

"Not boring here, in Russia."

"No, I'll grant you that. I do worry about my drinking, Raya. I have reason to. My dear lovely mother died of alcoholism. She was only forty-nine. She began drinking the moment she heard about my father's death and never stopped, all through her career as an actress. She was drinking the day she died."

"I am sorry, Miss Chase." Raya rose. She was wearing what was in Russia an expensive gray gabardine suit, with matching vinyl handbag. "Come on with Raya now. We go to dining car and eat. It will make you feel good again."

As they left the compartment, Tatty forgetfully started to turn left, toward the rear of the train, until Raya grabbed her arm.

"Dining car is this way. That way is to private car behind us."

"Private car?" said Tatty, trying to imagine such a thing in the workers' paradise.

"*Da.* Very important Soviet official aboard."

Tatty thought nothing more of that. She followed Raya meekly on into the dining car and was staggered by the heat. The Russians there, perspiring freely as they gulped and gorged, paid it no mind, but Tatty found it devastating. She was dizzy by the time they sat down.

"Ah," said Raya. "They have *kharcho,* and *lobio. Georgi* food."

"What?"

"Specialty of Georgia, where Stalin came from. *Kharcho* is a spicy meat soup. *Lobio* is butter beans in spicy sauce. You'll like."

Tatty nodded absently. Her mind was occupied with something else, a growing unhappy realization. Very important Soviet official indeed. The swine had affixed himself to her by rail car. After they returned to the compartment, there would no doubt be a rapping at the door and some servant or aide in the corridor with an imperious summons disguised as an invitation. Or worse, she might find him waiting in her compartment.

She was hopelessly unprepared for this now. There was no way to escape the train and no way to evade him while on it. If she refused him now, he might dismiss her as not worth the trouble and ruin Ramsey's scheme completely. But if she came to him, it would be for nothing. Ramsey would have no cameras inside an unexpected private railroad car. The beast would quickly have his fingers over more than her knee and, even if she succumbed, she'd accomplish not a bit of what was wanted. She'd have to repeat this sordid scene all over again in Moscow.

She would not sleep with that man. Not for America. Not for her murdered father. Not for the butchered grand duchess. Good God, why had Ramsey given her that pistol? If she still had it now, she'd probably use it. To shoot herself.

Halfway through the spicy butter beans, a solution to her predicament presented itself, though not one of her intentional devise.

She closed her eyes, but that only made it worse.

"Raya, I . . ."

126

She put her hand to her mouth, trying to resist the rising awful urges. Not a chance. Moving in desperate lunges, she did manage to get all the way out to the car's vestibule before disgracing herself. Raya, surprisingly helpful, came to her rescue before anyone drew near.

"Well, I suppose Chairman Griuchinov won't be so interested in having me to his private railroad car after all," said Tatty.

"What are you talking about? Very important official in private car is General Badim."

8

There was no snow in Moscow, but it was colder. Meadows, wearing what looked like a sable *shapka*, greeted them just inside the station, giving Tatty a hug and a brush kiss of the cheek, then stepping back to pat her hand.

"Welcome, welcome," he said, with much gushing. "Everyone thinks you were just fabulous in Leningrad, and the Soviet government is very, very pleased. They've given you the Maly Theater here. It's quite an honor." He moved them on toward the exit to the street. "We can drop Miss Postnikova off at Intourist and then take you on a little tour. Or, if you like, we'll go directly to your hotel."

"Please," said Tatty. "Directly to the hotel."

The car he had this time was much more elegant, a Lincoln. As she entered the back seat, Raya went around to the other side and heaved herself in, not wanting to ride up front with the driver, a mere servant. Meadows, once the luggage was put in the trunk, climbed in to the rear as well and there she was, held pinnioned by the large woman and the overly cologned and hand-patting male. She wondered if this was part of his Agency cover or if he actually was a fairy. The American foreign service, after all, wasn't the British.

It was too hot in the car.

"Tonight," said Meadows, "there's a small dinner for you at the home of our deputy chief of mission. Tomorrow night, you're to be the guest of honor at a really grand dinner given by the Soviet Foreign Ministry, and then Friday night the ambassador will reciprocate with a big bash for you at the residence."

"No thank you."

"Whatever are you saying? The ambassador—"

"No. I mean tonight. I couldn't possibly go to any dinner. As Raya and the railroad porters will not so happily attest, I am ill."

"Is true," said Raya, with disapproval.

"Oh dear. The DCM will be crushed. Are you sure that after a little sleep . . . ? He's put together quite a little feast."

"If you don't stop talking about dinners and food I'm going to lunch, as we used to say at Smith, all over your pretty car. I want to be by myself tonight. In the unlikely event I should get hungry, I'll get something from room service."

Cresting a brick-covered rise, the car swept by a conglomeration of brilliantly floodlit Russian Orthodox church buildings, which Tatty remembered from her first trip as the Cathedral of Saint Basil the Blessed, remembering also that it had been ordered built by Ivan the Terrible and that they used to execute people and issue imperial ukases in front of it. No doubt Raya could and would tell her volumes more.

Now they were in Red Square, once known as Beautiful Square. It wasn't beautiful, but it was awesome, a vast, bricked space that was the heart of Moscow, the heart of Russia. On one side was the floodlit art nouveau facade of the GUM Department Store; on the other, the dark, forbidding walls and towers of the Kremlin, huge illuminated red stars atop each. Prominent before one wide section of wall was Lenin's mausoleum, floodlit, very squat and square and much smaller than she remembered.

The driver hurried on, gliding downhill. In a moment they were before the largest building Tatty had ever seen.

"We tried to get you into the National," Meadows said.

"It's first class and certainly the most charming hotel in Moscow, but, when in Moscow, one must do as one is told. This is the Rossiya, the largest hotel in the world. The Russians call it the greatest. I think you'll find it quite grand."

She was given a room this time, not a suite. It was commodious, with an expansive double bed and high beautiful windows. Unfortunately they gave no view of the nearby Kremlin but instead one of the hotel's inner court. It was of a breadth to match the hotel's, and left the uppermost part of the windows filled with the night sky, but she felt confined and restricted nevertheless. The Rossiya had many of the aspects of a prison. The *spasibo* lady in this stretch of corridor was situated right outside her door.

On her first visit those many years ago, she had stayed at the Intourist Hotel in Gorky Street. Her room had been small, but it had looked out over the street.

There was again fruit and cheese in a basket on the bureau, no vodka this time but a bottle each of Armenian wine and Armenian brandy. A small card, printed in the Russian alphabet, bore the name V. Griuchinov.

She opened the wine, and found it execrably sweet and smoky, something to be drunk only in desperation. The brandy was nothing at all like cognac, but it was strong, and not unpleasant. She drank a glass, slowly, sitting on the bed, wondering when, and if, Griuchinov might call, then set the glass on the bedtable and fell back against the pillow. She had forgotten how many days were left of this ordeal.

The telephone jangled shrilly. She hesitated, then grabbed it up. It was a man's voice, speaking gruffly and rapidly in Russian. She caught only one word, *"Bystro!"* "Hurry."

Hurry? What for? Where? She asked the man to identify himself. There was a pause, then the word *"Prostite."* "Excuse me." Then he hung up.

Ignoring the angry grumblings and rumblings of her voided stomach, she poured another brandy. When it was finished, she let herself drift to sleep watching the stars in the upper window.

This time the telephone frightened her. She sat up, letting it ring, but the rings became insistent.

"*Kto tam?*" she said. "Who is it?"

The responding voice was deep, warm, and American, with a travel-worn Eastern accent. It was the most beautiful sound, she thought, she could possibly imagine hearing.

"Are you receiving stage-door Johnnies?" Spencer said. "If so, I volunteer."

"Jack! Dear Jack. Where are you?"

"Downstairs. Though, in this hotel, that could be half a mile away."

"I'll be right down. No, I need some repairing. Can you come up? No, that won't do, will it? I'll be along as soon as I can. Is there a bar?"

"The Rossiya, I think, has three dozen bars. But to make sure we don't lose each other, let's meet outside the main entrance. The one facing Red Square."

"Which is that?"

"Ask."

Hanging up, she tore through her luggage until she came to her favorite cocktail dress, a green silk sheath with low-cut bodice. She couldn't find her green shoes, only black ones. But it didn't matter. This was Russia.

Stepping from the elevator and hurrying outside, she almost did not recognize him. Dressed in a long dark coat and black fur *shapka,* he looked startlingly Russian. Had she not let her glance linger long enough to notice his eyes and the familiar scar across his left cheek, she might have passed him by. How severe he looked. When Chesley had first brought him home, leading him by hand from her Jaguar up the front steps of the Chase house in Connecticut as she might some prize horse, Tatty had thought him not only the handsomest man in the known world but the most untroubled person she had ever encountered. He seemed to take pleasure from everything about him. He had been charming, effortlessly so, in everything he had said and done.

Now, standing in the shadows of the night, dressed in black cloth and black fur, he looked like some character

131

from Dostoyevsky's most maddened tale, a man of secret demons.

As he pulled off his hat, she threw herself at him, holding him tightly, pressing warm cheek against cold. He held her close as well, but there was a perceptible frailty to his grasp. Chesley had said something about his being ill.

She stepped back, holding both his hands as might a little girl. "Hello again, John August Spencer II."

"Hello, *sestra.*"

"No, not sister. *Podruga.* Dear friend."

"Friend."

"Friends enough to have dinner? I've had nothing, nothing I could keep down, all day."

"Yes. Yes indeed. We'll go to the Metropole. It's just the other side of Red Square. Would you like to walk? Do famous actresses walk?"

"Yes they do. Especially when they are with legendary journalists in the heart of Moscow."

"Has Chesley been telling you legends about me? I'd more likely expect nasty stories."

She put her arm in his and they began to walk, hurriedly, as though to avoid the fact of Chesley. There was a wind blowing and, without her boots, it was bitter against her legs.

"You did well in Leningrad?"

"The last performance was not as glorious as the first."

"Just like life, Tatty. And how is my ex-wife?"

"I haven't seen Chesley in weeks and weeks. The last time was at a party in Greenwich. We only talked for a few minutes. As usual, she was the most beautiful woman there."

"Rubbish. How is Christopher?"

Chesley had won full custody of their son and had not been generous with visits. It was possibly two years since Jack had seen him.

"I gather he's fine. I've not seen him since last Christmas. Chesley has him in boarding school."

"I know. He sent me a letter from there once."

"I'm sorry, Jack, that all that hasn't gone better for you."

132

He shrugged. "It's gone as I should have expected. But tell me of your Russian triumph. How is it you're dating the dirtiest old man in the Soviet Union?"

"How did you hear about that?"

"Gossip. The Soviet Union is all police and gulags, corruption and gossip. Today's gossip has you in it. Especially over at the embassy."

"To what effect?"

"That the almighty deputy party secretary has become a stage-door Johnny."

"That's all?"

"Some versions have Comrade Griuchinov becoming a successful stage-door Johnny."

"Which he certainly has not."

"Of course not."

They were in the center of the square, and the wind had risen full against them. The floodlit colors of St. Basil seemed more intense, as though whipped into their brilliance like a fire flame by the blasts of cold air. She pulled him closer, till their arms touched.

"And what did you say? Did you tell them that was nonsense? That you were my brother-in-law and ought to know?"

"Actually, I've kept that a secret, Czarina. Otherwise they'd all be perstering me to arrange dates."

"Griuchinov is a swine."

"Is he? I'm sorry to hear that. He seemed the best of the bunch, a matter of some import with the premier having heart problems again."

A military vehicle, a small truck of sorts with four headlights blazing, came over the hill and proceeded across the square, rapidly but without urgency.

"He fondled my knee."

"Goodness gracious, Tatty. Your knee."

The Metropole Hotel and its adjoining restaurant were in Marx Prospekt, a major thoroughfare leading east from the square. The dining room, like the hotel lobby, was extremely old-fashioned but quite pleasant. The china and silver were also old. Tatty's plate was cracked, and her knife a little tarnished. She looked away from it, up into

Spencer's candlelit face. His eyes were an odd light brown; the candle flame brought out the green in them, but accentuated also the shadows beneath.

"You look tired, Jack."

"Not tired, Tat. Bone dead weary. I've had too much Russia."

"How long have you been here?"

"Nearly a year. It's enough. I'm a newspaperman, *sestra*. I've covered four wars and the Iranian revolution. I've gotten drunk with the prime minister of Ireland. Now here I am at the epicenter of the greatest menace to civilization since the mongol hordes, writing feature stories about cultural exchange, and occasional political pieces based on gossip, pieces that almost always turn out to be wrong."

The waiter, wearing a near-floor-length apron in the old world style, had brought them each a small carafe of vodka set in bowls of ice. Spencer drank, then turned to look at the dance floor, a raised stage at the rear of the room with a large band playing to one side.

"You make it sound so dreary."

"Not dreary, m'dear. Bleak."

"Why did you come?"

"I was told to. My newspaper chain has been threatening to fire me for a long time, Tatty. I don't argue with them, much. My bureau chief in Washington tried to look out for me as best he could. When the Moscow slot opened up, I suppose he thought it was a good place to keep me on ice. Everyone on the Moscow beat drinks."

"Are you drinking more than before?"

He smiled, to himself.

"Probably not, Tatiana. I'm just getting older. Getting old."

Tatty was distressed, in large part for selfish reasons. Jack Spencer had been the warmest, wittiest person she had ever known. She had been counting on him to lift her out of her depression. Instead, he was dragging her down into his own.

She took his hand.

"You're so sad, Jack. Is it because you're still in love with Chesley?"

"No." He shook his head for emphasis. "No, I'm not in love with Chesley, anymore. It's a question I've pondered as much as I have death and eternity. Do you believe that? It's true. She was all my life, Tatty."

"All?"

A guilty grin came and went. "Those girls and ladies were just what they always were. They had nothing to do with my marriage."

She almost said, "But everything to do with your divorce," yet could not. He was still holding her hand. She in no way wanted to increase his unhappiness.

"I'm not in love with Chesley. That's all drained and empty, what's left is cold and hard. That's what makes me so sad, Tat. Not that I love her but that I no longer do. I cannot understand how this has happened to me. What in bloody hell could have taken my love for Chesley away?"

He had let his shoulders slump. He straightened them, leaning stiffly against the back of his chair, his eyes watching her expression. "I'm sorry," he said. "This is a desperate place, Russia. It pulls the emotions close to the skin."

She squeezed his hand. "You don't need to apologize to me. Good Lord, Jack. Think of all the times I came to cry on your shoulder. You're entitled to at least one such occasion yourself."

He squeezed her hand back. "*Sestra.*"

"No, not *sestra. Podruga.* Friend."

"*Podruga.* Not quite accurate. A term insufficient." He turned in his chair again, observing the whirling and clomping on the dance floor as though it were an elaborate entertainment intended just for them. One couple dominated the stage, a tall attractive blond girl in a shapeless long dress and what appeared to be army combat boots, and a much taller black man in a blue suit and green turtleneck sweater, doubtless an exchange student from one of the leftist African countries. They looked utterly absurd, yet danced so beautifully together that one didn't notice. With such dancing, they would have looked marvelous dressed

135

in clown suits. Tatty felt jealous. For all her running and body care, she was a clod at dancing. This lack of a basic talent had cost her not a little in her career.

Spencer was watching the girl, appraising her face and form, perhaps calculating what chance he might have if he were to make some move on her. Could he possibly be thinking that, here in the company of his exquisite sister-in-law, reunited with her after so long a time? Chesley, very bitter, had said he was such a man, but Tatty had not believed it. Did she now? She didn't know.

"Would you like to dance?" he asked, suddenly very debonair.

"Not to this wild stuff, thank you. Perhaps if they play something slow. Do you think they will?"

"It won't be Peter Duchin, but I expect they will." He paused as the waiter served their food, chicken Kiev and potatoes for her; blini, pancakes with salmon, caviar, and sour cream, for him.

"You see," she said. "Russia isn't all gulags and police, corruption and gossip. It's food and drink, song and dance, too."

"Not to speak of ICBMs and yellow rain. And missiles that shoot down civilian airline passengers."

She ate her potatoes first, making it possible for her stomach to accept the rest. Such a wanton indulgence in calories. She hadn't gone running in weeks. Much more of this and she'd begin to get plump. What was going wrong with her? She glanced up at Spencer. He was staring at her, adoringly.

"Stop that," she said, "or I'll start giggling."

"No, please. It's not a night for giggles." Yet he continued to stare. "Do you hear what they're playing, my dear? I believe they're playing our song."

"Why, so they are. What is it?"

" 'Kalinka,' or as close to it as they can come."

"It's not exactly slow."

"I don't think they'll get much slower. Everyone here seems bent on a good romp."

"Very well, then. Let's have a good romp."

They danced with some clumsiness, and too slowly for

the music, but she didn't mind. She was happy to be in his arms. She had last danced with him at a summer party, on someone's terrace, but the woman with whom he was cheating on Chesley that night had cut in. The blond Russian girl in the combat boots was looking at Tatty and Spencer intently. Tatty was pleased that she was looking. Tatty would not let her cut in. Not anyone.

As they walked back across Red Square, he put his arm around her shoulders and held her close. The wind had subsided, but it was much colder nevertheless. Somewhere off in the black she could hear a distant but sharp ringing sound, as though someone were striking a club against the pavement. It was followed by another, and then another, the interval exact.

Spencer stopped, looking up at the clock face on the nearest Kremlin tower.

"Is this cold too much for you?" She shook her head. "There's something here you should see. The face of Russia. Of Soviet Russia."

He took her hand and led her toward the Kremlin wall and the Lenin mausoleum, all the way up to the chain and posts that marked the edge of the square.

There was still a soldier standing in the entranceway, stone still, his immobile face etched in shadow and the rimming glare of reflected floodlight. He was staring—at her, past her, through her—his eyes in the darkness lifeless and unblinking, the look of the dead.

The sharp, ringing blows continued, and drew nearer. They were footsteps, the fall of heavy boots, in slow march. She and Spencer looked to their left as toward them came a group of four soldiers, moving in exaggerated slow motion. In unison their legs swung out, and as their boots came down with that shattering crack, their left arms would swing up till their hands touched their rifle stocks, then fall back as their other legs were brought forth. This slow procession brought them to the tomb at precisely a minute to the hour. They stood at attention for a moment, then two of the soldiers, moving in the same slow, exaggerated step, made their formal way to their posts, one to the side of the mausoleum and the other to

the entrance, arriving just as the two men they were reliev-
ing joined the formation. After another moment's pause,
the formation turned about face and commenced its funereal retreat. Standing in the formation, the soldier now in
the entrance looked no more than eighteen. His too was
the face of death.

"He'll stand like that for an hour, never moving," Spencer said. "There are more than two million in the Soviet
Army just like him. In Peter the Great's day, everyone
served but the gentry, and conscription was for life. Now
it's only for two years, but eighty percent of the population
serves."

"You were drafted, weren't you Jack?"

"Yes, but I wasn't a soldier like that."

She steeled herself for one last look at that young dead
face in the entranceway, then pulled Spencer away and
toward the hotel. When they reached it, he hugged her,
kissing her gently on the neck just beneath her ear. Then
he stood back, smiling in his sad, weary way.

"One of the more memorable nights of my life, Czarina.
I thank you."

"I thank you, friend. Cher friend."

"I hope I'll see you again before you leave."

"Tomorrow."

"Tomorrow?"

"And all the days. Can't you, Jack?"

"We have a sort of death watch on. It's possible the premier had a heart attack. But if he should succumb, we'll
be the last to know. They'll no doubt call us in to hand
us two-day-old copies of the Paris *Herald Tribune* with
the story. If I'm with a VIP like you, I might get a beat
on it."

"Can you be with me tomorrow?"

"What about your high-ranking Sovietski swain?"

"I've not heard from him since Leningrad. I passed out
in a restaurant with him; fell face first into a plate of Russian hors d'oeuvres."

"And you a Greenwich girl."

"He may never ask me out again."

"Tatty, when I first met you, two sloe gin fizzes was a big night. Are you all right?"

"I'm fine, Jack. Can you come after breakfast tomorrow? I have this Intourist woman who no doubt has tours of seventeen museums planned, but I can get rid of her."

"Not after breakfast. I have an interview with the oldest man in the Lithuanian Soviet Socialist Republic. After lunch. That's fine. What about lunch?"

"Lunch. Twelve?"

"Oh dear. My interview is out in some nursing home in the country. It's scheduled for eleven, but as always they'll be late. I probably won't be back in Moscow until one. Why don't I call you when I get back? No. That means you hang around your room. This is so damn difficult. I'm sure they'll have you off on all sorts of official tours anyway."

"I'll do what I want."

"I'll call you, Tat. Let's leave it at that."

He backed away, bringing two fingers to his brow in farewell. He was all somber again, a man with dark looks in dark coat and dark hat. Behind him was dark Russia, ready to swallow him up. He seemed so forlorn, hurt, and lonely. She suddenly felt very angry with Chesley.

He moved off, with yet another odd wave.

"Jack!"

"Yes?"

"It's too cold a night. You need brandy. I have some brandy in my room. Please join me in one."

He halted. His eyes sought the depths of hers. She lowered her lids, protecting her thoughts.

"French brandy?"

"No. Armenian."

He pursed his lips and nodded, approvingly.

"There is one good fact about the Soviet Union. The Bolshies can lay claim to most of Armenia. If it weren't for them, it would be in thrall to the heathen Turks, and those bastards would outlaw brandy."

"I have a wonderful view of a courtyard," she said.

"The world's largest airshaft," he said, stepping forward and taking her hand. "I will come and marvel at it with you for a while."

They entered the hotel like an imperial husband and wife. Tatty took her key from the *spasibo* lady outside her room without an instant's notice of the disapproving grimace that accompanied it. Entering the large chamber, which was basically a bedroom, Tatty slammed and bolted the door behind her, turned on the lights, clicked on the radio set in the wall, and turned the tuner to the one station of the available three that was playing balalaika music, very romantic balalaika music. She pulled off her heavy red coat, then went to the bureau. In addition to the wine and brandy, there was a fresh carafe of vodka and a sealed full bottle of Stolichnaya behind it. And another calling card. She flicked it to the floor.

"People seem to come and go in my room as they wish," she said, "and one of them has left Stolichnaya. Would you like some instead of brandy?"

He had taken off his hat and coat. He put a hand to her waist and turned her around. "Give me a moment to think about it," he said. He pulled her close and kissed her, as she had hoped, prayed, and hungered he would do all evening, as she had wanted him to for all the years he had been part of her family life. She moved her hands to his back and, clinging tightly, moved them up to his still strong shoulders. He pulled her even closer, lowering his left hand to pull up the hem of her dress and, slipping it beneath, running it up the back of her leg to her hip and the top of her panty hose, reaching to her buttocks, lifting her, reaching further until his fingers touched the moistening warmth of her vagina.

"Not *podruga*, Jack," she said, reaching for his belt, stopping to take his kiss, then frantically pulling the buckle free. "*Lyubov*. Love."

They fell onto the bed. He knelt to free her of her clothes, then tore off his own with some violence. Yet when he came to her side again, his touch was gentle, his kisses tender. He touched and kissed her everywhere. At length he knelt once more and came forward, massaging the nipples of her breasts with the tip of his wonderfully

140

enlarged penis. He placed it between her breasts and squeezed them hard. Kissing her less tenderly now, he slid down upon her and moved his hand once more to her vagina, his fingers working her, playing her, with a virtuoso's touch and skill. She tried to hold herself back, wondering why he wasn't joining her, but he had taken her too far. Her hips began to pull and push, her pelvic bone riding beneath his hand. She began to make sounds she would never have thought herself capable of making. Her legs were trembling, shifting. Her chest was heaving. She reached for his shoulders, begging, but he kept on, till her entire body was in motion, till she had lost all thought, all perception of time and place, till she was driven to an agony of pleasure. Then at once he slid between her thrashing knees, moving her legs apart with his own and then, taking hold of her buttocks, thrust himself violently inside her, again and again and again, recapturing and recharging her pleasure just as it had begun to slip away, bringing it to a new intensity, his great force relentlessly producing a final flow of joy. At that last moment he pressed himself hard against her, his strong hands gripping her bottom till she feared his fingers might break through her skin, gasping, then relenting and relaxing and unfolding and finally rolling, with a happy sigh, onto his side.

Then he continued to please her, holding her in his arms and comforting her, stroking her cheek and her back, telling her lovely things about herself. It would have been wonderful to fall leisurely, warmly to sleep amidst all this, but she had lost her weariness despite the exuberance of their lovemaking. Her mind was working. She turned onto her back and, folding her arms over her breasts, looked out the tall window at the night full of stars. She had turned on only one lamp upon entering, and its light illuminated only a corner of the large room. There was no moon, but she could not imagine a Russian night with a moon. Russian nights should be cold and starry. Moons were for the Hamptons.

"What are you thinking?" he asked.

"I'm thinking about the sky."

"It's a sky worthy of thought. The Soviets haven't yet been able to change the sky, although I suppose there's enough in their nuclear arsenal to manage that."

"Chesley always thought you such a liberal. And you carry on about the Communists as though you were Ronald Reagan."

"I'm still a liberal. Communists are the most conservative people I know."

For some reason, the heavy scent of her own perfume came to her in a sudden rush, the chemistry of the heating and cooling of her body, she supposed. His would restore her warmth, but she resisted the urge to move nearer.

"I'm also sorting out reasons," she said.

"Reasons?"

"Reasons for your having done this. I can't narrow them down. I don't know if it was because you go to bed with women compulsively, or whether you had thought of seducing me all those years when you couldn't, or whether I'm a surrogate for Chesley, or whether this is a blow struck against Chesley, or whether you just haven't had a woman for a long while, or what."

"I can make this problem easier for you. I wanted to do this for all of those reasons. Every one of them. Plus one more."

"Yes?"

"*Lyubov.*"

"*Lyubov.* Indeed."

"Chesley demanded that she be the only woman in my life, but she made that impossible. To have been that faithful to Chesley would have meant being her possession entirely. Being her possession and nothing else. I could not imagine such a life. Not for me. Do you understand?"

"Well, in part."

"I could imagine a life in which there was no one else but you. No other woman. I've thought I could be happy having you and only you. I've thought about that many times. I thought that the first time I saw you on the stage. Do you understand that?"

"No."

"Do you believe me?"

He was leaning on an elbow, looking down at her. She kept her eyes on the window.

"No."

"Why not?"

"Because that was not a conclusion you could have come to without having had me."

"You'll see."

"Perhaps," she said.

"Now you tell me something. Why did you do this?"

"I can't tell you. That's something I have to sort out tomorrow."

They lay there close but not touching, in silence. If this were still an era in which people smoked, she supposed that in this interlude they would smoke. Finally, quietly, she began to sing.

> *"All night long, the glasses tinkle,*
> *While outside, the raindrops sprinkle,*
> *Do you think another drink'll*
> *Do us any harm?"*

"Chesley's song," he said. "I've not heard that in years."

"It's a lovely little song."

"She was afraid it encouraged me."

"I'm sure it did. It encourages me. Would you like the Armenian brandy or some vodka?"

"The brandy. To better remember you by. I drink vodka every day."

"Don't you want to remember me every day?"

"No. I want to save that for very special times."

She put on her coat, then went to the bureau and poured drinks. There was something odd about the room that made her hesitate before bringing his glass to him. She looked about it, but could see nothing amiss. Then she realized it was something she could only hear amiss. The volume of the radio had decreased dramatically.

She handed him the brandy. "Do you suppose that with all our gymnastics we somehow rattled the volume down? I can barely hear the radio."

He laughed, then put a finger to his lips.

"Did I tell you what I heard about the Soviet premier today?" he said, his voice falling to a whisper.

The radio turned off completely.

He began to laugh. Realizing what was happening, so did she. Their laughter became convulsive, hysterical. She laughed so that she spilled brandy on her bare knee, and kept on laughing. A minute or so later, the radio returned to full volume, very loud indeed, as though it were angry.

"You will find, dear Tatty, that conversation in the Soviet Union is an outdoor sport."

He drank. His bare shoulders were trembling. She was reminded of something that took away her happy moment. She sat down in a chair by the window before speaking to him, then realized that was the wrong place to be. She moved to the bed and sat down beside him, taking his hand.

"Chesley said you were seriously ill. You haven't seemed at all ill, but now you do."

He sighed, then gulped down most of his drink, ending with a cough.

"I suppose I must tell you then. Actually, it has nothing to do with how I feel now. I'm just cold, and run down. I suppose I've been drinking too much. I'm probably not really up to the Russian winter."

"Tell me what?"

"I have a bomb in my head."

"What?"

The radio volume lessened again.

"An aneurysm. A ballooning artery in the brain."

She gripped his hand quite tightly. Her own had suddenly gone cold.

"Jack. Dear Jack."

"No pity, please. We're all going to be pulled down by something. This could go off five minutes from now, or in twenty years, or it could never go off. It's just there."

"Does it, is it, hurting you? Is there anything that can be done?"

"The operative phrase is 'inoperable.' But it's no great

bother. Occasionally the vessel inflates a little and I get some spectacular headaches, but nothing strong drink can't cure."

"There's no medicine?"

"They gave me a prescription. I tried it for a while, but it didn't seem to make much difference. The headaches still came. I stopped after a few months. I'm still alive."

"Did Chesley . . . ? Was this why . . . ?"

"No, no. I discovered it months after she left me. It was just before I went to Iceland, if you recall my adventures there. Chesley is the noblest of women, Tatty. There's nothing that would fulfill her more than devoting hours to my sickbed."

She kissed his hand, then released it. "You need sleep, Jack. And so do I. It's no problem for me if you want to stay here."

"Well, it could be." He rose, went to the bureau, and poured himself another brandy. Then he dressed. When he was done, he picked up his drink. "God, Chesley—"

"Tatty."

"Tatty. God yes. I am tired. I'm twitterpated, Czarina. This has all rendered me bananas. I've got a lot of sorting out to do myself."

"When will I see you?"

"I'll pick you up at six o'clock. We can have cocktails and then I'll drop you at the theater."

"There'll be a rehearsal tomorrow. I'm to be there at six-thirty."

"Then I'll pick you up at five."

"Kiss me."

He did so very gently, without parting his lips, much as he did the first time he had kissed her, when she was still a teen-ager and he the courtly step-brother-in-law.

"I love you," he said.

"I love you, tonight. I think. I will see you tomorrow and I will look very much forward to it."

He said no more. When the door closed behind him, she went to the chair by the window to finish her brandy.

Mila. "Dear." That was the word she had wanted instead of *podruga.* But she had chosen *lyubov,* and now she was left with *lyubov.* She drank and looked to the Russian night sky, and saw that there was a moon after all. Wrapped in her coat, she fell asleep in her chair.

9

In the morning, having sometime in the night put herself to bed, Tatty awoke all rosy and flush, a woman in love. She sang to herself in the bath, closing her eyes as she savored the more physical memories of the past evening, leaving the tub with strong erotic urgings and needs she could not, alas, fulfill. She had not felt this way in years; she could not remember which man it was who had last made her feel this way. Perhaps none.

Later on, she was positively giddy at the Kremlin, going "oooh" and "ah" and laughing merrily even as Raya dragged her through the great armory and its exhibits of horrid medieval helmets worn by the likes of the father of Alexander Nevsky and Prince Ivan, son of Ivan the Terrible and murder victim of Ivan the Terrible. Finally, outside a golden-domed cathedral where the Terrible once, in his unique fashion, worshiped, Raya asked if she was drunk.

"A little," she said. "But I've been that every day. I'm just in good spirits. It's your wonderful country, so bright and gay. Who could help feeling so marvelous?"

Raya merely grunted.

After lunch, however, as fatigue returned and the repetitive boredom of all the touring accumulated, Tatty's rapture began to diminish, making room for some depressing thoughts—all about Jack Spencer. She had had them the night before, in the times when there had been no love-making, and they kept leading to the same unwanted conclusion: John August Spencer was a weak man. He drank out of weakness. He philandered out of weakness. He let Chesley leave him out of weakness, when a stronger man, a Captain David Paget, for example, might have dragged her screaming back to their marriage. Jack was a brave man. He flew sailplanes and strange little motorized aircraft called ultralights. She had seen him walk into a riding ring to quiet a hysterical horse with nothing more than a short crop. She had heard from others vivid accounts of his conduct in all his precious wars. But even in this bravery there was weakness. It and the wars it required were an escape constantly resorted to. When bullets are flying, one need only endure.

She chided herself. The man had an aneurysm. He had lost the most desirable woman he probably had ever known. He'd been exiled to Russia. There were reasons for his depression, for his dark looks and mournful gazes.

She and Raya were walking along the Kremlin Embankment adjoining the Moskva River.

"I take you to Alexander Gardens," Raya said. "Then you have seen Kremlin."

"I just remembered. Chairman Griuchinov promised to take me on a special tour of the Kremlin, and now I've gone and done it myself."

"So go again. Is worth seeing twice."

"He hasn't called."

"Maybe you offended him, becoming so drunk like that."

"He left gifts in my hotel room. Brandy, wine, and vodka."

Raya shrugged. "Why is this American newspaperman bothering you?"

"He isn't bothering me."

"He is with you all last night."

"It wasn't all last night and it didn't bother me."

"You say you know him for long time before. You know him well?"

"He's a good friend."

"Newspapermen are always trouble. Especially American."

"I don't feel troubled."

"After Alexander Gardens, I take you back to hotel. I think you need sleep."

She tried to sleep, as though to placate Raya, but it was no use. Love, depression, confusion, and her professional anticipation of tonight's Moscow debut kept her even from dozing. She worked on her scripts a while, then went for a walk around the hotel, which seemed greater in circumference than even the Kremlin. She continued walking, gripped by hard thoughts. As she completed her third circumnavigation, she saw Jack Spencer walking up from what Raya had said was a subway stop, walking with a serious limp.

There was a purple bruise above his right eye, and a purple and yellow one upon his swollen left cheek.

"Jack! My God! What happened?"

"No system is perfect. Even in the workers' paradise they have muggers. The son of a bitch jumped me as I was going into my building. Hit me twice with some sort of billy right across the face and had me down in a second. I kicked him in the balls before he could get my wallet. Unfortunately, that gave him an idea and he did the same thing to me, with far greater effect, I fear. I had an interesting morning with the good Sovietski doctor."

Jack had that ballooning artery. She reached and touched his face.

"I'm all right, Tat. I won't exactly be running the high hurdles today, but we'll survive. Always do."

He always did. Bravery was not his only game; there was also stoicism, almost to the point of masochism. She had seen him ride horseback—and take jumps—with a broken foot. Cold, heat, burns, great bloody cuts, nothing seemed to bother him. He took his pain from other things.

She took his hand, deciding to say nothing more about his injury, or anything else that had happened the previous night, unless he brought it up. He didn't, not until after a long walk around a wide curve of the river, a look through two small museums, and several cups of coffee in a warm, many-windowed restaurant. Finally, as she had expected, he ordered vodka for them both. She carefully sipped hers; he gulped down a glass and then refilled it from the carafe.

"Better," he said. "Everything." There was an odd look to his face, a boyish grin beneath sad old eyes. For all he had done to himself, he was still the handsomest man she had ever known, even with the two awful bruises. "Well," he continued. "What are we now?"

"Still you and I, but more, more to each other. This morning I was wildly in love with you."

"And this afternoon?"

"This afternoon I'm sad and terribly confused, but no less sure that I'll be wildly in love with you again."

"Not," he said, with a groan, "quite just yet."

She smiled, as demurely as possible. "Tonight I have to go to a Soviet dinner; tomorrow to one at our embassy. I know of nothing after that, yet."

"What about afternoons? Tomorrow afternoon?"

"I don't know. I have this very bossy Intourist nanny, who I don't think approves very much of you. She could complicate things. I suppose she could get me in trouble, or may have already. It was stupid of me, really, but I had this little pistol."

He put his hand on hers firmly, finished his drink, and rose. "I think we should resume our stroll. It will improve the conversation."

They didn't speak again until they were far down the street. "All right. What pistol?"

"I had it in my suitcase. I knew of course that they searched everything, but they didn't bother with it, not for several days. Then suddenly it was gone, taken from my bag. Is firearm possession a serious crime?"

"All crimes are serious in a Soviet Socialist Republic, but that one can get you the full fifteen years in a gulag. If they haven't bothered you about it, you may get a pass. They may even hand it to you in a sealed box at the airport when they return your passport. What in hell prompted you to bring a gun into this country? I can't imagine how you pulled it off."

"I didn't. It was given to me when I arrived, by the embassy, for self-protection. I had a bad experience in France last year. A man tried to rape me. The State Department knew about that." She let her revelations end there.

"So they gave you a gun. When those people aren't being fools, they're being complete idiots. Was it someone in their security section? The CIA people here wouldn't be that stupid."

"It was someone from the cultural section."

"Incredible. Well, be wary of your Russian nanny. Be wary of all the Russians."

"What about my Russian self?"

"It should be wary of my self, at least when I'm ready to run the high hurdles again."

The street opened onto a large square. She recognized one large building on it, embellished with grand colonnades and statues of horses, as was the Bolshoi.

"Your theater is there," he said, pointing to a smaller structure just to the right, the roofline of the great GUM department store visible above it. "It used to be called the Little Imperial Theater, back in the good old days."

"Is this called Bolshoi Square?"

"Oh no. It's Sverdlov Square."

"Sverdlov?"

"It's named after Jakov Sverdlov, Lord High Executioner and Great Comrade Hero of the Revolution. They have a city named for him also—"

"I know. In the Urals. Jack, I'd better go into the theater now. Do I have your number? I'll call you as soon as I can get free again."

He started to kiss her hand, but she pulled his to her lips instead.

"Your number."

He dug in his wallet for a card. "Here are all three. I'll stay close to one of them as long as you're here." Placing it in her hand, he kissed her softly on the lips, then turned to limp away. For a nervous moment, she wished he

151

wasn't leaving her, but she collected herself. The worst would soon be over. Only a few more Russian days.

The rehearsal went well, and the performance much better than that. The chamber orchestra was of a higher quality than the one in Leningrad and the printed translations of Tatty's readings had been replaced by a live actress who sat off to the side and repeated each of Tatty's lines in Russian. It was the same sad-faced blond woman who had come up to her at the Friendship and Cultural Ties Union reception in Leningrad. Whether for her or for Tatty, the theater was full, including all the VIP seats—though there was nothing to be seen of the Cheshire-cat face of Valeri Jakovich Griuchinov.

Her escort for the Foreign Ministry gala was the American ambassador himself, whom she had taken for a western-looking Russian when she had noticed him in the audience. His name was Crabtree and he was an extremely wealthy man, a benefactor who had donated an entire theater to a college in upstate New York where Tatty had once given readings much like these. The chairman of one of New York's largest banks, he was a busy, impatient man who sat leaning toward the glass partition of his limousine and drummed his fingers constantly on the leather seat.

"Damn big show tonight," he said. "Damn big show."

"Do you mean my readings, ambassador?"

He smiled politely, but shook his head with some irritation. He seemed at once displeased by the nuisance of her visit yet flattered to have an attractive woman in his company. He was a self-made man at or near sixty. She guessed his wife would be forty or less, elegant and beautiful, and not the first woman he had married.

"No. Sorry. I mean this dinner. Dobrynin, the foreign minister, is going to be host. Deputy Premier Popov is going to be there. Marshal Kuznetzov, the defense minister. Party Secretary Furtseva. Almost everyone except the premier and General Badim."

"Of the KGB."

"He is the KGB, that son of a bitch. Very cool character. Seldom comes to social events, though he has the best table manners of all of them."

"What has occasioned tonight's damn big show? Certainly not little me."

"You're a very charming lady, Miss Chase. And very talented. But I think they're seizing upon the occasion to break some new ice. We've had practically no social contact with them for over six months. In fact, four months ago the bastards started another fire in the embassy. Time to have the firemen change the microphones again, right? No, they're up to something new. Maybe something big. The premier's had another heart attack, you know. It could be . . ." He clamped shut his mouth, then sat back and gave a sheepish grin. "I talk too much. Excuse me."

"You said 'everyone,' Mr. Ambassador. Would that include Mr. Griuchinov, the chairman of the council of ministers? He was very nice to me in Leningrad."

"Yeah. I heard." A quick embarrassed smile. "Sure. He ought to be at something like this."

He was not. Dobrynin, whom Tatty remembered from innumerable newspaper photographs taken during his many years as ambassador to the United States, sat at the head of the table and put Tatty immediately to his right. Deputy Premier Popov, an amiable if slightly doddering old fellow, sat at the table's other end. Marshal Kuznetzov, sitting obliquely opposite her, stuck in Tatty's mind because of his great height. He was easily six and a half feet tall in an assemblage where most of the men were no more than five foot eight. He moved very clumsily; his gestures were awkward and nervous, and he kept pulling at his military collar. Tatty wondered how Ramsey could see him as such a great hope for the West. The only one there she found at all attractive and likeable was the venerable Dobrynin. Perhaps he had become irretrievably Americanized. He talked to her charmingly throughout the dinner. She hoped Ramsey's short list of possible heirs to the Bolshevik throne was longer than he had thought.

When she returned to her room at the Rossiya, there were fresh bottles of Armenian brandy and vodka waiting on the bureau, and another of Griuchinov's cards.

The next day, in a very wet snow, Raya drove her in a large purple car out to the Economic Achievement Exhibition in the suburbs. All morning she was marched by displays of consumer goods manifesting the Soviet Union's economic might, though most of the goods came from Eastern European satellites, especially the decent-looking furniture. After a bad lunch, Tatty was made to stand in the middle of a dizzying circular Cinerama that had great yellow Sovietski trucks and tractors bearing down on her from all directions. At the space achievement pavilion, Tatty decided she had had enough.

"How many warheads?" she said, looking up at a badly maintained old space rocket.

"Is Americans who began arms race," Raya said.

"Is not Americans who kill people with yellow rain. Or shoot down civilian jetliners."

"Is Americans who are only people ever to kill human beings with atom bombs."

"We must go back, Raya. Once again, I'm exhausted."

There was no message from Jack Spencer, nothing from Griuchinov. She slept, and was taken to the theater by the American ambassador's chauffeur. His dinner party afterward was the most impressive of her tour, of any of her tours, yet Dobrynin was the only Soviet luminary present, the places of the previous night's luminaries taken by cultural and trade officials. Most of the Americans there, aside from the ambassador, were relatively low-ranking as well, complete to Meadows leering at her from the far end of the table. It quickly became clear that the true purpose of this event was a private conversation between Dobrynin and the ambassador at some discreet opportunity during the evening. When it came, shortly after the serving of brandy and liqueurs, Tatty excused herself and summoned the chauffeur. As the guest of honor, it was de rigueur for her to leave before anyone else anyway.

Meadows escorted her home, chattering away in the embassy car about all the gossip he had picked up at the dinner. Approaching the Rossiya, he had the driver stop some distance from the entrance. As they got out, he said seriously, "Ramsey was not pleased with your performance in Leningrad."

"Ramsey? Someone in the USIA?"

"Stop being a twit. The drunk scene in the restaurant did us no good. Ramsey wanted pictures of you whispering intimately into Griuchinov's ear, not snoring in your plate."

"I'm sorry. I was very nervous. I drank too much vodka."

"We noticed. You're supposed to be portraying a clever spy, my dear, not a lush."

"I'm sorry."

They were almost to the entrance. Meadows stopped, turning to look into her face. They were standing very close, and he was not much taller than she.

"This has to be very, very convincing," he said. "We're not dealing with morons."

"I'm doing my best."

"It isn't very good. We were counting on his inviting you back to the little pied à terre he keeps in Leningrad. You ruined everything."

"This isn't exactly easy for me."

"There's still a chance he might ask you to his flat here in Moscow. We're going to count on that."

"He hasn't even called."

"Encourage him. If he takes you anywhere, suggest going to his place."

"Like a brazen hussy."

"You are not an unsubtle woman."

"He hasn't called. He hasn't come to the theater."

"There's still time."

"Unfortunately."

"If you didn't want to go through with this, my dear, what are you doing here?"

"You're right. I think I'll go back to New York."

"Oh no. Not now. You're going to do what's required of you. This isn't a trivial matter. You know what's at stake here."

"I might just get on a plane and go home."

His long, steady disquieting look made her turn away. "This is Russia," he said.

"The man at the door is watching," she said.

"He's always watching."

"They took away that pistol you gave me."

"I can get you another."

"No. I want nothing more to do with guns."

"We have many people here. They're looking out for you. We promise you, there'll be no surprises. Just do what you're supposed to, what you agreed to. Ramsey thinks very highly of you. Don't disappoint him."

She looked at the headlights moving along the roadway on the opposite bank of the river. "I'm cold," she said.

Meadows put his arm around her waist and they continued toward the doors. He began chattering again, about the new ballet at the Bolshoi. At the entrance, he kissed her cheek, whispering in her ear.

"Remember your father."

Again there were no messages. In her room, the opened brandy bottle had been replaced by a full one, but the untouched vodka was still there, joined by a second carafe. There was again a card. She had kept them all. If this went on long enough, she'd be able to hand them out as party favors on some mad Hamptons evening.

And how long might this go on? He should have been at the Soviet party; he could have been at the Americans'. He ought to have been at the theater. She damn well ought to be in his apartment.

She took off her clothes, then put on her robe, poured vodka, and went to the chair by the window, turning it completely around so that she would not see the bed she had so recently shared with Spencer, that she so badly wanted to share again now. *Lyubov.* Love. "Love alters not with his brief hours and weeks, but bears it out even to the edge of doom." Glorious Shakespeare. No one had ever let her play Shakespeare, except in college. She raised her cold glass. She wanted to drink to the Russian moon again, but there was none. There were not even stars. It had begun to snow.

After the strangest breakfast of her stay, breaded boiled

eggs called *tkhum-dulma,* she and Raya went to the Museum of the Revolution in Gorky Street, a former noblemen's club that had been crammed full of memorabilia from the Bolshevik rising; precious little of the general revolution that had brought the Kerensky moderates briefly to power and made Bolshevism possible. There were endless dioramas and paintings of the Russian civil war, doubtless many of Tatty's relatives depicted in the slaughter.

They came to a horse-drawn cart bearing an antique machine gun. "Look," said Raya. "Machine gun cart of Red First Cavalry Army."

Tatty had used up her illness excuse, her fatigue excuse, her "I-have-to-go-over-my-readings" excuse. She went to the cart, pounded her gloved fist against the wheel, and shouted, "Look! I'm damned tired of your revolution!"

Raya was a restrained volcano, topped with ice.

"Miss Chase, you are stupid woman. Come now. We go to Marx and Engels Museum."

"No! No more. I'm going back to the hotel."

If only she could go back to the United States. If only she could take Jack Spencer with her.

Once again, there were no messages. She had lunch alone at the Rossiya's twenty-first-floor restaurant. Staring out the window at the Stalinesque grotesqueries that were Moscow's skyline, she ate her pilaf, as most of the men in the room stared at her unabashedly.

Feeling lonely, she returned to her room. She drank, read, slept, read, slept, drank, and paced her room. The Russian sky darkened toward night. Finally the phone rang.

"I have a health bulletin. I no longer hobble."

"Jack?"

"I still don't walk very rapidly, but I don't cry out vulgarly."

"You're feeling better?"

"I'm feeling more than better. I'm feeling lustful. It seems like centuries since, since . . ."

"I cannot tonight, Jack."

"No?"

157

"Jack, this tour. There are some things that must come first."

"That's why I'm calling."

"Jack, please."

"I understand."

"No you don't. We shall have lunch tomorrow, come what may. And I mean that. I have sworn off revolutionary points of interest."

"Too bad. I have one in mind. Lefortovo. It's somewhat distant. Leave at noon. You'll be there by twelve-forty-five. Tell your taxi driver you want the restaurant, not the prison."

"Lefortovo. *Lyubov.*"

"*Lyubov.*"

She hung up the receiver reluctantly. Tomorrow at noon, she could be having lunch with Griuchinov.

He didn't call. Raya picked her up at the appointed hour and drove her to the theater in the purple car. A third or more of the auditorium seats were empty. As in Leningrad, her audiences seemed to dwindle with each performance. This night, it did not include Griuchinov. Raya spoke only perfunctorily on the short drive back, and once again there were no messages. The evening's alcoholic gift this time was not brandy or vodka but Johnnie Walker Black Label. She glanced at his card on the bureau; it looked quite the same. What did this move mean in his silly game? Was something so special as the West's best Scotch intended as a good-bye gift? Was he pulling out of this fruitless pursuit?

She lay on her bed nearly an hour before accepting reality and ordering a lone dinner for herself from room service. It was another hour before it came. She ate in silence. When she had shoved the service cart back out into the hall, irritating the *spasibo* lady, she changed into her nightgown, turned the room radio to the least depressing of the three channels, and then went to work on the good chairman's Scotch.

With all the lights on in the room, her trim bare feet propped up on a table, she set her mind to how she might yet improve her performance before the tour ended, how she would handle Griuchinov if the final invitation ever materialized. She had made her decision. She could bring herself to have sex with him, to do whatever such an old man might require for his pleasure.

Ramsey was right. What was needed was the stuff of an airtight divorce case. Flagrante delicto, captured by clever Ramsey's tapes and cameras. Then they would have to get rid of him. Then she would truly have administered the coup de grace, her body for her father's blood, for so much blood.

She imagined Griuchinov in some ragged, padded labor camp uniform, trudging a daily path to death in a snowy, Arctic gulag east of the Urals. She saw him kneeling on the cold stone floor of a Moscow prison, as a bullet was fired into his brain for treason. Or would they do something worse? Was it possible that in some fashion her own father's death might be approximated?

No it was not. They would do nothing to Comrade Chairman Griuchinov. Because he would never call her. With her foolish, drunken antics in Leningrad, she had thoroughly frightened him away. The continuing gifts of liquor were meant to insult her. Each one of them said to her, "You are a disgusting little decadent lush."

She drank, then set down her glass to squeeze tears away from her eyes with the heels of her hands. She was a failure, a loser. This Russian journey had affirmed that in every way. Nothing so well represented the pathetic decline of her theatrical career as the dwindling attendance at her readings. Nothing so well defined her general ineptitude at life than her inability to lure one demonstrably lascivious old man to her convenient bed. An obnoxious actor she had once worked with had said her only talent was being pretty. He was probably right.

How had she come to such misery? Had she kept to the course set for her by the kindly Mr. Chase—logically following Miss Porter's and Smith and her marriage to the pleasant young stockbroker, to her own house in Greenwich, the Junior League, children, and work in Republican politics—she might now be quite well content. Surely those things were all that poor Gwen had asked from life.

159

But Gwen was not sister to Chesley Anne Hammond Chase. With Chesley her most proximate example of the fully lived life, Tatty could never be content.

And now she had Chesley's most prized possession, the man Chesley had taken to the altar when no other woman could, the man who had driven Chesley to extraordinary passions just by refusing to be completely possessed by her. He belonged to Tatty now, as much as he had ever belonged to Chesley, as much as he would ever belong to any woman again. Tatty had a sure instinct for that. She was as certain of Jack Spencer's feelings for her as she had been of Dexter Johns's or so many others before him.

Yet the value of Jack's love seemed diminished by his giving it to her. She still cared for him, dearly, for all the things he still was as well as for what he had been. But he was much the loser now, a burned-out newsman whose best future meant simply keeping his job, an aging man who already had an ailment that could kill him at any time, a man discarded by Chesley. That he would turn now to her made him seem all the more the loser.

If she called him now he would come to her room or she to his apartment and they would lose themselves in vodka and frantic sex, two forlorn people clinging to each other in the middle of this huge, cold, oppressive country.

No. Lunch tomorrow would have to do. Their relationship ought to be after Russia, more than Russia. She really ought to bloody well finish her goddamn job here before doing anything else.

She would have one last Scotch before retiring, she thought. She had three. Her last thought was of a reproachful, disdainful, unforgiving Ramsey Saylor, greeting her upon her return with a cold, murderous stare.

Raya was angry that Tatty declined breakfast, angrier that Tatty declined a tour of the Battle of Borodino Museum, and confused when Tatty asked her to drive her out to the Lefortovo Restaurant—for lunch with a friend. Tatty dressed with great care, choosing again her black suit and red silk blouse, almost defiantly adding the antique jeweled pin. On the way out, she glanced again at

160

Griuchinov's card, stopping to put it in the drawer with the others. As she had not noticed the night before, there was writing on the back, in Russian, and a telephone number. He was asking her to call. The message, as best she could translate it, said he hoped she was feeling better and that, if she was, she was to call. Please to call.

She was running late. She started for the door, hesitated, then hurried to the phone, dialing quickly.

Jack was certainly correct. Without Raya to tell her, it was difficult to determine which was prison and which was restaurant. Raya was sullen, having been told this was a private luncheon to which she was not invited and then being dismissed for the day.

"By yourself, you may get in big trouble," she said, and then sped away, no doubt no further than just around the corner.

Jack was at a side table, his back to the wall, looking strikingly civilian amidst so many military officers; looking haggard, too. He took her hand, his smile suddenly that of a small, happy boy.

"Czarina."

"Why have you chosen this dreadful barracks as a place to eat?"

"The set lunch is only one ruble, making it popular for Soviet army types. I'm working, you see. Vodka?"

"Yes. Working how? Drinking vodka?"

"It clears the brain. We have a big story today." He handed her a carbon flimsy.

BY JOHN A. SPENCER
   MID-STATES NEWS SERVICE
   MOSCOW—THE SOVIET GOVERNMENT TODAY AN-
NOUNCED SWEEPING NEW PENALTIES FOR PROFITEER-
ING AND OTHER ECONOMIC CRIMES IN WHAT IS VIEWED
AS AN UNPRECEDENTED KREMLIN CRACKDOWN ON IN-
TERNAL CORRUPTION.

"With the premier in intensive care, as this morning's

rumor has it," Jack said, "Badim is finally making a move, a hell of a move."

"You mean General Badim, who runs the KGB?"

"He's a purist. As we might judge by his art collection alone, he believes in the Soviet good life, but as a reward of rank and service to the CPSU, service such as gassing Afghans and bullying dissidents. He refuses to tolerate it as the end product of skimming, winky dink, and collectivist wheelie-dealie. The penalties he seems to have pushed through include a minimum of three years' forced labor for taking a bribe, the smallest bribe. Every bureaucrat in Moscow could be in danger of a gulag. Your friend Griuchinov ought to be a little nervous, not to speak of Popov, Sukhanov, and Yevgeni the Great."

"Who?"

"The oversized Marshal Kuznetzov. You dined with him, remember? Badim has put the fear of Lenin into the entire ruling circle. The premier may not let him get away with it, but right now the premier is on a respirator."

"He is?"

"Or so I've heard."

"What has all that to do with this ghastly restaurant?"

The dining room was now filled with gray and brown-green uniforms, most with bright red trim. Some of the officers were watching them, too boldly, but most in the room were talking excitedly among themselves. Thick cigarette smoke hung low, much like clouds over the sea on a rainy day.

"My story thus far is based on a terse handout from the Foreign Ministry and all sorts of rumor and gossip. None of us has any real sources here, you know. The State Department never tells us what it knows, which is well, because it's usually nothing. You can't even get the embassy CIA types to exchange information. We all have people among the dissidents, but those underground groups are so infiltrated by the KGB and GRU that the stuff they give us might as well be in Pravda. So we turn to other sources. This is one of mine."

"One-ruble lunches?"

"One-ruble lunches here at Lefortovo. I look for sudden

162

changes, anything different. Rapid comings and goings. Military traffic. Arrests. Excitement." He gestured at the Russians in the room. "These fellows now are carrying on as though the Chinese had just attacked on a thousand-mile front. It's clear the army had nothing to do with this, had no idea it was coming. I've overheard some of these fellows calling it a great insult to Kuznetzov. He must be very angry."

"Can we go now?"

"Oh no. First the delightful one-ruble lunch. Today it's not bad. *Kvas.* Borshch. *Pirog.* You know that? It's a pie made of cabbage, eggs, and mushrooms. *Halva* for dessert. And vodka. Vodka costs another two rubles."

"These soldiers make me nervous."

"That's their job. Is Russia getting to you? I would have thought you'd be in heaven."

"Heaven and hell, all in the same place."

"I'll find a better place for dinner."

"Jack, I can't. I have to meet with some Russians."

His look turned to that of a small, hurt child, and then a very clever one. "The very charming Comrade Griuchinov."

She let her expression turn cold.

"What would all your czars and nobles say, Tatty?"

"Please, Jack. Let it drop."

A waiter brought the borshch. Jack took a spoonful, and grimaced. "Well then," he said. "When next, for you and me?"

"I don't know. I'll have to call you."

"Is there a you and me?"

"Yes. Of course. Obviously. That has nothing to do with it." She tried the borshch, pushed it aside, then pulled it back and began eating.

Looking up, she touched his hand. "Jack. This isn't a lark for me, you know. This isn't some Caribbean cruise. This is business for me, and it's not over."

"Perhaps there's just been too much vodka." He drank some, a lot.

"Oh, shut up."

They did not say another word throughout lunch. The

moment she set down her fork for the last time, he rose. She followed him to the foyer, where he paid a waiter or manager a ruble to telephone for a cab. Crossing the street to stand and wait on the opposite curb, they were almost run down by a convoy of military vehicles, including a long green staff car, that came careening around the corner. Jack pulled her tight against him and out of the way, then released her, still not speaking.

They waited for so long that Tatty was almost at the point of marching around the corner where she was sure Raya was lurking in her purple car, but with everything else, she was in no mood to see what might result from mixing Raya and Jack together. Matters were combustible enough.

The cab that finally came was a large Volga. Their bodies did not touch. They did not speak. The taxi followed much the same route Raya had followed outbound, but when they neared what looked to Tatty to be Karl Marx Prospekt, Spencer leaned over and said something to the driver in Russian. He immediately turned left, and then pulled up at the curb.

"Dzerzhinsky Square," said Jack, helping her out. "No one should leave Russia without seeing it. Many who see it never see anything else again."

As the cab pulled away, she saw that the square was actually a circle. Opposite was a very large, grim, old-fashioned office building with narrow windows, and a more modern annex that looked even grimmer. In the center of the circle was a statue of a man in early twentieth-century dress.

"Felix Dzerzhinsky," Jack said. "Father of Soviet terrorism, mastermind of Lenin's beloved Cheka, and all-around great guy. Also Polish. The big building over there is where General Badim does his thing. It used to be an insurance company in the czar's time. The Bolsheviks made certain modifications." He urged her on, and they began walking around the circle, he with some obvious lingering pain, she with much reluctance.

"Is that where Lubyanka Prison is?"

"The most terrifying basement in the world."

There was a fair amount of traffic around the square, but few pedestrians. Tatty felt as though there were dozens of pairs of eyes upon them, staring coldly from those narrow windows.

"Do you think the premier is going to die?" she asked.

"Not with the certainty everyone had about Brezhnev, but it's a good possibility. This is heart attack two."

"What would happen if he does?"

"The *New York Times* lads don't agree with me, but I think it would quickly narrow down to a knock-down drag-out between Griuchinov and Marshal Kuznetzov, with the worst man winning."

"Griuchinov."

"No, Kuznetzov."

They crossed a street, continuing around the circle. Tatty's eyes were tearing from the cold wind.

"What about old Popov?"

"Too old. The premier made him his deputy just to keep his rivals out of striking distance."

"And General Badim?"

"The sentimental favorite in some Western circles, but very doubtful. It's too soon after Andropov's ascension. The others in the Politburo don't want to see the KGB established as the only avenue to the CPSU chairmanship. And there's a strangely Western feeling that a nation of spies should be run by someone who is not a spy."

"Why do you say Kuznetzov is worse than Griuchinov?"

"Because, for all his use of slave labor on his irrigation projects, Griuchinov is what used to be called a 'good Communist,' like Dobrynin. The jolly giant is a murderous butcher."

"Kuznetzov is a butcher?"

"The butcher of Kabul, among many other places. When he was head of the GRU, he was in charge of the butchery in Angola, North Yemen, Somalia, and Ethiopia. He has some American blood on his hands as well."

"What do you mean?"

"In the sixties, he was chief of Soviet military intelligence in Southeast Asia. A lot of our fliers went to their unmarked graves in little pieces because of that son of a bitch, especially in the early days."

"Of the Vietnam War?"

"Vietnam, Laos, Cambodia, Thailand. He's worked with all the red guerrillas there."

"You call Griuchinov a 'good Communist.' Wasn't he in Southeast Asia, too? Working with guerrillas?"

"He may have been there. They don't let me leaf through their personnel files. But as far as I know, his background is strictly farmboy. I doubt if he's ever picked up anything more lethal than a pitchfork."

"You're sure?"

"I'm sure of nothing about this place. But that's the best we news types have on him. If the CIA has something better, they're not telling."

"Are you saying we should want Griuchinov to win? That that would be best for the world?"

"Tatty. Comrade Griuchinov may well be a fiend who would sell all of the women of Europe into white slavery, as you may have occasion to discover. But Kuznetzov is the only one of these bastards who I feel would have no compunction about ordering a preemptive nuclear strike if he thought it necessary."

She bit down hard on her lip. He'd been holding her hand, but now she pulled it away.

"I know too little about politics," she said.

"Be grateful."

They were standing now just outside the building of narrow windows. She could not see dozens of pairs of eyes, but there was a man looking at them from the second floor, with apparent displeasure.

"Please, Jack. I want to get away from this place."

"That's fine with me. I've seen what I came to see. Business as usual at Chez Badim. No excitement. Everything under control."

She pulled his arm, hurrying him away.

"I think I'll nip by the Kremlin," he said. "Will you join me? Your hotel's just down the street."

"I think I'll go directly to it. I need to lie down."

"In that case . . ."

"No, Jack. I need bed rest. Not bed."

"Of course. You have to perform."

"What do you mean by that?"

"Nothing. You have a performance tonight."

"Let's get a cab."

"Let's not. Red Square's very near. We can walk. I find it improves my condition."

Reaching Khmelintsk Street, he took her on a short diversion, turning a corner into a dark, narrow public way that was little more than an alley. People in scruffy clothes were sitting or standing in doorways, drinking. A few, despite the cold, were sleeping.

"As good a place to get drunk in as there is in Moscow," he said, "and there are streets like this all over Moscow. The great Soviet alcoholism problem. Lacking solution, it's kept out of sight."

"Please, let's go on," Tatty said. Some of the drunks were women.

"Don't be so contemptuous, Tat. What's the difference between us and them? We just sit on chairs and drink a better grade of vodka."

She stepped back, moving away from him.

"I'm going to go on by myself, Jack. I'll call you. As soon as I can."

She began to walk quickly toward Red Square.

"Tatty. Don't wear that czarist pin of yours in front of Griuchinov."

"Stop it, Jack. Or I won't call you at all."

After a long nap in her hotel room, she took a long hot bath. Laying out a black evening gown, she then thought better of it. The gown was perhaps more seductive than she wished, and it didn't go well with her pin, which she now most definitely intended to wear. She decided to take the gown with her to the theater and wear it only for her reading. Afterward, she'd change back to her red blouse and black suit, and Czar Nicholas pin. If Griuchinov was not amused by it, too bad. It came with the rest of her.

The telephone rang. Still in her lingerie, she answered

it, hoping it was Jack, regretting her stupid churlishness. When this was over, she would make it up to him, in ways that would please them both.

It was not Spencer, but Meadows. Tatty wished she had more clothes on.

"My dear," he said. "I was just checking to see if you managed to get a Russian invitation."

"Everything's fine, thank you."

"You haven't had a Russian invitation?"

"I'm doing just fine, Mr. Meadows. Just fine."

"If you should get an invitation from the Soviets, well, I know you're seeing an American friend here, but, my dear, it would not do well to insult your Soviet hosts, if you know what I mean."

"I'm not sure I do, Mr. Meadows, but you have nothing to worry about. I've no intention of insulting anyone. Now I really must go. Thank you so much for your solicitousness."

She hung up the phone sharply.

The Russian limousine driver was waiting outside her dressing-room door when she emerged after changing. The audience had been slightly larger this night, but Griuchinov did not come. Neither was he in the car.

"Are we going far?" Tatty asked, in Russian, as she eased herself into the back seat.

"Nyet, gospozha. Blyzko."

Near. And the driver used the old style, prerevolutionary term for madame. She sat very quietly.

Her rendezvous was much more than near; it was at the Kremlin. The chauffeur pulled up abruptly at the gate of the Nikolsky Tower at the northernmost point of the Kremlin walls, then escorted her through a tunnel to the interior, where she was met by a man in a soldier's uniform, who introduced himself as Chairman Griuchinov's servant. He led her to what she recognized from Raya's tour as the Council of Ministers Building, an old classical palace with a big dome on top. Raya had said Lenin had lived and worked there. He had lived none so well as the "good Communist" Griuchinov. The servant ushered her into an apartment on the second floor that was as elegant and decadent as Ramsey Saylor's pied à terre in Georgetown, done in reds, blacks, and assorted greens, with heavy draperies and expensive paintings.

She seated herself on a plush velvet dark green sofa in what she took to be the drawing room, edging close to the adjacent fire, which was blazing with six or seven logs. The waiter brought her a small carafe of vodka in ice and a chilled glass, then retired. As she sipped her drink, she had a moment of panic. Of what possible use was this? What cameras, tape recorders, or eavesdropping devices could Ramsey Saylor possibly have intruded into this Kremlin palace? Was CIA penetration so marvelous it could reach into this innermost sanctum of the Soviet government? All for nought. *Rien. Nichevo.* Nothing. She would be making this sacrifice, enduring this ordeal, to no purpose.

She calmed herself. She would do what was asked of her, and, win or lose, leave the rest to Ramsey. That would be that. She had no reason to doubt the CIA's capabilities. She was working for the Agency, after all, and here she sat.

Griuchinov entered smiling, reaching to take both of her hands. He was wearing a black belted peasant blouse of the old Russian style, black trousers, and soft black leather boots. With his longish gray hair, he looked something of a poet, or musician; a circus-bear trainer perhaps, anything but a Soviet bureaucrat.

"Miss Chase," he said, getting the "Chase" right this time if not the "Meese." "I am so pleased that you could join me this evening."

Kissing both of her hands, he released them and sat himself beside her, reaching to light an American cigarette. The servant, whom Griuchinov addressed as "Sergeant Lev," brought a carafe of vodka for his master, then bent to whisper in his ear. Griuchinov frowned and said a few sharp words in Russian.

"Our dinner will be a little late," he said, as the army servant retired. "The cook is ailing and another had to be found. In meantime, he is preparing an ample *zakuski.* You will enjoy, yes?"

There was a spark of mischief in his eyes.

"I have learned to appreciate your country's excellent vodka more slowly now, Mr. Chairman. And I look forward to enjoying your *zakuski.*"

It was more than ample. The sergeant set down a huge tray with sturgeon, herring, two kinds of caviar, sausage, spicy cheese, anchovies, and dark bread set on plates in a bed of ice. Dinner might not be necessary.

Something had bothered her from the moment she entered the apartment, and she realized what it was: the music. He had a tape or record system hidden away somewhere and it was playing very Western music, indeed, a jazzy version of "Southern Nights."

She smiled, and so did he. He was quite charming, really, and it infuriated her.

"That's very interesting music, Mr. Chairman, to be hearing inside the Kremlin."

"Yes? You like it?"

"I do, thank you. But I am very fond of Russian music as well. There's a song, 'Evening Bells.' Would you have a recording of it?"

"Oh yes, yes." He clapped his hands twice and called Sergeant Lev's name. When that produced nothing, he went to a small box affixed to the wall near the doorway and pushed a button, twice. This finally produced Lev, who received his instructions dutifully and then disappeared. By the time Griuchinov returned to his seat and raised his vodka glass to his lips, "Southern Nights" was replaced by a strong Russian basso. The song was "Evening Bells," but sung playfully rather than traditionally. The singer had an extraordinary range, and used the song to exercise it as he might the scales.

"Is Ivan Rebroff," Griuchinov said. "His parents were born Russian, but not Sovietski. He was born in Germany. But we accept him. He has remarkable voice. Five octaves, perhaps more. He has sung at your Carnegie Hall."

Tatty sipped, closed her eyes, put back her head, and listened. Her feet were too warm in her boots. With another man, with Jack Spencer, she would remove them now. Her evening with Griuchinov was still too formal.

"You are called Tatty, Miss Chase. Your name is actually Tatiana?"

"Tatiana Alexandra."

"Beautiful Russian names. And your Russian family name? What was it?"

"Iovashchenko. It was my grandmother's name. She married a man named Hoops. My mother, Chloe, married a man named Bobby Shaw. Not very Russian, that. Would I be called Tatiana Bobbyevna?"

He smiled, patting her knee as he reached to pour her and himself more vodka. "I think perhaps here he would be called Boris. So, Tatiana Borisevna Iovashchenko, except you are Hoops and Shaw. How are you then called Chase? Husband?"

"No. My father was killed and my mother married a very nice man named Chase. I'm divorced. When I was married, my name was Dewey."

"Tatiana Dewey. No, it does not go."

"It certainly didn't." Eyes wide open, she stared over the rim of her glass at the fire. "You are named Valeri Jakovich, Mr. Chairman. Your father was Jakov?"

"*Da.* Jakov Petrovich."

"Griuchinov."

"No. I say this to you in discretion, Miss Chase, yes? Well, my mother and father never married. They would have, but he was killed in Civil War. Very turbulent times."

"And he was Jakov Sverdlov."

"What? Oh no." He laughed. "If he was Jakov Sverdlov I would have so many fewer troubles in my young life. No, my father was Jakov Petrovich Nikulin, close not to Lenin like Sverdlov but to the unfortunate Trotsky. My mother's name was Griuchinov, but I was known as son of Trotsky's favorite general nevertheless. It was not easy for me until Khrushchev came to power. Much better then for all Russians, though not so good as now. Our premier is very brilliant man."

She took some caviar on a piece of bread, licked her lips clean afterward, then sat back, taking the chairman's warm, strong hand. It was indeed a farmer's hand. It became more than warm in the grasp of hers. He would be off balance now, more disposed to candor.

"I like your hand," she said.

"Miss Chase, I am so pleased that you feel comfortable here."

With a quick motion of her free hand, she both pulled open the jacket of her suit and the top button of her red blouse, exposing both the czarist pin and the curve of her breast.

"I am comfortable here," she said.

The basso Ivan Rebroff was now singing "Kalinka," much more robustly than the band had played it that night in the Metropole. Poor Jack; how disgusted he'd be to see her now.

"The other evening," she said. "We were talking about your being in Southeast Asia."

He laughed. "No, Miss Chase. We were talking about not talking about my being in Southeast Asia. Very public place, yes? But I was there, yes. During unhappy times there for our two countries."

"My father was there."

"Yes?"

She bit down hard on her lip. She had to do this. Something was wrong.

"He was a pilot. For our air force."

"Yes? My son was pilot with Soviet air forces, with Fighter Aviation of the Air Defense Forces of the Homeland. He is now with Aeroflot. You have flown Aeroflot, yes? Very nice?"

"My father was killed flying in Southeast Asia, in Laos, after he was shot down."

He frowned and squeezed her hand sympathetically. "Miss Chase, I am so sorry to hear. This is terrible thing about war; so many fatherless children. I know so well."

"You were not involved in the war there, Mr. Chairman?"

He shook his head. "No. I was involved only with rice. And manure. Rice paddies are fertilized very primitively in Vietnam. I tried to teach them less primitive methods, but they are a very insular, stubborn people. Oh. I say undiplomatic thing."

She turned abruptly and looked up into his eyes.

"You were strictly an agronomist? You were never involved with the military, say, with prisoner-of-war camps?"

His eyes answered her before his words did. "I am a farmer, Miss Chase. Please, let us talk of other things."

As an actress, she knew acting, and there was none of it in his eyes. There was only truth.

"For your sake, Mr. Chairman. And I mean this very sincerely, for I think I like you. For your sake, I think I had better leave here at once. Something is very wrong. I've been misinformed."

"Miss Chase . . . ?"

Sergeant Lev the servant entered, unsummoned. He came toward the table as though to remove the *zakuski,* though they were far from done with it. Instead, he reached inside his tunic, pulled forth a small pistol, and shot Griuchinov in the face, a spray of blood bursting from the back of the chairman's head. Griuchinov, hands raised, eyes bulging, rose from the sofa, but did so as a dead man, falling forward onto the table, his face in the *zakuski,* his blood running into the bed of ice.

Lev set down the pistol on the table. It was the one she had had in her bag, the one Meadows had given her, the same blue-gray finish, the same mother-of-pearl on the grip.

Sergeant Lev was wearing white gloves. He had been from the first.

He went to Griuchinov's body and pulled down the chairman's trousers until his buttocks and genitals were exposed. Then he stood straight, looking at Tatty with all the impassivity of an alien being.

"You have shot Chairman," he said, loudly, as though for a microphone. "You resisted his advances by murdering him. I am now calling authorities. Stay where you are."

10

Tatty sat transfixed, watching the ice fill with blood.

Sergeant Lev had gone to the telephone. There were armed militiamen all over the building. She had passed two at the entrance. Yet the man was telephoning. That meant something. What it meant she would decide later. At this instant, she knew only that, if she was to survive, to escape, to live, he could not be allowed to complete his call. He was dialing.

He had set her pistol on the table. That was a mistake. She picked it up and got to her feet. There were moral questions about what she was to do, but she hadn't time to consider them. There was the possibility that she might threaten him away from the telephone with the gun, that she might overpower him in some way, find something with which to knock him out. But there were no longer even seconds left. He had stopped dialing.

Aiming the pistol with both hands, she fired twice. The first shot hit him in the small of the back, causing paralysis and pain. The second, the trigger pulled as the gun rose in recoil, struck the back of his head, splashing blood against the wall. She should run now, but where? To the embassy. But Meadows was at the embassy, and Meadows had given her the gun. Meadows was Ramsey's man. There might be many of Ramsey's people at the embassy.

Where then, with so little time to think? No time, so she must make her own call. She had no one else, nothing else. It was crazy, but everything else was crazier. She had to know what to do. Stepping over Lev's body, fighting back images of another man's dead body lying atop her own in France, she frantically began to dial. There was no answer at the first number. She dialed the second. Spencer answered on the fourth ring. She could not understand why police were not crashing through the door.

"Jack, thank God."

"Czarina. I should have thought you'd be making merry with the good chairman right about now."

"Jack, Griuchinov's dead! He's been shot, murdered! I killed the man who did it. I don't know what to do!"

Spencer paused a second or two, then swore. "Where are you?"

"In the Kremlin."

"The Kremlin? For God's sake, Tatty!"

"It just happened, Jack. What do I do?"

He paused again, then said, "Get drunk, Tatty. Grab a bottle of vodka and go to as good a place to get drunk in as there is in Moscow. Do you know what I mean?"

"No. Yes! You mean—"

"Be quiet! Gather up everything you have there, everything that could be identified with you. Then go where I said. Go now. Hurry. Run, Tatty! Run!"

She found her coat and hat in a front closet and pulled them on hastily. Throwing the pistol into her purse and snatching up a bottle of Stolichnaya, she searched through the rooms of the apartment until she found the kitchen, a pantry beyond that, and a rear door leading to a dark, gloomy set of service stairs. As she fled down them, she heard a pounding at the front door of the flat. There was a passageway at the bottom, leading outside, but Tatty could see the outline of a militiaman and his rifle at the end. Another door led to an interior corridor illuminated by old-fashioned lamps along the wall. The door at its end was locked, but there was a passageway leading off to the right. She followed it until she came to a door that did open, revealing an ornate auditorium, the chambers of the

Council of Ministers. It looked deserted. Staying close to the walls, Tatty moved through it, passing by the great double doors she presumed to be the main entrance, instead slipping out a side exit further along. This put her in a wide hall. It was empty, but she could hear voices around the corner, which she took to be those of militiamen at the building's entrance. Darting across the hall, she entered a doorway opposite, finding herself in a small conference room, dark but for faint light from the exterior windows.

Were they exterior? The building had interior courtyards. She could be climbing down into a trap, an animal pit, into death. But she must keep moving. She must run. The windows were locked only with latches. She undid one and slowly raised the sash, opening it wide. She peered outside. It was a courtyard, a deadly dead end. In brightly lit windows opposite, she could see militiamen, drinking something from cups.

Closing the window quickly, she almost panicked, almost began to cry. But not yet. There were other rooms and other windows. Returning to the hall, hurrying in the opposite direction from the building entrance, she found one at the very end. There was nothing but dark wall to be seen out its windows. It was no dead end. It was the Kremlin wall.

The drop was even greater. She guessed ten feet. Stuffing the bottle of vodka into a coat pocket, she looked out, seeing no one in either direction. But she could hear loud voices, and distant sirens. She lowered herself from the window ledge, painfully scraping a knee, then let go, falling too heavily. Her right ankle gave way and she landed with a jarring thud on her backside, some vodka sloshing over her coat. She rose quickly. She could stand. There was no time for pain.

Down the wall, at the far corner of the building to her left was the Nikolsky Tower gate through which she had come. To her right was another tower she did not know. She walked toward it, limping, keeping to the building wall. Reaching the corner, her cheek pressed to the abrasive masonry, she moved her head slowly forward until

176

she could see around it. At the next corner down were some military vehicles, with lights on and engines running, and some men standing around them—soldiers, not militia. The tower gate itself was closed, militia or soldiers visible through its steel bars at the other end, stark silhouettes against the lights of Red Square.

Directly opposite her was another building, the one Raya had so proudly pointed out to her as the center of the world, the building of the Supreme Soviet of the USSR. Streaming past on the other side were people—not soldiers or police, but ordinary people. Raya had said the nearby Palace of Congresses was used at night for theatrical productions, the ballet, and balalaika orchestras. They were theatergoers, heading home.

Crossing the bright space between the two buildings, she walked very stiffly and erect, in hopes she might be taken at such distance for a soldier on some duty. Reaching the shadows once more, she ran, her heels sharp and clattering against the pavement; ran with mad, frantic, lurching steps, but she ran very fast. Never in all her beach mornings at the Hamptons had she run with such passion and abandon. Run, Tatty, run. Her boots rang out the cadence, the sound urging her on. She glanced just once over her shoulder, seeing no one. Nearing the crowd, caution slowed her. Finally, she stumbled to a halt and fell back against the building wall, catching her breath.

The theater seated two or three thousand people. They were still coming. Calming herself, buttoning her long coat about her and smoothing its skirts, adopting the smile of someone who had been wonderfully entertained for an evening, she swept to the side of the procession, sidling quickly into its midst. Though she detected two groups of American tourists, each led by their indomitable Intourist guide, most of the people were Russian, with the Russian people's propensity for crushing together in a great human clot. As they flowed on toward the pedestrian tunnel by Spassky Tower that led out to Red Square, as she heard more sirens, motor traffic, and military shouting behind her, she felt strangely secure.

But it could last only until they emerged upon the

square. Then the people would disperse and leave her na-kedly alone; a beautiful blond woman in a bright red coat, alone in the middle of Red Square—with all of Soviet security searching for her.

She had seen the two young men as she swept into the crowd. They were now much ahead of her in the crowded tunnel, but she began to fight her way forward. The pressure eased as they surged out onto the square, and she raced up between them, bottle of vodka in hand. With her free hand, she took the arm of the young man on her left. He was dark. The one on her right was fair, and more merry, though both seemed in good spirits. She was in surprisingly good spirits herself, as elated as she had been stealing liquor from that beach party with Captain Paget, in much the same way. She had escaped the Kremlin. All that stood in her way now was the city of Moscow and all the reaches of the Soviet Empire.

"*Za vashe zdorovoye!*" she said, raising the bottle in a toast and drinking. She handed it to the merry one, who drank generously. The dark one shook his head in refusal.

"*Myetro?*" she asked, deliberately pointing the wrong way to the subway, comporting herself as drunkenly as possible.

"No," said the blond one in Russian, "is this way."

"*Pokazhitye mnye, pozhaluista?*"

"Yes. We show you. Come."

The dark one hung back, but stayed with them, which was well. Alone, the blond one would have doubtless followed her into the subway. With only him at her side, she would be even more noticeable, and there were now more military trucks and jeeps pulling into the square.

Many in the theater crowd were also heading for the metro, and she hurried the two young men to keep up with them. At the subway entrance, she kissed the blond one on the cheek, said "*Spasibo*" cheerily, then dashed way, burrowing into a jam-up of short, burly Russians trying to get onto the down escalator. With some resentment they made way for her, and at last she was on the moving stairs, descending. Pausing a moment to catch her breath, she began pushing her way forward again, New York style, though her effort seemed to little diminish the eternity it took to reach the cavernous depths of the platform below. Ignoring the gleaming statuary and other socialist wonders Raya had pointed out so smugly, she stopped only to quickly consult the wall map and glance back at the escalator. Her pulse jumped as though with a jolt of current. There were no policemen—none she could recognize as such—but the blond man was there, scarcely twenty feet from the platform.

Remembering as best she could, trying to follow the Russian signs, she darted through an archway and along a short tunnel, eventually emerging on another platform she hoped was the correct one and leaping onto a train she prayed was going in the right direction. As the door closed behind her, she closed her eyes in silent thanks. She had now escaped Red Square, for the price of only a swallow of vodka and five kopecks. That so many of her fellow passengers were staring at her did not matter. She was only going one stop.

She had picked the right train. As she emerged from the up escalator and the metro exit, she saw there were many lights on in the building of narrow windows, though not so many as must be on in the basement. She stood a moment in somber contemplation. She had not escaped if she had only reached Dzerzhinsky Square. Her earlier elation was now abandoning her. Cold, increasingly unhappy, she had a fleeting impulse to walk up to the building and surrender, to state her case and submit to the surrealities of Soviet justice, to spare herself what she realized was going to be a painful and probably pointless ordeal of flight. But it would be madness.

Perhaps because of the increasing bitterness of the cold, there were few in the street of drunks. Glad of the darkness that hid the expensiveness of her clothing, she stumbled to a doorway distant from the others and sat with her arms hugging her knees, drinking what remained of the vodka against the falling temperature.

A better warmth was provided by the quiet fury that came when she put her mind to the subject of Ramsey Saylor. Silently, she called him every vile name she could think of, but none sufficed. That cold, scheming, amoral, passionless, cruel, rotten son of a bitch had planned this with such wonderful perfection. His marvelous, intricate, perverted mind had not overlooked a single subtlety. Working for the CIA, she had killed a KGB operative in France, because he had tried to rape her. It would now be shown that, working for the CIA, she had killed a Soviet official in the heart of the Kremlin, because he was trying to rape her, her chronic drunkenness the reason for such bizarre, irrational behavior. When had Ramsey devised this? When had he chosen her as his unwitting instrument, decided he could exploit her person and her weaknesses so cleverly? So foully?

A better question was why? To what end would an official of the Central Intelligence Agency attempt to implicate the agency in the murder of one of the highest-ranking Soviet leaders, especially at a time when the Soviet Union was still suffering universal scorn for its plot to assassinate Pope John Paul II and its murder of the passengers and crew of a civilian jet? Why do such a thing to the United States? Why kill the one Kremlin figure who had shown any apparent friendliness toward policies benefiting American interests? Ramsey was a patriot, a conservative intellectual.

She thought of the expensive furnishings in Ramsey's expensive Georgetown house, of the John Singer Sargent painting that, upon reflection, probably cost several hundred thousand dollars. Harvard or no, Ramsey was the son of a gun salesman.

A sick feeling came into her stomach.

One of the dark figures along the street, a man, rose and stood looking at her. What had once repelled Chairman Griuchinov would not repel the denizens of this wretched place. He started toward her with a shuffling step. Her nerves were so numbed she doubted if she could make herself vomit and doubted if even that would dissuade him. She began to cry, unpleasantly, insanely—working in little growls and tiny shrieks, shaking her head frantically. He paused. *"Smyert!"* she cried. "Death!" He hurried back to his place. A moment later, he left the street. She drank.

Had the horrible Sergeant Lev not made the mistake of arranging the props before he made his telephone call, had she not found within herself the wit, desperation, and violence to snatch up the pistol and kill him, she would now be lying against the cold stone not of this alley but of Lubyanka prison.

She would not give in to despair. Jack was coming, strong, handsome Jack Spencer, her life's hero. He would take her from this—he would save her.

She pictured her generational cousin, the Grand Duchess Tatiana, leaning against some cold Siberian wall six decades before and thinking similar thoughts. Heroes to come, who never did.

Spencer did not arrive for almost an hour. She had by then consumed all of her vodka and nearly all her hope. Jack brought more vodka, two bottles of a cheap brand. He seated himself and pulled her close to him, handing her a bottle.

"Drink," he said, "and speak softly."

She drank, seeking and finding warmth, but for a moment could say nothing.

"You must hate me for taking so long," he said, "but I had no choice. I have an automatic tail wherever I go—we all do—and it took every trick I could think of to lose them. I'm not even sure I have. But we might as well stay here for the time being. I can't think of any safer place to go to right now."

"Jack, what do I do?"

"You are in the most serious trouble anyone could invent, Tatty. You are very close to being dead."

She sniffled, wiping tears from her eyes with her gloved hand. "That's so encouraging to hear."

"Tell me now how this happened."

"The servant did it, an army sergeant. He came into the room and without any hesitation shot Griuchinov through the head. Then he said I had murdered the chairman. He put down the gun and started to telephone. I shot him. Then I called you. I was set up for this, Jack. They picked me out for this when I was back in New York."

"Who did?"

"Some people in the CIA. I, I've done some work for them in the past. For a friend from college days. His name is Ramsey Saylor."

Spencer swallowed vodka, and said nothing for a minute.

"It's a damn strange thing," he said finally. "The Soviet army is all over the place. Convoys, military police patrols, everywhere. But the militia hasn't stirred. Dzerzhinsky Square is quiet. When Brezhnev died, every window was ablaze. There was nothing on the Tass wire. I'm not even sure that the news about Griuchinov is out. The KGB has a tap on my line, yet, despite your call, they've done nothing. I think Marshal Kuznetzov has a real problem on his hands."

"What do you mean? Did he arrange this?"

"It's my best guess. But he didn't arrange it well enough. You're here, not there. He needs you. With your beautiful corpus in hand, in Griuchinov's apartment delicto flagrante, he discredits Griuchinov and his followers. He discredits General Badim and the KGB for letting you get to Griuchinov. He brings glory on himself and his GRU by apprehending you. And he acquires proof."

"Proof of what?"

"That he didn't kill Griuchinov. But he doesn't have you. Here you are." He took another, very big swallow. "But does the KGB know where you are?"

"Jack, are you drunk?"

"Not yet. I'm just thinking, thinking as hard as I can."

"Why did the CIA let Ramsey do this to me?"

"The CIA did not let him do it to you. He did it on his own. Have you any idea why?"

"Yes. I'm sure it was for money. But how would he be in contact with Marshal Kuznetzov?"

"I know of Mr. Saylor. He's in the Agency's Soviet section. He has a hundred ways of communicating with Soviets."

"How do you know of Ramsey? How do you know the CIA didn't let him do this?"

"Tatty, I've done work for the CIA—many of us newsboys have. Some out of patriotism. Some in exchange for information. Some for money. I do it for all three reasons, especially the last. Thanks to your step-sister's lawyers, I'm paying for Christopher's boarding school, among a great many other things."

"What sort of work do you do for them?"

"Most of the time I just bring them rumors and gossip. Sometimes I do odd jobs. In Iceland, once, I helped sink a Russian trawler."

"Did you know why I was coming?"

"I was told only that it was part of an attempt to embarrass and cajole the Kremlin into letting the Bolshoi come back to the United States. My job was to ask the embarrassing question at the news conference. Your job, I was told, was to cajole the lascivious Griuchinov, who has authority over Bolshoi tours."

"Who told you this?"

"My resident case officer, the faggot Meadows."

"Why didn't you talk to me about it?"

"The faggot Meadows told me not to. I was going to anyway, after you were done with Griuchinov. Surprise, surprise. A family of spies."

A sudden flare of light shot along the street. At the corner two armed, long-coated militiamen—one with an enormous flashlight—were peering into the passageway, examining the drunks. The light flickered back and forth, moving down the street. As it neared them, Jack sat forward, shielding Tatty, and raised his vodka bottle in toast. The light paused, then continued its zigzag course to the end. Then it went out.

"Do not stay here all night!" one of the militiamen shouted in Russian. "Is going to be very cold!" And then they were gone.

"Can't we go some place?" she said. The militiaman's words had made her feel the harsh temperature more now than at any time since coming to Russia.

"We can't go to my place, because there must be a dozen microphones in my bathroom alone, which happens to give me great joy on bad mornings. There is an apartment of a Russian friend where I take . . . where I occasionally entertain lady friends, but there must be even more microphones there, and probably cameras. I know a great many dissidents, the so-called Soviet underground, but half of them probably work for General Badim or Kuznetzov. Our options narrow."

"Perhaps we should go to the American embassy. The ambassador is very nice."

"The faggot Meadows. And friends."

"Aren't there any good CIA people?"

"That is a philosophical question for which there is no time now to ponder. I'm sorry, Tatty. We can't have you surface anywhere in Russia, especially in the embassy. Then Kuznetzov has his proof. If he can't lay hands on you, he would still be able to point to you."

"He doesn't have the pistol. I took the pistol."

"That was wise. It would be more proof. And also, you may need it."

"What am I going to do, Jack? Look at these people. They're going to sleep. Am I just to go to sleep here, Jack? Freeze here? My God, dammit, Jack, what do I *do?*"

"I'm going to get you a cab."

"You are drunk."

"I'm trying, Tat. After this, I'm not going to be able to do much drinking for a while. But I'll get you out."

He set down his bottle and reached inside his coat.

"Here is all the money I could lay hands on in the bureau. There's about seven hundred eighty dollars in rubles and five hundred in greenbacks. Hide the greenbacks in your underwear, Tat, because in this country, American currency is golden and you can even get killed for it." He reached into another pocket. "Here is my State Department press card with my photograph on it. It will identify you to some people I want you to try to find. Here is a list of their names and their last addresses, as best I can remember them."

She peered closely at the paper, but could not read from it in the dark.

"You memorize the lines of plays, Tatty. I want you to memorize these names and addresses, and then destroy that paper. That paper could get them killed as dead as you."

"Who are they?"

"The first is Waldemar Jozef Rodnieski. He's a Pole, in Warsaw. He's the foreman of a sausage plant. He was a leader of sorts in Solidarity, when there really was a Solidarity, and a good source of mine, but he went over to Jaruzelski. One of the first. But it was to spy for Walesa and Solidarity. Trust him with your life. I have.

"If you can get to him, he can possibly get you onto a boat. A ship. Some stinking freighter. The Baltic's still ice-free. If you get to Western Europe, try for the next people on the list. McLaren is an Australian with Reuters in London. We've saved each other's lives a couple of times and gotten drunk together a million times. Brigitta Glaesner is our bureau chief in Bonn. Explain your situation and she will do everything she can for you. She was a young girl in Berlin when the Soviets came in 1945. She went out to the country because she thought she'd be safer. She was wrong. She'll do everything for you, believe me."

"Jack—"

"If Rodnieski can get you onto an Icelandic boat, one of the refrigerator freighters, all the better. The Russians don't bother them much. If you can make it to Iceland, go to the man who's last on the list, Sverrir Axelsson. He's with a newspaper in Reykjavik called *Kvoldbladid.* He can get you home."

"These are all?"

"All I can come up with at the moment, at least in the way of people I absolutely trust, and who owe me one."

"Can't I just go to an American embassy, the embassy in Poland?"

"That's your draw, Tat. I wouldn't. Marshal Kuznetzov has a long reach. And once he's aware of this, General Badim will do his duty as well."

"Jack, what do we do right now?"

"In a minute. Do you have any money in your purse?"

"A lot. Three hundred dollars in American money and I don't know how many rubles. I also have some traveler's checks."

"Never mind those. Take out the money and give the

185

purse to me. All your ID, everything else, leave that in. And you've got to get rid of that damn red coat. I wouldn't be surprised if they could pick that up from a satellite."

"But what will I wear?"

He glanced along the street. There was a woman curled up against the wall, snoring. Taking Tatty's coat, he moved her to a sitting position. When she did not awaken, he gently removed her long black coat and pulled Tatty's on in its place.

"There," he said. "If she doesn't lose her toes and fingers tonight, she'll wake up thinking she's gone to Soviet heaven. It would take a year for a well-paid worker to earn enough for that coat."

Tatty put on the woman's wretched shapeless garment with much distaste. "It probably has fleas."

"Be thankful if it doesn't have lice. You can't keep that fur hat. It's much too expensive."

"I need something."

"Take mine. It's only rabbit. Thirty-five rubles." He untied the ear flaps and pulled them down around her head. "There, with your collar up, you can't even see your blond hair. I wish we could get rid of your other things, but there's no time."

"Jack, how are we going to get to Poland? How are we going to get away from here?"

"It's more than seven hundred fifty miles to Warsaw. I wish I could put you in a cab, tell the driver, 'Byelorussia Station,' and have you snug in a sleeping compartment on the overnight express. That's impossible, and not just because it left hours ago. But I can put you in a cab."

"What do you mean?" Dread and doubts, unhappy thoughts about all the bad things Jack Spencer might actually be, began crowding into her mind.

"No trains, no planes. You have no travel papers, Tatty, and there's no way to get you any. You'll have to bribe your way to Warsaw, and you'll start by bribing your way out of Moscow by taxicab. It's not an unreliable way to get about, Tatty. Many Russians on discreet business use it. Remember, this is one of the most corrupt countries in the world. It has a black market like postwar Italy's.

You can buy anything you want with the right money. All you have to buy is seven hundred and fifty miles."

He took a long, long pull of his vodka.

"You're a swine, Jack. You're a shit. You're just as weak and cowardly and self-centered as Chesley said. You're just going to throw me out into the dark like a stray cat and go back to your booze. And when you get transferred out of here you'll call up my stepfather, if you can work up the nerve, and ask if I ever made it."

"You've got it wrong, Tat."

"The hell I do. I hate you so much right now I can hardly tell I'm scared, and I am truly very scared, Jack Spencer."

He sighed, and leaned even closer to her. "Tatty, I'm death to you. There must be a dozen, two dozen people who do nothing more all day than keep track of everything I do and every place I go. That's the way it is for all of us correspondents. When they get around to transcribing the tape with that last phone conversation of ours, every militiaman in Moscow will be looking for me. I expect I'll be picked up five minutes after I leave you. I hope not. There are still some things I can do to help you. But damn it, Tatty, I can't help you by traveling with you. The two of us together make for ten times the target. I want you to have every chance out of this!"

"That's a crock."

"Listen to what I say. There's a village about thirty miles southwest of here called Olinksovo, on the railroad. Country women gather there in the mornings to take the train to the Cheremushki free market in the city. Bribe a taxi driver to take you out there. Tell him you had a fight with your husband and you want to go home to your mother. It's within the fifty-mile limit so you shouldn't have much trouble with checkpoints unless Kuznetzov really goes berserk. Bribe the man well, but haggle. Act a little drunk. Act."

She stared at him stonily.

"All those women are operators, survivors. Befriend them, help them, tell them about your awful husband. They can find a westbound truck for you. A trustworthy driver. You won't get to Warsaw in one crack. The cities en route are Smolensk, Minsk, and Brest."

"Swine."

He got to his feet and pulled her to hers, then reached into her purse, removing the pistol. "You forgot this."

She let him slip it into her pocket.

"There's an all-night taxi stand not far," he said. "The bureaucrats in this interesting neighborhood work late."

She kept her eyes away from his. Her limbs were stiff and cold from all that sitting. She needed to go to the bathroom.

"Tatty. It's time to go. It's more than time."

The street was bright with orange light. It was empty, though traffic could be heard not far away. A few flakes of snow were falling, blown and tossed by the wind. He put his arm around her. She pulled herself away.

"Tatty. For the few minutes we'll walk together now we've got to be something normal and logical. Tipsy lovers might be out like this. We must be tipsy lovers."

She accepted his arm then, grudgingly glad for the warmth.

"We will never see each other again, John Spencer. Never."

"I think that may very well be. But, Tatty, I want you to be the one to live through this. I wish it more than anything."

There were two cabs parked at the taxi stand, green lights glowing on their windshields, the drivers standing outside and stamping their feet like Dostoyevsky's coachmen. Spencer hung back against the wall, releasing her.

"Go, Tat. Luck and prayers."

She began walking away. The taxi men saw her and stared.

"Remember that I love you, Tatty."

His unwanted words hastened her step. She didn't look back. She was more alone than she had ever been.

11

As they pulled away from the cab stand, she began her performance for the driver, wailing and moaning about her drunken beast of a husband and how he had beaten her up at a party. She had not told the driver exactly where she wanted to go. When she did, he refused. She offered him twenty rubles for the trip, half again as much as the meter fare would be, but he still refused. When she gave him five rubles on account and a drink of her vodka, he agreed at least to take her to someone who might help her. He also took her to a place to go to the bathroom, a cold, wretched public toilet with a drunken man sleeping in it. And rats.

The someone who might help her proved to be an off-duty driver who lived in one of the poorer sections of west Moscow, his cab parked in front of his drab, nondescript apartment house. He was ten or fifteen minutes coming out of the building, still buttoning his trousers and coat. He and the other driver said the deal would be thirty rubles. Twenty-five for the man who would take her and another five for the first. She swore and began to cry. She was not rich, she said. She only wanted to get to her mother's. She would pay the man twenty rubles and the other one already had his five. The new driver, a younger man in a cheap *shapka* and yellow vinyl coat, shrugged. He wouldn't earn twenty rubles any other way that night.

He smoked, sang, and coughed as they drove out the deserted streets, the singing as unpleasant as the coughing. She abided it gladly. She was in no mood to deal with the possible dangers of a conversation.

As they entered the first of the suburbs, passing a group of militiamen standing beside a truck, he began to talk, asking, as had the first driver, about her strange accent. She told him, as she had the first driver, that she was Polish. She then realized she was portraying herself as a Pole who came from a village just outside Moscow. She quickly explained that her mother, a widow, had married a Russian army captain who had brought them here to this miserable country to a miserable life that now included her miserable husband. The word *kapitan* worked its magic. He grumbled some about how good the Poles had it, then fell silent.

How good the Poles had it. She remembered driving by a store on one of Moscow's main thoroughfares with Raya. It was crammed with humanity to the point of such excess that the people seemed packed for shipping. "Is Polish goods store," Raya had said. "Is very popular."

Buildings and houses fell away and they were soon traveling in darkness except for the patch of road held in the headlights. An occasional military vehicle would roar by them on the narrow road, frightening Tatty each time, but none ever stopped.

At last he bumped over railroad tracks and entered the village, pulling to a stop by the little square. He turned in the seat, raising his eyebrows and shoulders in question. She told him to proceed straight ahead and then, choosing the darkest street she could see, told him to turn right. She picked a darkened house with a wall and gate five doors down. Giving him an extra ruble and fifty kopecks, she let him take two drinks of her vodka and then said good night. She closed the door and went to the gate. The cab had not moved. She waited as long as she could, then, sweating despite the numbing cold, pushed the latch of the gate. It gave a loud clank, a noise that seemed to her as loud as thunder, and gave way. She slipped inside, closed the gate behind her, and stood motionless in the black shadows of the narrow yard, fearing that she had awakened everyone in the house, that the people here might have dogs. There was only silence. At last, the cab drove away.

The village railroad station was small and empty. A short ways down the line, a man was standing in the dimly lit window of a squat signal tower. The station door was open. In a country that so prized security, secrecy, and paranoia, she was amazed to find so many unlocked doors.

The stationmaster would be there in the morning. She did not want her sleeping body to welcome him. Waiting for her eyes to adjust to the darkness, she sought out the women's room and slipped inside. She curled up on the floor, wondering what she might be lying in, wondering if there would be rats.

The morning came with much noise outside, but it was not the kind she feared. The women were arriving with their goods for the Moscow free market. One of them barged into the lavatory, stepping over Tatty, going about her crude toilette as though there were always someone lying on the floor. Tatty sat up, murmuring good morning, and went to wash her face and hands in the ice-cold water of the rusty sink. The outside air was even colder on her skin.

The women, perhaps three dozen of them, were sturdy-looking, though many were old. Their sacks, satchels, and baskets contained a market full of things—chickens, eggs, gathered roots, nuts, milk, knitting, homemade beer, wine, and vodka, odd household objects—anything that could be sold for profit at the chief form of capitalism openly tolerated in Moscow.

Tatty bought a sack containing four live if silent chickens from one, a weary-looking babushka, paying what she judged from the woman's expression to be a fair Moscow price. She then slung it over her shoulder and moved about the others who had gathered on the platform, looking for the friendliest face. She quickly changed her mind,

191

seeking out instead the craftiest. She settled on a brown-faced woman dressed more warmly than the others, who had a large, long-handled square basket. There was cloth peeping out from the top but Tatty guessed by the way the sides bulged that it contained something heavier, probably liquor, illegal homemade liquor.

"The train comes soon?" Tatty asked.

The woman scowled at the track. "Some days." She looked up at Tatty, then down, assessing her top to bottom in a quick glance, her Asiatic eyes lingering on Tatty's boots. "You are not from here. You are going to Moscow?"

"*Nyet,*" said Tatty. "Minsk."

"Train to Minsk stops not here."

"I'm not traveling by train."

The woman stared at her.

"Have you vodka for sale?" Tatty asked.

The woman's stare darkened. "You want vodka?"

"Yes." Tatty did. She had left the bottle Spencer had given her on the filthy women's room floor and did not want to go back for it.

The woman studied her very carefully this time. "Five rubles. Very good vodka."

The price was inflated, but that did not matter. Tatty gave her a ten-ruble note. The woman quickly opened the basket, pulled out a bottle wrapped in newspaper, and put it into Tatty's sack with the unprotesting chickens.

"You are not traveling by train? How are you going to Minsk?"

"I don't know." Tatty went into her lines about the wife-beating in Moscow, this time saying she was fleeing to her Polish mother in Minsk, a Polish mother without a husband of any kind. For a long moment, she was afraid the woman was going to ask her something in Polish. Tatty spoke not a word of Polish, except for *kilbasa,* which she thought meant sausage.

"You are in trouble?"

She nodded, beginning to cry. "My husband knows officials."

"You have internal passport?"

192

The sound of the English word startled her. Then she remembered. The Russian word for passport was *pasport*.

"No. He has all my papers. I ran away. I was drunk. I took a taxi here. I have to get away. To Minsk."

"You have money?"

"*Da.* A little."

The woman folded her arms and looked off in the direction of the train.

"Do you know anyone going west, who could give me a ride?"

The woman's distant gaze did not change. "No. I know no one with car."

"Do you know anyone with truck? Going to Minsk?"

The woman didn't move. Tatty crumpled up a five-ruble note and put it in the woman's hand. She looked at it, and then down at Tatty's boots, staring hard. They were black, like her own, but they were Louis Jourdan. Tatty gave her another five rubles.

She looked back down the tracks, but her demeanor changed. "Is road leading west from square. Follow it four kilometers to main highway. Is café there. Roti and Valentina manage café. Valentina is good woman. I sell her vodka. Tell her I send you. Olga. Give her money. She will find you ride. Valentina has many friends among truck drivers. Go now. You are with me too long."

Tatty picked up her chicken sack. The woman was looking at her boots again.

"You are Polish?"

"*Da. Polska.*" It sounded right.

"You Polish have it too good."

Once out of sight of the village, Tatty paused to roughen up her boots with a stick and muddy snow, an act that she expected would be rendered unnecessary after a day or two more on the road. She lingered to take two swallows of the woman's vodka, a strong, raw stuff that had about as much in common with the good Stolichnaya as cheap California chablis did with Bollinger. She was thankful for it, nevertheless.

She reached the café ravenous, weak from the walk and

the night. The man Roti had only just opened up, but was able to provide her with *kvas,* fish, sausage, and cheese while he heated up the stove. She ate wolfishly, embarrassed by her slovenly looks until she reminded herself how much her safety might depend on her scruffy appearance. Roti kept looking at her in such lusting fashion she wished she looked ten times scruffier. She was hot now in Jack's lumpy fur hat, but she kept it on to cover her stylish blond hair.

Others came, ate, and left, including two militiamen. They studied her, but as men, not police, and finally departed as well. Tatty had let herself feel secure because they were only militia. She supposed this was a mistake.

Valentina proved to be an attractive, fat, blonde, blowzy, cheerful—and, for so small a place—somewhat worldly woman, who accepted the mention of Olga's name and a folded ten-ruble note as crude protocol to be dispensed with as quickly as possible. Once it was, she carried on as though she and Tatty were old friends, taking her back to the kitchen, asking about Moscow, asking about Warsaw, accepting everything Tatty told her. She readily agreed to arrange Tatty a ride as a matter of course between chums, and just as chummily pocketed another ten rubles. She eyed Tatty's boots with friendliness as well, but her own legs were much too short and plump. Tatty gave her the chickens instead.

The truck driver Valentina procured was named Pavl, a youngish, not unattractive man with a bluish cast of beard on his cheeks and a brown birthmark on his forehead. Though thin, he had very wide cheekbones. His eyes were of a blue much darker than Tatty's. When he laughed and joked, he seemed something of a leering, country dolt. When serious, he looked quite wise.

He agreed to take her to Minsk only after much thought and two cups of *kvas.* She offered a hundred rubles. He ended up with twice that.

As they pulled out onto the road, he began to talk, about himself, about anything that seemed to come into his mind. Many of his words she did not understand, but she murmured what she hoped were appropriate responses at appropriate times. For all her fatigue, she sat erect and very much awake. The traffic on the highway was sparse, but regular. Her feeling of security had vanished with the heat of Valentina's kitchen. Out in all this morning brightness, out in this forbidding countryside she knew nothing about, so far from safety on the map of Russia in her mind, she was quite afraid.

But they saw no one who threatened them. There was little to see but dirty patches of earth and muddy snow; bare trees, birch trees, and pines; occasional streams; and the long empty road. After an hour or so, she let him have the vodka bottle and crumpled against the corner of the cab, falling immediately asleep.

He seemed to awaken her an instant later, though opening her eyes she saw they were in a much different place.

"Checkpoint coming up," he said. "You must get in back."

"Will there be trouble? You know I have no internal passport."

"No. Easy checkpoint. I know this road well. They will not look in back. But you must get in there."

He helped her, but with more interest in grabbing a feel of her backside than in preventing injury, for she scraped and bloodied her knee again on the tailgate. The truck was carrying crates wrapped in burlap. She climbed over them and dropped out of sight beyond, sitting huddled in the darkness as he put the lumbering vehicle into gear again.

A short distance later, when he slowed, her pulse began to beat faster, hammering furiously by the time he stopped. All but holding her breath, she heard Pavl say good morning and then another voice respond with words she could not clearly discern. For a long terrifying moment, there was no sound at all, then the other spoke once more, very briefly. Pavl lurched the truck forward, rumbling up through the gears with no great haste. Except for her clumsy climb to the rear, there'd been no more inconvenience than at a change booth on the Connecticut Turnpike.

"*Zhenshchina,*" he called her. "Woman. Hurry."

"What?"

195

"Around bend is bad checkpoint. You must get out, *zhenshchina*. You must walk."

"Through checkpoint?"

"No, no. Go north here into woods. Walk kilometer, maybe. Then go west. Walk to river. Then follow river back to road. I wait by bridge. Go now. Hurry."

Standing on the road, watching as Pavl's truck noisily dwindled into the distance, she felt as though she'd been left on another planet. She bit down on her lip, holding back tears, and anger. Tatiana Romanov would have thought it divine deliverance to be able to stand free and alone on this road those many decades ago, no matter what dangers might still have awaited her.

Tatty leapt the shallow ditch at the side of the road and started into the woods, thinking how ridiculously visible she would be if she was still wearing her red coat, thinking of her friends so many thousands of miles away in New York, dining at the Edwardian Room. She trudged on, bending branches back from her path. Tatiana Romanov probably thought of friends in Paris.

Reaching the river, she slumped to the ground, leaning back against a tree, so exhausted she could have slept right there. How wonderfully easy to give up now. How perfectly right to do so. She had done nothing wrong. There had been nothing but wrong done to her. Privations, indignities, terrors, all unwarranted and unjust, heaped upon her by grim, squalid people in dutiful, national purpose. They had no right to do this to her. Not to a person like her. They must know that.

A large bird flew in swoops along the stream, lighting briefly on a branch, then darting away, so free.

They dared do it to her, all right. They dared do it to anyone. They had tried to murder the Pope. They slaughtered those airline passengers.

Pushing herself to her feet, she resumed her ordeal, following the river in the direction from which the bird had come, from which the bird had fled.

She was actually surprised to find Pavl's truck pulled off the road just a few yards past the bridge. He was putting papers and small personal possessions back into the glove compartment.

"They search everything," he said. "Very bad check-point." He pulled the bottle of vodka out from under the dashboard. "They search almost everything." He smiled, then pinched her thigh, painfully, and started the engine. She slid down in her seat, looking up and out the window at the tops of the trees. So many millions of Russian trees.

She took the bottle of vodka from him, and drank.

"We are almost to Smolensk," he said, as two army trucks rumbled by them from the other direction. "There I must leave you."

"What? You agreed!"

"*Nyet*. Valentina said you want to go to Minsk. I say only I give you ride. I do not say how far. I go only to Smolensk. My freight is for Smolensk. I cannot go farther."

"Why didn't you tell me? I paid you all that money."

"If I tell you, you might not come. You would pay me no money."

"You'll get not a kopeck more."

"I don't care. I like you. You are pretty little woman. I find you ride in Smolensk going west. You know anyone in Smolensk?"

"Is there a Smolensk Social Register?" she muttered to herself.

"What you say?"

"I know no one in Smolensk."

"If I cannot find you ride west, I find you place to stay night in Smolensk."

"*Spasibo*."

"Maybe I find you place to stay where I stay." He reached and pinched her again. He was steering the truck unsteadily. It was good that the vodka was all gone.

"I must get to Minsk."

"You could be nice to me. I have been very nice to you."

A large bus careened past them, swaying, and roared off down the road. Pavl was not driving fast. He was stroking her knee.

There were violent things she could do to stop this. Possibly, the threat of violent things would suffice. But she was afraid to try either. She was traveling toward safety, but, strangely, the farther they got from Moscow, the more insecure she felt. Pavl could cause her a lot of trouble if she displeased him. Anyone could cause her trouble.

She took his hand. "I like you, Pavl Andreyevich, but I cannot be nice to you—to any man—for several days. Do you understand me?"

He pondered this very seriously, then at last smiled, as though at a joke he had just come to appreciate. A very clever joke.

"Ha, ha. Pavl is going to Smolensk on wrong day." He began to laugh uproariously at this. The truck began to swerve.

Tatty closed her eyes. She would not worry about his driving. There seemed to be some divinity looking out for her.

As they approached the city, he had her sit on the floor out of sight. Her head kept banging sharply against the knob of the window crank in this position, but she endured. Her knee was a bloody mess. Taking off her gloves, she saw that she had broken off two fingernails, one torn so far back there was bleeding. In Manhattan, this would have been a major disaster.

Pavl looked down at her hands with much fascination. "You are Polish, *zhenshchina?* You say you are Polish?"

She nodded, then so did he. He didn't speak after that until they were well into Smolensk, and gritty brick building fronts were all to be seen when she looked up out the window.

When he finally stopped, dusk was gathering. They were parked in a dirt yard filled with piles of old metal and debris. There were no people in view. Beside the truck was a crude wooden shed with a small window.

"You are to wait in there," he said, a colder tone to his voice now. "If I can get to another driver, I will send him to you here. If not, I will come back and take you to place to stay."

"*Spasibo.*"

"I will need money to give to other driver. To make deal."

"How much?"

"Two hundred rubles."

"But that's what I gave you for this entire trip."

"One hundred is for other driver. One hundred is for me. For being so nice. I know you are in big trouble, *zhenshchina*. I take big risk."

She pulled some crumpled notes from her pocket. During one of the stays in the rear of Pavl's truck, she had used the time to carefully hide the bulk of her money in various parts of her clothing.

"And now I want to feel your breast."

"You what?"

"I want to feel your tit! That's all I will do!"

She bit her lip, to no point. She sighed, then opened her coat, unbuttoning her red silk blouse part way lest he tear it. Then she closed her eyes. He moved his rough hand over her skin with surprising gentleness, rubbing her nipple with his thumb.

"You said this was all you would do."

He pulled his hand away. "Yes, and now I have done it. Pavl Andreyevich Sanko has felt your tit. Very nice, but not so nice as Valentina. Now go. I will do as I promised."

The shack seemed to contain as much debris as the yard outside. She seated herself on the floor, leaning back against a huge pile of rags, hugging her knees, feeling very sorry for herself. Pavl was probably the most honest man she would encounter in this ordeal, and her best guess was that he would pocket the two hundred rubles and do nothing more to help her, considering himself a noble fellow for not having tipped off the police. If he did not come, if no one came, she would spend the night in this place, and tomorrow, she would just do her best. That was what the grand duchesses had done day after terrifying day: their best. While there was still a glimmer of light, she would start trying to memorize the list of names and addresses Spencer had given her, a list too sadly short.

When the door to the shed at last crashed open, it was

completely dark outside. She heard the chugging idle of a large truck engine, but could see little out the doorway because of the immensity of the man who stood in it. Though he was in silhouette, she could see that he wore a long, sleeveless coat over a heavy, old-fashioned jacket. His fur hat was high and thick, almost the headdress of some wild tribesman. He seemed altogether out of another century, a caravan man, or an overseer of serfs.

"You are woman who wants to go to Minsk?" His voice boomed like Ivan Rebroff's at its lowest octave.

"Yes," she said, rising.

"Give me five hundred rubles now or I leave you here for police to find, and kick in your head before I go."

"But . . ."

"Do not be stupid!"

She stepped to the doorway and its light, assembling the sum from her pockets. He snatched the money from her with one hand and shoved her out into the yard with the other, with such force she almost fell sprawling.

"Hurry! Is space for you in compartment under seat. Keep feet off battery or you will get shock."

It was the space of a coffin, for a small person.

"How long will I—"

"Shut up! Get in! You will get to Minsk."

She did, barely able to arrange herself comfortably before he slammed the seat bottom back into position again. Slamming the doors with equal violence, he heaved himself inside, causing one of the springs to press down against her scalp. With much clashing of gears and gunning of the engine, he got the big rig underway. By the time, as best Tatty could tell, they were out of the city, he had all that weight hurtling along quite rapidly.

Her comfort lasted only a few minutes. Pain began to gnaw at the bones and muscles of her shoulders, neck, and hip. She was beset by oily fumes from beneath and flatulence from the big man above. She was fiercely hungry. She was enraged. But she was learning to endure. She wept, but only with tears. No sound.

She could not calculate how much time or distance had passed when he finally liberated her and let her sit up on the seat beside him. Since leaving Smolensk they had made two brief stops, with only a few words exchanged between the driver and what Tatty had assumed were local militia. A third time, he had been compelled to shut down the engine and leave the truck. There had been a number of voices and people banging about in the cargo section of the truck. The passenger door had been opened and someone had carried out an examination of the glove compartment and cab. Tatty, biting her lip, had held her hand over her mouth to muffle her breathing. If she were religious, she wondered what she would have promised God to be spared. She promised nothing, but she had been spared.

"Where are we?" she asked, as the driver rumbled the truck back onto the highway again from where he had pulled off to free her from the compartment.

"We have passed from Moscow Military District to Byelorussia Military District," he said, gruffly. "We are on Warsaw-Moscow highway. Soon we cross Leningrad-Kiev highway at place called Orsha. There is hostelry there where we stay overnight."

He rubbed the back of his neck. In the dim light of the dashboard she could see that he had a face as massive as his body, with features in hugely similar proportion, but he seemed to have no eyes. She looked more closely. Though he otherwise appeared a European Russian, his eyes were oriental, two long slits.

"What is your name?" she asked. He became angry.

"Never mind my name! I do not want to know your name. You are only baggage. Special cargo. Big trouble. You pay me for trouble. I take you to Minsk. Now be quiet. Do not irritate me any further."

He smelled terribly, but by then, Tatty supposed, so did she.

There were a number of trucks parked around the hostelry at Orsha. The establishment consisted of a small refueling facility, a restaurant, and a long, sorry-looking barracks building. Tatty was thankful for the darkness. The place would look even more forbidding in daylight.

After dealing with the formalities in the office, the driver took her from the truck and through the shadows to the rear of the barracks building, yanking her along like a led calf. The door opened to a rude staircase and a dimly lit corridor above.

"Here no questions asked," he said, in what was as close as he could come to a whisper. "But you don't exist. *Ponimayu?* You are not to be seen."

She nodded. He enveloped her with his great arm and its overpowering odors, as though to persuade his fellow drivers she was merely some road tramp he had snatched up, and half dragged her up the stairs, not releasing her until they came to a door at the end of the hall.

"Is best they have," he said, opening the door to what looked like a furnished cell in Lubyanka. He pushed her inside and closed door behind them. "You sleep in corner. Bed is for me."

She had no interest in his bed. The only furnishing that attracted her was the chamber pot. She had come a long way from the Hamptons. The only self-indulgence allowed her now was going to the bathroom.

"I am going to restaurant," said the giant. "I bring you back food later." She nodded, meekly.

He was gone for two hours or more, and returned quite drunk. She wondered what volume of vodka it would take to make such a man that drunk. He had brought back a large bottle, but it didn't have much in it. She grimaced when she opened the crumpled paper parcel he dropped on the floor beside her. It contained a round of black bread and a lump of greasy, soiled cheese.

"I'm thirsty," she said, cautiously eyeing the vodka.

"I get you mineral water in morning," he said, going to the bed and lowering himself onto it with a great creak. He reached and turned out the small lamp on the table, the only light in the room. She could hear him drink. As her eyes adjusted, she could see him.

"You are sick?" he asked, after belching.

"What?"

"*Bolna.* Woman's trouble. Pavl said you have woman's trouble."

"Yes. Yes, I do."

He drank and belched again, then set the vodka on the

table. In a moment, he was snoring, as grotesquely as he did everything else. She had been aching for vodka for hours, but putting the slimy mouth of that bottle to her lips would be more than she could bear even now.

In the middle of the night, though, shivering and shaking in her wretched coat, she went up to the bottle and drank. She couldn't help it.

In the morning, he refused to buy her vodka from the restaurant, saying a drunken woman was trouble. But he did bring her a large bottle of mineral water and some decent food. She ate it with fingers revoltingly filthy, but ate it all.

He allowed her to ride on the seat instead of beneath it, but warned her to keep down. Traffic on the highway had increased. It occurred to Tatty that she could not recall the day of the week. His face had softened in daylight, making him seem almost human, but she was not going to provoke him with any question about the calendar. She would remain silent, as he wished.

Then she had to speak. Nature had inconvenienced her again.

He pulled off onto the gravel shoulder near some trees. She hurried off deep within them; leafless, they didn't provide much cover. She went about her business quickly, rising and turning to discover the giant not twenty feet distant, blithefully pissing all over a bush. Looking away, she hurried past him.

"Where in Minsk do you go?" he asked, after they had passed through a town called Borisov. She could not tell how much of his dark expression was hangover.

"I'm not sure."

"I have no time for driving all over Minsk. I have long drive yet to go after Minsk. I drop you at city center and go. Good riddance."

"Where are you going after Minsk?"

"I go to Warsaw." He smiled, proudly, revealing a missing molar. "I am long-haul driver. I once drive to Vladivostok."

"I'm going beyond Minsk also. I would like to go to Warsaw. May I go with you?"

He scowled. "*Nyet.* Impossible. Transport person without passport across Soviet frontier? I am in very big trouble. They take driver's license, send me to work camp. Depending on who you are, I could get shot."

"Warsaw is where I'm going. I'm Polish."

"You are not Polish. You are not Russian, but you are not Polish." She froze. "I think you are maybe Lithuanian. Not Polish."

"How close can you get me to Poland?"

He scowled, but this time in thought. "Brest. Is at Soviet-Polish border. I could take you to Brest. But I want more money. Taking you so close to border is very dangerous. I want much more money."

"Another five hundred rubles?"

"More than that. How much have you?"

"I will pay you five hundred more rubles and one hundred in American currency."

"You have American dollars?"

"I have one-hundred-dollar American bill."

He beamed, and slapped her leg. "For that, Viktor Feodorovich Kolshov will take you to Brest. I also buy you vodka."

In his new amiable phase, he proved worthy of his word. He bought her Stolichnaya, got them through Minsk without pause or incident, and pursued the highway beyond with great enthusiasm. She thought she might yet persuade him to take her across the border to Warsaw. Certainly she was not feeling the spurious elation she had upon escaping the Kremlin walls, but her dread and anxiety were easing. Unlike the Romanov girls as they were dragged off into the hostile vastness of Siberia, it was her sense at last that she was actually moving nearer to safety, that she might actually succeed.

Kolshov seemed happy, too. He sang, and picked at his ears.

The early Russian dusk had come and turned to night when he finally pulled off the road. They had just passed a sign saying BREST, 18 KM, making Tatty fearful he was going to dump her here in these woods and make her walk the rest of the way, but he kept driving, arriving finally at another hostelry. Their quarters this time were much less crude and shabby, but similar in dimension and furnishings. She would spend another night on the floor.

He invited her to share the bed. He had brought her back hot food and another bottle of vodka from the restaurant. Both had made her feel fairly cheery and cozy, but not that cozy. She declined sweetly, reminding him in her best Russian of her woman's problem. Her Russian had come back to her so fully that she could speak in subtleties now. This language that had for so long been only an unwanted vestige of her childhood had become a vital resource. After this, she must cherish it and speak it often, in gratitude, for it was saving her life.

Leaving him to grunt and stare at her from the bed, she rolled over on the floor and closed her eyes. As she had the last two nights, she pretended she was lying in the hard sand of the beach at East Hampton. She could almost hear the waves. Other sounds intruded, Kolshov taking off his clothes for the night. Soon he would be asleep. Soon it would be morning. Soon she would be in Poland, then home. The warmth of spring and summer would come, and we shall all go to the seashore.

He pulled her up and threw her onto the bed as he might a log into a fire. He was completely naked, glistening with sweat, his face half angry, half calculating. He hit her a numbing blow on the side of the face and yanked up her skirt, tearing back her pantyhose.

"You lie, *gospozha!* You have no woman's sickness. I watch you in trees this morning. You lie!"

Swearing, he struck her again, and ripped open her blouse. She tore at his face, ripping flesh with her fingernails. Once more he bashed her, nearly knocking her out. She lay reeling, as he pulled at her coat, finally jerking it, her suit jacket, and her blouse off in a single violent motion and throwing her over onto her stomach. As he reached to roll her back again, she turned and hit him hard in the nose with the flat of her hand. He paused, startled, as blood flowed down over his mouth, then went after her again, hitting her ribs, seizing the waistband of her skirt and pulling, ripping, falling back against the wall as it came free. He seemed dazed. Her brassiere had somehow come loose in the struggle and, except for her boots and the shredded remnants of her pantyhose, she was entirely naked. She had a moment's chance to get past him and out the door, but to what end? Where could she go like this?

He regained his senses, and stood over her now. Despite the pain she had inflicted, the great slavering beast was beginning to have an erection. She thought of poor wretched Jack Spencer, and his pain. Spreading her legs now, bending her knees as though she was submitting and preparing to receive him, she waited until Kolshov moved closer, then shot out her right leg, smashing into his genitals with her boot. He shrieked thunderously and stumbled backward. Sitting up, she kicked at him again, this time striking a less wounding blow. He slid to the floor, clutching himself, his face full of fury. She hurried from the bed back to the table on the other side of the room. There were angry shouts somewhere in the building, but no one seemed to be coming to the door.

The lout was sitting atop all of her clothes. The pistol was in the pocket of her coat. If she had it in her hand she would kill him, notwithstanding that the gunshot would bring everyone in the hostelry at a run.

Groaning, whimpering like some injured animal, he got to his knees, and then staggered to his feet.

"You will suffer for what you have done to Viktor Feodorovich Kolshov!" he said. "You think you are hurt now, *zhenshchina?* I am going to smash your pretty face to bloody garbage! You will not live much longer, *zhenshchina.*" He gathered up her clothes and dropped them on the bed. "But first we must find out things about you. I think you are very rich woman. You wear expensive ring, Western clothes. You give me hundred-dollar American bill. I think you have much money, *zhenshchina.*" He stuck a hand into a pocket of her coat. As he bent over to look at the wad of currency he thus retrieved, she did as instinct commanded and snatched up one of the vodka

206

bottles, rushing up and cracking it so hard over his skull that it broke.

If it had contained more vodka, it might have killed him. He slid to his knees but, struggling, rose again. She clawed at the side of his face with the broken remains, but he rose too quickly and she caught him instead in the chest. Raging, he knocked the bottle out of her hand and sent it crashing against the wall. As he recovered his balance for a final lunge, she kicked him again in the groin with the fullest possible swing of her leg. He fell forward, wailing. She needed a final weapon, but not the gun. She went to the small chair and, finding a strength in her arms she could not possibly have imagined there, hit him over the head with it—once, twice, three times. His body flattened, and he fell silent. Whether she had killed him or only rendered him unconscious, she did not know, or care.

She could not wait now even to catch her breath. Amazed to find buttons still on her suit jacket and coat, she dressed as best she could, tearing off the strips of pantyhose that hung from her boot tops. Making certain of all her belongings, she took one of the bottles of vodka and left. The corridor, for all that shouting, was empty. The night outside was very cold.

The vodka kept her going. Exhausted again, hungry again, in increasing pain from the truck driver's beating, suffering bitterly from her lack of underwear, she plodded along the Brest highway as though through a terrible dream. Occasionally, a tiny set of headlights would prick the darkness in the distance, or she'd hear the dull rumble of a vehicle far behind her. Each time, she'd stumble off into the brush, woods, or frozen fields to the side, then stumble back. The Polish border was not much further away. Thoughts of Jack Spencer forced her ahead, because he had cast her adrift, because she was going to survive despite him. Thoughts of Ramsey Saylor kept her moving as well.

Because she was going to kill him.

The grand duchesses were put away each night with armed Cheka seated just outside their open door. Here was Tatty, alone in the dead of night, still free.

When dawn came quickly, her pace increased, but it became more difficult to detect the approach of vehicles in time. Woods were sparse here, and one could see seemingly for miles. She took to scurrying twenty or thirty yards off the road and just dropping in the snow.

As she did so for perhaps the twentieth time, something disturbed her about the sound of the truck that approached from behind. It was too familiar. She lifted her head from the snow just in time to see Kolshov's huge rig come slowly by and stop on the shoulder, idling with cloudy spasms of exhaust. She reached into her pocket for her pistol.

He rolled down the passenger window. His face looked discolored and there was a bandage around his massive head.

"You will die very soon now, *zhenshchina!* Viktor Feodorovich Kolshov will see to it!"

As he pulled away, she got to her feet and began to run from the road. She would follow the line of the highway into Brest, but at a distance. It was slower going in the snow, but it could not be helped.

A stream too wide to cross halted her three or four kilometers later, making her turn back toward the road. She had not gone five steps when she saw that it made no difference, that nothing could make any difference to her now. There were two trucks stopped on the highway, brownish-green with military markings. Men with rifles were moving toward her through the snow. She took a drink of vodka. It would be her last.

They took her to what appeared to be a country militia or military police station not far from the outskirts of Brest. Two other small military trucks were parked in the graveled yard, plus Kolshov's rig. He stood by the entrance of the building with a sergeant and spat on her as they dragged her inside.

She was thrust into a wooden chair by a desk, her head snapping back against the wall. A young officer behind the desk asked her several questions—what was her name, where was she going, where had she come from? She only glared sullenly. When she refused to respond to the third

208

round of the questions, the young man gestured to the two who had brought her in. She was taken to the rear, stripped of all her clothing, and made to stand with hands against the brick wall while they searched her vaginal and anal cavities, using a flashlight. Then she was dragged into a small cell and dumped on the bare cot that was its only furnishing. Speaking her first words to them, she asked for a blanket. They brought her instead a towel. It was grimy and damp, and too small to do anything with but drape over her shoulders.

The Princess Irina. Throughout her flight she had been comparing herself to the grand duchesses when it should have been to Mathilde's cousin, the Princess Irina, the ballet dancer who had tried to escape the 1917 terror by reaching Poland, and had failed. Peasants had found her naked, bullet-ridden body in the river. Where would they find Tatty's?

She lay down upon the cot, pulling the towel down to cover her hips. She would sleep. For now, it was almost as good as death.

A deafening burst of gunfire snapped her awake. Into her mind flickered the image of the Romanovs meeting their end in the Ekaterinburg cellar, and her eyes opened in full expectation of seeing men there with pistols, shooting her.

But they opened to an empty cell. The gunfire was elsewhere in the police station, and outside. Then it abruptly ceased, leaving a silence as overwhelming as had been the shattering noise. There came shouts, running footsteps, and someone barking orders. A moment later, her cell door opened and a man in a black overcoat and hat stepped in, carrying her clothes. He set them down beside her on the cot, then said, "Get dressed. Is necessary you hurry."

The police station had become a charnel house. Everyone she remembered being in it was dead, their bodies flung and splayed grotesquely among overturned furniture, bullet holes and blood everywhere. Outside lay the body of the truck driver Kolshov. He had been shot in many places, but also the face. She went to the wall and vomited. The czar and his family must have died like that. That could have been the Grand Duchess Tatiana's face.

When she recovered, another man in a dark overcoat was settling a still-smoking automatic into Kolshov's arms. There were two others in civilian clothes moving around the yard, and two civilian cars parked on the gravel. The man who had released her from the cell now pulled her arm, firmly but gently. He took her to one of the cars and opened the trunk.

"Get in, *pozhaluista.*" She did so without question, with his assistance. "You are comfortable?"

"Yes." It was a horrible lie.

He slammed down the trunk lid. A moment later, the car was speeding away. They drove a considerable distance, stopped in one place for perhaps fifteen minutes with the engine running, roared off again following a route with many turns, passed near a railroad, and then accelerated onto a highway or country road that enabled them to drive very fast. In the darkness, all she could see was the giant's face. When they stopped this time, the driver opened the trunk immediately. The light came as a blessing.

"You are to do exactly as I say," he said, as she stepped onto the ground. "Nothing else. Do not try to run away. Only safety for you is in doing exactly as I say."

She nodded. The man did not have a friendly face. In a few minutes, she could be dead.

"Go through trees." He pointed east, to where the morning sun had risen into a broken overcast, its rays lighting individual trunks and branches among the forest of stark silhouettes. "Go directly across for half a kilometer until you come to a road. You will see two black cars, small one in front, large one in back, stopped on road. If there is no other traffic in view, run to large black car and get in. Take this with you and give to person in car."

He handed her a briefcase with a combination lock. She clutched it to her chest as a schoolgirl might her books.

"Go now. Hurry!"

She wanted to run, but hadn't the strength. Slipping and sliding in the snow, she moved as quickly as she could, not even pausing to look back as she heard the car drive away behind her. For all his helpfulness, he was not a man she wished to ever see again.

Though she had tried to keep the rays of sunlight coming from the same portion of the sky, her clumsy progress took her obliquely askew. She emerged from the woods some distance from the cars, which were parked on the shoulder with engines running. As she at last drew near them, she saw that the long one in back had dark curtains drawn across the side windows in the rear, rather like a hearse. Pausing to take a deep breath, as she might before attempting a high dive or some other risky stunt, she darted to the car's side and snapped open the door, climbing hurriedly within. For a startling moment the limousine's lone passenger looked to be Griuchinov.

He was not, of course. He was merely of Griuchinov's age and hair coloring, and shared the dead man's fondness for the color black. His coat was extremely expensive-looking, but black. His suit and vest were the same hue, as was his tie, and he wore a black homburg, a hat she'd not seen except in old photographs. His face was thin and his features most un-Russian, as were the metal-framed eyeglasses set on his long, thin nose. He smoked an American cigarette in a holder and wore a shirt with a collar too large for his thin neck, a style doubtless copied from Andropov. He did not speak, but the moment she closed the door behind her both cars sped away.

"General Badim?"

"Do not speak my name. Not again."

Frightened, she said nothing.

They moved at great speed even as they entered Brest. Both cars had special red flags flying from their front fenders and they occasioned much respect. Peeking out through an opening of the curtain, Tatty saw a militiaman on the street corner snap to attention as they passed.

"*Nyet,*" said the man, with a gesture at the curtain.

She dropped her hand at once, and turned to him, but he said nothing more. Smoking in silence again, he stared straight ahead.

Hurrying through the little city, they came to a sizable

array of railroad tracks, crossing them by means of a high bridge. A short ways farther, they turned to follow a large barge canal, crossing it on a lower span with a drawbridge at the center. A short stretch of open countryside followed, on the other side of which was a high tower and what proved to be a military checkpoint. She could see only out the front windshield, but there appeared to be many soldiers. She lifted her head to see better.

"Down." He spoke softly but harshly. She obeyed, dropping down onto the seat just as she saw the barrier gate fly up. The two cars approached without slowing and sped through, the first car honking irritably as though dissatisfied with the barrier operator's slow response.

"You may sit up now," said the man in the homburg. "Now you are in Poland."

She pushed herself upright. Sure enough. A roadside sign flashed by and it was in Polish.

"Are you going to kill me?"

He switched to English. His grammar was slightly off, but his pronunciation was beautiful.

"I was friend of Griuchinov," he said. She looked startled, and then afraid.

"No, *dochka*. Be calm. I know what happened in apartments of Council of Ministers. All that happened."

"How did you know I was in the police station?"

"*Dochka*. I have known where you were from very beginning."

He took the briefcase from her and removed his glove to work the combination. When it opened, he pulled on the glove again, then reached inside and removed her pistol. He took out the clip, checking to see that the chamber was clear, then handed both parts to her.

"This must stay with you," he said. She put the two pieces into separate pockets as he reached again and took out Jack Spencer's press card, shaking his head somewhat sadly. Next he handed her the red and gold czarist pin.

"You offended many people with this," he said. "An antique design but manufacture is very new." He frowned. "I do not know who would want to manufacture something so odious nowadays. This, however, is very old." He held up the grand duke's emerald ring that the military police had nearly broken her finger in taking off. "Also very Russian. If it belongs to nobility, should be in Soviet museum. If belong to you, you are fortunate and wealthy woman."

She accepted it without comment. He reached for the last time, taking out a thick fold of currency and closing the briefcase. He counted out her American dollars carefully, placing the small stack in her hand, and then counted out the rubles, but put those in his pocket. Taking out a large black leather wallet, he pulled another kind of currency from its folds, handing her a carefully calculated amount.

"Polish zlotys," he said. "Is illegal to take rubles out of Soviet Union."

"You're going to set me free?"

They left the highway they'd been traveling, bouncing onto a side road that led into another and much thicker forest.

"Yes, of course. But you must go. You have friends in Poland." He said it as much as statement as question.

"I know of some."

"They can adequately assist you, arrange for your departure?"

"That's what I've been told."

"Say nothing more of them."

Slowing, they turned from the country road onto a rough logging trail, bouncing to a halt deep within the trees. A small brown van was parked a few yards away. He looked at his watch, a handsome silver one of Western manufacture.

"Will be quiet in Poland, very stable in Poland, for at least forty-eight hours. You understand? Will be especially quiet in Gdansk. Very unusual for Gdansk. You know my meaning?"

"I'm very grateful."

He looked at his watch again. "Driver in van will take you where you must go. Is less than two hundred kilometers to Warsaw. Find your friends. Avoid all soldiers, Polish or Soviet. Go now." He reached across her to open her door.

"Thank you," she said.

He smiled, grimly. "Go now. Find refuge. Do not ever come back. You may never return to Russia. Good-bye."

As she stepped outside and turned to shut the door, she saw that he was staring ahead again, wreathed in cigarette smoke and his own thoughts. As she started to climb into the rear of the brown van, the two black cars, wheels spinning, accelerated out of the logging cut in reverse, swerved back up on the country road, and were gone. A bird flew across the cut, calling shrilly. The van driver closed the rear door in her face, locking it.

She gave the van driver only the name of the street she wanted in Warsaw, not the number. He drove to within a block of it, having waited until darkness fell to do so, pulling into an ancient alleyway traversed by arches. In the shadows of one, he set her free.

The address Spencer had given her was that of a small, narrow house. He would doubtless be amazed that she had lived to use it. She was surprised that it was a house instead of an apartment building. Jack's friend must be of some consequence.

The van driver had warned her of the curfew. She could not stand out in the doorway for long. She rapped the iron knocker twice, somewhat timidly, then chided herself. In Poland, that was no way to get a door to open. She began pounding on it with great thuds, ignoring the pain it brought to her battered hand.

It opened a bit, revealing the face of a small dark-haired woman with a lovely mouth and a sharp nose.

"Waldemar Jozef Rodnieski!" Tatty said.

The dark-haired woman's eyes widened, but she still said nothing.

"I come from Jack Spencer," Tatty said, more softly. "I need help."

The woman stepped back half a pace, but without invitation.

"Jack Spencer," Tatty said, lowering her voice. "Amer-

214

ican newspaperman. John A. Spencer. John August Spencer."

A hand reached from behind the door, opening it and pulling her inside with great force. Losing her balance, she crashed back against the hallway wall, hurting her shoulder. The man who had been standing behind the door slammed it shut, and shoved home the lock bolt. He looked at her intently. He was her height, or perhaps a bit shorter, handsome in an elfin way that belied his years, which were more than forty. He was slender, but muscular. He had a small face, too narrow for his mouth. A long, drooping mustache masked deep lines. His eyes, exactly the color of his dark brown, too long hair, were quick and intelligent, almost merry beneath quizzical eyebrows that resembled inverted Vs.

"You have come to the most watched house in all Warsaw, woman," he said in English. Not thinking, she had addressed them in Russian.

"I'm sorry," she said, speaking English now herself. She pulled Spencer's press ID from her pocket and gave it to him. "Jack said you . . ." Her voice trailed off. She glanced at the dark-haired woman, whose eyes were much more friendly now.

Rodnieski studied the press card with great care, then returned it. "From where do you come, woman?"

"From Moscow. I am in trouble. I need to get to the West."

"How did you get here?"

"Money. I bought friends. I bought rides. I walked. I ran." She gestured at her dirty, tattered clothing.

"How did you cross the border?"

"In a car. A man who took all my rubles. I still have money." She took out her roll of Polish notes. "I can give you Polish money."

He put his hand over hers and gently pushed it away.

"For Jack Spencer," he said, "I would do anything." He studied her face. "You are girlfriend?"

"I am his sister-in-law."

His seriousness vanished. He took her in his arms and hugged her tightly, reminding her suddenly of a diminutive Polish writer who had pursued her for a summer in the Hamptons.

"We will help you, sister of Jack Spencer. It is very difficult now in Poland, but we are getting people out. We will get you out." He grinned. "But first we must give you thorough cleaning. You smell too much of Russia. Sabina will draw you a bath. You are in Poland now."

Before stepping into the tub, steeling herself, she turned to the bathroom mirror, sadly transfixed by what she saw. Her face was mottled with bruises, dirt, and dried blood. Her lips were chapped and bleeding, her hair a filthy tangle. No wonder Rodnieski's wife had looked at her so strangely.

There were bruises on her side and her breast, and long scratches on both thighs. She possibly had broken a rib. Lowering herself painfully into the hot bath, she leaned back and closed her eyes. It would take a very long time for the hatred to dissipate that she felt toward so many men, though one of them, through some act of generosity to these Polish people, had made it possible for her now to survive. She wondered what a man like Jack Spencer could possibly have done to warrant the fierce loyalty the Rodnieskis displayed. Perhaps he had just given them money.

She sat up and began to scrub almost savagely at the dirt, as though she could wash away with it the last few weeks of her life, wash away all her memories of John A. Spencer. Ramsey Saylor she would remember.

12

Waldemar Jozef Rodnieski got it all wrong. She tried to impress upon him the need for haste. She talked of Gdansk as though a godlike Jack Spencer had commanded her to go there. She intimated a knowledge of great and secret matters beyond his ken though not too forcefully, fearing he might respond with a line of inquisition that would lead to the old man in the black homburg.

He would have none of her wishes. He talked volubly, angrily, endlessly of Jaruzelski's suppressions, of mass arrests, of crackdowns in Gdansk. He said she must remain in his house for several days, until the situation was exactly right. He liked her suggestion about trying an Icelandic ship. The Russians tended to treat them as innocents, he said. Iceland, though a member of NATO, had a strong Communist Party, so he could get her aboard an Icelandic boat easy—though she might have to go back into the Soviet Union.

He visited her several times a day, twice suggesting that they sleep together. She declined with strong references to her familial relationship with Spencer. When he waved those aside, she cited her injuries. He accepted that. He made her accept an elaborate escape scheme, which included her traveling within a crate two hundred and sixty kilometers to Kaliningrad. Rodnieski said he had a Polish girlfriend whose Russian husband was a port official at Kaliningrad, which was just the other side of the Polish border due north of Warsaw. Difficulties could be eased. The money she had would help, though he himself would not take a zloty.

No. All he wanted was her flesh. She wondered if he was so loyal to Spencer only because Jack had provided him with women. But he was a very nice man, and an important one. People from both the defunct Solidarity and the Polish government came to the house and treated him with great deference.

She remained in his house eight days. As she feared, when the forty-eight hours passed, security tightened throughout Poland, especially along the Soviet border. Rodnieski told of widespread arrests in Gdansk, Warsaw, and Cracow. Word came of a massacre at a police station near Brest. It was blamed on black marketeers, but Jaruzelski's security police took the view that the Polish underground, such as it was, might be involved. They shot a man in Lublin, Rodnieski said.

Tatty said nothing of what she knew. She concentrated on getting well and feigning continued infirmity. It became apparent she had not broken a rib but she pretended that she had. He made no more advances upon her, but clearly found her refusal very frustrating. Because of this, not to speak of boredom and the paranoia bred by remaining behind the Iron Curtain, she longed to be gone.

He came to agree. An Icelandic refrigeration ship that had been in dangerous Gdansk was now in less dangerous Kaliningrad. The police crackdown in Poland was intensifying. Having kept her in his home for her own safety, Rodnieski now wanted her out for the sake of his. Arrangements were made, arrangements that required most of her remaining money. The Icelandic captain agreed, though with some reservation, to take her aboard as a cabin boy whose name had inadvertently been left off the ship's manifest; he had been relieved to hear she was very blond and had blue-gray eyes, and could easily pass for Icelandic.

All this Rodnieski told her when he came home one

night and informed her they would have to leave within the hour. He provided her with workman's clothes and a floppy fisherman's cap in which to hide her hair.

Rodnieski, posing as a driver's helper, accompanied her on the journey, in the beginning riding with her in the back of the truck with all the crates. Room had been made in one for her, but, once clear of Warsaw, it seemed safe enough for her to ride outside of it until they neared the border.

Not long out of Warsaw they crossed a border that wasn't there.

"Before World War II, this was Prussia. East Prussia," Rodnieski said. "The Russians treated these people more terribly than any other. Stalin understood Nazis but was paranoid about Prussian military. All Prussian people who were not killed were moved away. Most of Prussia was given to Poland. A small part was kept by Soviets. Kaliningrad, where we go, was Prussian city of Königsberg."

Tatty remembered the old duke's telling her that her connection with the Romanovs was not through her Russian relations but Prussian ones: she was in some part Prussian. This dark countryside they were now traversing was to a degree an ancestral homeland, home to ancestors she knew nothing about. Royalty? Peasantry? All family trees were rooted in peasantry. She wondered if in some recent century there had been an ancestor, a blond Prussian girl, much like her. Someone who lived in this strange, flat country, who loved it well.

Now it was owned and inhabited by Poles. Prussians, Poles, Russians, Balts, fighting and fornicating with each other over all those centuries, armies and camp followers surging back and forth until they all became the same people. Yet how they still fought and hated each other.

"Why are you so loyal to Jack Spencer?" she said, abruptly.

Rodnieski did not speak for a very long time, then cocked his head to one side and smiled.

"I was in great danger once. Jack Spencer saved me from it."

"How?"

"He killed a man."

"Jack killed someone? In a fight?"

"No." He frowned. "You are leaving Poland. You must never speak of this. I would not want him to know I told you."

She nodded.

"The Jaruzelski government knows I still deal with the Solidarity people but they think I do it as their agent. There was a police spy who found proof that it was other way around. He put me under arrest and was taking me away. Jack hit him over the head. He broke the man's skull. We threw the body under a train."

Tatty sat in silence, listening to the thumps and groans of the speeding truck, taking her north to the sea, but back into Russia.

"But I would be Jack Spencer's friend even if that had not happened. He was very good to us."

After crossing what she was told was the Lyna River, she was put back in her crate. The truck was stopped several times, once for a very long time, but no one disturbed the cargo. Perhaps the likelihood of Poles fleeing into the Soviet Union was too small. Perhaps Rodnieski knew best after all, though she still suspected she might now be in West Germany if she had gotten to Gdansk within that first forty-eight-hour period.

She could tell when they reached the city, sensing as soon as they reached the dockyard area that they were in trouble. The driver suddenly accelerated, swerving and weaving the truck violently around what Tatty guessed were other vehicles or stacks of cargo. All at once the truck lurched to a stop. She heard someone tumble into the rear and begin to jab open the lid of the crate with a small crowbar.

"Tatiana," said Rodnieski, prying it open. "You must find the ship yourself. It is the *Rän.* The *Rän.*" He pulled her out of the crate and all but threw her out of the truck. "Go, Tatiana! Good luck! Good-bye!" He pounded twice on the wall of the truck and the driver jammed it into gear,

jerking forward. She could hear a siren, and running footsteps. In the distance was a searchlight.

She ducked into the stacks of cargo, listening as the
truck drove away rapidly. Soon she could not hear it anymore. Then she heard gunshots.

The Icelandic captain was gruff and unfriendly, obviously displeased with her presence and very worried about
the disturbances in the dockyard. A police car with
searchlight blazing had pulled into view just as she had
scrambled up the *Rän*'s gangway.

"You must go below at once to the galley. If they come
aboard, I want you working. Cleaning fish. Peeling potatoes. I'm not going to hide you. If they were to search the
ship and find you, we could all go to Polish jail. You are
here as a cabin boy. If they discover you, I will admit to
taking you aboard without papers but will say nothing else
about you. I can do nothing more for you. I did not expect
all this trouble." He turned to his second officer, a young
man with a full black beard. "Take her below."

The young officer was very nice. He explained that, in
Norse mythology, Rän was the name of the wife of Aegir,
god of the sea. All the waves of the sea were her children.
It was a lucky ship, he said. She recalled the sailors' superstition about a woman aboard a ship.

The cook was an old but pleasant man. The young officer spoke to him quite firmly in Icelandic; Tatty hoped
he was telling him to be considerate to her. There was an
actual cabin boy, a teenage youth with long dark hair who
looked more feminine than she did.

"It will be a long, hard night for you," the officer said.
"We are not to get underway until late tomorrow morning. We must onload more cargo."

When he left, the cook smiled, patted the top of her fisherman's cap, and proceeded to give her every dirty job he
could find. He and the feminine boy sat and watched her
work through much of the night.

Parties of men came aboard twice, but no one came
below.

Once they had left the harbor, the captain became friendlier, but he refused to free her from her galley rigors. "You come aboard as cabin boy, you stay cabin boy." But she was given increasing amounts of time for herself, much of which she spent out on the deck, in good weather, standing up at the prow, staring at the sea, in her mind's eye at all the seas toward which they sailed. She spent much of Christmas Day this way. As the Danish coast receded behind them in the winter dusk, Russia seemed thousands and thousands of miles away, the Romanovs merely names in books. She would cleanse herself of all this. She would return to life.

After they had passed the northern capes of Scotland and were on their final course setting for Iceland, the captain relented and freed her from her galley duties entirely. For her last night, he even provided her with a large, well-furnished cabin on the deck level just beneath his, quarters comparable to a stateroom on the old liners. With her sailor's clothes off, lying between the clean, crisp sheets with her eyes closed, she could have been in her Fifty-seventh Street apartment, but for the ship's roll. It amazed her that she could ever have been unhappy in that place, such a short time ago.

The captain, almost fatherly at the end, walked her up from the Reykjavik docks to the taxi stand near the little Icelandic capital's central square. Sverrir Axelsson's apartment was in what amounted to suburbs, though they were quite near. She had no idea whether he was home, but in Reykjavik, with only eighty-five thousand people, there were so few places he could be.

He was at home, coming to the door in stocking feet, sleeves rolled up and tie askew, a glass of beer in his hand. He was probably Spencer's age or older, but he looked almost boyish and something of a scholar, pale blue eyes behind thick black-rimmed glasses. Jack had said he was a columnist for Iceland's largest afternoon newspaper.

He appeared curious, and perhaps a little irritated. It was very late in the evening.

"Are you Sverrir Axelsson?"

"Yes. What is it?"

222

"My name is Tatiana Chase. I am the sister-in-law of Jack Spencer. He said you were his friend. He said I should come to you. I'm in trouble."

Curiosity and irritation abruptly vanished, replaced by horror, disbelief, and then confusion.

"Don't you believe me?"

"Oh yes, yes. But you are supposed to be dead. Jack Spencer has been arrested in Moscow for your murder."

She quickly pushed past him into the flat, as though escaping some dark, unseen danger in the street. They stood awkwardly in the hallway for a moment, then he took her coat and cap, and ushered her into a very modern, very expensively furnished living room. She sat down on a leather couch, still feeling awkward, not to speak of frightened and confused.

He studied her face. "Yes, it's you. Just like the newspaper picture. I'll show you. But first, would you like something to drink? A beer? Or something stronger? Almost anything is stronger than Icelandic beer."

"Something very strong, please."

"Brennivin, then. Our local firewater. There is nothing stronger than our Icelandic brennivin. We call it 'Black Death.'"

He brought her a clear liquid in a tall, narrow Scandinavian glass. He was right about its murderous strength. She coughed. She had had nothing alcoholic to drink since leaving the Rodnieskis' house, and poor Waldemar had been very sparing with his vodka.

He then gave her a newspaper called *Kvoldbladid,* turning it to page four. There was a small wire service photo of her, a theatrical agency portrait probably six years old. She could not read the short, accompanying article, which was in Icelandic.

"I'm sorry," he said. "Wait. There was also a story in the Paris *International Herald Tribune.*"

It was very short, but told her all she needed to know. American news correspondent John Spencer had been arrested by Moscow police for the murder of Broadway actress Tatty Chase, who was on a tour of the Soviet Union. Spencer, the estranged husband of Miss Chase's sister, surrendered to police and confessed to beating her to death and throwing her body in the Moscow River. He blamed an alcoholic rage. Though her purse, hat, and coat were recovered, her body was not found. The article concluded with a reference to her last starring Broadway role, three years before.

She set the paper down, drank the strange liqueur, and then pressed her hands against her eyes. Jack Spencer was now in some basement cell in Lubyanka. He had done that for her. When she took her hands away, they were moist. She drank more, and asked for another.

"How did you get here?" he asked, as he poured it.

"On an Icelandic freighter. Jack suggested it, when he suggested that I might come to you. There were other things I could have done, but it worked out this way. I had gotten as far as Poland, and there was an Icelandic ship in Kaliningrad." He seated himself opposite her, looking very serious.

"What is this all about?"

She wondered how good a friend of Spencer's this Icelander was. She must presume a good one indeed, for Jack had sent her to him.

"It's about murder, Mr. Axelsson, but not mine. Some Soviets, some very nasty men, tried to implicate me in something very awful. Tried to set me up as a patsy. Jack rescued me. Well, he helped me get out of Moscow. I'd no idea he'd done this, too. I feel very bad about it. God, is there any other news of him?"

Axelsson shook his head. "It's been only a short while. I'm sure he's all right. For now. Tell me more of this."

Axelsson was a newspaperman. She had already told him too much.

"You shouldn't know any more, Mr. Axelsson. For my sake, for Jack's. For your own sake. People have been killed. Do you understand?"

He smiled, but it was a serious expression.

"In Iceland, we are not very familiar with such things."

She drank. For the first time, she realized there was music playing, a woman's voice, very sad and lonely, singing in Icelandic. A book, what looked like an American war novel, entitled *Fragments* lay open and face down on the coffee table. She glanced about the room. There was nothing to indicate if he was married. She wondered where she would sleep. She wondered if he would allow her to stay.

"You must excuse me. I'm a little distraught. I feel sort of helpless at this point. Getting from Moscow, I've gone from man to man. I mean, it's been like chapters in a book, but now I've come to the last of them. I don't know what to do."

"What to do? That's simple enough. You go to the American embassy. It's not two miles from here. They will inform the Russians you are alive and Jack will be let go."

As simple as that. End of story. Except that Ramsey Saylor and Marshal Kuznetzov would not want it to be the end of the story. They would write new chapters, their own chapters, ending with her and Jack Spencer dead. Jack might never get out of Russia alive.

She wondered why Badim had not simply had her killed, had her remains liquefied in some acid, as the Cheka butchers had failed to do successfully with the Romanovs. The man in black must kill people every day, bureaucratically, signing papers. That would have foiled Kuznetzov thoroughly.

Axelsson's apartment was well heated, but she felt cold to the bone.

"Miss Chase?"

"I'm sorry. I'm afraid my mind's a mess."

"Do you want to go to the American embassy?"

"No. I don't want anyone to know where I am, that I'm alive. Not yet. I'm afraid of what might happen to me."

"And Jack?"

"And of what might happen to Jack."

"What do you want to do? My wife is visiting her parents in Norway. You could stay here, for a few days."

"No. I want to get back to the United States. The answer to my problems is in the United States."

"Have you money for air fare?"

She smiled, embarrassed. "I have two hundred fifty-six dollars. Also Jack's press ID and some jewelry. That's all

I have. My ring, I think, is fairly valuable. If necessary, I could . . ."

He shook his head. "Flying is perhaps not a good idea. Our customs people are, well, they can be tolerant on occasion, if necessary. But in New York, I don't know how you could get through. It's worse in Chicago. Icelandair doesn't fly anywhere else."

"What do I do?" She made a weak joke. "Your train and bus service is so poor."

He smiled politely. "I think you must go to sea again. Because of our winter storms, some of our trawlermen work the Grand Banks this time of year. One could take you to Canada. Is it easy to cross the U.S.–Canadian border?"

"Yes. Especially into New England."

"The fishermen would do it for nothing, for the sister-in-law of Jack Spencer."

And whom had Jack killed in befriending the Icelanders? "The captain who brought me here never heard of him."

"A freighterman, no. But some fishermen revere him. He covered our 1975–1976 cod war with Britain. The damned British were destroying our export fishing industry, and that's the basis of our economy. Jack sailed in our coast guard boats against the British. He got into a couple of the fights. He wrote a series of articles taking our side, warning that we would throw NATO out of the big air base at Keflavik if the British did not withdraw from our fishing grounds. A short time after they appeared, the American government ordered the British to stop it and they did. Everyone in Iceland who knows of this is most respectful of Jack Spencer."

And so she'd be handed off to another man, someone else obligated to Jack. In Canada, at least, at last, she'd be on her own.

"All right. I'll do it."

"It will be a very rough voyage."

"I'll make it."

"It will take a long time."

"That's all right. I have time. I need time."

And every day she took, Jack Spencer spent in some wretched Russian cell.

With her mind full of fresh and unwanted memories of mountainous waves, seasickness, the stench of fish and diesel fumes, and the coarse talk and behavior of open-sea fishermen, Tatty set foot on the North American continent near a fishing town called Port Dufferin up the Nova Scotia coast from Halifax. Three days later she crossed the U.S.–Canadian border on a Greyhound bus near St. Albans, Vermont. She reached Bridgeport, Connecticut, that night.

It was raining when she came up the street. The neighborhood was quite old and the houses very modest, but they were well kept up. She found the one with the right number and, joyously, saw lights in the window. Hesitating, Tatty glanced up and down the street, so paranoid that she even looked for shadowy figures in the nearby cars. She was being ridiculous. This was sanctuary. She rang the bell.

Gwen showed neither shock, horror, disbelief, nor confusion; only inordinate happiness. Her eyes shining, she threw her arms around her friend, hugging and kissing her almost ferociously, saying over and over, "I knew you weren't dead. I knew you weren't dead. I knew you'd come back to me."

PART THREE

In revenge and in love woman is more barbarous than man.

—Friedrich Wilhelm Nietzsche

13

Gwen had a small spinet piano, and it became the saving grace of Tatty's confinement. For much of every day while Gwen was away teaching school, Tatty sat plinking and plunking at it until, after a few weeks, despite the piano's being slightly out of tune, her playing sounded respectable again. As her roughened, battered hands healed, she improved still further. This day she felt confident enough to attempt her favorite pieces, all by Erik Satie, his three *Gymnopédies* and the five *Gnossiennes*. Her favorite of all, the *Cinquième Gnossienne,* she did over and over until she could lift her mind from the keys and just listen to the music, her left hand producing the slow, somber chords, her right the strong dramatic notes and trilling interludes and responses. The strange, melancholy timing of the piece had always made it seem, surreally, a man and woman dancing in a large, elegant room at twilight, yet a dance so slow and macabre that they might be dead.

Her fingers lingering, she finished the last notes, and once more found she wanted to hear them again. She suppressed this desire, gently closing the lid. It was her rule never to drink while playing, and now, under new rules, it was past noon, and time to drink. She had abandoned vodka; she thought she would never drink it again. At great expense on her small teacher's salary, Gwen kept her supplied with Scotch. If this odd exile in her own country kept on much longer, Tatty would have her switch to cheaper bourbon, or gin. She didn't mind martinis, even in the winter's cold.

She filled half a large glass with Johnnie Walker Red, added a small amount of water from the kitchen tap, and then went to a window that overlooked the surprisingly expansive rear yard. It was snowing again. That first night, the dull, steady rain had changed to snow and become something magical, falling heavily and clinging to every surface of roof, branch, and twig, until everything in view was wonderfully white.

Gwen had put her arm around her and said encouragingly, "It's a whole new world, beginning again."

But there were reminders enough of Tatty's old world. She sought them out. More than she indulged herself with the piano, she read. Gwen already took *The New York Times*. Tatty, promising to pay her back, had her subscribe as well to the *Washington Post* and several magazines that dealt with foreign affairs, anything that might contain news of developments in Russia.

Gwen had saved the stories that had appeared in the *Times* about her. The first, announcing her murder and Jack's confession and arrest, had begun on page one, though at the bottom of the page. Those that followed, stating basically that nothing had changed, that her body had not been found and that Jack had not yet been brought to trial, dwindled in size and crept deeper and deeper into the paper. The last one, a statement from her stepfather that the family was not satisfied she was actually dead, had appeared in the "People in the News" column.

There was news of another kind as well. The same edition that first announced her murder also carried the notice that Sid Greene's play starring the rock star was closing after only five performances. Curiously, the item brought Tatty her most cheering moment in weeks.

There was other news from Russia. Every day seemed to bring a story that the Soviet premier was still ailing—one day that he was in rapid decline, the next that he was showing improvement, the true nature of his ailment never authoritatively stated. Twice in these several winter weeks both the *Times* and the *Washington Post* had printed rumors that he had died, only to report him alive again a few days later.

Griuchinov's name appeared briefly in the *Times* dispatches, first in a Tass report announcing that he had become seriously ill, then as a mention in the stories about the ailing premier.

On Christmas Day, the old deputy premier, Feliks Alekseyevich Popov, died, or so Tass reported. Shortly after, it was announced that Popov had been replaced as deputy premier by Defense Minister Kuznetzov, who would retain his military offices.

Tatty pressed her face against the window pane. She gathered that the old man in the black car was still alive, but he had not prospered. He was probably in deep political trouble. It perhaps should be no wonder he had not killed her. She was his only witness to the fact that Kuznetzov was a murderer.

What she could not comprehend was why he had let her go, indeed, helped her to escape; why he hadn't snatched her away to some secret protective custody in the Urals or Siberia?

But, for the KGB, a safer place would be much farther away, in another country, even the United States. Perhaps especially the United States.

Could the KGB now know she was here? Could they reach out and take her whenever they wished?

Standing with face pressed against the glass, watching the wind pile up snow against Gwen's small garage and the elm tree beside it, she could not answer that question with any certainty. She could not say there was not some Russian, or some Russian operative like Ramsey, watching her at this very moment.

Russian. She was Russian. She was talking about Soviets. Communists. Scum.

The next morning's *Times* had said that the new deputy premier was coming to the United States in March, to address the United Nations General Assembly. The good

Marshal Kuznetzov was going to enhance his foreign policy credentials, an initiative necessary for an heir to the Soviet throne.

Tatty left the window and refilled her glass. She turned the radio to a station playing "beautiful music," and began to read a copy of *The New Yorker,* devouring every distracting word.

Gwen returned a short time after four in the afternoon, as she always did. She set down her notebook and papers, fetched Tatty another drink, and went into the kitchen to prepare dinner. She came out of the kitchen intermittently, to talk of her day, chattering on through dinner and as they did the dishes. She loved most to talk of early times, not of their marriages or the summer in the Hamptons, never of any of the men they knew, but of when they were young girls together, playmates, schoolgirls, college roommates.

Some of it Tatty enjoyed; much of it she did not. Gwen was almost giddy. Tatty had never seen her so happy.

Tonight she would not be.

As Gwen prepared to go to bed, leaving Tatty to her whisky, her newspapers, her deep and intense thoughts, Tatty, slightly tipsy, said, "Gwen. I'm going to try to reach my family. Probably tomorrow night."

Gwen sank against the door frame, her expression slack, her hands somewhat aflutter. She had been such a beautiful girl in her youth. Now just thirty, she was becoming thin and pale, too old for her years, hell-bent for scrawny, spinsterish middle age. David Paget could have—should have—spared her that.

"Tatty, from all that you've said, it could be very dangerous."

Tatty had told her nothing more than that she and Jack Spencer had gotten into serious trouble in Russia and that Jack was in jail and she was in danger. Tatty wondered why Gwen hadn't pressed her further. She suspected that Gwen wanted to do nothing that would jeopardize this windfall of a circumstance. A life of her and Tatty, no one else.

"You've been wonderful," Tatty said. "But it can't go

234

on much longer this way. You go to school. I play the piano. I read. I get drunk. You come home, we eat, you go to bed. I stay up and drink some more. This might seem paradise to some, even to you, but it's been too long. I've got to resolve this, Gwen. I can't just become a recluse stuck away in Bridgeport, Connecticut. I've just been resting up, Gwen. Now I want to fight back."

Gwen pushed her hair back from her forehead, then sat on the arm of an upholstered chair.

"Whatever you need to do, Tatty." She spoke almost in a whimper. Her eyes were glassy with tears.

Tatty set down her glass.

"Gwen. I still may have to stay here for some time. And you've been extraordinarily kind. But I have to get started now. And the place I must start first is with my family. I have to try to reach my stepfather, my sister."

"I know, but it could be very dangerous, Tatty. You said so."

"I'll be very careful. If I could, I'd like to borrow your car."

"Of course. Anything."

She came and kissed Tatty on the cheek, then hurried off to bed.

When Tatty finally went to bed, close to two A.M., she stopped for a long time in the bathroom to look at herself in the mirror above the washbasin. Gwen had said something that first night, that Tatty had changed, that her face had gone hard. When Tatty pressed her on this, Gwen recanted, saying she meant merely that Tatty looked tired.

Tatty stared intently at the blond woman in the mirror, studying, examining her face inch by inch, following each line and curve of bone, finding only herself. There was some bitterness there, yes; some sadness, and much seriousness. But she hadn't changed. The cuts had healed and the bruises had faded. She had not aged. Only a few weeks had passed. She was still only thirty.

She leaned closer, this time concentrating on her blue-gray eyes, the color of the Arctic sea.

Now she saw what Gwen had seen. She had killed a second man. Another man had died violently in front of her.

Men had died all around her. Because of her, more men might be dying still. The woman Raya might be dying.

It showed in her eyes.

She left the next night after dinner, borrowing not only Gwen's old battered Volkswagen but some money and Gwen's driver's license as well. Except for the difference in hair color, they resembled each other enough for the license to suffice as identification should some policeman stop her in the darkness. Gwen insisted she take it. Tatty did, though it was not policemen she was worried about.

It was a cold night, with flurries of blowing snow. It wasn't far to Greenwich on the Connecticut Turnpike, but Tatty took a longer route, following Highway 25 up to the Merritt Parkway and using that instead, approaching her stepfather's estate from the open countryside up near Westchester. Once off the parkway, she stayed on back roads, traversing a reservoir she remembered as a necking spot, finding remembered trees and houses at the end of remembered curves in the road. She had come this way with Ramsey once, during their second affair, shortly after she was married. She was still in her early twenties then, but had fancied herself much the worldly woman, sophisticated in the brittle fashion of Noel Coward heroines. As Ramsey had always been that way, their affair proceeded famously. There was a television film the two of them had seen, *Edward and Mrs. Simpson*. Ramsey had always made much of his resemblance to Edward VIII, contending that if he had been blond they would have looked like brothers. Though he complained that the actor playing Edward did not look like him, that he was "unbeautiful," Ramsey was transfixed by every aspect of the king's behavior. Tatty was much more taken with the music, all period pieces from the time. She had bought a record of the sound track, and learned all the songs.

She memorized all the lyrics, practiced them in the English style of the thirties. She had sung them with Ramsey in the car, which came to irritate him; and sung them by herself, driving at high speeds the country roads of Connecticut and Westchester.

236

She sang them again now.

> *"I've danced with a man,*
> *who's danced with a girl,*
> *who'd danced with the Prince of Wales . . ."*

She sang them again, twice, three times, then fell silent. She was on her road, a road she had traveled home, schoolgirl, debutante, Smith girl, and woman, thousands of times.

Turning off onto a side road perhaps a half-mile short of her stepfather's drive, she followed it up and over a hill, pulling off into a wooded area just shy of a small stone bridge over a frozen creek. She had walked this creek many times. She knew every bend.

Gwen had lent her an old pair of boots. They were a bit tight in the calves, but Tatty was grateful for them. There was old, deep snow on the hillside leading up to the house's rear lawn. She crept up through the vineyard, past the old stables, up along the steep grade of the strange swimming pool that fell from a depth of one foot to fifteen in only sixty feet. She remembered it all so well: the tool shed, the formal gardens to the right, the large garage and its apartments for servants above to the left.

There were many lights on in the house. Tatty waited, then darted across the expanse of snow and winter grass. She heard nothing, except perhaps an unseen animal in the brush beyond the formal garden. She could hear a television set on somewhere within the house. The back door, leading to the large pantry and kitchen, was locked. She moved around to the left, to the cellar window whose latch had never been properly repaired, through which the teen-aged Tatty had gained surreptitious entrance to the house at all hours of the night.

It still opened. She pulled it up and slipped inside, dropping to the cellar floor with little noise, just like always. There were things in her way she couldn't possibly have remembered, but she felt her way around them, at last reaching the wooden stairs, climbing them quietly. She

237

pushed the door open, entering the dark kitchen, hearing the television quite clearly.

It was Chesley there, in the sitting room off the main hall, watching one of those sex-laden prime time soap operas. Chesley had a master's degree in fine arts, had had a book published on the history of windows, and had for two years held a job as curator of a Connecticut art museum.

Tatty had been offered a role in one of those television series, and had declined. It was her first and last encounter with Hollywood. The producer, an extraordinarily unpleasant man, had asked her out to his beach house in Malibu to discuss it. She didn't go.

Tatty stepped into the room, moving silently to where Chesley was curled up in a thick, antique unpholstered chair, eating caviar on melba toast and drinking white wine resting in an ice bucket. Tatty grasped her shoulder and kissed the top of her head, her lips touching the silken finish of Chesley's rich, dark hair.

"What? Tatty? Tatty?" Chesley untangled her legs and quickly rose, turning to face Tatty directly. "Good God. Tatty! It is you. My God, it's you. Why aren't you dead?"

"I'm just not."

Chesley, totally without expression, stared at her, her dark eyes full and hesitant. Then at once she stepped forward and pulled Tatty to her, holding her more tightly than Tatty remembered her ever doing before. She kissed Tatty's cheek, a glancing brush of lips, perfectly soft despite the harsh winter weather.

Then she stepped back. Taking her wine glass, she snapped off the television, and seated herself on one of the four couches in the room, as though Tatty had been away only a few days.

Chesley was thirty-six. She looked the same as she had at twenty-five, as she would at forty-five. She was so utterly perfect, a "great beauty" in every best sense of the term. In the England of Sargent, Whistler, Oscar Wilde, and such philanderers as Edward VII, she would have been one of the "PBs"—"professional beauties." She could have been mistress to anyone in the realm, including and especially the king. Except that Chesley was not a woman to be mistress to anyone.

"What's happened? Why did the *Times* say you were dead? Why is Jack in jail?"

Tatty went to the fire. She had borrowed one of Gwen's dresses, and it was too thin for the cold.

"I got into trouble in Russia, very serious trouble. It was worth my life to get out of there, and I did so only with great difficulty. Jack's claiming that he murdered me was his way of helping. It was a lot of help. It was a very selfless, brave thing for him to do. I was surprised."

"Surprised?"

"Never mind. Is Daddy home?"

A dark look passed over Chesley's face, but was quickly gone. When Tatty and her mother had first entered the Chase household, she had taken to calling her stepfather Daddy Chase. He had insisted on just Daddy. Chesley had been greatly irritated.

"He's in the city, working late. He's been spending much of his time trying to get friends in the State Department to do something about you, to find out what happened to you. He never believed you were dead. He never believed Jack would have done you any harm, though I did."

Their eyes held each other, then Chesley looked away.

"What do you mean?" Tatty said.

"There's a lot you don't know about Jack."

Tatty could have said the same thing to Chesley, but did not. Here was Chesley eating caviar and watching television soap operas. There was Jack in some cold stone cell, or worse.

"May I have something to drink, Chesley? Not wine. Gin, or Scotch. I'm so very cold, and my nerves are shot. I've had a very bad time."

Chesley started to ring for a servant, but Tatty shook her head violently. With a shrug, Chesley went out of the room, returning shortly afterward with a bottle of her father's rare unblended Scotch and a crystal glass.

"What sort of trouble did you get into, in Russia?" she asked, as Tatty drank.

"I suppose you could say it was political. I don't want to tell you any more. I don't want to involve you or Daddy in this in any way. It could be very dangerous for you. I mean that. Some people have been killed."

Chesley made a face. "Really, now."

"Yes, really, Chesley. I killed one of them myself."

They stared at each other. This time Chesley did not look away. "How did you get involved in it? You went there for some theatrical reason. A one-woman show."

"It has to do with my ancestors. My Russian grandmother's people."

"Meaning?"

"The Romanov connection."

Chesley again made a face, and gave her bitterest laugh. "That's twaddle, Tatty."

"I beg your pardon?"

"Twaddle. Or, as Jack would put it, a lot of crap. I'm sorry, but I've never believed it. I've never had reason to believe it. If you don't know it by now, I'm sorry, but you ought to. Your grandmother was a fraud, my dear. She was a very attractive and extraordinary woman. And I don't doubt her people were well off. But royalty? Nobility? Please, Tatty. If there had been as many Russian 'nobles' in St. Petersburg as there are now in Westchester, the Communists wouldn't have stood a chance."

"Why are you saying this to me? Why now?"

"Because it's true. It was bad enough your grandmother and mother traipsing through the house babbling endlessly in Russian; but the pretension, Tatty. All that condescension to us mere mortals. It got a bit thick, especially when it turned out to be so phony."

Tatty turned and looked into the fire. If someone didn't attend to it shortly, it would begin to go out. But she didn't want to touch it, or anything else in the house. Chesley was making her feel very much the stranger.

"I've seen proof of what she said."

"Please, Tatty. After your mother died, Daddy tried to find out everything he could, to settle her affairs. There was nothing, Tatty, not even a birth certificate. Not for your grandmother, not for your mother. It wasn't easy making you the sole heir to your grandfather Hoops's estate. Daddy even had trouble getting you your father's military benefits. He had to go to Washington and work through friends."

Tatty stared at the fading flames, and drank the rest of her whisky. Finally, she went to where Chesley had put the bottle on the coffee table and refilled the glass, this time all the way.

"You're going to end up like your mother if you keep drinking like that."

"You're being very unpleasant, Chesley."

"I'm sorry. My own nerves are in a bad way. It's not been easy, with Daddy so upset. With Christopher asking about his father. And now you suddenly appear, breaking into the house."

"It's my house, too, damn it!"

"Yes. I know. Daddy made you that promise. But you've been with us so little in recent years. You've become such a Long Island person. All those strange people."

Tatty took a sip of her drink. "Look, Chesley. We can find a better time to play out all these old grudges, all this sibling rivalry. At the moment, I need help. I'm in a great deal of trouble. I'm going to need some money."

Chesley frowned, as though Tatty's grandmother, mother, and Tatty herself were always sponging money from the almighty Chases.

"I mean my own money! I just can't get to it myself, right now. I'm sure there are people looking for me right now. Some very bad people. If you can advance me something, I'll repay you from one of my accounts as soon as I can."

"Anything, Tatty. You know that."

"Five thousand dollars. I'm going to need at least that."

Chesley frowned again. Tatty almost threw her glass into that oh-so-perfect face. She wondered how that porcelain visage would look with cuts and bruises, wondered how Chesley would have fared with that drunken, savage Russian giant.

"I'll do my best, Tatty."

"Look, if I could get to my safe-deposit box, I'd happily sign over all my negotiable securities to you. I'd sign over my apartment, my jewelry. But I don't dare do that." She sipped the whisky, remembered something. "Do you have the combination to Daddy's study safe? I did, but I've forgotten it."

"Yes. But why? What do you want?"

"There's that bond, the ten-thousand-dollar bond he gave us jointly when I came into the family. He said it would bind us together. A joke. I guess. I'll sign it and you can do with it what you want. Just have five thousand dollars for me."

"When?"

"Tomorrow. Please. I have to get moving."

"All right. When shall we meet? Where?"

"At six P.M. Some place in Westchester. In Pound Ridge, in the bar of Emily Shaw's Inn."

"You really don't have to sign that bond, Tatty. You know that."

"Chesley. Just get it. Hurry. I've been here too long. This is one place where they could be looking for me."

Chesley did as she was asked, leaving the room as regally as a prima ballerina leaving the stage. When she returned, Tatty had poured a third glass of whisky, and was drinking it fast. Setting the glass down clumsily, she signed the bond in the appropriate places, predating the entry to a time prior to her departure for Russia.

"It's yours, Chesley. We are no longer bound."

With that, Chesley began to cry. She pulled Tatty to her again. "I'm sorry, Tatty. I'm so damned sorry. I've been horrid tonight. It's been a horrid time. I . . ."

Tatty patted her back, then pushed her gently away, looking into Chesley's tearful eyes.

"Chesley. Tell Daddy I'm alive, that I'm all right. That I love him and can't wait to see him again. But tell him to call off the dogs. I'll get myself out of this, but I need as little attention drawn to me as possible, especially in Washington. Tell him that, please."

"I will." Her eyes were terribly cloudy. In distress, she

had lost control over her face. It now showed some of her age. "Tatty. How is Jack?"

Tatty stepped completely away from her now. This time it was she who averted her gaze.

"Chesley. I don't think you will ever see Jack alive again, and I fear it's all because of me."

She left by the front door. It was brazen, perhaps foolish, but she was tired of all this craven skulking. No one had followed her. As she made her way along the roadside toward her car, she detected no one. To make absolutely sure, as she drove back toward Gwen's, she kept on past the Merritt Parkway, proceeding north all the way to Westchester, taking side and back roads and at one point turning off her headlights and driving in the glow of returning moonlight, ducking off suddenly into a remembered cul de sac in the woods. No one passed by, with lights on or off.

She turned her own back on, reversing her direction and driving fast. Contrary to her expectations, to her logic, her confrontation with Chesley had not depressed her. She felt liberated, enlarged by it. She had moved beyond the reach of Chesley's scorn and domination. She no longer felt meek and ashamed about her sexual encounter with Jack Spencer in Moscow. It now seemed fitting and proper, altogether logical. Perhaps, were it not for poor Jack's miserable situation, an occasion for rejoicing. She and Chesley were now certifiably equals.

She kept thinking of Ramsey and that Prince of Wales film; those songs, that illicit summer. They knew from the beginning it would end. They had counted upon it.

A country club one night. The band knew some of those songs. Ramsey then bribed them to bring their memory to full color.

Ramsey had pressed his chest against her breasts, had brushed his lips against her cheek, had danced her near the open doors to the terrace.

The music ran thrillingly through her mind, memories of that passionate interlude mingling with cold lovely thoughts of how she would delight in one last dance with

Ramsey Saylor, at the end of which, like the black widow spider, she would kill him.

There were headlights steady in her rear view mirror. She let them stay there awhile, but at the next side road, she abruptly pulled off. The other car, a large station wagon, drove by without pause. Killing her own lights, Tatty turned around and pulled back onto the main highway, pursuing the station wagon with her own car in darkness. The other driver continued steadily on, his speed comfortably below the limit. As they neared the Merritt Parkway, she slowed to let him gain distance from her, then turned her lights back on as she ascended the entrance ramp.

It was becoming clear to her what she must do now, and the prospect of doing it made her at once sad, fearful, and excited. Gwen would not like it. Her family would not like it, but what family had she, really? Her father, mother, and grandmother were dead. Except for a few distant cousins in Massachusetts and Virginia, there was only her stepfather and Chesley. Daddy Chase loved her as dearly as she loved him, but that love had flourished only as compensation for the lack of family bond. As for Chesley, she was full of love, but had shared not a drop of it with anyone but a few men and her child. In a strange way that had mostly to do with Russia, she felt closest now to Jack Spencer.

She had driven away all thoughts of Russia as soon as she had gotten free of the place, but now they were returning. She was beginning to think of herself as Russian, almost as intensely as she had at Czarskoe Selo. Chesley's petty, cruel attempt at debunking notwithstanding, she was once again thinking of herself as Tatiana Alexandra Iovashchenko, cousin of czars. Could she become this? Was that wise? Whether it was or not, she could not remain Tatty Chase.

Gwen did not like it at all when Tatty informed her of her plans. She flew into a tearful rage, marching angrily about the room, flailing the air with her thin arms, screaming that Tatty was making an enormous mistake, that she was going to expose herself to great danger, for all practical purposes kill herself, for nothing. Gwen then collapsed in a chair, sobbing. She was providing a haven for Tatty, providing her with everything she needed. Tatty had been so wonderfully kind and generous for so many years, and now she was so happy to be able to pay her back, and Tatty was throwing that aside, rejecting her help, rejecting her. She sobbed until Tatty felt she must have expended her every tear, till Tatty could stand no more and went to the kitchen to pour herself a glassful of Scotch. When she returned, Gwen had largely recovered. She stood forlornly in the middle of the room, her arms slack at her side, her head held absurdly, like a martyr's at the stake. When she spoke, her voice was tremulous, and exaggeratedly tragic.

"You've absolutely made up your mind? You're going to leave? You're going to do this foolish thing?"

"Yes, Gwen. I absolutely must."

Gwen left the room without another word or look, whimpering all the way up the stairs. Tatty sat and drank, going to the piano finally to play Satie's *Fifth Gnossienne* again, to calm herself. When she was sure Gwen was asleep, she went to bed. She would have to get up early the next morning.

She fell asleep at once. She knew she would awaken at three or four in the morning and have to fight her way back to slumber, as alcoholics do. Her new plans must involve doing away with all this drink. She was very near to becoming her mother.

She awakened well before three. At first she thought it part of some dream, for she had been dreaming lately with such regularity, sexual dreams, with Jack, Ramsey, and the horrible Russian giant all interchangeable, all naked. There was now a naked body next to her, and a warm small hand reaching beneath her night-gown.

"Tatty. Dear, dear Tatty."

The hand touched her breast. Fury brought Tatty completely awake now, but she lay frozen, her anger silent, as helpless as she was raging.

"Tatty, Tatty. I love you so." There were kisses now. "I have loved you for so terribly long. I thought you understood that. I thought I'd made that known to you. So let me tell you now. I love you, love you, love you. You mustn't go. Dear Tatty. I can be so good to you."

There were kisses again, and the small hand moved down her belly.

Tatty struck with both knee and elbow, with as much violence as she had in her struggle with the giant Kolshov. Gwen was knocked from the bed, striking the floor and the bedside table with a simultaneous crash.

"No, goddamn it!" shouted Tatty. "I won't have it. I am not like that! I have never been like that! I won't let you do this to me! Damn you, Gwen!"

She calmed herself, letting her heaving breathing fall to sighs. Gwen made no sound. Alarmed, Tatty turned on the light. Gwen lay curled and huddled on the floor, her eyes open in the wild stare of some injured animal. A gash on the side of her head was turning her strawberry hair dark with the crimson of blood.

"Oh God, Gwen. I didn't mean for that to happen. I'm sorry."

She helped Gwen to her feet, then took her into the bathroom, washed out the cut, and applied antiseptic and a bandage to it. Gwen's right eye was swelling and what looked to be the beginning of a large bruise was forming on her hip.

"I'm so sorry, Gwen. You startled me in my sleep. I've just been through a lot. I . . ." She took Gwen by her thin shoulders and looked emphatically into her eyes. "Gwen, this is all for the best. It is probably a very good thing that each of us knows exactly how the other feels about this."

Gwen turned her head away.

"We can still be friends," Tatty said. "We've always been friends."

Gwen pulled herself away and walked into her darkened bedroom, not saying a word.

In the morning, Tatty was afraid Gwen would go back on her promise. Before the dreadful scene the night before, Gwen had said she would let her have her car for the day. If Tatty would drop her off at her school, she would get another teacher to drive her home in the afternoon. Gwen said nothing at all about this, about anything at all, eating her breakfast in silence, the flesh about her eye all purple and black.

After breakfast, Gwen came up and handed her the car keys, then started toward the door. When they reached her school, Gwen got out, still not having spoken a word, but paused before slamming shut the door.

"You'll come back tonight?"

"Yes," said Tatty. "In time for dinner. We can have a long talk. But I'll be leaving in the morning."

Gwen shut the door. Tatty watched her slender, tragic form until it disappeared into the school's main entrance, then slammed the car into gear and drove hurriedly away. She had awakened at daylight feeling sick and depressed, but that eased now with every mile that brought her closer to the state line and Westchester County, New York.

She had tied a scarf tightly about her head, much like an old Russian babushka, feeling sufficiently disguised upon arriving at the village of Braddock Wells. Driving swiftly through, she followed Pommel Ridge Road, slowing as she passed her grandmother's old house, still sad to see a stranger's cars in the drive. Turning onto the dirt road beyond, she found it frozen hard with winter. Speeding the Volkswagen past the old mill and across the stone bridge, she ground it into lower gear for its struggle up the hill. The old duke's great stone house was just as she remembered it, except there was no smoke from the chimneys, the windows were darkened, and there was a chain across the driveway.

Tatty parked in the gravel just in front, stepped over the chain, and trudged up the sloping drive. The duke could answer many questions, if he were still there. If he were not, many questions might still be answered, another way.

No one came to the door. She pounded on it, rang the bell, remembering that the aged man was hard of hearing. But no one came. No duke, no servants. Nothing. With a sigh of irritation, she left the front steps and went around to a window, peering within. The room was empty, devoid of furniture. She hurried past a long line of bushes and went to one of the windows of the library where she, the Grand Duke, and Ramsey had had drinks by the fire. It was empty; the furniture gone. For a frightening moment, she thought herself part of some particularly scary John Cheever story, but she quickly brought herself back to reality. She was merely caught up in one of Ramsey Saylor's more elaborate schemes. And that was scarier.

She had to make sure. She had plans to deal with Ramsey, but she was not going to accept her stepsister's disdainful dismissal of her heritage until she had made sure. Dead sure.

It required her talents as an actress. The role, she decided, would have to be that of a blasé, haughty, social-climbing Westchester housewife whose husband had almost but not quite the financial means to advance their social station by advancing their residential one. It meant filling out a card, going on at length about fictional family finances, looking through a large notebook of photographs and descriptions of properties on the market—including some Tatty recognized as belonging to families of friends—discussing some houses she had seen for sale in the vicinity of the village, and finally mentioning the one at the top of the hill on Old Tarleton Road that looked empty and deserted.

"Oh, I know the one you mean," said the real estate saleslady, an attractive, gray-haired woman of about fifty. "That's not on the market. It's been held in a private trust for years."

"Are you sure? I thought it was owned by some Russian. A General Suvorov."

"Let me check the computer."

They went to an inner recess that, in clashing contrast to the colonial furnishings of the outer office area, looked like the working area of a space station. The woman flicked the fingers of her hands over the keys rapidly.

"No. That property's been held in a private trust for years and years. No Suvorov. There was a Russian house nearer the village, on Pommel Ridge Road; the name was Iochenko or something. But it's owned now by somebody named Brady." She smiled, sweetly but professionally.

"You seem to be very interested in that old Tarleton Road house, but I'm sorry, it's just not for sale. If it were, I fear the price would be, well, prohibitive. It's the sort of place that will ultimately end up being bought by a religious order or sanitarium or something." Another sweet smile.

Tatty asked to look at something comparable but less expensive. The woman suggested she come in the next Saturday and she'd show her a few. Tatty nodded and hurried out; once in the cold, she realized her face was covered with perspiration.

She halted. She had to make perfectly, absolutely sure. She went into another real estate office on the other side of the Braddock Wells village green, and got more or less the same answer, with some amplification. The property was not only held in trust but was tied up in probate proceedings.

She drove aimlessly away into the winter afternoon in some despair, passing many remembered places, then with much purpose, passing many, many more, devoting the remainder of the day to a nostalgic perambulation.

All right. Once again, the perfect Chesley was perfectly right. She was no relation to the Romanovs. She was merely victim of Ramsey Saylor's clever exploitation of her credulity. Her grandmother's origins were probably as murky a mystery as Tatty had always felt them to be. All right, it was a fraud. She was no more Romanov royalty than she was a Chase.

But it didn't matter. Whatever she actually was, she could no longer be. She had to become something, someone, completely different. And fast. Dear Jack had been in Lubyanka far too long.

Tatty pulled into Emily Shaw's parking lot, handed over Gwen's old Volkswagen to the youthful attendant at the entrance, and hurried into the warmth inside. Chesley sat alone at a table near the fire, her beauty striking even in silhouette. Tatty touched her hand, in hopes they might recommence in a different mood than that in which they had parted. Her hopes were well founded. Chesley took her hand and gripped it warmly.

"I'm so sorry about last night," she said. "You took me

by surprise. I was feeling so much anger and resentment, toward you and Jack, for what you were doing to the family, putting me and Daddy through. He's overjoyed, by the way. It was all I could do to keep him from coming with me."

Tatty wished he had. She could in no way guarantee to herself that she would ever see him again.

"Did you bring the money?"

"Yes." Chesley's lips formed an embarrassed smile. "I didn't cash in the bond. Daddy was very upset at the idea. Instead he got you most of the cash he had in that little savings account he keeps in the bank in Greenwich. It comes to about seventy-eight hundred dollars. Will that do?"

"Yes. That's wonderful. Where is it?"

Chesley gestured at a small overnight bag on the floor beside her. "It's in there. I put in a few clothes as well. And your mail. Daddy's been collecting it from your apartment. I didn't put in all of it; just what looked personal or important. There's a slip from the post office, too. You have a registered letter waiting for you there."

The very last thing she needed at that point was a stack of mail addressed to Tatiana Chase. She would deal with it as quickly as possible. She would ignore the registered letter, having a very good idea who might have sent it, who might have someone waiting every day for her to pick it up. Clever, clever Ramsey.

Chesley was having a sweet Dubonnet. Tatty ordered a Manhattan. She had little time to linger and a great thirst for alcohol. Many in the room were looking at them; certainly all the men were. Here were what Jack had called the two best-looking women in New York, seated at the same table in this country village inn. They should have met in some gas station women's room, but Chesley would have hated that, and probably would have balked at it.

"What do you want to do about your apartment?"

"Keep up the rent, if you would. For a while. I'll get in touch with you about it. After a while."

Tatty's drink came and she sipped it gratefully. Perhaps

this was not a bad choice of rendezvous. They must look nothing more than a couple of Westchester ladies having a late afternoon drink, discussing their husbands, or their affairs.

"What are you going to do, Tatty?"

"I can't tell you. For one reason, I haven't figured it all out yet. For another, you and Daddy shouldn't know. I wasn't exaggerating about people getting killed."

"What more can we do to help you?"

"Nothing. Just stay out of it, and let everything quiet down. That will help me." She glanced at the door as a man entered; no one she knew. "And don't talk to, don't have anything to do with a swine named Ramsey Saylor."

"I remember him. A boy from Westchester. Harvard. One of your beaux." A more characteristic smile crept onto Tatty's face. "Several times."

"Don't let him near you. He's part of this, and very dangerous. I don't want to tell you anything more, but stay away from him."

Chesley nodded. She seemed at a loss for what next to say. Tatty feared she might lapse into that great forte of their class—small talk.

"What you said about my grandmother and mother, their origins," Tatty said. Chesley's face became blank. "I was very angry about that at first, but thinking about it today, well, I have reason to believe you may well be right."

She hadn't fully concluded that yet. She was fishing, provoking. But Chesley did not respond in the way Tatty hoped she would. She only patted Tatty's hand, recanting nothing—sympathetic and affectionate, almost smug. Her belief in the nobility of the Iovashchenkos had been Tatty's only bolster of self-respect when she and her mother had come to the Chase household. Now it was gone. She finished her drink.

"I must go."

Chesley quickly drank her Dubonnet.

"No, Chesley. You stay awhile. Let me just sort of vanish." She rose, and kissed her stepsister's forehead. "I love you. I love Daddy. I'll find a way to get in touch. Good-bye."

She picked up the overnight bag and the purse Gwen had loaned her, and walked away. The parking attendant took too long getting her car, making her nervous. She almost didn't tip him, but quickly realized that would make her stick in his mind. She didn't want to be remembered by anyone.

Once gone from the place, taking a series of back roads she knew east across the line into Connecticut, she felt an extraordinary sense of freedom. She was escaping herself. Her life had not been quite so pointless and meaningless as Ramsey had insisted, but he had now irrevocably driven her from it. Tatty Chase could no longer be, nor could Tatiana Iovashchenko. She was free to become whoever she wished.

There was a car behind her, but she was not going to worry about it. There were too many cars for her to become paranoid about each one.

She could go to Canada, when this was done. She was very fond of Canada. Better, Australia or New Zealand, lovely places, and out of harm's way.

There would be one more night in Bridgeport, and then Tatty Chase would disappear.

There were no lights on in Gwen's house, but as she went to put the key in the front door, Tatty heard the radio playing quite loudly. If Gwen had not yet come home, there was no way the radio could have been turned on. If she had gone to bed, she would not have left it on, certainly not at such a volume. Perplexed, Tatty hesitated, then pushed open the door, eyes straining against the darkness, wincing at the din.

She called out Gwen's name. Hearing no answer, she shouted it out. The radio was insufferable. It was a wonder the neighbors hadn't called the police. She started toward the kitchen to turn it off, when her peripheral vision caught the movement. It was a strange motion, too high above the floor. Blinking in the dark, she peered more closely. It was the slow, profound spin of a mobile, such as one might see at the Museum of Modern Art, only this had no such metallic delicacy.

She quickly flicked on the hallway light, as she should have done from the first. Then she screamed.

Gwen was much as she had been at the conclusion of that living room scene, her arms slack at her sides, her legs akimbo, her head bent forward oddly. But she was hanging naked from a length of clothesline tied to the upstairs balustrade. Her eyes were not sad but madly strained and bulging. Her face was a puffy crimson, her mouth full of a ghastly purple tongue.

Tatty stood immobile, as she had when Griuchinov had pitched forward into the tray of ice. She didn't know what to do. The radio had to be turned off. Gwen had to be cut down. Tatty had to flee.

There was a note on the hall table. Tatty snatched it up. It was a sorrowful farewell, Gwen proclaiming her overwhelming love, and her utter inability to go on living without Tatty's love in return. It was the perfect suicide note, except for one small matter.

It was entirely in Tatty's handwriting.

14

Tatty ran to the kitchen, turned on the light, and snapped off the radio. She looked frantically about, and grabbed a carving knife, hurrying back to the hall. Scrambling up the stairs, she sawed frantically at the clothesline until it finally gave way, and Gwen's body fell to the floor with a horrible thump, landing in a tangle, her genitals exposed from the rear. Tatty rushed to her side, turning the body over to a more seemly pose, pointlessly loosening the cord around Gwen's neck, sick at the sight of the deep, ugly line it had cut into the flesh. She closed Gwen's staring eyes, then rose to go upstairs to get a blanket and cover the body. She stopped.

No. She must run now, just as she had run from the Kremlin. She had her small suitcase, the borrowed purse with all her other possessions, the keys to Gwen's car. Except for her collection of newspaper articles about events in Russia, there was nothing else of hers in the house. She had thrown out the clothes in which she had returned to America. Everything else she had used was Gwen's.

She jammed the spurious suicide note into her coat pocket, clicked off the hall light, and, with overnight bag and purse in hand, ran outside and down the front steps. Feeling a thousand eyes upon her, though she saw no faces in the windows across the street, she backed Gwen's Volkswagen out of the drive, and roared off, taking streets and a road that led north toward Danbury. In her panic, her intent was to keep driving all the way to Canada, but before long she thought better of it. Canada would mean no deliverance. Not yet. She needed help. She needed friends. Friends were in New York.

She left the car in a supermarket parking lot a few blocks from the commuter railroad station in suburban North White Plains. It was an hour-and-ten-minute wait, which passed slowly and horribly, her mind beset with images of Gwen's disfigured face and fears of what would happen next, perhaps at any moment. She wanted a drink.

Nothing did happen. She boarded the last car of the train and took the last seat in the rear, assured that everyone in front of her would be facing forward. When the train finally lurched under way, gathering speed for the short run to the city, she allowed herself to feel a little more secure, enough to take her eyes from the others in the car and open the little suitcase.

The money was there, nearly all of it in hundred-dollar bills. Remembering Russia, she rolled it tightly and quickly stuck it into the top of her bra and in her coat pockets. Chesley had also put in a nightgown, a pair of her Ferragamo shoes, one of her more expensive afternoon dresses, and, thoughtfully, several pairs of panty hose. As Tatty hadn't requested, her birth certificate was there. Angry, she took this as a snide gesture of Chesley's, but at length realized it was probably her stepfather's idea—and a good one. Though she'd legally taken the name Chase, her birth certificate was under the name of Shaw, her real father's name. She could use it to acquire a new passport, without attracting trouble. Here she'd so blithely decided upon Australia or New Zealand as her eventual haven, without stopping to think that her passport was in some Moscow police file.

The forward door to the car banged open. She looked up, her hand going instantly to the coat pocket in which she kept the pistol. Seeing it was only the conductor, wondering if she looked too fearful, she closed the lid of the suitcase and composed herself. When he finally reached her, she was able to say, "Grand Central, one way," almost nonchalantly. He lingered overlong after handing her her change and ticket, but she could only hope it was for the usual reason.

When he was gone again, she quickly went through the mail. The "important-looking" pieces proved to be mostly investment offers and charity requests, though there was an old letter from her tax lawyer advising her of a new change in the internal revenue code that would be of advantage to her. The "personal" ones were largely invitations to formal parties and theatrical previews. One, however, was from her ex-husband, asking if she would be willing to sell him her interest in the cottage they both still jointly owned in Chatham, on Cape Cod. She'd forgotten she still had it. She read on. He wanted it because he was remarrying. Well, hurray for him. The bride was no doubt the sort of Smith girl who'd be more than content with suburban Republican politics and the Junior League. She read further. Good God, he was marrying someone named Levatino.

There was another letter from an actor friend in London, who was writing to say he was in London, and an old one from Dexter Johns, proposing marriage.

The final piece of correspondence was a small, elegant card stuck in a side pocket of the bag. It said, "Remember that we love you, daughter, and will always be waiting." It was signed, "Daddy." After that, in her own hand, was Chesley's name.

Tatty shut the case and slipped it onto the seat beside her. She closed her eyes, but that did not hold back the tears. When they reached Grand Central, the conductor looked at her with some concern as she left the train.

Wiping her eyes, she passed through the gate into the terminal much as she had hundreds of times before. She could now be returning from just another visit to the country. It would be so easy to turn and walk out the Lexington Avenue exit, hail a cab, and return home to her apartment, there to watch the late news with a cozy drink and then go to bed.

But Tatty would not want to see what would be on the news that night.

She thought of stopping for a drink in the Oyster Bar, where she had met so many dates in her college days, preferring it to the Biltmore's silly "under the clock."

She should not go where she had ever been before. She should not be in this city. Yet she needed a drink. Good God, she caught herself thinking of going to the Algonquin.

She hurried up the ramp to Forty-second Street, settling finally on a grubby little Irish bar near Murray Hill, not far from the Morgan Library. It was fairly crowded, and the bartender was busy. She ordered a double Scotch on ice when he finally came, and when he went away again, she looked through Gwen's purse, taking the small amount of money that was there but leaving the driver's license and the few other items that were Gwen's.

The drink was not enough. She had another, quickly, then left. Passing a small alleyway, not dissimilar to the one she had hidden in in Moscow, she threw the purse into a pile of uncollected garbage, and hurried on. Heading west, Tatty crossed a stretch of Fifth Avenue she had paid little attention to in years before, startled to see an entire block of Korean storefronts. She kept on, into the darkness of the shabby side street, moving around sacks of garbage but remembering to stay close to the curb, away from the doorways. Reaching Herald Square, alarmed at its sleaziness—the bums, bag ladies, and winos, the hulking young men—she turned north on Sixth Avenue, walking quickly, almost at a run.

It was a puzzle. It was a game. How many people could Ramsey and the Russians have at their disposal? How many of her friends could they watch? Ramsey had not thought of Gwen but he had had someone at the Chase estate. He had someone, no doubt, at Tatty's Fifty-seventh Street apartment. Where else? Which of her friends would he choose? The likeliest? The least likely? He was more than clever. He was ingenious. She would have to avoid the obvious. She would have to avoid the ingenious.

The warmth and glow of the whiskies was wearing off.

Tears were returning, tears for Gwen, tears for Jack, tears for Chesley and Daddy Chase. Tears for herself. She was enveloped by layers of melancholy, helplessness, and paranoia. But inside her was still the anger. It kept her going, hurrying along, stumbling over broken pavement, dodging through traffic, until she finally found herself back in her own country, on Central Park South, the St. Moritz just down the street.

She looked diagonally across the park toward the Upper West Side, a neighborhood like all those south of 96th Street becoming rapidly expensive, but still with its grubby, grimy sections.

She rolled her dice. Ramsey had already rolled his.

Cyril Greene, barefoot, wearing jeans and a T-shirt, unshaven, though his red mustache was gone, opened his door an inch or two on its chain. He seemed not to recognize her. The television set was on. He smelled of beer, and something else. Marijuana.

"It's me, Cyril. Tatty Chase. I need your help."

His expression focused. "Tatty Chase." He shook his head.

"Please, let me in."

He shook his head again, then he produced his obnoxious old grin. He let her stand there a few seconds more. After another shake of the head, he pushed the door forward and slipped off the chain, opening the door wide and ushering her inside like the maître d' of a grand restaurant.

Closing the door behind her, he leaned back against it and stood there, arms folded.

"Amazing."

"Yes. I'm alive."

"That's not amazing. What's amazing is that you've come here, that you're standing here in the middle of Chez Greene. Chez Cyril Greene. Chez Sid would not be amazing."

"It would tonight." She looked around. The place smelled rancid and stale. There were several empty cans of beer standing on the principal table and a pile of clothing in the corner. Four doors opened onto the room: the one through which she had entered, one leading to a kitch-

258

enette, another to the bathroom, and a very wide one behind which was likely to be found a Murphy bed. "Cyril, I need a place to stay."

"You certainly must. Desperately, for you to be here."

"I'm in trouble."

"Obviously."

"Just for tonight. I'll be gone tomorrow. The day after at the latest. I need sleep and some food. I have to figure out what to do next. I'll be no trouble."

"Tatty, by any calculation, I must owe you six hundred consecutive days in the Helmsley Palace's best suite." He shoved an old *New York Times* off what appeared to be his best chair, and motioned her to it, seating himself on a sagging couch. She kept her eyes from his bare feet.

"I need a drink," she said.

"I have beer."

"Anything."

"You don't drink beer, do you? I have some wine, but it's rather old, and there isn't much of it."

"Anything."

"Wait. I've a pint of Rock 'n' Rye. I keep it just for when I have a cold. I've had a few sniffles, lately, but nothing—"

"I'll take it. In a large glass, straight. Please."

He leaned forward, hesitating. She quickly reached into her coat and pulled a bill free from the roll. It was a hundred. She set it on the water-stained table next to her.

"Buy another. And with the change, get me a large bottle of something decent."

She pressed the heels of her hands against her temples. She was shaking.

"Tatty, are you all right?"

"I'm fine!"

She moved her hands again to cover her eyes. Tears were streaming from them.

"Tatty?"

"Just get me the damned drink, will you?"

She heard his bare feet crossing the wooden floor to the kitchenette. Taking her hands away, she found herself looking at a Seurat print on the dingy wall opposite. She folded her arms, hugging herself, still trembling. She was wearing one of Gwen's dresses and it was making her ill. She caught herself searching frantically over it, as though for bloodstains. Her mind was unraveling. She could not think.

Cyril slammed a cabinet. "Do you want to tell me what's going on?"

"No," she said. It wasn't true. She wanted to tell him, someone, anyone, everything—to let it all pour out, purge herself of the entire horror, and then crawl into someone's arms, even Cyril's, for a protective embrace of warmth and comfort.

"Did your brother-in-law really try to murder you?"

"No."

"Was someone murdered?"

"I don't want to tell you anything, Cyril. Not a word. I haven't told anyone anything. I'm just in trouble, and I need your help. Just for tonight. Please."

"Sure, Tatty. Anything." He came back with a jelly glass filled to the brim with the candied whiskey. "Here. It's all I've got."

She drank, gratefully and desperately. He eyed the hundred-dollar-bill.

"Take it, Cyril. It's yours. I'll give you more if you want it. Money's not among my worries."

"I'm really not a sponge, Tatty. People are unfair about that. I've just had a long streak of bad luck."

"I understand that, Cyril. You have no idea how much I do. It's just that money is not what matters right now. What matters is that I'd like a bottle of good Scotch and something decent to eat. I have money for me and for you. The money is unimportant." She hugged herself still closer, spilling some of her drink.

"Would you like a blanket?"

"No. That's all right." She took another large swallow. It was awful, but wonderful. She had drunk quite a lot of Rock 'n' Rye as a college girl.

"That *Times* story about you was the biggest thing to happen to our crowd in years," he said. She resented the "our crowd," but fought herself. It was despicable of her to resent anything about Cyril Greene at this juncture. And "our crowd" had always included a large number of people like Cyril, although they tended to take better care of themselves.

"Did you know there was a memorial service for you one night in Elaine's?" he asked. He had brought a can of beer out with him, and popped it open.

She laughed, nervously. The sound came out more a stifled shriek. "Doubtless everyone raised a glass of Stolichnaya."

He shrugged. "I drink Campari when I go there. When someone's buying. Sydney, by the way, was absolutely devastated by what happened."

"Happened to me?"

"To you, and to his play. He was drunk for days. He kept staggering around at parties, saying that if he had cast you in that part you'd still be alive, and if he'd cast you in that part, so would the play."

Tatty managed a tremulous smile. "Cyril, please. I'm glad to see you. I want to talk to you, all night. But will you please go get something to eat? Chinese food. Pizza. Anything hot. And get some Scotch."

"Yes, yes." He rose and went to a corner near a stack of old magazines, sticking his bare feet into a pair of L. L. Bean rubber-bottomed Maine outdoor shoes. He added an old army field jacket and an Irish walking hat. This time her smile was not so tremulous.

"Mexican," he said, pausing at the door as he slipped the hundred-dollar-bill into his jacket pocket. "Tamales. Refried beans. Chile peppers. Some Chivas Regal, and some Mexican beer."

"Hurry back," she said. "I want to talk."

When he closed the door behind him, she had an urge to leap up and walk madly about the little apartment. She was still frantic, still fighting back tears. She sat and drank. She remembered the very nice times with Cyril. There had been some. There had been quite a few, actually, when she had first moved into New York after college and Europe. He had not been living in such a hovel then. She had thought him quite brilliant and witty, though her romantic interest then had been a hard driving advertising man with a passion for flying sailplanes.

She looked at her watch just seconds before he came back through the door, so she was able to know that her sanctuary with Cyril Greene had lasted exactly forty-seven minutes. Cyril came through the door headfirst, with his face bloodied and two men behind him, one white with extremely short hair and a mustache, a flowered shirt, and a white leather jacket; the other a muscular black, in dark clothes, with an earring. Tatty's pistol was in her coat and it was folded atop her suitcase. She threw her glass into the face of the white man, then picked up the old floor lamp, yanking the cord out of the socket and heaving it against both of them. Cyril, his parcel now a glob of steaming food on the floor, leapt up and hit the white man in the eye with his elbow. He began clawing at the white man's face. "Run, Tatty! Go!"

They blocked the outside door. She hesitated. The black man was coming toward her. If they had meant to kill her, she'd now be dead. They wanted her breathing.

Tatty lunged for the bathroom door, slamming it on his fingers. She fell back, then slammed it again, fixing the hook. She turned on the light. There was a small window of frosted glass, open a crack. She jumped up on the toilet seat and, with painful, grunting effort, wrenched the window sash free of its sticky old paint and up ten or twelve inches. She pulled herself up and through it, hanging head down, the sill sharp and suffocating against her belly. There was nothing below her but the cold, wet bottom of a gangway four stories below. She looked to her left and saw an empty, darkened window. To her right, perhaps three feet away, was a fire escape.

There were screams behind her. She squirmed, turning, sitting up, sitting backward, her hands holding her back from a fall, her legs still inside. She kicked off her shoes, and, with great difficulty, swung her legs out, holding tight to the window frame. There was a sort of ledge, barely an inch wide, above the window of the floor below. She set toes upon it, and looked across at the fire escape. If she swung hard from the window, she could grab the iron rail. There was a heavy crash against the door, amazingly insufficient against the hook. The next would not be. She stepped hard against the tiny ledge and, with right hand gripping and sliding free, swung toward the fire escape.

Her left hand caught the railing and slipped down. Her right, the palm bloody, caught the brick wall and then the bottom of the railing. Her body swung onto the fire escape the floor below. She crumpled, then rose. There were more screams and another, more successful crash from the open window. She started down the cold, wet, slippery stairs, faster and faster as she made the turns. If he had a gun, if he was ready to shoot her, she did not care. She could only run.

She landed on the pavement of the gangway, slipping. Pausing just a millisecond to glimpse the building rooflinesaroundher,shedashedforthenearbystreet.Itwascolder and wetter. A taxicab was moving slowly down it toward her.

No. Inside Cyril's apartment was the suitcase with all that mail with her name on it. And her gun. The gun from Russia.

Slipping again, her feet in agony where they were not numb, she raced up the front steps of the adjoining building, rolling into the vestibule and slamming the door shut behind her. The white man ran by. The black man might have gotten stuck in the bathroom window. He might be on the roof, or on the street running the other way, or still waiting in the apartment. He might be anywhere.

She had to go back to the apartment. They would not figure on that. They needed her, alive, needed her fast. They would look first where they expected her most.

The inner door from the vestibule was ajar, held open by many years' layers of thick, ugly paint. Crouching, she pulled it open quickly, then crawled inside. She waited a long time. No one came in after her.

They had closed the door to Cyril's apartment, locking it. She had to go back to the roof and down the fire escape. The open bathroom window seemed a hundred yards away. She began to cry. Crying gave her nothing. It would not get her to the window.

She climbed the fire escape to the level above, clambered over the railing, then lowered herself. She had gotten from the window to here. It was physically possible to get back there—not probable, not safe. She would likely kill herself. But there was no other way.

With a hard swing, she pushed herself away, aiming her foot at the window opening. Her leg shot through. Her pelvic bone thudded against the sill and her shoulder struck the window sash violently. But her hand, nails scraping, caught hold of the window frame, and then the sash. She sat motionless for a long moment, breathing with heavy sighs that came close to becoming sobs, then ducked her head and pulled and fell inside.

Cyril was on his back, pale blue eyes staring, mouth agape, his T-shirt soaked red with his blood, blood that had spread in great pools to either side. Her cold, battered stocking feet were now warm. She was standing in his blood. She bit her lip, fighting nausea, fixing her eyes on the Seurat print until the sickness passed.

Her bag was in the corner where she had left it, the coat she had borrowed from Gwen still folded atop it. She moved quickly, putting on the coat, snapping open the suitcase. She put on the Ferragamo shoes. Retrieving Gwen's shoes that she had kicked off in the bathroom, and the bottle of Chivas Regal that had rolled free of Cyril's grocery bag, she dumped them in the overnight bag and closed it. There was nothing left to do.

But there was. She set down the suitcase, then knelt by Cyril's head, careful to avoid the blood. Gently, she closed his vacant eyes. He had proved himself her friend after all, more than any other friend, and she had killed him, just as she had killed Gwen. He had once said to her, with some embarrassment, that his life would be complete, indeed, a triumphant success, if she would kiss him just once. She lowered her head and touched his cool lips with her own. Standing again, she hesitated. She knew no Jewish prayer to say for him. She quietly spoke a Christian one. It must be all the same.

No one was in the street, but that was small comfort. There was no safety in this city. She had no idea when she would know safety again. She walked quickly, heading east. She crossed the garish brightness of upper Broadway almost at a run, continuing east. Reaching Central Park West, she waited for some cars to pass and then hurried across, plunging into the darkness of the park. There were a thousand kinds of fiends and thugs in that dark, urban wilderness, but she had this advantage. Those people would not be looking for her.

And she had her pistol. She kept it in her hand, once having to stick it in the face of some drunken lout who lurched out of the shadows of an underpass. When she finally reached Fifth Avenue on the other side, she was amazed she had not actually fired it.

There were doormen, canopied entrances, well-dressed people alighting from cabs. She passed an apartment building where, just a few months before, she had gone to a party with Sid Greene and found herself talking to Norman Mailer, Arthur Miller, and later, Tom Wolfe. She was back in her own country, but with no place to go. She tottered on, her legs still hurting from her bout with the window. The pain became a driving force. She kept going, east, toward the river, relentless but without purpose, moving because it was the most acceptable form of waiting. She had to wait, for her mind to come together, for an idea to come.

She reached the river, almost bumping into it unexpectedly. The street ended in a cul de sac. There was a railing, the late-night traffic on the FDR Drive humming beneath her feet. There was no one around. She took the whisky from her suitcase and drank. She found herself strangely calm, strangely untired. Her system was devoid of emotion, drained. But her mind was working.

Sunrise caught her leaning on the iron fence before the United Nations. She watched as the bright orange crimson on the horizon faded, and all the other colors of the river and city came brightly to life. Her eyes glanced along the familiar outlines of the General Assembly building and the Secretariat. She had been to the UN many times, not merely in the public areas but in the sanctums of the elite, meeting in the restaurants for lunch or in the delegates' lounge for drinks with diplomatically connected friends.

Ramsey Saylor had been a diplomatically connected friend. He could come and go through this fence whenever he wished. Marshal Kuznetzov could as well. Tatty was a fugitive in her own city, hunted down like some vermin before an exterminator. Marshal Kuznetzov would be here as a guest, free to do as he wished, go where he would, as though welcome.

A guard in a glassed-in sentry box was watching her. She raised her bottle in toast, and drank. He looked away. She looked at the Secretariat building, all the way to the top. She felt a drunken desire to fly to the top, to stand there in command, to reorder the world about her as she wished, as though she were the czar. The czar to whom she was no longer related.

In a grubby little all-night café smelling of a morning's strongly antiseptic mopping, she had coffee and something warm to eat. She was in the West Thirties again, heading toward Herald Square, coming full circle.

But not quite. She was not in desperate flight this time. Herald Square was now part of an incipient plan, a launching point.

She descended the grimy, littered stairs to the subway. At their bottom was a wide expanse of underground passageways leading off in every direction, some to the department stores, some to office buildings. There were a few little shops and vendors' stalls down here, newsstands, posters, and endless graffiti; a shoeshine stand. Meager streams of people moved along this Dantean landscape, the poorest and scruffiest sort, all looking tired in the early hour. She must look more than tired, something horrible. There was a mirror in a chewing-gum dispenser bolted on a steel girder pillar. She quickly passed it by.

Two pillars down was an unfortunate, unattractive, dirty-looking girl, though probably no more unfortunate and unattractive than Tatty felt. She wore thick glasses, and her dark hair had not been washed in days, perhaps months. She held in her folded arms a thick sheaf of leaflets. Tatty accepted one, as she always did. It was a superstition with her. She had always passed such people by when she was young, but once, on the opening night of the play in which she had her first leading role, she had taken one from SANE demonstrators. The *New York Times* review that night had been wonderful.

This flyer was headlined SAVE SOVIET JEWS. A star of David followed, and after that was a raging text: "The Holocaust goes on! The Soviets are the new Nazis!"

Tatty supposed that was true.

The concluding line was "Death to the Kremlin!" At the end was emblazoned the "Jewish Revenge Committee."

Her plans now advanced by bounds. She went back to the dark-haired girl.

"Give me more of these," she said. "I'll hand them out where I'm going."

The girl was suspicious. "Are you Jewish?"

Tatty looked at her with great seriousness. "That doesn't matter," she said.

The girl pursed her lips and shrugged. She handed her perhaps fifty more leaflets. Tatty rolled them up and stuck them in her coat pocket, then walked quickly away. Ahead were steps beneath a sign saying PATH TUBES TO NEW JERSEY.

The train was a long time in coming, but it got her to Newark. A succession of grungy cabs, taking her from suburb to suburb and town to town, finally landed her at the railroad station in Trenton. A metroliner bound for Washington arrived in twenty minutes. She stopped in the ladies' room to wash thoroughly and change into better clothes, then went to her seat and slept all the way to the capital. At Union Station, she took a subway train to National Airport. Using cash and the name of Shaw, she bought a ticket on Piedmont Airlines.

The DC-9 gained altitude following the Potomac River, then banked, and turned south.

15

The overweight waitress in the skimpy costume that seemed endemic to Holiday Inn saloons brought Tatty's Manhattan on the rocks quickly. There were few other customers in the lounge, and Tatty felt very obvious. When one of the traveling salesmen at the bar looked at her, she turned pointedly away.

Paget entered in uniform—camouflage fatigues, combat boots, green beret worn low on his forehead. He looked very grim. She had told him about Gwen over the phone, but she was not sure that was the reason for his expression. In uniform, he might always look grim.

He pulled off the beret and touched her shoulder. His hand was gentle, but she could feel its strength.

"Good to see you again," he said. "Under the circumstances, it's very good to see you."

The waitress came almost immediately after he had seated himself. He ordered beer. They didn't speak until the waitress had brought it and left.

"Let me see if I have it straight," he said. "You were in Russia. You got here. The hard way."

"Yes. The very hard way."

His eyes were studying her face, a very careful assessment.

"I've never done anything like that," he said, finally. "You must be quite a lady."

"I'd rather not be quite a lady. I've had two friends killed and my brother-in-law is in a Russian prison."

"And the people who killed Gwen are after you."

"Yes. You've met one of them. He was at my place in East Hampton the weekend you were. Ramsey Saylor."

He sipped his beer. "I don't think we should talk any more in here."

"We can go up to my room. I have a bottle."

"Your room."

"Yes."

"A bottle."

"Yes. Scotch."

He drained his beer in a few gulps. She left half her Manhattan.

She had opened the drapes, exposing the room's view of the motel parking lot and the screen of pine trees beyond. She poured two strong whiskies and water, without ice. As she stirred them with her finger, he took her shoulders and kissed the back of her neck. She froze.

"Perhaps I misunderstood."

"I think you did."

"You don't want to go to bed with me."

"No."

"Yet here we are."

"If you want to, I'll do it. At this point, I'll do anything. I need your help. I need it badly. I'll do whatever you want. But I don't want to. No."

"Entendu." He released her shoulders.

She turned around. "Please. Don't consider this a rejection. You're an attractive man. I thought Gwen very lucky. But I have no taste for sex right now—I'm all cold inside."

He took his drink to the table by the window and sat. "Tell me what I can do to help you."

"I want you to come with me to New York. I want you to help me make the Russians very, very mad at Ramsey Saylor, so mad they'll want to kill him."

He leaned back until his chair was tilted against the

wall, then sipped his drink. Paget stared at her a long while before speaking.

"Why don't we kill him ourselves?"

"That won't accomplish what I want."

"And what is that?"

"I want Jack Spencer out of Lubyanka prison."

"Are you in love with him?"

"Maybe. But most important, I am obligated to him. It's the greatest debt I've ever owed."

"Tell me what you have in mind. Tell me as much as you can."

"Captain Paget, I'll tell you everything."

"You trust me."

"Yes."

"Why? I could turn you in to those people. I could sell you to them. How do you know I wouldn't? How can you trust me?"

"Captain Paget, at this point I have no one else to trust."

"You don't know very much about me."

"I know everything Gwen told me. I first met you twelve years ago, you know."

He looked unhappy. He let his chair come forward and set his drink down on the table loudly. He stared into it.

"Tell me what happened to Gwen," he said, quietly. His face was handsome in a way, but the scar and his visible torment overwhelmed that.

Tatty sighed. "They strangled her. They hanged her from the bannister in her house. It was arranged to look like suicide, except they put the suicide note in my handwriting."

"They?"

"Ramsey, or his friends. He's very perverse. He's very clever."

"You're sure it wasn't suicide? You're sure she didn't write the note?"

"Yes. Even if the handwriting had been hers, it wouldn't have sounded right. It was, it was a love note. It wasn't written the way she said things."

"A note to you."

270

"Yes."

"Were you lovers?"

She was angry, but hid that. "No. Of course not. I knew Gwen had problems, but I had no idea they had gone that far."

He slammed his fist down hard on the table, causing his glass to jump. Whisky sloshed over its sides, but the glass did not fall over. He stood up and went to the window, standing with legs spread stiffly apart in military fashion, his hands gripping each other tightly behind his back.

"I could have stopped what happened to her. I could have prevented it. She told me that. But she wouldn't let me. She used to say she loved me, you know, but she always kept me at arm's length."

"She was extremely fond of you. You were the only person, the only man, except for her husband, she ever felt kind about, concerned about. She used to worry about you, especially when you went into the army."

"She didn't write much."

"She wanted to write you, but she didn't want to answer your letters. They were full of so much anger and violence. She could never understand why you joined the army. She used to say you were the most sensitive, caring man she ever met. You used to write her poetry. She kept some. She had a few of your poems in that house in Bridgeport. She showed me one. It was called 'Song of the Reveler.'"

"Did you know her mother had me and my family investigated? To see how much money we had? When she found out that my father's income came mostly from a military pension, she tried to stop Gwen from seeing me."

"Her mother's been dead a long time."

"She was worse than you people, her mother. You were born what you are. Her mother wanted to become that, above all else. She used Gwen to do it."

"Gwen kept seeing you anyway. It just threw her when you joined the army. Especially when you wrote that long letter about killing a Viet Cong. She was very upset when she got that letter."

"What she never realized was that I joined the army because of her."

"And did you kill that man for her? She thought you did. Your letter sounded like some Hemingway story. A hunting trophy."

He swore, quietly. "No. I killed that one for me."

She stared at him. There seemed nothing left in this man capable of creating poetry, or weeping, or treating anyone or any thing with gentleness. But that was all to the good.

He was thinking. She waited, watching him, then looked away.

"What about Gwen's body?" he asked.

"I don't know. I was going to call my stepsister, but I ran into trouble in the city. There was another killing."

"Call your sister. I'll get you to a safe phone. I want Gwen taken care of. I want her buried decently. The best."

"Yes, certainly. But we have to be careful. Ramsey is very dangerous, very ruthless. It's going to be hard for us . . ."

There was an odd touch of a smile in his grim face.

"Us," he said.

"Will you help me?"

He looked at her very steadily.

"No," he said.

"No?"

Anger, fear, and hopelessness—helplessness—beset her at once. She sank back in her chair, her mouth slack.

Now he smiled. "I'll help you. Of course I will."

"But you said . . ."

"I wanted to see how serious you are about this. I see you are very serious."

"You'll do it?"

"I said yes."

"Why? Because of Gwen?"

"I'll explain while you drive me back to the post."

"I don't have a car. I have no driver's license with me."

"You can use my car. And I want you to move to a motel closer to the fort. I'm going to stay with you until we go to New York."

"All right. As you wish." She frowned.

272

"It's not that, Tatty. No sex. Not unless you want it. But if your Mr. Saylor makes a move on you, I want to be there."

Paget owned an old Ford Mustang convertible, bright red with a black top, dating back perhaps to 1965. The steering wheel felt oddly large in her hands. The engine sounded strong, as though it had been rebuilt. She drove too fast on the expressway leading to Fort Bragg. Remembering the need for caution, for anonymity, she slowed. They passed through the front gate to the fort without being halted. Apparently traffic flowed through all the time.

"Here we are at the fort and you haven't explained a thing."

"We've got a long way to go, yet. Take the next left."

She obeyed. "All right. Now tell me."

"In a month, I'm going to be thirty-five."

"Midlife crisis."

"I'm only a captain. Haven't you found that strange? I'll make it even stranger. I went to West Point. Veterans of the Corps of Cadets are guaranteed colonel. I should be a lieutenant colonel by now, in time to get my eagle by forty. I was a captain ten years ago, in Vietnam."

"All right. Why are you still a captain?"

A huge green army truck lurched around a corner into her lane. She swerved around it.

"I left the army in 1975, after Saigon fell. My work after that was highly extracurricular."

"What do you mean?"

"Gwen didn't tell you anything about me?"

"A little. That you've killed people."

"I've killed a lot of people. Free-lance and government service. In Zimbabwe. In Namibia. In Central America. You say you've done work for the CIA, for Saylor? I've bumped into a few of those people myself."

"You've worked for the CIA?"

"No. I'd never do that. Hate the bastards. Ivy grads and all dirty. But I worked with some free Cubans who were financed by the CIA. We went beyond our brief a few times. Shot up a couple of Castro police stations. Finally, the CIA got tired of me messing around in South Florida. They pushed the right buttons and I was activated from the reserves. My only way out would have been to resign my commission. And I wouldn't do that."

"Why not?"

"Because I was at the Point. Because I have this thing about making major. I want to make major before cutting loose. My father was a major. Mike Hoare's a major. I should have made major in Vietnam. I would have if I hadn't been court-martialed."

"What for?"

He paused. "For killing some people. In an unauthorized way."

She would not ask further. "You've been back in the army for some time, now. Why haven't you been promoted?"

"They know I want to make major. They dangle it over my head. They use it to make me be a good boy."

"You still haven't explained yourself."

"I'm getting tired of being a good boy."

"And?"

"And it would please me very much to make the Russians mad."

"And?"

"And it would please me for them to kill Ramsey Saylor."

"Because of Gwen?"

"No. Because of you."

She followed his directions onto a dirt road. It took them deep into the piney barrens. When he finally told her to stop, she was amazed they were still on the post. He got out, then hesitated, resting his foot on the door frame.

"Something I'd like to know," he said. "Last Labor Day, the night we raided that beach party, I got the idea. Well, you . . ."

"I was interested in you, Captain Paget. I thought of trying to borrow you from Gwen, which I didn't think would have been all that difficult. I had a need for someone like you. But not now. For now, this is strictly business."

"*D'accord.* I just wanted to have that, to be able to keep it in my mind."

Paget picked a rainy afternoon, a cold and miserable one for Washington. Early spring was usually nicer to the capital. He seemed pleased. Such weather kept people inside, and away from their depressing windows. He said he needed ten seconds to get over the rear patio wall and up to the sliding doors. Ten seconds in his business was a long time, he said.

"Why daylight then? Why not wait until dark?"

"In neighborhoods like Georgetown, daytime is burglar time. People are gone. At night, there's too much going on."

"We'll be going into the house of a CIA officer. There could be some nasty surprises."

"I'll be looking for them. I've been up against most. He has a roommate, or did I tell you? He's not a CIA officer. He's a football player who arranges flowers in the off-season."

"Flowers?"

"I don't know how he ever made first string at Notre Dame."

Pondering this, she dropped him at the corner, driving on to find a parking place, having to go almost all the way down the hill to M Street. He said to give him fifteen minutes. The walk back took almost all of that. She paused before turning down the walk to the front courtyard. According to the State Department locator in Washington, Ramsey was on assignment in New York. He had to be, with Marshal Kuznetzov coming to the United Nations. As the third-ranking man in the agency's Soviet section, he would be needed to help coordinate surveillance and analysis. Kuznetzov might want to talk to him, too.

She strode forward quickly and rang the doorbell three times in rapid succession, as planned. There was no response.

They might have miscalculated. New York was just a short air shuttle flight away. Ramsey might have come back, might have been called back by Langley. The football player could be home, and not at his nearby flower shop. They had telephoned just a few minutes before, but in a few minutes much could change. Paget might not have been able to get through the back door, or even over the patio wall.

She was about to turn and run when the door opened, no one in view. "Get inside, Tatty. Stop looking so nervous."

She hurried within as he slammed the door shut. He was holding what looked to be a small pile of laundry, and something else.

"Sorry," he said. "I was in so quick, I went immediately upstairs."

"You had no trouble?"

"He has an explosive device attached to his upstairs safe, but we've no interest in that. Otherwise, it was easy shit. One burglar alarm, rather cheap, not activated. I had the door lifted out in a few seconds."

"You sound like a professional burglar."

"I was, for a time, in Florida."

She stared at him and he stared right back.

"You tell me too much."

"We can go now," he said. "I have everything we need." She glanced at the laundry. "I went into his dirty clothes. Shirt, underdrawers, and socks." He opened his other hand. "And prescription medicine with his name on it. Your friend Mr. Saylor has high blood pressure."

"You're right. That's as convincing as we need."

"I'll put the door back in place, and we'll go."

"No. There's something I have to do, something I promised myself at a bad point in Russia."

When Paget, unhappily, left her and went downstairs, she proceeded to Ramsey's sitting room. She stood in the middle, staring at the enormous, wonderful John Singer Sargent painting. There was nothing she had done in her life that was as terrible as this would be, not even killing those two men.

Tatty sought courage, but found only anger, just as good. She stood defiantly a moment more, then moved to the fireplace, and grabbed a poker. She climbed atop the

276

plush sofa, bit her lip, then rammed the poker through the fabric of the canvas. She hesitated. The hole she'd made was large, but could be repaired. She pulled down and to the side, violently. The canvas made a sickening ripping sound.

"Did that do us any good?" Paget said, when he rejoined her.

"Probably not. It did me a lot of good."

"It was a beautiful painting."

"Yes it was, one of the most beautiful I've ever seen. Now I hate Ramsey even more for making me do that."

"You could be wrong. It could do us some good. Sun-tzu."

"What?"

"Sun-tzu. He was a Chinese philosopher of war. Fifth century B.C., I think. He was the father of guerrilla warfare. He wrote a book called *The Art of War*. Clausewitz read it. Mao Tse-tung read it. There's a passage in it about a jar of urine."

"I don't understand."

"Sun-tzu was once military advisor to a king at war with a rival warlord with an enormous ego. Before their first battle commenced, Sun-tzu had the king send the enemy general a gift to honor him, an expensive jade jar of wine. Only it was not of wine. Sun-tzu had it filled with urine. When the warlord drank it, he flew into an insane rage and ordered an immediate attack. Sun-tzu's army was waiting for it. The warlord's force was annihilated."

"And?"

"You've given Ramsey Saylor a jar of urine."

They arrived in New York separately, she on an Eastern Airlines shuttle; Paget, back in uniform, riding the Amtrak Metroliner as just another military man. Tatty wore a dark red wig, very large designer sunglasses, a drab black sweater and wool skirt, expensive but drab sensible shoes, and a nondescript trenchcoat. The clothes in her suitcase were much the same. Paget carried her pistol.

She was traveling under the name of Golda Isaacs, speaking with a discernibly Jewish and slightly foreign accent. She carried a copy of the *New York Review of Books* and *Commentary* magazine, which as usual had a cover line about Soviet Jews.

At LaGuardia, she pushed past other passengers in the cab line to snatch a cab. She snapped at the driver, and demanded he turn off his radio. Checking into the Beaton Place Hotel, she was rude to the desk clerk and paid for her room for the week with a deposit of eleven brand new hundred-dollar bills. She snarled at the bellman and tipped him only a quarter. She wanted to be remembered.

As soon as the bellman left, she called the front desk and, exaggerating her accent, asked to be connected to Ramsey Saylor's room. The clerk icily informed her she would need room information, and transferred her. She was rude to the room information woman, and to the hotel operator when she asked her to ring Ramsey's room. Listening to his phone ring four times, five times, six times, seven, she feared he might still walk in and answer. That connection, followed immediately by her hanging up, would create very much the wrong impression. Finally, after the fifteenth ring, the operator returned.

"There's no answer," she said, much as she might have said, "There's a leech on your cheek."

"Did you dial the right number?" Tatty demanded. "Ring again."

This time the operator let it ring on into infinity. After another twenty times, Tatty hung up. She stood up, stretched, and went to her suitcase, taking out a bottle of vodka—Polish vodka. She forgave herself for that. Vodka was nearly odorless. It would not do to be reeking of Scotch or gin these next few days. Golda Isaacs wasn't like that.

She filled half a glass and went to her window, her eyes darting over everything and everyone moving in the street not far below. She was home, and yet the view seemed as magically alien as the one from her window in the hotel in Leningrad. Alien and forbidding.

One drink was all she allowed herself. It was time to create Selma Peabody. She took the stairs the four short flights to the lobby. She had reserved a room on a lower floor so she wouldn't have to use the elevator. Ramsey's room was on the ninth floor. She had no interest in stepping into an elevator car in which she would be greeted by him.

Once out on the street again, her anxiety eased. As she walked along, moving north and west past so many well-remembered places, glimpsing, through windows, hair dressers and sales clerks who would have recognized her in an instant but did not, she began to feel a surge of confidence. She was invisible to these New Yorkers, much as Greta Garbo had been for so many years.

Invisible, perhaps only a ghost.

Selma Peabody would not be merely a ghost.

Paying cash, she began to assemble Selma—a long and quite necessarily expensive black wig from a shop up on Madison Avenue, a wardrobe of four very sporty outfits and one large brown leather handbag from Lord and Taylor's, a Sony tape recorder and reporter's notebooks from stores on Sixth Avenue. Except for the tape recorder and notebooks, she had everything delivered to the hotel. The wig shop, catering to the wealthiest of Upper East Side ladies, would remember that. As Golda Isaacs, she had made quite a point of making the salespeople there not like her.

On the way back, as a test, she stopped in an Italian restaurant on Second Avenue she used to frequent on nights between plays when she was not up to preparing dinner for herself. As Golda, she ordered fettucine Alfredo, her favorite dish. The waiter, who had occasionally borrowed money from Tatty, showed no recognition. She was perhaps being excessive with Golda's bad manners. He slammed the plate down on the table and left the bottle of wine on the table without pouring it.

When she returned to the hotel, the wig had been delivered but the clothes had not. She had paid an extra charge, to assure delivery, but New York was New York, not London.

Paget didn't arrive until after eight P.M. A three-piece, pin-striped, dark blue suit, Burberry trench coat, and

Hartmann briefcase had transformed him. An Irish walking hat covered his too-short hair.

"You're extremely late," she said, slightly annoyed. She had taken off the dark red wig and sunglasses. "I was about to go out and eat without you."

"Wouldn't do. We need room service tonight. Establish that you have a male visitor. Is the food any good here? What does Ramsey usually eat?"

"Ramsey enjoys caviar, snails, lobster, truffles, and the paté at Fortnum and Mason's."

"Shit," he said, looking at the room-service menu. "I was going to have the prime rib."

"Have it. I'll eat for Ramsey tonight."

He opened his briefcase, taking out a half-gallon bottle of whisky and Tatty's pistol. "Where?"

"Put it in the Tampax box in my suitcase."

"Tampax?"

"A good place to hide things. Very off-putting."

"We should both use the bed tonight."

"Yes, but not much."

He poured whisky and knocked it back. So formal a suit looked odd on such shoulders.

"You didn't ask why I was late."

"I presumed that being a proper Westchester gentleman, you'd tell me."

He sat down in a chair and removed his shoes, which were brand new and appeared to pain him. Soldiers were kindest to their feet.

"I followed Ramsey Saylor."

"You what?"

"I made only two passes. Once when he went from here to the U.N., and later, when he took a cab from the U.N. to the Upper East Side. It dropped him within five blocks of the Russian consulate."

"He has an extraordinary memory for faces, for everything."

"He didn't see my face." Paget rose, and went to the window with his drink. "I went to the *Times* and bought some back issues. I found only one story about Gwen."

"Was there any mention of me?"

"Nothing at all. It was only five paragraphs long, three or four pages into the metropolitan section. 'School Teacher Found Hanged In Bridgeport.' The police suspect a sex criminal or burglar."

"I reached my sister-in-law. Gwen will be buried in Greenwich. Did you really love her?"

"Yes. With a real passion, once."

"Her mother wanted someone really rich for Gwen, someone old line. She wanted Gwen's engagement picture in the Sunday *New York Times*."

"That architect she married; he was old line."

"Massachusetts old line. And the family had no money anymore."

"Gwen got into *The New York Times*."

They stopped talking. They drank, not looking at each other. He went again to his bottle.

"Call room service," he said. "And order a bottle of wine with dinner. I intend to get just a little drunk tonight. Want to join me?"

"No, David. After this, I don't want anything more to drink tonight."

"We'll see about that."

"I mean it." She went to the phone and dialed room service. Before picking it up she looked at him and said, "I really do. For the first time, David, I believe that we can do what we mean to do."

Black wig in place, wearing lavender-shaded sunglasses and the most sporty and Southern of the four outfits, Tatty strolled through the gate outside the United Nations Secretariat building and then turned to the uniformed guard in the adjacent booth. She took a letter from the huge handbag, typewritten on the stationery of a North Carolina newspaper they had obtained by stopping by the paper's advertising office to take out a spurious classified asking a reward for a lost, nonexistent dog.

"Can y'all direct me to where I go to pick up press credentials?"

The letter identified her as Selma Peabody, a reporter for the paper, and said she would be at the United Nations for a week, gathering material for some feature articles, and asked for temporary credentials to cover the period. It was signed, fraudulently, with the name of the paper's managing editor.

The guard sent her in to a reception desk just inside the lobby of the Secretariat, where a rude English woman glanced at her letter, made a telephone call, and sent her up to the second floor. Following a long corridor past some news offices, cable desks, and some of the weariest and most jaded-looking people she had ever seen, she came to a large press bullpen where more of these people were shuffling along endless bins, all stuffed with sheafs of paper. A French girl at a nearby counter directed her to the office of the deputy press officer, an ebullient little man with thick black hair whose nameplate identified him as Greek.

He glanced at her letter, dropped it in a file box, then, humming merrily, filled out a temporary pass for her that was good for an entire month.

"That's all?" she asked. That's what they had told Paget, posing as the editor, when he had called, but it seemed odd.

"That's all," he said, smiling generously. "Just so we have something on a letterhead."

Penetrating U.N. security was as easy as that. The pass was good for access anywhere in the complex, even to the top floor where the secretary-general's offices were.

"If you have a moment, would y'all mind showing me around a little?"

He indicated that doing so might well prove to be the very best part of his day.

Tatty knew nothing about the news business except what she had learned from Jack Spencer, but the press corps here, most of them foreign, all behaved so strangely she had no fears of standing out. She quickly fell into their routine. The endless bins were full of press releases and official reports, and were combed through at least twice a day. There were briefings every morning, usually followed by press conferences. She interviewed an English undersecretary general in his office on the top floor, asking him rather recklessly about Marshal Kuznetzov's visit. He replied charmingly but with some rather stock remarks about the Russians being incompetent and not really quite the threat they seemed. She interviewed an equally charming Irish ambassador who, over lunch, offered the most eloquent argument on behalf of a United Nations she had ever heard. In another interview, this with a Latin American ambassador, she was treated to a passionate vilification of the United States.

She covered meetings of the General Assembly and Security Council, which were attended by only a scattering of press, and the open sessions of the Trusteeship Council and the various U.N. committees, which were covered by no press at all, the labyrinth of storage and workrooms and mazelike corridors to the rear deserted and echoing. Riding all the elevators in the Secretariat, she discovered those that went to the basement and subbasement, and that the floor buttons to them could only be worked by an operator with a key. Prowling the lower levels, she found easy access out to the public areas and their gift shops and crowds of tourists. In the press room, she spent hours typing up meaningless notes and making useless telephone calls. She found out, as most of the other reporters apparently knew well, that most of the real work at the U.N. was done in the huge and extravagantly furnished delegates' lounge, which had an extraordinary view of the East River and an excellent bar. An African delegate made a pass at her there, but retreated before her quickly thickened Southern accent.

On her fourth day, she went to the Greek and announced almost tearfully that she had lost her pass. He quickly wrote out another, which that night she gave to Paget. The Greek's scribble was such that the name on it could have been Sidney Porkbelly.

The day before Marshal Kuznetzov's visit, she felt bold enough to take a front-row seat in the press-conference room for the Soviet briefing, bold enough indeed to ask a question.

"Mr. Ambassador, will the deputy premier's news conference be before or after he meets with the secretary general?"

"Press conference will be at ten o'clock. Meeting with secretary general at eleven. Private reception at twelve o'clock. Private luncheon at twelve thirty o'clock. Speech to General Assembly at two o'clock. Afterward return to Soviet embassy."

He stared at her after answering, but was quickly distracted by an English reporter who had a long sonorous question about arms control that the Russian ambassador declined to answer.

She felt pleased with herself for her audacity, but her nervousness returned as she paused in the delegates' lounge for her midmorning Bloody Mary. She had just sat down with it at a table by the window when Paget strolled in. He walked nonchalantly past her, briefcase and *New York Times* in hand, and bought a bottle of beer at the bar. Returning, he took a seat at the empty table next to her, facing away from the window. After a sip of the beer, he opened the newspaper wide.

"I thought I'd find you in here," he said, quietly.

"Why did you come?" She put her hand up in front of her mouth, resting her face against it as though in thought.

"Dress rehearsal."

"They accepted your pass?"

"Didn't even ask for it. If you wear a pin-striped suit, carry a briefcase, look bored and tired and act insufferably arrogant, they let you past as one of the boys."

She gulped down most of her drink.

"This is crazy," she said. "I'm going to go."

That afternoon, long after Paget had gone away again, her nervousness abruptly became terror. She was walking down the long, wide, carpeted and high-ceilinged corridor that led from the Secretariat escalators to the General Assembly, when her eyes suddenly filled with the sight of Ramsey Saylor walking toward her.

He was dressed in exactly the same sort of suit as Paget, but looked much more natural in it. His hair was uncharacteristically mussed in front, as though he had simply forgotten to comb it. His mouth, more typically, was slightly open, tongue against the tips of his upper teeth. His heavy-lidded, feminine eyes were vacant and staring, but straight ahead, not at her. He seemed totally absorbed by thought, as though pondering some great and frightening truth about the universe that had just been revealed to him.

She was clutching a sheaf of press releases, as she had taken to doing while walking about the complex, an effective badge to ease the suspicion of any of the pale blue-uniformed security guards. She pulled one release out quickly and, head down, began to read it. She and Ramsey passed. Her cheeks were moist with sweat. Proceeding on twenty or so feet, she glanced quickly back. Ramsey kept on at the same pace, unfazed, still transfixed by his thoughts, looking as though he might walk on and into the wall at the far end of the corridor, as though he might walk through it.

"You're absolutely sure he didn't notice you, didn't notice anything about you?" Paget asked that night.

They were lying in bed, both in their underwear, late-night street traffic filling the quiet between their words. Paget was drinking whiskey.

"Yes."

"You said he's very observant."

"He's the most observant person I've ever met, but we all have our lapses. He looked extremely preoccupied."

"We'll have to be maximum careful leaving the hotel tomorrow morning. If he sees you again, here in this hotel, he'll notice."

"I understand. We can take the service stairs."

"He probably uses the service stairs. We'll just be careful." He drank. "You're not drinking again tonight?"

"No." She was staring up at the gloomy ceiling. He was sitting up on one elbow, his powerful arm muscles delineated by the window light.

"I suppose I could observe that, if we were to ever make a thing of it, this would be our last opportunity."

"You could."

"You're not interested?"

"No."

"I've fallen a little in love with you."

"I know. I'm flattered."

"But no."

"Perhaps we'll meet again sometime, Captain Paget."

"You're all cold inside."

"David. I am absolutely nothing inside. I keep telling you, this is not rejection. It is impossibility. If we did it you'd feel even more rejected."

He finished his drink, sighed, then after a long silence set his empty glass on the night table.

"What are you thinking about?" he asked.

"I am thinking about a great many dead people."

"Why?"

"It helps."

He rolled over onto his stomach, his head turned away from her.

"Never think of dead people," he said. "They're not worth it."

16

They rose very early, washing and dressing quickly, then setting about arranging the room as planned. Ramsey's dirty laundry was dropped in a corner of the closet, on the floor beneath the neatly hung clothes of Golda Isaacs and Selma Peabody. Ramsey's blood-pressure pills, the prescription label with name and address turned to the fore, were set on the bathroom's marble sink, next to an assortment of make-up jars. The stack of anti-Soviet leaflets Tatty had taken from the girl by the subway were put as though carelessly on the dresser top. Nearby were the copies of *Commentary* and the *New York Review of Books,* along with a paperback edition of *O, Jerusalem!* In a dresser drawer were put the stacks of press releases she had collected from the bins, along with the notebooks and tape recorder.

Paget set a museum catalogue from an exhibit of turn-of-the-century American painters featuring John Singer Sargent on the night table, and in the drawer beneath, a half-dozen Ramses condoms.

"You don't think we're being a little obvious," she said.

"The Russians are not a subtle people."

She was dressed in Selma Peabody's tackiest Southern outfit, the one she had worn when she had first gone to the Greek for her press pass. In the large handbag, folded tightly, she had clothes more suitable for a Smith girl—a Diane von Furstenberg wrap dress, a pair of stacked-heel Gucci loafers, and a Burberry raincoat. She had hidden the pistol in a storeroom in the U.N. building in case people were being searched this morning.

There was nothing left to do.

"Do you want a last drink?" he asked.

She shook her head. He stood looking at her.

"May I kiss you?"

"Yes."

The touch of his lips was surprisingly gentle. When her body did not respond to him, he stepped back.

"Perhaps we'll meet again sometime," he said.

"Perhaps, David."

"You want to go through with this?"

"Yes."

"So do I. All the way."

There was a large number of New York City police outside the U.N. compound, but the security personnel inside, if more alert, were no more numerous than usual. There were no searches, though she was twice asked for her pass.

She went through her usual morning routine, stopping to chat briefly with the Greek. He would wonder why she didn't attend the Kuznetzov press conference, but she dared not appear. She told him she had to write a story about the Law of the Sea Treaty her editor wanted sent off that morning. He said there'd be a summary of the news conference and he'd be happy to give her a fill, but that it would all be in *The New York Times* the next morning anyway. She smiled sweetly.

As the other reporters rushed down the hall to the conference room, she sat at a typewriter and banged away until the Greek and the Asian girl were also gone and the only one left in the press-room area was a swarthy young man behind the counter collating press releases. She picked up her coat and bag, and walked quietly away.

As Tatty had observed all week, the girl who operated the elevator assigned to the personal use of the secretary general customarily took a coffee break at 10:20 every morning. Her habit was to take the elevator down to the first basement, leave it open and locked, and walk through the basement and a lower-office-level corridor to a coffee bar in the bottom of the General Assembly building.

She was there, though less relaxed than usual, gulping her coffee and glancing frequently at her watch. An Anglo-Saxon with dark brown hair, though not so dark as Tatty's Selma Peabody wig, she was slightly shorter and heavier than Tatty, but not so much that her clothes would look noticeably ill-fitting, or so Tatty hoped.

When the girl finished, Tatty waited only until she had turned her back and started for the corridor. Once she was in it, Tatty brushed past her, walking briskly along the curve of the hall until she reached a metal door to the right. Opening it, she looked back down the corridor beyond the girl. There was no one in view. Standing back against the open door as the girl drew near, Tatty contorted her face into a look of horror, and said, "My God, look at this!"

The girl hurried up and looked in, whereupon Paget yanked her inside as he might pull a fish from water. He gripped her mouth with one hand and her arms with the other, pulling her up tight against him. Tatty shoved the muzzle of her pistol into the girl's throat.

"What is your name?" she said. "Tell us your name!"

The girl's face was bathed in sweat. She was shaking. Paget relaxed his hand.

"Sondra Hochmeister," the girl said.

With that, Paget reached into his pocket, took out the chloroform-soaked rag he had prepared, and put it over her nose and mouth. In a moment, she slumped.

"Now," he said, "up the stairs."

The short flight of concrete steps took them up to another empty corridor off which were a number of press and broadcast workrooms. Like the meeting chambers they overlooked, they were dark and deserted. Lugging the girl's inert form to the farthest of the rooms, they set her down on the floor near a closet. As Paget began taking off her pale blue uniform, Tatty removed her clothes.

"Hurry," he said, once she had put on the uniform.

Her eyes lingered on his a brief moment, then she darted away.

The elevator was there, dark, open, and waiting. Taking the key from a uniform pocket, she activated it and turned on the lights. Then she brought it up to the second floor, biting her lip as the doors opened. There was a cordon of half a dozen U.N. security men waiting outside. The nearest one looked at her, startled.

"Sondra took sick in the coffee shop," she said. "They sent her home and asked me to take her place."

As though still unsure, he studied her a moment, then turned away. He was a Latin, probably South American, not much disposed to see threat in a woman. And she was in the same uniform as he. She had brought the elevator at the right time.

She looked at her watch. It was ten minutes to eleven. The trip from the press conference room to the secretary general's floor could take no more than two to three minutes. Kuznetzov would want to arrive exactly on time. So she had five or more minutes to stand here and wait.

Leaning back against the wall of the elevator car, she looked at her nails, assuming as bored an expression as possible. A minute passed. The Latin guard stood straighter. The others stiffened as well. Anyone could come around the corner, into the elevator. Another minute. There'd be nowhere for her to go.

No. The security guards would keep "anyone" away, just as they did when the secretary general came and went. Another minute. She rubbed her eyes. Paget had wiped the hotel room free of their fingerprints. Had he gotten them all? Was there some odd place she had reached? Would it matter? Hotel rooms must have thousands of fingerprints all over them. They didn't exactly scrub the walls every day. She had no fingerprints in anyone's file. She had never been arrested in all her life except in Russia, and there they had only stripped her of her clothes and thrown her in a cell.

Another minute passed. The elevator was a jail cell. What if Ramsey had her fingerprints? He'd have had ample opportunity to get them. What if Kuznetzov and his party were accompanied by the head of U.N. building security? He'd not recognize her. He'd think something wrong. She'd opened the panel that allowed her to operate the elevator manually. She could close the doors at will. But could she close them in time?

She stopped looking at her watch and stood stiffly erect, remembering the sentry at Lenin's tomb. It would be only a short while before Kuznetzov came. Then she'd be free. Almost.

The security guards stirred again. A group of people were approaching. She could hear their voices and footsteps. The guards assumed new positions to let them pass. Tatty squinted to mask her eyes. She'd abandoned her now too-recognizable sunglasses.

They were closer now. She lowered her head, as though subserviently. How many people looked at the faces of elevator girls? How many at doormen or parking attendants? These would all be high-ranking Russian officials. An elevator girl would be a mere servant.

The first figure appeared, a tall European, undoubtedly a U.N. official. He looked not at her but at his charges following behind, standing aside and ushering them into the car. There were so many, four or five short burly men, then a much taller woman and the giant Kuznetzov, and then two men almost his height, probably GRU security agents.

She pushed the button that closed the doors, taking a longer glance at Kuznetzov and the woman. Her stomach contracted into a tight, hard, painful knot. She felt dizzy. It was Raya.

Tatty kept her head averted, her eyes fixed on the panel before her. She had to go through with it. There was no way out. She reached to touch the button for the top floor, which lighted. But with her right hand, with a slight, surreptitious pressure of her little finger, she depressed the manual switch for "down."

The Russians began talking as the elevator descended. Tatty looked up at the little screen indicating their floor number, as though puzzled. The Russians were becoming excited. It was only a short way to the subbasement, and they reached it, the doors opening.

"Something's wrong," she said. "I'll get the engineer. Wait."

She squeezed by one of the GRU agents, quickly pressing the "close" button as she did so. He needed only to reach and grab her shoulder. He did not move to make room for her, as Russians never move in crowded conveyances, but he did not stop her. She got past and out the doors as they began to close.

"Ustanovityes!" shouted Raya, frantically. Halt!

Tatty was free, lunging away. She heard one of the Russians hit at the safety bar in one of the moving doors, halting it.

But he was too late. Paget's arm moved in front of Tatty's vision, throwing an ignited grenade. She looked back to see it explode, the great flare of strangely sputtering, sparkling flame. Horrified, she saw Raya's hair catch fire and all the Russians' faces whiten in the brilliance of the incandescent pyre. Their screams became a din, but were quickly muffled as the doors finally closed for good.

"You said it would be a gas grenade!" Tatty shrieked at Paget. "A nausea gas that would knock them out. All those people are burning alive!"

Paget gave her a rude shove, almost sending her sprawling.

"Shut up!" he said. "Get moving!"

She cursed him, hating him, but did as he said. Back in the darkened press workroom, she took off the elevator girl's uniform and Selma Peabody's shoes, and put on the clothes from her bag. Sondra Hochmeister was unconscious but still alive. Tatty dropped the uniform on the closet floor beside her, along with the wig. She checked again, to make sure her memory and mind had not failed her. Yes, a label with the name of the Madison Avenue wig shop was there. Everything was done.

"Let's go!" he said. "Move!"

Reaching the curving corridor, they fell into a slow step, as planned. They talked gaily, she responding from time to time with brittle, almost theatrical laughter. Pushing through the doors into the public area, they strolled on past another pale blue–uniformed guard, who observed them without much interest.

"Into the gift shop," he said.

Paget bought a Chinese basket, because its bulk would require a large plastic shopping bag with a U.N. logo on the side, enhancing their image as innocent tourists. She purchased a *matryoshka*, the traditional Russian nest of wooden dolls, each but one with another inside. Her mother had given her one once, but she had lost it. She had been planning to buy another on her last trip to Russia.

Tatty had just paid for it when they heard a great commotion. Security guards were herding the tourists out of the shops and up the staircase to the main level above. "We're evacuating the building! Please leave at once!" People looked unsure, but no one panicked. From the top of the stairs, it was a short distance to the main doors leading out to the north terrace.

"What is it?" Paget said to one of the guards.

"Nothing to worry about."

"Then why are we having to leave?"

"There's an elevator fire in the Secretariat, sir. Nothing to worry about. But you'll have to go."

They stayed with the crowd, moving tightly together up the stairs, then easing apart as they reached the upper lobby and fanned through the doors leading outside. Most of the crowd simply reformed once on the terrace, entranced as fire engines and police cars arrived seemingly by the dozen. Tatty and Paget moved back to the rear, and then a slight ways further, where no one could hear.

"How soon will you call your Cuban friends?" she asked.

"In fifteen or twenty minutes."

She looked directly up at the sky. It was a clear, pale blue but for a few dirty cumulus clouds.

"Could there be a war because of this?"

"No. That's the first question I asked myself. I can't see them doing it. They helped Castro and the mob kill Kennedy, and we took no reprisal. No, Kuznetzov wouldn't be worth the risk. The Kremlin's going to be a torn-up anthill for the next few weeks, Tatty. There'll be no one in enough control to be ordering ICBM strikes."

A hand gripped her shoulder. She looked up into a policeman's face.

"Excuse me, miss."

He pushed his way through. Two other policemen followed.

"Let's go," she said to Paget.

Walking slowly, Tatty swinging her shopping bag like some carefree tourist, they made their way west to Second Avenue, and finally to an Irish bar and restaurant neither of them had ever been in before. They took a table at the window, as tourists would do and fugitives would not. Paget ordered a beer for himself and a Bloody Mary for her without consultation. The waiter brought menus with the drinks. She caught herself thinking it was better to have a waiter than a waitress. He would notice only that she was an attractive woman. The waitress would notice details.

Was her mind always going to work this way? What had she become?

"I'll call now," he said. He crossed the room toward a short hallway leading to the lavatories, looking much too military, stopping at the pay phone. There were entirely too few people in this place.

The police would not be looking for them. They would presently be looking for Golda Isaacs. And the Russians for Ramsey.

She opened the menu, glanced over the items, and then closed the menu cover as though to some unpleasant sight. She could not eat now. Her stomach was hard and knotted.

"He left at once," Paget said, returning to his seat. "Within two or three minutes of the sirens he was out of his office and into a cab. It went up First Avenue instead of turning west. He may not be going to his hotel. I think maybe the airport."

The drinks came, her Bloody Mary unusually spicy and hot.

"Are they any good, these Cubans?"

"The best. They do this sort of thing all the time."

"What do you mean?"

"I told them Saylor double-crossed us in a drug deal. They'd take him out for us if we wanted. If we paid."

"You mean kill him."

"They do it all the time."

"No. I just want to know where he's going."

Her drink was so red. Her mind's eye filled with Raya's flaming, screaming, dying face.

"Why did you use that grenade, Captain Paget?"

"That son of a bitch blew away a lot of my people in Vietnam."

"That's why you decided to help me. You planned to kill Kuznetzov from the start. It had nothing really to do with me at all."

"Don't say that. He wasted your father, too."

"The others in the elevator had nothing to do with that."

"They weren't the Russian Red Cross, lady."

She looked down at her expensive new shoes. They could still hear sirens in the distance.

"What was in that horrible grenade?"

"Whitey Pete," he said.

"What?"

"White phosphorous. Incendiary grenade. We used them in Vietnam. They used them in Korea. It'll burn through a tank. After incinerating those people, it probably burned its way through the elevator floor. Look, Tatty, it's not a nice way to die but it's fast."

"What if it's all for nothing? What if Ramsey just disappears and the Russians don't even go after him?"

"They'll go after him. The police may back off when they discover there's a CIA man involved, but the Sovietski will be relentless."

"What if they find him before we do?"

"My Cubans are good. I'll call them again in a few minutes. If he's going to LaGuardia, we should know soon."

He ordered a sandwich and another beer, then left to make another call. Tatty turned away to look out the window. She wanted to leave this man, wanted never to see him again. They had had a bond in Gwen, in youthful memories, in the place where they had grown up. But that was gone now.

Paget took his seat and grinned.

"He went to LaGuardia, all right. He went into the Eastern shuttle terminal, then out the other side and onto an airport bus for Kennedy."

She finished her drink. There were many strollers on the sidewalk. Normal people, as she had once been.

Tatty gathered up her belongings.

"I'm going to Kennedy," she said. "You stay here."

"I told you before, we can leave everything to the Cubans."

"I'll call you when I get there. Where will you be? Here?"

"No. Some place more likely. A hotel bar."

"The Waldorf. The bar in the Bull and Bear. I'll call you there."

She rose. He remained seated.

"Am I going to see you again, Tatty?"

"That's hard to say, isn't it, Captain Paget?" She took his hand. It was as warm as hers was cold. "Be there when I call."

He was. The bar sounded rather crowded. All to the good.

"I'm at the Pan Am Terminal," she said.

"You're in the wrong place. My friends tracked him to Eastern."

"I'll get over there."

"You're too late. He's airborne. He bought a ticket to Bermuda, under the name Sargent. Flight One Hundred. Can you believe that? How does anyone hide in Bermuda?"

"Thank you, Captain."

"It's two hours' flying time. You can cut your deal with

296

the Russians for Ramsey's flight number, and we can be out of here tonight."

Two hours was not long enough to get Jack Spencer out of Russia.

"Good-bye, Captain. Have a nice life."

17

She lay on her back in the sand, naked, eyes closed against the late morning sun. She had brought a towel with her, along with a small waterproof beach bag, holding both of them high above her head as she had splashed through the surf around the sharp black rocks to this hidden cove. But having now removed her bathing suit, she wanted no other fabric against her, only the cool, silky Bermuda sand. The sun was warm, though the sea water was cold, no more than sixty-five degrees. The great black lumps of barnacled rock behind her and to either side were fortress walls against the wind, but occasionally a shift of breeze would bring a swift, cool puff through the opening to the sea, tickling over her legs and belly, breasts and face and hair, then subsiding, like the small, lapping waves that splashed near her feet.

Tatty felt none of it. Her body responded instantly to every tactile sensation, but her mind did not. As from her first day here, when she had plunged into the cold surf without any care of it. If a great wave were now to come smashing up between the walls of rock and boil over this sandy floor, her mind would continue with its thoughts as though undisturbed. Colonel T. E. Lawrence, Lawrence of Arabia, a great hero of her father's, had been fond of amusing himself in front of others by putting out matches and cigarettes with his fingers. A corporal once tried it and cried out in pain, exclaiming, "It hurts!" "The secret," Lawrence said, "is not to mind that it hurts." Tatty no longer minded. Whatever happened to her now could not matter. She did not much believe in souls, but it seemed as though hers had become detached from the confines of her body.

She now realized it was this she had sought in those interludes in that quiet retreat behind her house in the Hamptons. A form of peace transcending all around her, all within her. It had always been elusive; now it enveloped her, even here at the edge of the blustery, noisy sea.

Lines of plays and verse stirred from her memory. Rimbaud had written: *I have bathed in the poem of the sea.*

She had lain like this that odd morning at the end of the last summer, eyes closed and exhausted on the cold Hamptons beach after her mad, frantic run.

If she kept her eyes closed she might again hear Gwen's feet in the long grass, Gwen delivering her her grandmother's leather-bound book of death. So many people were now dead because Gwen had brought her that, dead for much the same reason that all the people in the book had died, rendered dead in much the same manner. The grand duchess had died no more horribly than had Gwen or Cyril, Griuchinov or the woman Raya. And Tatty had been death's messenger, bridging, though fraudulently, the violent past of 1918 to the violent present.

In a way she was grateful to Chesley for her cruel revelations, grateful to learn that she was not related to those people, that she had no czarist blood. What she had done was not just another selfish act by one of that all too selfish royal Russian tribe. What she had done was merely a mistake.

Squinting, she opened her eyes to find the sun and measure its level. It was nearly time to go. She had made a schedule for herself here on Bermuda, and she kept to it.

A moment more of this cold, still, quintessential peace. She recalled Jack Spencer arguing with someone, most likely Chesley, in one of her more liberal moods.

"You keep insisting that the alternative to war is

peace," he said. "The alternative to war is not peace, it is slavery, degradation, robbery, and murder."

The first principle of war, then: The alternative to death is death.

Perhaps it was not some transcending peace she felt. Perhaps she had simply moved through all this into a dimension closer to death.

Perhaps death was the only peace there was.

She stood up, stretching, staring out at the sea and the sunlight dancing upon it. The tide was rising. If she did not hurry, she might have to swim instead of wade around the rocks to regain the hotel beach. She brushed the sand from her skin and then pulled on her bathing suit. Striding out to the waves, she brushed her hand against the wall of barnacled rock. The sand was so smooth beneath her bare feet; the rock seemed covered with a thousand tiny knives.

Her custom here after rising was to go for an early run and swim, dress, have breakfast in the hotel's main dining room, return to the beach for her interlude in the cove, then retreat to beneath the sun umbrella of a table on the hotel's swimming-pool deck for a Bloody Mary and a read of the newspapers.

She had registered as Ann Shaw, and the black, supremely courteous waiter greeted her as that. Because of her theatrical, Greenwich, Miss Porter's accent, he like many in the hotel thought she was English. Tatty didn't mind that at all. She certainly felt less Russian than she ever had in her life.

The Bloody Mary, which she ordered with gin instead of vodka, was perfect. If the Windsor Beach Hotel was not the very finest hotel in Bermuda, it was quite close, and it was certainly the most English.

The news about the Soviet Union in the *Washington Post* and *The New York Times* the waiter brought her was much like that she had read throughout the past week. The premier was still ailing, but improving, and had been seen muffled in black overcoat, scarf, and fur hat, on the balcony of his dacha. Acting in his stead, supervising the government day to day, was a committee of Politburo

300

members including Foreign Minister Dobrynin and KGB Chairman Badim. Relations with the United States were moderating after the initial hysteria. Both countries had put military forces on alert and the Soviet ambassador in Washington had been recalled. Ambassador Crabtree in Moscow remained at his post, seeking, without success, an audience with Dobrynin. The U.N. secretary general offered to resign, and several Eastern bloc nations suggested it would be a good idea. As Tatty feared, flinching when she read the headline of the story, the Arab delegations, led by Syria but with Egypt abstaining, denounced Isreal as a threat to world peace and renewed demands for its ouster from the General Assembly.

The police aspects of the story were reported in the *Times*'s metropolitan section. Raids had been made on the Committee for Jewish Revenge, and most of the group's few members had been arrested, three of them injured in the process. Tatty had told Paget how troubled she was by the prospect of this, but he shrugged her off.

"They've bombed two Russian consulates," he'd said. "The streets'll be healthier without them."

Tatty thought of the girl in the subway in prison. But the *Times* reported that most of these people were being released, only those who had fought the police in the initial arrests being kept in custody.

There was no mention of any other arrests. There was no mention of any kind, anywhere, of Ramsey Saylor. The Russians might well have gotten to Tatty's hotel room before the police. The police might have turned that aspect of the case over to the tight-lipped FBI. The CIA might have moved in before anyone else.

She opened the morning's Bermuda *Mid-Ocean News*. There was a wire-service story from Moscow. Dobrynin had been named deputy premier. He had agreed to meet with Crabtree at the end of the week. The president had ordered U.S. forces to stand down from alert, except for those in West Germany. Israeli and Syrian aircraft had clashed over Lebanon, but there was no major ground fighting.

Tatty closed the paper, folding it, and set it on the table.

301

She had no more need of such news. But now she had to concern herself with life and death as it would be fought for on this small, fragrant, enchanting island. The few miles it stretched from St. George to Dockyard were the universe, the quantitative limits of her universe. Ramsey Saylor was now both God and devil in her life.

Finishing her drink, she returned to her room and showered the sea salt from her hair and body, changing into a blouse, khaki Bermuda shorts, and Topsiders, as she did every day at this time. In a parking area adjacent to the hotel's main entrance was the powder blue mini motorbike she had rented for her stay. She set her purse into its wicker front basket—carefully, for she had her pistol in it—then pulled on the required safety helmet. The security guard at the end of the drive waved at her as she roared past him into South Road, accelerating into the left-hand lane and the first of the swinging curves that led down the hill toward Hamilton. When she had first come to Bermuda, some twelve years before, there were few cars and more bicycles and horse-drawn carriages than these noisy little machines. Now every road and street was as frantic as a Go-cart track. The speed limit was still twenty miles an hour, but no one seemed to respect it. She had nearly been driven off the road three times until she had gotten the hang of the traffic. Twisting the handlebar throttle to maximum speed, she swung around two old women on mopeds then raced along after a taxicab.

Turning around the rotary at the eastern edge of Hamilton Harbour, nearly colliding with a large pink bus coming out of Trimingham Road, she glanced quickly to the left, twice, three times, capturing the view of moored sailboats and turquoise water in fragmented segments. She let her eyes savor all this, but her mind stuck to its cold business.

Entering the broad expanse and thick traffic of Front Street, the great cruise liners moored at the quay on the left, blocks of stores, shops, and offices with gaily painted British colonial facades on the right, she slowed, put-putting along, just another British or American lady going shopping. But she was hard at work. Tatty moved along with the traffic, looking quick and hard at every face she passed. She made a complete circuit of the town center, as she did every day. Finally, she descended the hill back down to Front Street again, pulling up in a carpark and locking the silenced motorbike's front wheel. She went through the same area now on foot, stopping in Trimingham's to buy a straw hat and a khaki skirt, the store's plastic shopping bag a badge of identity as she moved back out onto the street. Then up Queen Street to the central art gallery. She looked into all the little art galleries nearby, the campy little shops, all the very British places, all the places he would most enjoy. Again Tatty found nothing, not even a false alarm, no one who even resembled him. As always.

She took lunch in a second-floor restaurant on Front Street, asking for a table on the veranda, which overlooked the quay and harbor just opposite the Hamilton ferry terminal. She ordered an avocado salad, with Bermuda's spicy pepper pot soup to begin, and a gin and tonic to be served at once. It was her second drink of the day, and she savored it.

All the world's secret armies of cold-minded, bloody-handed, soulless spies would be looking for Ramsey. The West would seek him in the East, the East in the West. They'd look for him in the slums of Mexico City, the slums of Calcutta, the high-rises of Singapore, the villas of Cap d'Antibes. They'd seek him in farmhouses in North Dakota and steambaths in Tokyo. But the smartest would look for him here; the rabbit would run to his own secret briar patch, his own thicket of brambles and thorns. Ramsey knew every foot, every beach, road and house of Bermuda. Of all the hiding holes in the world, it was the one where he'd fit in most naturally, indeed, perfectly. It was the single place in all the world that he loved best. If he were finally to be cut down, he would want it to be here.

Yet it was proving extraordinarily difficult for her to find his exact hiding hole on this little island. She had spent her first week prowling St. George and all the communities east of Hamilton, being especially cautious near the U.S. Naval Air Station of St. David's Island, working her way back every day until she had covered all the territory west to Grape Bay. This afternoon she planned to devote to scouting the yachting clubs in and near Hamilton, and if that was unsuccessful, turning that night to some of the bars in Hamilton most popular with gays.

She would search and search until she found him. Ramsey was here, somewhere.

And now at last she had her proof, for there they were, pulling up in a black compact station wagon with red upholstery, Ramsey's favorite colors, at the sidewalk leading to the ferry terminal, the same muscular black man with the same massive forehead getting out the passenger side. He wore an earring and a gold chain, a black T-shirt, tight blue jeans, and white tennis shoes, dancer's clothes. As Tatty quickly drained her gin and tonic, the black man went to the rear of the station wagon. The driver, the same man who had been at Cyril's that dreadful night, complete to flowered shirt, close-cropped hair, and mustache, got out and opened the hatch for him, handing out two shopping bags. There was a third person in the rear seat of the car, but Tatty could only see a portion of his back and shoulder.

Bags in hand, the black man started toward the ferry. The driver returned to his seat and restarted the engine. Tatty pulled a twenty-dollar bill out of her purse and rushed through the veranda doors, thrusting it upon a waiter. She hurried through the restaurant along the bar, then, putting on her sunglasses and her new straw hat, down the stairs. She had just a few seconds in which to decide—run for the car park and her motorbike in hopes of catching up to them, or follow the black man.

She chose the latter. Running might draw their attention without getting her to her motorbike in time. Whatever happened on the ferry, it was bound to take her closer to Ramsey. If the black man recognized her, she had her pistol.

There weren't many on the ferry. Tatty took a seat up by the bow, facing slightly to the rear, the entire deck within her field of vision. The black man had seated himself against the rail on the starboard side. He looked at her, but as he looked at everyone else on board. Then he crossed his legs and tilted back his head, closing his eyes as the ferryboat chugged backward from the dock.

The grinning black captain spun the helm till the wallowing boat had reversed its course, then thrust the engines into forward, heading out past Point Shares through Two Rock Passage into Bermuda's Great Sound. Tatty looked about her, at the passing islands and houses, ahead to the opening waters where a cruise liner was steaming in through the channel by Spanish Point.

The black man got off at the Watford Bridge dock, a narrows far up the left hook of the island not far from Dockyard, the first of three stops the ferry would make before returning to Hamilton. Tatty let him gain some distance from her, realizing her mistake as she stepped onto the quay. He dropped his two bags into the oversized basket of a yellow minibike, unlocked it, and, with an athletic stomp on the starting pedal, pushed off the kickstand and roared away. By the time, half-running, she reached the road, he had disappeared. She had to wait fifteen minutes before one of the pink buses came. She took the rearmost seat, the one over the engine, accepting the bouncing discomfort in return for the greater visibility.

The visibility was useless. She saw nothing of the black man, or his minibike, or anything that might have anything to do with Ramsey Saylor. This was one of the oldest and poorest parts of Bermuda, a section favored by middle-class English tourists. The building exteriors seemed more drab than on the rest of the island, more weary from the years of sea and weather, the vegetation more overgrown. Here and there beneath the lowering limbs of great green trees she could glimpse the facades of great gray houses. It was her guess that Ramsey was in one of these, but she could not know.

After the bus crossed Somerset Bridge, a ten-foot wooden span purported to be the shortest drawbridge in the world, she gave up looking for the black man. She eased back against the seat, ignoring the spectacular view, thinking.

The long bus ride back to Hamilton took nearly all the rest of the afternoon. Returning to the Windsor Beach Hotel tired and disgruntled, she went out onto the balcony of her room for her third drink of the day, a rum and Coca-Cola. With a pistol close to her chair and her straw hat pulled down almost to the top of her sunglasses, she sipped it sparingly, looking down the hillside of meandering paths and pines and banana trees to the beach with its squealing children, supine adults, and the sparkling waters beyond.

She spent an hour with her drink and her thoughts, then went inside and napped. Afterward she showered, changing into another Diane von Furstenberg dress. She would dine at the hotel tonight. Foregoing the gay joints this time, she would pass the rest of the evening at the hotel's nightclub. The Esso Steel Drum Band was appearing, the finest in the West Indies. She hoped that, with his deep fondness for the islands, Ramsey might appear.

She watched the skies darken to night, then dined on Vichyssoise, crabmeat, tournedos of beef, asparagus, potatoes Anna, and a glass of St. Julien. She descended to the nightclub and nursed a Cointreau for an entire performance of the extraordinary musicians, who played Beethoven's Fifth Symphony on the inverted halves of fifty-five-gallon gasoline drums. Ramsey did not appear. Neither did his friends.

In her room she mixed a stinger, changed back into shorts and a blouse, foregoing underwear and shoes, and then walked down a meandering path to the concrete promenade, and down the stone steps to the beach, which the hotel kept floodlit until well after midnight. The sand was quite cold, but refreshingly so. She crossed the beach's wide expanse and stood for a moment with the waves lapping to her toes and ankles. She walked forward, until the sea reached her knees. There were stars in the sky, and far out, the rocking lights of a large boat. She moved about in the cold waters, stirring it against her cold flesh, finding something sexual in that. Then she stood still again, legs parted and taut in almost military fashion. She felt immensely strong.

She turned abruptly. On the promenade, back from the stone railing but caught in outline by the beach floodlights, she saw the slight figure of a formally dressed man, clothed in a white suit and dark tie. He seemed to have white hair. Stepping back, he disappeared into shadow.

Tatty stood, her back to the sea. If she were to survive, or even succeed with her plan, she could consider no one, not the slightest shadowy figure, innocent. If she went back now, up the steps and path to the main hotel building, she could be shortly dead. But she could not stay here, exposed in the midst of these floodlights. She could not stand still. She must keep moving, moving forward, pressing him, pressing them all.

With both the doors to the interior hall and her balcony locked, chairs tilted against them beneath the doorknobs, and her pistol on the bed beside her, Tatty prepared for bed.

She had brought her nest of wooden *matryoshka* dolls with her, separating them and lining them up in their descending order on her dresser. She looked at them over the rim of her glass. She still wore the emerald ring the spurious czarist duke had given her. She would keep that much. It was perhaps the only thing in all of this that was genuine. The red imperial pin that Ramsey had given her she had thrown into the sea.

She sipped, and turned out the last of the lights.

The next day arrived with the sky bright though the sun was not yet up. She put on her bathing suit, a covering jacket, and a towel, and ran down to the beach. The surf was higher and colder than it had been since her arrival. The cold and violent force brought her body very close to her mind.

Retreating much farther up the sandy floor of her secret cove than usual, she looked all about her. There was nothing, no one, to be seen. She pulled off the two pieces of her bathing suit and stood naked, the nipples of her breasts becoming erect in the stimulation of the cold, vigorous wind. She owed herself this interlude, at the beginning of what could prove to be the climactic day. It could be a most important indulgence. It could be her last.

Nothing happened; not until she had finished her usual shopping and luncheon rituals, her perambulating reconnaisance of the town. She was on her way back to the hotel again, going eastbound past the main stretch of Front Street, put-putting by a dusty wine and spirits shop on the left. There was the little black station wagon, its hatch open, revealing the same red upholstery. Tatty had not remembered the license-plate number, but it did not strike her as different.

She slowed, glancing inside the shop. She saw the close-cropped man in the flowered shirt at the counter, standing next to a taller, more youthful man with long blond hair.

Tatty pulled off into a side street, swerved her motorbike up onto the sidewalk, then jerked it around, leaning over it as though tinkering with the throttle. She had her safety helmet on, and her sunglasses.

The black station wagon roared by. Tatty lunged the motorbike off the sidewalk and after it, barely avoiding a following truck. She skidded into the right-hand lane momentarily, then regained control and sped along Crow Lane toward the rotary. The station wagon accelerated around the circle, turning into The Lane, the main road leading to the west. But just beyond a small park, it snapped into a sharp right-hand turn, following a twisting, turning shore road leading out along the southern reaches of the harbor. Keeping the motorbike at top speed, using the soles of her Topsiders to brake, skip, and skid around the tight corners, she stayed with it. She could see that the driver was watching her in the rearview mirror. The other man had turned in the seat, his eyes fixed on her. She wondered if he might suddenly start shooting. They couldn't recognize her, with her safety helmet and sunglasses, but they might guess.

She opened the flap of her handbag, pulling the pistol up to where she could easily reach it. The road now wound up a grade, a sharp cliff falling steeply on her right to the harbor. She could see the city of Hamilton, rising uphill from behind two ocean liners, the pink fortress of the Princess Hotel just beyond. The station wagon was escaping her now. She could only hope to catch up once they reached the top of the hill.

At the top, the little station wagon spun left into Chapel Road, heading south across the island. Shoe to the ground, Tatty slid around after it. The road was straight, allowing the car to accelerate and gain more ground. But it had to slow for a left turn into the Middle Road, and then right again for Pinnacle Hill. Disregarding even the thought of other traffic, Tatty sped after it, narrowing the distance.

After another straight stretch, the road swung violently into three S turns leading up one of the steepest grades on the island. It was all she could do to keep her cycle upright and prevent herself from skidding across the abrasive pavement on her knees.

At the top, she found them now too far away for any hope of catching up. Descending the grade beyond, they'd connect with the main thoroughfare that was South Road, leaving her far behind, caught in traffic. All she could do was watch the car recede toward the line of trees on the horizon.

Tatty slammed to a stop and took the pistol from her bag. Holding it with both hands, leading the station wagon with the gunsight, she fired, the echoing shot a sound seldom heard in Bermuda.

Now they would know it was she.

For the rest of the day and evening, she fairly much followed her routine, though again remaining at the hotel instead of prowling the Hamilton bars. At bedtime, however, taking blanket and pistol, she slipped out of her room and down the hall to a back stairs. The hotel was set against a hillside. Taking the stairs up two flights, she emerged on a concrete walkway that led to the spongy grass of the slope. She gathered the blanket under and around her, and nestled against the trunk of a pine tree far enough along the ridge to allow her a view of her balcony. She had also brought along a bottle of rum. Her nerves were chafing now. She needed the rum.

Sometime after midnight, it began to rain, and kept up

for more than an hour. Huddling beneath her blanket, sipping the liquor, she endured. It could be worse. She could be slogging through winter Russian woods.

No one came. She dozed off several times, but never for long. When morning light broke the grayness, she returned to her room. Nothing was disturbed, most especially, the talcum powder she had sprinkled over the carpet just inside the door. No one had stepped in it.

She had two hours for sleep before her scheduled morning swim and breakfast. She bolted the doors and fell into a gentle slumber, the pistol in her hand. When she awoke, the sun and a warm southern breeze seemed to have driven the rain and its harboring clouds away.

The morning gradually became hot, especially in the enclave of her private cove. Her bathing suit removed, she first lay on her belly, the sun's heat tingling her buttocks, but faced toward the waves, toward the only access anyone could have to her. She closed her eyes, keeping her ears alert for every unexpected sound, the pistol in her waterproof bag inches from her hand.

But then she slept, face on arm, sliding into the slumber as though rolling down a gentle hill. She lolled in sun heat and sea sounds seemingly forever. When she awoke, she could not tell why, whether it was her body's clock reminding her that her hour's interlude had expired, or something more disturbing. She opened her eyes, rising on her elbows. There was nothing she could see or hear. But there was something she could sense. She snapped her head to her left. These black rock walls were ridden with sea-torn clefts and caves, holes and tunnels. A few feet beyond her elbow was a hole half filled with seawater, half empty space, between waves. It connected to the next chamber in the rocks. Through it, she could see a foot, a black man's foot. She had last seen the thin gold chain around the ankle just two days before, on the ferry to Watford Bridge. He was waiting, the one foot pressed firmly on flat, water-covered rock, supporting his weight, the other flexed, toes down, heel raised.

Tatty moved closer to the hole. Then, rolling over almost onto her back, she inched forward, her head half submerged, her temple just inches from the arch of jagged rock, her face at once splashed by a scurrying wave. She waited for it to subside, then opened her eyes, blinking, looking up.

She could not see all of him. She could not take in head or face, but she could see enough. He held a knife. He could have come through the sea opening while she slept and killed her, but he could not have known that. The man could only be bearing in mind that she had gunned down a Russian soldier in the Kremlin, had helped burn the Soviet defense minister and seven others to death in a United Nations elevator, had fired a gunshot at their retreating car. He would be waiting for her to leave at her customary time, and it was likely past time. Who had told them of this habit of hers, she could not say, but he was taking advantage of it. The rocks to her left projected a shorter distance into the sea than did those she would have to wade around to attain the hotel's beach. As she started out, turning to the right, the knife would go into her back with no one to see.

But that would not happen. She took two more waves in the face, annoying, but tolerable. She waited, taking another, and another.

She heard the big one coming, rushing up over the sand and rock with a crashing whoosh. As it struck, she grabbed the foot, twisting, and pulled. He fell with a thudding smack, and crack. He cried out, though she could not tell whether it was because he had hit his head or because of the gaping wound in his knee caused by her yanking his leg through the jagged hole. Rolling back, rising to her knees, she pulled again, wedging his leg by the calf in a cleft. Weakly, he tried to move it. It held fast, the foot and ankle extending from the rock. She stood up, gripped a ledge, and jumped hard on the ankle. It broke, the foot dropping downwards, another rushing wave drowning his scream.

The tide would be rising. If he could not get free, he would drown. If he was willing to endure extreme pain, he might get free. In either case, he would hardly be able to pursue her.

She put on her bathing suit, closed her waterproof beach bag, and walked slowly into the water, a wave dashing up between her knees. If her ears heard his muffled crying, her mind did not. It was hearing Cyril's screams.

They did not find the black man until early afternoon. She was on her balcony then, sipping a gin and tonic. She watched the police and medics run down the path and across the beach. She watched them trudge grimly and slowly back up again, the body slung in a bag.

They came in the middle of the night, the one with the clipped mustache and the one with the long blond hair, opening her locked door in whatever well-practiced way they used, and slipping inside, moving, finally, out onto her balcony. From her hilltop, she watched them move to her railing. Then, dropping her blanket, she began climbing the hill to the road.

As she expected, the black station wagon was parked on the side of the road, perhaps a hundred yards down. She had left her motorbike in a cul de sac a similar distance in the opposite direction. She ran to it.

She did not see them emerge from the hedge and cross to their car. But she saw its taillights go on as they started the engine. Her cycle's was already going. As soon as they moved, headlights piercing the darkness, speeding into the left-hand lane, she followed, with no lights on at all.

It required keeping fairly close to them, though not close enough to avoid a few panicky moments when they swept ahead over a hilltop or around a sudden curve, leaving her in blackness, but she managed, rattling along behind them, moving west on the coast road. They were heading where she expected, toward that reach of the island where the black man had gotten off the ferry after it crossed Bermuda's Great Sound.

At that hour, there was little traffic. Only three cars and a cycle came by from the other direction, nothing drawing up from behind. Past the Sonesta Beach Hotel, however, where the road curved right and crossed the island to the shore of the Great Sound, a car approached rapidly from the rear. The driver did not see Tatty's unlit cycle until

312

the very last moment, and had to swerve suddenly into the right-hand lane. Honking angrily, he sped by, then slid into the left-hand lane again, snugly close to the black station wagon. Swerving once more, he passed the station wagon quickly, then accelerated off into the night. She raced ahead, gunning the little two-cycle engine as fast as it could strain, but there was nothing but open pavement ahead. Her quarry had disappeared. Passing beyond the town lights, she turned her own headlamp on just in time. A moment later, she would have hurtled off the side of the approach to Watford Bridge.

Tatty pressed on, meaning to take the road to its end. If she encountered nothing, she'd double back, driving more slowly, looking again. She knew she was closing on them; she sensed that Ramsey Saylor was very near.

The headlights behind her seemed to explode into view, incandescent. The driver had them on bright, and showed no inclination to dim them as he closed on her, driving very fast.

She knew who it was before the gunshot rang out, the bullet striking sparks in the road far ahead. She yanked the handlebars to the right, almost toppling, then back to the left, sliding, skidding, swerving, back and forth.

There was another shot, passing through trees above and to her left. She dared not turn and try to fire back. It would slow her, immobilize her for the instant it would take the shooter to aim true. She ground on, shuddering over the road's shoulder, skidding in sprays of gravel, at one point lunging up onto a narrow side road. The station wagon kept on relentlessly, gaining inches, gaining feet. The secondary road proved to be only an unfortunate loop, leading right back onto Malabar Road. She turned, bouncing, to the right, regaining traction and hurtling on, the little mixmaster engine making echoes as she passed along some high stone walls.

Cresting a small rise, she could see an expanse of sound and open sea ahead and to the right. The moon was rising through wispy clouds in the northeast. There was a breakwater of some sort, and a ship.

Another gunshot, almost stinging her ear. She hunched

forward, lowering her head, swerving again from side to side. They were at Dockyard. The road straightened and ran alongside the quay. Still swerving, she saw the ship was some sort of small British naval vessel. But she dared not stop. Her back would be filled with bullets before she got within a hundred yards of the gangplank.

A sharp turn loomed ahead. If she didn't make it, she'd go flying into the black water. Setting down her foot, wondering why the soles of her Topsiders hadn't been torn open, she slid crazily around the angle, whizzing off between a building and a line of trees. The road then yanked her to the right again, and then right once more. There was another breakwater, a large, two-masted sailboat tied against it, sheltering in its lee, a radio blaring forth loud music from within.

She roared by, making two abrupt and nearly fatal turns to the left, racing between a long warehouse building and a high wall, the following station wagon lagging not a second. The road made a circuit. She went around again. This time she would save herself. Instead of preparing for the sharp left, she kept accelerating along the high stone wall, at the last moment bouncing the bike up onto some rock-strewn mounds of grass.

The cycle, leaping, lurched up two of the mounds, then twisted and fell from under her. She hurtled somersaulting into the blackness, landing with a surprisingly soft thud. She lay a moment, catching her breath, listening as the cycle's idling engine coughed and died. Down the slope, she saw the little station wagon halted, the two men stepping outside.

Tatty crawled back toward the cycle, finding her purse and its strewn contents, including the gun. She snatched it up, and hurried toward the top of the slope. The stone wall was shorter there. The closer to the top she got, the shorter the wall. She stumbled. Swearing, pistol still in hand, she clambered forward, to where the wall was only about five feet high. Sticking the pistol in her belt, cold against her belly, she grabbed the edge of the wall and pulled, struggling all the way up, the slipping toes of her shoes clawing at the mortar, ignoring the painful scrape of her knees. With an extra lunge, she pulled herself over the top and rolled onto her back, her chest heaving, just as they fired again, twice.

It occurred to her that the smartest, safest move would have been to have hidden behind a safe rock on the slope and waited for them to come after her, shooting them as they came near. Useless hindsight.

Another shot was fired. She rolled over again and, her mind refusing to acknowledge the pain, hurried away on her hands and knees. To her left, down another grassy slope, was a castle keep—a parade ground and a number of old stone military buildings, all dark. She remembered. This was all a museum now.

Tatty dropped from the wall, landing awkwardly on the inner slope and rolling. When her battered body came to rest she staggered to her feet and ran, down to the grassy parade, on toward the stone buildings, running and running despite the bang, hiss, and metallic clatter of more gunshots, running until she could find her own ground.

Gripping the stone casement with an outflung hand as she swept by, she swung around the corner of one of the museum buildings, falling and tumbling. Just ahead, the building's shadows shrouding it from the increasing moonlight, was a huge ship's anchor set into masonry. She scrambled for it, crawling up into its shelter and shadow, bringing forth the pistol and aiming it with both hands at the corner she had just come around.

The one with the short hair and mustache was the first to appear, his flowery shirt bright in the moonlight. She let him keep coming, into her protective shadows, until the second man, the long-haired one, arrived. Then she raised the pistol slightly and fired, hitting the first man in the chest, apparently killing him instantly. He fell sprawling. The other kept coming, no longer toward her, but past her, skimming the side of the building as he came near.

Leading him slightly, she fired again. Her bullet, or a chink of struck stone, hit him glancingly in the ribs. He gave a quick, high shriek, stumbled, but kept on.

Tatty rose to her knees and fired again, this time at his

back, striking him in the right shoulder. He fell, sliding, but got to his feet. Limping, almost staggering, he lurched on. She knelt, and watched him go. There was a rectangular stone pond carved into the floor of the castle keep, an outboard motorboat moored in it, a long iron gate barring egress through a channel cut through the wall of the outer rocks to the sea. He limped in his wounded way around and alongside the pond, then struggled up some metal stairs to the top of the old fort walls.

He was now moving so slowly she could almost catch up with him at a walk, but she hung back, stalking, not taking to the stairs until he was some distance along the wall. Reaching the top, she followed along at his slowed pace, crouching in case he turned and tried to fire. But he did not. He seemed so grievously injured his every thought was concentrated on escape, on sanctuary.

"Stop," she said.

Dragging a leg, he kept moving.

"Stop, damn it!"

He would not.

"Is Ramsey in that sailboat?"

He swung around, clumsily raising his gun. Her own lifted into his face; she fired. He fell with outflung arms and legs onto his back.

He was dead. From the distant two-master, she again heard the loud music, 1930s country-club dance music. She dropped off the wall and started toward it.

The boat had raked masts and an old-fashioned design. She had noticed it anchored near Watford Bridge when she had stepped from the ferry after the black man two days before. She had noticed the name on the prow: the *Dorian Gray*. She should have known then.

No one was in the cockpit. It was a long boat, perhaps forty-five feet, not counting the bow pulpit. She crept forward. The main entryway from the cockpit would not do. That is where he would look at the first sound, if he could hear it in the din from the radio. Moving past the main cabin windows, she stepped quietly aboard and, pistol in hand, reached the forward hatch. It was open and ajar, for ventilation. She lifted it and pushed it back, opening the hatchway completely. There was a big Styrofoam fender tied with plastic line to the rail. She untied it, hurling it aft into the cockpit.

As the back of Ramsey's head popped up from behind the main cabin, Tatty lowered herself through the forward hatch, hanging, and then dropping, quietly. When he came back down the companionway ladder, she was seated by his table, the pistol leveled at his belly.

He was completely naked. He stared at her with his languid eyes, showing no emotion, no surprise.

"The rara avis returns," he said. He sat down, almost casually crossing his bare legs. He had a mug of something resting in a cup holder, rum and hot tea from the smell of it. The thirties music on the radio was overpowering.

"Turn that off!" she said.

He did so, quickly. She held the pistol higher, fearing he might try to throw the mug's contents at her. He did not. He demurely sipped.

"Please pardon the au naturel," he said. "I never wear clothes when I sail in these waters. I once crossed the Atlantic to the Canaries wearing not a stitch."

"Ramsey. I've killed three of your friends. The black man on the beach—"

"I know. Armand said he was sure it was you, but I doubted him. I thought it was the Agency. What misdo."

"I don't know which was Armand, but he's dead. They're both dead. One inside that old fort, the other out on the quay. I shot them."

"I didn't hear that. Kept the damn radio on too loud. Another agenotypic misdo. I am the most intelligent person ever to work for Central Intelligence, yet now I am undone. Comes from too much association with the thick-headed Russians, if you'll pardon the ethnic slur."

"Ramsey. I want you to put some clothes on. You're coming with me."

He leaned back, putting his hands behind his head. He uncrossed his legs, exposing his genitals.

The pistol wavered slightly in her hand. She realized at that moment that it was empty. She had checked it very carefully day by day. Its magazine had initially contained eight rounds. The first had killed Griuchinov, the next two, his murderer. One had been fired as a bow chaser at the disappearing station wagon speeding toward South Road. One was in the chest of the man with a mustache. Three others were in the body of the long-haired blond man. She had nothing left.

She raised the pistol higher, aiming at his face.

"Damn you, Ramsey! I mean it! You're coming with me!"

"I'm sure you mean it, Tatty, whatever it is you mean. But whatever it is, I'm not leaving this boat. Not with you."

He spread his legs a bit farther apart. She glanced away, then corrected that mistake.

"I'm not, Tatty. It strikes me you have three alternatives at this moment. One is to kill me." He sipped his drink, nonchalantly, but his eyes fixed on hers. "You could do that very easily, and very justly, I suppose. But you have not. That you have not, I'm wagering, means that you will not."

"Don't be so certain."

"Unless I do something rash, of course. But I never do anything rash. I'm quite the systematic man, don't you know. Immovably Socratic. I shan't stir from this spot as long as you're here."

"Get your clothes on!"

"Don't be prudish. It doesn't become a Russian. Your second alternative, Tatty, is to let me go."

"What?"

"Yes. If you're not going to kill me—and you're not—you'll simply have to. In a few days I'll have disappeared into the Caribbean. Drug-running, the modern piracy, is rife and rampant. I'll find friends. I expect I'd be a very valuable acquisition for some partnership. I know just about all there is to know about our government's capabilities. But once among them, that would be that. There's no leaving them. Unless you made some solo sail to Jamaica or the Bahamas, I'd be out of your way forever."

318

She wondered at this long discourse. Was he stalling her? Was he expecting others?

"You said three alternatives."

"Yes. The third is that you come with me."

"Are you insane!"

"Heavens, no. I'm being utterly Socratic. You've no place to go back to. I've ruined your life, your career, devastated your friends. You've no one to go back to except your aging stepfather and a stepsister who secretly loathes you. You've no one else."

"There's Jack Spencer."

"That poor devil. He's gone, isn't he? At any rate, Tattykins, wherever you go, there'll be as many nasty gentlemen looking for you as there are for me."

He crossed his legs again, setting his hand on his knee. He drank. "This is the alternative I'd choose for you, Tatty. It's very important to me."

She was sweating now. It was very hard to keep the gun securely aimed. She lowered it to the table in front of her, muzzle raised.

"I want you, Tatty. I want you to bear my child. I want a son by you, Tatiana Alexandra Iovashchenko. The seminal man speaks and seeks."

"Ramsey, you're a damned faggot!"

"Not entirely, dear Tatiana, as you've good reason to know. But that's not what matters. What matters is that I have a son, a lineal descendant whose mother is you. What matters is that I am father, grandfather, ancestor of royals."

"What are you talking about?"

"Tatty. All these American WASP princesses whose great-grandfathers were storekeepers. All these Smith girls, Tatty, descended from meat-cart pushers. All the great fortunes, the great families of America, Tatty. They rose from dire poverty, from slime. The first Astor was a German barkeep. The first Vanderbilt piloted a Staten Island garbage scow. Gustavas Swift sold raw meat from a cart on Cape Cod. The Rockefellers came from a vermin-infested pigsty on the Rhine called Rockenfeld. You, Tatty. You are royalty. You have centuries of it in you."

"That's a lot of crap, Ramsey. I've good reason to know."

"You've no reason at all. I'm the systematic, Socratic man, Tatty. I've researched your background as I have no one else's. I've thought upon it, pondered it well. This is what I mean to do. I suppose what I've always meant to do."

"Do you realize that you have been a threat to my life for months now? You've slaughtered my friends. You tried to set me up for the worst kind of murder in Russia. You've made me a hopeless fugitive. Your friends, your slimy, beastly lovers, have been trying to kill me for days. And you sit here, naked, sipping rum, talking about fathering my child?"

"Sincerely, Tatiana. It was never my arrangement with the Russian gentlemen that you were to be killed. You were merely to be tried and convicted. After the trial, you were to disappear, as though off into the gulags. Instead, you'd have been turned over to me. That was my agreement with them, Tatiana. For them, Griuchinov dead, you tried and convicted; for me, a considerable sum of money, plus you."

"Plus me. A little objet d'art picked up on the Russian market. And what would happen after I performed for you and produced your little heir, which thank God would probably be medically impossible for me? What would you do then? Trade me for a painting? Sell me to some brothel? Have me rendered for the chemicals in my body? Have you any idea how appalling you are?"

"Ease up, Tatty. You're not coming out of this so badly. You're alive. You're free of the Bolsheviks. You may even be able to reclaim your fortune some day. I'm ruined for good. They're all hunting me. I've no clear idea yet where I can find sanctuary. I've only this boat. You caught me completely off balance, completely out of position. It's damned amazing. I drop you, the fluffy-headed innocent, into this, in medias res, and whammo, it's I who ends up hanging from the cliff."

"You're just outrageous! You have no measure whatsoever of how disgusting and monstrous you are! There's not

320

a shred of morality to you, is there? There's only what you want and don't want, and you do anything you want. You stroll into innocent people's lives and smash them up like so much crystal on the shelf, and then walk away whistling."

Her heart was beginning to pound, her rising anger bringing a flush to her face, making her hand shake. Her mind was reeling, but suddenly she stopped it cold, catching herself, regaining control. He was provoking this, distracting her with her own fury, pushing her off balance.

"Are they all like you in the CIA, Ramsey? Have they all had moral lobotomies like you? At least the others who've been as ruthless as you in this, Kuznetzov, Badim, Captain Paget, they did what they did for some comprehensible reason, to serve some rational end. You just do it because it can be done."

"Paget?"

"You met him at my place in the Hamptons. A soldier. Poor Gwen's friend."

He smiled, nodding. "So that's how you managed that U.N. tour de force. I thought that was beyond your capabilities. I hadn't expected you'd be able to find help, certainly not help that talented. Yet another agenotypic blundering."

He was studying her, his dark-lashed eyes filled with caution and cunning, the cheetah in the grass raising his head to plot his run. He glanced at her pistol, the quick look so penetrating she half feared he could tell it no longer held ammunition.

"We can talk this out, Tatiana. Let me get you a drink. You're always good for a drink." He started to rise.

"No. Keep away from me!" She moved slightly forward, lifting the pistol for better aim. "Get over there, by the galley. Move, damn you!"

Her tone intimidated him just enough. Rising again, moving carefully to the side and backward, he did as she said, his eyes never leaving her.

"A gin and tonic, Tatty. A Scotch. A Cuba libre. I've so much booze aboard it's ballast. Come on. One last frosty drink."

As he moved to the galley, she herself moved to the short ladder leading to the cockpit and afterdeck. She put a foot on the step, holding the pistol as menacingly as possible.

"We're quits, Ramsey. You live, I live. You go your way, I'll go mine. Just don't ever cross my path again."

She climbed backward, step by step, their eyes in a tense, desperate marriage. With left foot finally on the deck, she moved back quickly to the rail. As she expected, he came to the companionway, peering out. He put his hands on the brass grips on either side, gaining leverage enough to propel himself rapidly forward.

Tatty threw the pistol hard into his face, striking him in the forehead. It was the first injury she had caused Ramsey in all her life. A joyful release exploded inside her like some powerful potion as the gun struck. She did not linger to watch the blood flow. Joy evaporated, leaving animal fear. She hurtled over the rail, landing on her knees on the breakwater, but quickly rising, running, head down in the fastest wind sprint she had ever run.

Ramsey had not cried out. He would recover quickly. It was possible he might pause to snatch up the pistol and quickly check to see if it was loaded, if it had indeed been a bluffing game. But his mind was too quick for that. He could leave that indulgence until later. He would move immediately to take up a weapon he was sure of and come scrambling after her. She likely had only seconds.

She reached the end of the breakwater at full gallop, leaping up onto the quay, stumbling, careening on toward the body of the long-haired man and then tripping again, falling, sprawling, rolling. Shaking her head, ignoring a twisted ankle and more screaming pain in her knees, she scrambled over the concrete and grabbed up the dead man's pistol, a long-barrelled automatic with a heavy grip. She had no idea how much ammunition it still contained, but was sure it was not empty.

She jerked her head up, ready to fire at a hulking Ramsey Saylor only a few feet away, but there was no one. He had not followed her. He had used the time to slip the lines and free his boat from the breakwater. In a moment, she heard the engine start. She rose as the graceful craft, Ramsey a shadowy figure at the wheel, turned in an arc and began to move with increasing speed toward the two exits that would take it out of Dockyard into the sea.

Quickly, she found the release for the pistol's clip. It was still heavy with bullets, and she guessed there was a round yet in the chamber. She slammed back the clip, but did nothing further. He was too far away. She had in fact let him live.

While her voice carried on their grotesquely absurd conversation in the cabin of Ramsey's boat, her mind had been dealing with the future. She had one more move to make. Though her most human, fearing instincts impelled her to run down the long quay to the British ship and whatever sanctuary it might provide, a more dutiful impulse kept her back. What she needed most, needed fast, was a telephone with which to contact the Russians. They had trawlers and fast submarines all along the coast. She had read an article about them in a recent *Newsweek*. If she told the Soviets Ramsey's plans, his location and probable course, it would be the same as delivering him up, almost the same. It ought to be enough of the bargain to free Jack Spencer. It was as much as they could rightly ask.

Ramsey was raising his mainsail. If he headed east upon emerging from Dockyard, he'd have a beam reach on a strong north wind. He'd have good speed and a long head start. He'd have a huge mid-Atlantic into which to disappear. If he were to go west and south to the Bahamas and the Caribbean, however, he'd have to first tack his way up against that strong north wind. He'd be slowed.

But she'd have to go all the way back to her hotel for a phone to use, nearly an hour's drive on her motorbike, if it was still functioning. Turning, trotting, her breath very hard now, she hurried along the roadway back toward the slope that had taken her to the top of the fortress wall. She climbed up, slipping and sliding, at last finding the cycle upended by a big rock, its front wheel prominent in the moonlight, and very bent.

She sank to the ground and began to sob. She cried and

cried, like some little girl whose mommy had scolded her with unusual violence. Then at once she stopped, cursing her tears away, standing again and looking down the hill at Ramsey's boat moving through the Dockyard basin, clenching her fists.

The Russians might no longer care. They might be seeking Ramsey only as benefactors, intent on rescuing a once-useful agent who had played the wrong side in a power struggle but was still of value. They might have nothing in the area that could find him in time. Jack Spencer might already be dead. She could be sure of nothing.

She could not leave it at this. She could not leave Gwen hanging from her own staircase, leave Cyril in his pool of blood, Griuchinov bleeding into the crushed ice, the young grand duchesses lying bullet-ridden in the Ekaterinburg basement. This had to end somewhere; this chain of death after death had to be broken. She would try now, at this place, this time. She would not let Ramsey Saylor, who had affected so much of her life, intrude himself on anyone else's. She would purge the infection.

"It doesn't matter if you don't make it, Tatty. What matters is that you try."

What strange, warm, ancient voice had said that to her? Her father, her real father, Bobby Shaw—sun-creased face, short gray hair, the strongest hands and arms she had ever touched, the gentlest voice she had ever heard, slow and Southern. It had been a school race, kindergarten or first grade, on some air force post. She'd fallen down, and all the others had scampered on past her. She'd gotten up and finished the race last of all, crying. Some of her classmates began laughing at her.

She'd try. She'd already thought of a way.

Once again climbing the wall, she found a place to drop to the other side, then ran to the keep and its pond with the outboard motorboat. Releasing the painter, clambering to the stern, she pulled hard on the starting cord, too hard. She fell back into the boat's bottom, her blouse wet from the standing water. She tried again, and again. The sixth time the engine sputtered, then caught. She pushed herself away from the stonework, shifting the motor into a slow speed forward and heading toward the wide iron gate, shifting again into neutral and coasting with a bump to a stop.

The gate was held by a rope, thick and stout. The knot would be more than she could manage. Grasping it, she looked back into the boat bottom, in the ridiculous hope there might be a knife. There was not, of course, nothing at all sharp.

Shaking her head hard into thought, she pulled the long-haired man's pistol from the belt of her shorts. Putting the muzzle to the knot, she fired, blowing half of it away. Steadying the knot again, she shifted the aiming point and fired once more. The rope fell in two. Holding to the gate, shifting the outboard into reverse, she pulled the great antique frame back, much as British seamen might have done on some eighteenth-century mission.

Pausing, Tatty caught her breath, then shifted into forward and high speed, plowing out to the windy sea.

The boat was little more than a skiff, seaworthy though, with a sharp prow and wide beam. Calming herself, remembering that coconut shells crossed oceans, she turned the boat to climb the swells, remembering to turn the boat again at the last moment to take the bigger waves on the bow quarter, then falling off to renew her easterly progress.

In the spreading moonlight, the sails of Ramsey's boat were stark, knife-sharp silhouettes. He was not steering east. He was hellbent for the Caribbean. He was struggling hard in his tacks against the north wind, sailing close-hauled to the razor's point short of irons, water and spray cascading over his bow with rhythmic redundancy.

Ramsey was flying a huge Genoa jib. It made for frantic, arduous winching when he came about, but would carry him forth against the wind with greater speed and force. It also obscured his forward vision greatly.

Crouching down into the watery boat bottom, her right elbow on the aftmost seat and her left hand holding the engine throttle and tiller, she steered her way toward him: tacking much as he was, hiding behind the elephantine swells, keeping her boat's stern from a direct assault by the sea. Swinging in alternating zigs and zags, swinging widely apart, then extraordinarily close, then away again, the boats were actually on a collision course—if she worked it right.

She did. She had pulled off to his port side, off his bow, just after he had come about onto a starboard tack. The big Genoa would keep her from view. She motored the little skiff sideways over a great heaving wave, accelerating forward until she was on an intersecting course, then turning sharply to starboard, closing directly, bow to bow. Shutting the engine down almost to idle, keeping just enough power to maintain steerage, she grabbed up the skiff's painter and looped it. As the great, sail-laden boat of Ramsey's drove steadily upon her, she steered the skiff abruptly to the side, taking the impact on the little boat's beam, hooking the painter over a cleat with a quick, desperate action.

He would immediately hear the thump, note the drag and the sudden weather helm.

She flung herself up onto his deck, crawling, slithering, losing a boat shoe, until she gained the starboard side, clinging to a mast stay. Ramsey abruptly came about, winching the jib to the other side, rising to look at the skiff as its painter slipped off the cleat and it fell off and away. Then he saw her.

"By God, Tatty, back for more? Do you love me so?"

Tatty rose to one knee, gripping the cabin rail with her left hand as she emptied the automatic loudly into Ramsey. From the jerks of his body, she could tell she had hit him at least four times.

Letting his body slip like ooze into the cockpit, she hurried to the helm, kicking his dead arm from where it had caught in the wheel. She yanked the main sheet free of its cleat, letting it play out, spinning the wheel as the boat fell off into a gentler point of sail that led back toward Bermuda. Settling finally into a run, the boom of the mainsail swung far out in the perpendicular, she looked down to examine Ramsey's naked body as it sprawled in the moonlight. Through some perverse mischance or chance of fate,

326

one shot had disfigured his "beautiful" face and another had destroyed his genitals.

Tying the helm on a course sufficiently to port to avoid an unexpected and disastrous gybe, she pulled up the body and shoved it down the companionway into the cabin. Then she threw her pistol into the sea.

The final maneuver required some nimbleness. She drove the yacht on toward the northern front of the Dockyard breakwater, spun the helm around through a violent gybe that almost capsized her, and then tied the wheel so the boat would go back out to sea. Then she rolled over the side, losing her other boat shoe, swimming frantically for a moment, then relaxing into a slow, surviving breast stroke.

She clambered up the rocks and then up over the breakwater. There was a man standing on the quay, in a white suit with white hair. She recognized him as the man by the hotel beach the night before, and at the Canadian embassy dinner party. The CIA man.

She got to her feet. He kept his place. They stood motionless, each observing the other's dark figure in the silvery gray of the moonlight on stone. Then he began walking toward her.

Tatty had nowhere to go. Nothing to fight with. No strength left for fighting. No strength at all; nothing but tears. Though even those were gone. She stood, shivering in her own thin arms. He came nearer. She lowered her head, waiting for the death blow, the gunshot, the knife slash.

He put his arm around her.

"Come, Miss Chase. There's a blanket in the car."

"You're Mr. Lovelace," she said, huddled within a warm knit Afghan against the corner of the seat, but still close to him, because of the smallness of the car. Another old man. She was much reminded of Griuchinov. And Badim.

"Laidlaw," he said, looking straight ahead. The driver, a very large man, drove the little car with precise grace,

327

maintaining the same speed no matter whether they climbed or descended hills or rounded curves.

Laidlaw turned to her. "I have some brandy. The sea must have been cold. Would you like some?"

"Yes," she said, still shivering. "Just for the cold."

He smiled. "I understand." He handed her an elegant silver flask. She meant only to sip from it, but she drank almost a third of its contents.

It helped. It warmed. It calmed.

"What about my motorbike?" she asked, finally—as it occurred to her, ridiculously.

"My associates are tending to it, among other things. Don't worry, it will be at your hotel's garage in the morning."

"And those men I killed?"

"We shall leave them where they are. They will make Mr. Saylor's fate more explicable, in their way. And they shall certainly preoccupy the Bermudan police authorities. We intend to have you out of here on a morning flight, before they can quite collect themselves."

"And Ramsey?"

"We shall let him sail on, until within the jurisdiction of our own Coast Guard. These dead men share a certain common denominator, or uncommon denominator. Their sexual preference. And there will be substantial evidence of a narcotics enterprise. We'll have added to it, of course, but Mr. Saylor had a fair-sized stock aboard. He was a cocaine addict, or didn't you know?"

"I didn't." She gripped the flask. She began to cry.

"What is it, Miss Chase?"

"I've a friend, in a Russian prison. When I killed Ramsey, I killed my friend."

He coughed, politely.

"John Spencer is now in Helsinki. He shall be in a much safer place by week's end."

"You know Jack?"

"Has he told you of Iceland?"

"A little."

"Suffice it to say I know him very well. We were there together. The relationship continues."

"How did you get him out? The Soviets were very emphatic about what I had to do to free him."

"They are always so emphatic. They have such bad manners. I have a friend, perhaps I should say counterpart, among their embassy staff in Washington. We both function as a convenient short cut for each other's side. He explained General Badim's predicament. I solved it for him. I had the chief Washington correspondent, and spy, for Tass, arrested for espionage. Badim immediately agreed to an exchange." He touched her hand. "Do not misunderstand Badim. Many Westerners love him because he is an intellectual, but he is the quintessential Bolshevik."

They thumped over the tiny wooden drawbridge. There were tiny lights off by the horizon to the southwest, some stars, some boats.

"But I think Badim trusts me, and that he is glad to be rid of Spencer, and of you. If you were to go into Russia again, he'd have to kill you at once. But outside, I think he'll leave you alone. If you keep quiet."

"I've no interest in interviews."

He smiled, and took a quick sip of the brandy himself.

"Miss Chase, would you be interested in going into Russia again?"

She looked at him as though at someone gone mad.

"I'm joking, in a way, but there's something you should know; something I believe you should want to know. Do you remember getting a notice of a registered letter?"

"Yes. At the Greenwich post office. I didn't dare pick it up. How do you know about that?"

The smile this time was fainter. He reached over the front seat and pulled up a briefcase. Setting it on his lap, he fingered the combination deftly in the dark, then sprung the catches.

"We're able to make . . . certain arrangements. This should have come to your attention weeks ago. Events, and all those interesting personalities, intervened. It could have been months before you were finally able to lay hands on this; possibly years. I thought you should have it now. It's germane."

She ripped open the thick envelope, then stopped.

"I'm supposed to sign for this."

He coughed. "You did."

A truck roared by them in the opposite lane. He handed her a small penlight.

The stationery was from a major law firm she recognized as being in the same building as her stepfather's. There were three pages of single-spaced letter, with a bulky sheaf of photocopied legal documents affixed beyond.

For all its length, the letter was much to the point. The big stone house and hilltop estate off Pommel Ridge Road in Westchester belonging to the late Grand Duke Suvorov had been deeded to her in secret trust in the year 1957. When the grand duke had died in late December of the previous year, some Romanovs in New York had contested the deed, but the probate judge in Westchester had held for her, presuming the ability of the courts to locate her, or one of her heirs.

She had no heirs, just those glimpsed in Ramsey's imagination, or perhaps Jack Spencer's.

"He was a grand duke, then? He was genuine?"

"Oh yes, the youngest and I think last recipient of a general's promotion in the Imperial army."

"And my grandmother knew him."

"Oh yes. Very much so."

"Then she might have been what she said."

"I don't know what she said; I can't say."

"She said she was a cousin to the czars."

"That I can't say, yes or no. But the grand duke was most definitely the cousin of Nicholas Romanov. He worked with us for many years."

The driver had his window opened slightly. As they swept down into a depression between hedges, she caught a heavy scent of flowers.

"Why did he give me his house? Just because he and my grandmother were friends, distant relatives?" All this talk of Russians was bringing music back to her, "Evening Bells," even now at the prelude to dawn.

"When you more closely examine the affixed legal papers, you will find it all spelled out, rather frankly. I mean to be very polite, Miss Chase, but let me say it. Your mother, Chloe, was an illegitimate child. She was not the daughter of Elwood Hoops. She was the daughter of Mathilde Iovashchenko and General Suvorov. Miss Chase, you are the duke's granddaughter. That is why you have his house."

She held the flask, trembling, then drank. She closed her eyes, sinking back against the seat. The coldness was draining from her nervous system—warmth, fatigue, and sleepiness flowing in behind it.

"The house does me no good."

"Not for a while."

She thought of Spencer in Helsinki, in a wood-paneled hotel room, under the protection of CIA agents, under guard.

She cranked down her own window as they reached the south coast by the Sonesta Beach Hotel, moonlight waves among the rocks.

"You said you would put me on a plane today. Mr. Laidlaw, I've no place to go. I've no place left to go."

"Oh no, Miss Chase. You shall always have a place to go. For the rest of your life."

"Why? What do you mean?"

"Miss Chase. Now you are one of us."

Acknowledgments

My grandmother Caroline, whose father was a czarist civil servant, came to the United States with her family from Poland in 1907, finding sanctuary from the troubles that began with the uprising outside the Winter Palace in 1905 and culminated in the permanent establishment of Bolshevik tyranny.

When I was a child, she told me many stories of her early life in the Russian Empire. I still recall vividly her recounting a ride with her father in a sleigh on a street in St. Petersburg as a troop of scarlet-coated Cossacks, singing, rode along a parallel route, silhouetted against the Russian winter sunset.

Those stories, long forgotten, recently remembered, were what led to this book. As I should have made better known to her while she was alive, I am much grateful to her for that, as I am grateful that I have belatedly learned to honor my Polish and Russian heritage as much as I have the English and Prussian.

James O. Jackson, a friend, colleague, and veteran foreign correspondent with few rivals in his understanding of the Soviet state, provided invaluable advice and expertise. Tom Dunne, Dianne Rowe, Deborah Daly, and Pam Dorman of St. Martin's provided what they always do, the best.

I am also grateful for the good counsel of Dominick Abel, Jack Fuller, and a dear friend and wonderful artist, Ellen Morgan Williams.

About the Author

Michael Kilian, 44, is a Washington columnist for the *Chicago Tribune* and the *Knight-News-Tribune Wire*, which distributes his column to more than one hundred newspapers in the United States and Canada. He is also a member of the *Chicago Tribune* editorial board and an annual contributor to the *Encyclopaedia Britannica* Book of the Year.

Born in the Midwest, he spent his childhood in Chicago and New York's Westchester County, and was educated in the East. His travels have taken him from Korea to the Soviet Union, Iceland to the mountains of Mexico, and his reporting has included Kremlin politics, Latin American unrest, the war in Northern Ireland, and Canadian separatism and constitutional reform. He is the author of four other books, including *The Valkyrie Project* and *Northern Exposure*, novels both published by St. Martin's.

He, his wife, Pamela, and their sons, Eric and Colin, live in Falls Church, Virginia.

Now that you've enjoyed this book, discover other exciting paperbacks from St. Martin's Press